DISILLUSIONS

SETH MARGOLIS

DIVERSIONBOOKS

Also by Seth Margolis

Closing Costs
False Faces
Losing Isaiah
Perfect Angel
Vanishing Act

Diversion Books
A Division of Diversion Publishing Corp.
443 Park Avenue South, Suite 1008
New York, New York 10016
www.DiversionBooks.com

For more information, email info@diversionbooks.com

First Diversion Books edition June 2015.
Print ISBN: 978-1-68230-095-4
eBook ISBN: 978-1-62681-858-3

Can our love subsist, except by sacrifices, by not asking for everything? Can you change the fact that you are not wholly mine—I not wholly yours?

My heart is overflowing with thoughts that I want to tell you. O I think there are moments when language means nothing.

O God, why must one leave what one loves so much?

Eternally yours.

Eternally mine.

Eternally we.

—Ludwig van Beethoven to his "Immortal Beloved,"
July 6, 1812

PROLOGUE

Because Jimmy Amiel's bedroom overlooked the front yard, he saw the two men get out of the car, stop at the end of the walk, and stare at the house. He hoped they wouldn't look that hard at the lawn. The grass was mostly brown and it needed cutting. With everything that had happened—or was probably going to happen—what difference would it make if two men in suits noticed that the lawn looked bad?

He moved to the side of the window so if they looked up they wouldn't see him. He was only six, but it probably wouldn't be smart to look like he was spying. His breath fogged up the pane; then he breathed in and the cloudy area shrunk a little. He watched that for a few seconds, the fog expanding, then shrinking, like something alive.

Why were the men out front? What were they waiting for? Nothing good, that much he knew. Everything had been kind of lousy lately. He should tell his mom. She was downstairs, in the kitchen, probably sitting on one of the high stools and staring outside.

The kitchen window faced the backyard, where the browned-out grass looked even worse than the front. She had promised him a swing set when they moved in, and he'd reminded her of the promise every Friday, when she got paid. But then things got crazy for them and he stopped asking.

He should tell her what was happening, except he wasn't sure she could stand any more bad news, and two men in suits watching your house was bad news, especially after what she'd been through. What they'd both been through.

Should he call his mom or keep on watching? He could use a brother right now, or even a sister. He knew grown-ups felt sorry for an "only" child, even though they never told you; they just smiled extra hard and said things to your mom like, "Isn't it nice that Jimmy's made a new friend?" But he liked having his mom to himself—they got along pretty good, better than most brothers and sisters he'd known. He'd worried that maybe Mr. Lawrence's little girl would end up his sister somehow, once his mother started working for him. He didn't want a sister, especially a one-year-old with twitchy fingers and a scream like a siren.

But right now, a brother or sister, an older one, would be okay. Someone to ask advice from. A father might know what to do—not his dad, of course; *he* made everything worse, much worse. Anyway, his dad hadn't been around at all lately.

He felt a rush of relief when he saw the Pearsons' dark blue car pull into the street and stop behind the other car, just like he felt every afternoon when they picked him up after camp. Mr. and Mrs. Pearson would know what to do. They didn't think much of his mom, he could tell just from the way they said her name when she opened the door. "Hello, Gwen," making the name shorter than it already was, as if they didn't want to waste even an extra letter on her.

The Pearsons walked around their car and stood next to the two men and talked for a few minutes. Finally Mr. Pearson nodded and they walked up the path, the two men in front.

"Mom!" He tore down the stairs and raced into the kitchen. "Mom, there are two men outside—no, I mean on their way inside, with Mr. and Mrs. Pearson, and I think they're…"

She just stared at him for a minute, so spooky he didn't know whether to go hug her or run back upstairs. But then the doorbell rang, and she got off the stool and went to answer it.

"You stay here," she said.

He started to follow her anyway.

"*Stay. Here.*"

She sounded like someone else, someone he'd better listen to. She closed the kitchen door behind her. He walked over to it but couldn't hear much, just a man's voice, like it was coming from under water or something.

A few minutes later the door almost hit his head. His mom got down in front of him and put her hands on his shoulders.

"Jimmy, listen to me…" He saw the younger man standing outside the kitchen, watching. "I'm going away now, just for a little while. I saw the Pearsons out front. They're going to take care of you while I'm…"

"I'll try to be back by dinnertime, but just in case, you should get your pj's and toothbrush and…"

"Mr. Meeko," Jimmy said. He never went anywhere without his panda.

"Right. Just in case, okay? You'll show the Pearsons where everything is, okay, sweetie? I may not have time to help you pack."

She wrapped her arms around him, holding him so hard he almost coughed.

"You'll have to come with us now," the older man said.

"Hey, back off for a minute, okay?" she said. "My son is here, in case you haven't noticed." Her old voice was back, the strong, I'm-in-charge, New York voice.

Jimmy felt better just hearing her talk that way. He saw Mrs. Pearson staring at the ground; a teardrop fell onto the small brick patio.

"Take care of him?" she said quietly to the Pearsons. Mr. Pearson nodded, Mrs. Pearson snuffled.

She knelt down and hugged him tight.

"I'll be back soon."

He just nodded. If he tried to say anything he'd probably start crying, and that was definitely something she didn't need right now. She needed him to be strong for her.

She kissed his cheek, stood up, and headed for the door. He'd be strong for her, he would. If he just didn't move, didn't open his mouth, he wouldn't—

"Wait!" He sprang at her, leaped right into her arms. "You can't go, you *can't go!*"

Now he'd done it. She was crying, he was crying, both of them holding on to each other; then somebody was pulling at him, hard. He wouldn't let go. They'd have to take both of them, together, he'd just—

"Go with the Pearsons, Jimmy."

"No."

"Come on, Jimmy." Mrs. Pearson yanked his right arm.

"No!"

His mom put her hands over his fingertips, which he was digging into her shoulders, and slowly forced them open.

"I don't *want* you to go!"

His mom took a step back. Mrs. Pearson finally pulled him away.

"Jimmy—"

The older man put a hand on her arm. She shook it off but walked with him anyway, right through the door and out to the car, then got into the backseat with the younger man. People were standing outside their houses on both sides of the street, watching. Mrs. Pearson held Jimmy close to her, which made it worse.

In the car window he could see his mom's face, already kind of like a ghost, practically invisible. She put a hand flat against the pane, watching him while the car pulled away from the curb and drove off.

"Let's go collect your things," Mr. Pearson said.

"She's coming probably back tonight," Jimmy said. "She promised."

Mr. Pearson held the door to their house open.

"I don't think so," he said. "Not tonight."

As soon as they were inside, Jimmy turned around and faced them in the hallway.

"She's coming back tonight," he said. "She told me."

They looked at each other, then back at him.

"Of course," Mr. Pearson said. "If she told you, it must be true."

But being an only child, Jimmy was good at reading the looks grown-ups give each other. They didn't believe him, and they didn't believe his mom one bit.

PART I

PART I

CHAPTER 1

Gwen Amiel figured the Mecca Diner would have been considered chic back in Manhattan. The booths had orange vinyl seats and speckled Formica tables with individual juke boxes that played twenty-year-old pop hits; Peter Frampton and the Bee Gees were still very big at the Mecca. Along the counter, pies and cakes and the cheese danish they could never sell were displayed under glass domes like antiques, which is what they were.

All of which, back in Manhattan, would have cost the owners a fortune to re-create, and people would have lined up on the sidewalk to get in. But in Sohegan, New York, two hundred miles to the north, population five thousand, give or take, the Mecca Diner looked just plain dreary.

Like the town itself, really. The big textile mills had gone out of business decades ago. Their hulking carcasses loomed over downtown Sohegan, keeping three-quarters of the town in shadow most of the day. During bad storms, bits of siding or roofing would break off and plunge into the Ondaiga River, then float downstream to God knew where.

Sohegan Tack & Hardware was the only significant business left in town. Most of the people who lived in Sohegan were employed by T & H, churning out nuts and bolts—literally—and switch plates and phone jacks and other things that people never really think about being *made* anyplace. But they *were* made some place, and that place was Sohegan. Last year, the town threw a big party when the company was added to the Fortune 1000. Not the Fortune 500. The Fortune 1000.

Some days she didn't know whether to laugh or cry, stuck in a town that made nuts and bolts, for chrissake, and threw a party for itself because its one and only employer had made the Fortune 1000.

Gwen sponged off the counter and sighed. All that had mattered earlier that spring was getting the hell out of Manhattan. She'd strapped Jimmy in his booster seat and driven north from Manhattan until she was too tired to keep going. Checked into the Fishs Corner Motel, just outside of Sohegan, which didn't know from grammar or housekeeping but was dirt cheap and close to the highway. The next morning she'd found the Mecca Diner in the middle of town, gone in for breakfast, and come out with a job. The next day she had a small rented house on Glen Road, Jimmy was enrolled in first grade, and Gwen was taking orders for the blue plate special. Jump-starting a life was a lot easier outside the big city, that much she'd learned.

"You got a customer, Gwen, if you're done mooning over there."

She made a face at Mike Contaldi, who was working the grill. Forty something, fleshy as a Cabbage Patch Doll and about as bright, he'd inherited the place from his parents and couldn't keep his hands off the waitresses, which explained the high turnover. The first time he'd touched her ass she wheeled around and jabbed a bread knife at his groin. "Do that again, Mike, and you'll be singing soprano." In Sohegan, a line like that from a woman actually worked. He never came near her again.

She looked around the restaurant, found the customer, grabbed her order pad from the counter, and walked over to the booth at the far end of the restaurant.

"Morning," she said as she removed the pen from over her ear. Yes, she kept it there—it had taken her a month to succumb, but after losing at least a dozen pens and having to replace them at her own expense, she'd given in.

"Just coffee for now."

He glanced up at her and something went soft inside. It was the eyes. Gray blue, wide and narrow, pale yet somehow insistent, and haloed with a trace of shimmering mauve.

She wrote *coffee* on the pad, all six letters.

He patted the plastic-covered menu in front of him. "I'll just take a look at this."

"Right." She turned and headed for the counter. "I'll get your coffee."

"You know who that is?" Mike Contaldi stood as close to her as he dared while she poured coffee. The diner's coffee always managed to smell bitter and watery at the same time, just the way it tasted. If Starbucks came to town Contaldi would be out of business in an hour.

She shook her head.

"Nick Lawrence," Mike whispered. "*The* Nick Lawrence."

"What kind of name is *the?*"

"Ha, ha. He's married to Priscilla Cunningham."

"Daughter of *the* Cunninghams?" Whoever they were.

"Owners of most of this town, including Tack and Hardware."

She turned and studied Nick Lawrence. He had a strong profile, a long nose with a slight bump halfway down, and thick brown hair that curled somewhat at his collar. Handsome and aloof—just the aristocratic type of son-in-law you'd choose for your heiress daughter. Except it was nine-thirty in the morning on a Tuesday and he was wearing a denim shirt and khaki pants, eating a late breakfast.

"How come he's not at the plant?"

"You mean and getting his hands dirty?" Mike rolled his eyes, but he sounded more awestruck than contemptuous. She brought the son-in-law his coffee.

"Something for breakfast?" She held her order pad chest-high, the nib of her pen pressed against the top line.

"Just rye toast," he said. "Strawberry jam, if you have any, no butter. Who's Jimmy?"

"Who's—"

He pointed to her order pad with the longest, most elegant finger she'd ever seen on a man.

"On your pad?" he said.

She turned it over and smiled. Jimmy had written his name on the cardboard backing, along with a self-portrait.

"My son. He comes by sometimes after school."

Back behind the counter, she tried to recall what he'd ordered. Rye toast with no butter was easy enough to remember—not too many people in Sohegan worried about saturated fats. But what else had he asked for? She popped two slices of rye in the toaster and took breakfast orders from a couple of phone company workers at the counter.

"I guess you don't have strawberry jam," he said when she placed the rye toast in front of him.

Damn. "We do, actually." She fetched the jam from behind the counter. "Homemade just yesterday," she said as she placed two tiny sealed packets next to his plate.

His laugh brought out a fine cross-hatching of wrinkles on either side of his eyes. About thirty-five, she guessed, or a really fit forty.

"You don't sound like you're from around here," he said as he tried to peel off the top of a jam packet.

"I'm not."

"Downstate," he said. "Not the city…Long Island?"

She felt her face warm. "Somewhere like that."

"I'm good at accents." His own voice, deep and precise, offered no geographical clues.

"I moved here from the city." He spread jam over one-half of a rye slice. "I've been doing time up here for almost a year and a half."

Doing time? The son-in-law of the man who owned most of Sohegan?

"My condolences."

He left her a twenty-cent tip on the $1.35 bill. Fifteen percent to the penny.

Sheila came in at noon for her chicken salad on rye, iced tea with lemon, black coffee.

"Nice suit," Gwen said. "New?"

"Just arrived yesterday." Everything Sheila wore came from a catalog. You couldn't buy good clothes anywhere local, and Sheila liked to dress the part she was paid to play: assistant director of the local savings and loan. She smoothed the lapels of the pale peach suit with her palms. "You think it's a keeper?"

"Definitely."

Gwen got her iced tea, placed it on the counter in front of Sheila, and took care of a few other customers.

"I met Nick Lawrence today," she said when she brought the chicken salad sandwich.

"Here?" Sheila crinkled her nose and glanced around.

"He came for breakfast. I was beginning to think they didn't let men that good-looking into Sohegan."

"Not my type. The penis, you know."

The man sitting a few stools away glanced at her and frowned. Everybody in town knew about Sheila Stewart. She and Betsy made no secret of their living arrangement.

"Although, to hear some people talk, he had his"—Sheila turned to the man at the counter and smiled—"his *organ* removed the day he moved up here to Sohegan."

"Huh?"

"The old man, Russell Cunningham? Almost had a cow when his precious Priscilla married him. Insisted they move up here or he'd cut them both off without a cent. So sonny boy did as he was told. How's his voice, kind of high and squeaky?"

Gwen laughed. "Low and sexy. I'd say his vital parts are still functioning."

"You're glad we moved here, aren't you, Jimmy?"

They were playing go fish, an after-dinner ritual. She worried sometimes that they were getting too close, too sealed off.

"Sure. Got any twos?"

"Go fish. School's okay?"

"I guess. What do you want?"

"Just wondering."

"No, I mean what *card* do you want?"

"Oh. Got any kings?" He frowned and handed her a king. "Do you have a special friend at school yet?"

"Not really."

She hoped all the time that her wariness of people hadn't rubbed off on Jimmy. Lord knew, what Barry had done to him—

"You get to ask again, Ma."

His eyes darted at her, then back at his cards.

"Oh, sorry. Give me all your fours."

"Go fish."

She picked a card and watched him study his hand, brows knitted. He was a serious child. And earnest, like his father.

"Do you have any…" He looked up from his cards and squinted at her, pursing his lips. She blinked three times. "…Any threes?"

She rolled her eyes and handed him a three. "How did you know?"

He took the cards and tapped the side of his head with his free hand.

"ESPN."

"ESP," she said with a smile. He might be earnest, like Barry, but Jimmy had a sense of fun. Surely the other kids had noticed by now.

Once Jimmy was asleep she resumed painting the living room. When they'd found the house that spring she'd liked the idea of living in a rental—no point to renovating, and the sense of transience suited her. But a week after moving in she decided to touch up the landlord's paint job in her bedroom. Before she knew it she was repainting the entire room robin's-egg blue, working slowly and meticulously every evening after putting Jimmy to bed. The tart smell of new paint was reassuring, and in bed at night she'd look up from her book and find herself staring at the clean, decisive edge where white trim met pale blue wall. She painted Jimmy's room next—mission yellow, it was called—then the spare bedroom in a linen white.

She was painting the trim around the living room windows a semigloss white. She'd never liked painting, especially the detail work. But lately she couldn't stop, and she was doing a much more fastidious job than the house called for, given the flaky condition of the plaster walls, the shabbiness of the furniture that had come with the house, and the fact that she'd signed a one-year lease. She'd already spent a full week on the living-room windows alone.

Later, after washing up, she had trouble getting to sleep. Waiting tables was exhausting enough, but she always left the diner feeling restless. Painting and keeping Jimmy occupied until bedtime made the evening go quickly, but then she'd turn off the light, lie down in bed, and feel a resurgence of jittery energy. Part of the problem was that almost every channel of thought was off limits. Her past— too much anxiety in that. Her present—the less thought given to Sohegan and the Mecca the better. The future? She'd promised herself to take things one day at a time. Hell, it worked for alcoholics.

That left Jimmy, usually, and sometimes she'd call up an event from *his* past, play it back in her mind, savoring one detail or another. His first birthday party was a favorite nighttime stop. She'd lavished so much unnecessary planning and cash on that party; afterward, as she scraped dried frosting from the living-room rug, she realized for the thousandth time how over-the-top her love for him really was, how easily it annihilated all competing claims.

But even that wasn't working tonight. She called up a trip to the Bronx Zoo…the night she'd allowed him to sleep between her and Barry, then willed herself awake every half hour to make sure she wasn't smothering him.

Nothing worked that night, nothing worked because every time she played out a scene in her mind all she could focus on were eyes: gray blue, wide and narrow, pale yet somehow insistent, and haloed with a trace of shimmering mauve.

CHAPTER 2

Gwen stood on the third-base line, watching the T-ball game through a camera lens. Jimmy swung the bat hard but connected with the tee, not the ball, which plopped onto the dirt in front of home plate. His eyes narrowed as his lips bunched into a resolute frown. She liked that expression of his, the look of a survivor, and snapped a few pictures. His next swing sent the ball into shallow right field. A series of comical defensive errors enabled him to circle the bases and score. He looked over at her and smiled shyly as he accepted high-fives from his teammates. She thrust a fist in the air in salute.

With Jimmy on the bench, Gwen lost interest in the game. She glanced up at the low mountains in the distance. Sohegan was bordered on the north and south by the Ondaigas, craggy, undistinguished stepchildren to the more majestic Catskill Mountains to the east. The Ondaigas forced the town into a narrow valley of inhabitable land, limiting its expansion, back when the town had been actually growing, to the east and west. Which was why the town always felt crowded, almost claustrophobic, despite its small population. Sohegan offered neither the serenity of the countryside nor the excitement of the city. "They should call this place 'Neither Here nor There,'" she'd once told Mike Contaldi. He didn't find that clever at all.

"I see the artist is also an athlete."

She turned toward the deep-set voice. Nick Lawrence stood a yard or so away, holding a young girl, about a year old, she guessed. Gwen smiled and looked back at the game, but she could tell from his eyes that he knew she remembered him from the Mecca.

"Your son has a good swing. Are you his coach?" He put the

baby down.

She shrugged, crossed her arms in front of her, and wished she'd worn a bra under the T-shirt.

"He must be seven or eight?"

"Six."

"Ah. Young to be in Little League."

"It's T-ball," she said as a batter popped one over the shortstop. The reaction from the crowd was unexpectedly muted. Gwen looked over and saw at least ten pairs of eyes glance away from them and commence the obligatory cheering. *The son-in-law and the waitress—* much more interesting than T-ball.

"We haven't introduced ourselves," he said. "Nick Lawrence." He extended a hand to her.

"Nice to meet you," she said, lifting the camera to take a shot of Jimmy on the bench.

"And you are…"

"Oh, no!"

Gwen tore off in front of him, heading for the batting cage. The little girl had managed to pull herself onto the third tier of an empty bleacher. Gwen scooped her up as she toddled toward the edge. Nick Lawrence joined her seconds later.

"Thank you, I…"

She handed over the child, who was howling.

"Poor Tess," he said as he patted the baby's back.

"Tess?" She smiled.

"My wife detested the idea of naming her for a tragic heroine."

"But you prevailed."

"A rare victory. Is your husband one of the coaches?"

"That wouldn't be practical. He lives in New York City."

"I see. So how did you come to live in Sohegan?"

"I came here for the waters."

He laughed. "But there are no waters in Sohegan," he said with a perfect German accent.

"I was misinformed."

She'd given up trying to explain her presence in Sohegan. No one could accept the fact that she'd voluntarily moved there. Even the national chain stores had overlooked the place, and the only strip mall to threaten downtown Sohegan with a bit of competition had closed less than a year after opening. Still, Sohegan retained a homey if homely character, the downtown shops the center of local life. The towering husks of shuttered textile mills might block the sunlight most days, but shadows suited Sohegan, somehow. It had one of everything—pharmacy, diner, shoe store, tavern, even a taxidermist's studio for the local hunters. And the shopkeepers greeted customers by name, usually offering credit when asked.

"My wife thinks Sohegan is paradise," he said. "She insisted we move up here after Tess was born."

"Insisted?"

He considered her a beat. "Her father owns practically the entire town. I assume you figured that out since our first meeting."

She flushed and glanced away. "Not really."

"Priscilla even looks better up here," he said. "In Manhattan she seemed out of place, somehow, always wore Armani, which wasn't her style, really. Here in Sohegan she doesn't bother trying to look chic, and ends up looking perpetually radiant."

Gwen forced a smile at this rather unexpected information and tried to focus on the game. He assumed an intimacy between them, perhaps because both were outsiders in Sohegan. But they had little in common beyond that fact, she felt certain. She stole a look at him; his face was lean and angular, but his lips were full, nearly to the point of poutiness. And those eyes, a pale, elusive gray blue—hard to turn away from, somehow.

"I often wonder if her father didn't have the entire valley tectonically engineered to flatter her appearance."

His smile did nothing to soften a suddenly grave expression.

"It's probably the fresh air," she said.

He shook his head slightly but replied, "I suppose so." Then he added, "Anyway, I should be getting Tessie home. Our baby-sitter quit last week. I haven't been able to practice."

She saw Jimmy leave the bench and head for home plate.

"Piano," he said, and she flushed again. "Priscilla refuses to even consider a local baby-sitter, says they'll gossip about what goes on at the house. Nothing goes on, I keep telling her."

Another unexpected revelation. He seemed almost desperate to unload all this information, and she couldn't help but be intrigued— she was pretty desperate herself for intelligent conversation. Still, how was she to respond?

"We're working with an employment agency in New York," he said after a short pause.

"Jimmy's up at bat," she said "I need to concentrate."

She headed closer to home plate.

"You never told me your name," he called after her.

"Gwen Amiel," she said over her shoulder as she raised the camera. Waiting for the first pitch, Jimmy had that determined expression again, the one that never failed to hearten her.

"Tess and I are very much in your debt, Gwen Amiel."

She nodded as Jimmy popped the ball over the shortstop and charged toward first base.

CHAPTER 3

Gwen waved to Jimmy as he climbed into the yellow school bus Monday morning. She thought he waved back, but the windows were nearly opaque in the sharp morning light. The bus turned right and disappeared down Union Avenue, leaving her with a sense of abandonment all the more absurd for being so familiar.

"Mrs. Amiel?"

She turned. The woman approaching from the direction of the house was tall, not quite heavyset, with short hair that looked unusually black against flawless pale skin. Cream blouse, white linen slacks, expensive-looking tan leather flats. Not someone you'd expect to call your name on Glen Road in Sohegan at 7:30 in the morning.

"I thought it must be you." The voice was throaty, assured, musical. A sleek, low-to-the-ground sports car was parked in front of the house. The woman walked to within shaking distance and extended a hand. The perfectly rounded nails were short and lacquered a subdued, lustrous red.

"Priscilla Lawrence. My husband Nick met you in the park on Saturday."

The craziest notions raced through Gwen's mind as she shook the proffered hand. She was going to be accused of having an affair with Nick Lawrence. She would be offered a million-dollar reward for saving their daughter's life on the bleacher. No, a *multi*million dollar reward, payable in equal annual installments of one hundred and fifty thousand—

"Do you have a few minutes? I'd like to chat."

Chat?

"I need to get ready for work," Gwen said. "I have to be there by eight."

"Perhaps I could walk back to your house with you, then."

Gwen shrugged and they set off.

"Nick told me about your saving Tess from what might have been a terrible fall."

Gwen shrugged again. "Kids that age are always falling off of something."

"Really?" A questioning look, then a nod. It struck Gwen that Priscilla Lawrence didn't have a clue about kids that age.

"My son was one big black-and-blue mark until he turned two," Gwen said. "You can't catch them every time they fall." Here she was talking her way out of a lifetime annuity! "But you try, of course, you have to try."

"I wanted to chat this morning because…you see, our daughter's nanny resigned a short while ago and Nick thought you might be interested in taking over." She took a deep breath and blew it out like cigarette smoke. "Not live-in, of course, and the hours are somewhat flexible since—"

"A nanny?" Gwen almost snorted the word. Priscilla Lawrence took a step back and placed a hand over her chest.

"Of course, what I meant was an au pair."

"Thank you, but…" She stopped as they'd reached the end of the walk in front of her house. "I have to get ready. I'll…see you around."

As she walked toward the house she heard Priscilla Lawrence following her.

"I'd get someone to live in, but I don't want anyone local, you see. My family…"

Gwen opened the screen door and turned to face her. "I'm really not interested."

"The agencies in New York haven't exactly been inundating us with candidates." Priscilla climbed onto the small brick stoop and angled through the open door. Gwen shook her head at the woman's gall and followed her inside.

"This is so…" Priscilla's glance from right to left took in the small living room, the tiny kitchen and dining room—the entire ground floor, visible from the meager hallway. She seemed, for the first time, at a loss for words. "This is so…how in the world did you find this place?"

"From a newspaper ad."

"And I see you're having it painted."

"Sparing no expense," Gwen muttered.

"And you furnished it so *quickly*. Nick tells me you've only been in town for a few months."

"It came this way." Lumpy sofa, yellowed shades, stained rug, bookshelves crammed with dusty paperbacks, gardening manuals, ancient cookbooks.

Gwen squeezed by Priscilla and into the kitchen, where she began rinsing the breakfast dishes. She wasn't alone for more than a second or two.

"No housework, of course. We have a couple, the Piacevics, who handle that." She watched intently as Gwen did the dishes, as if she were witnessing some new medical procedure. "They're Albanian. Very hard workers."

"I'm happy with the job I have." When Priscilla chuckled at this Gwen lifted a wad of suds from the sink and considered flinging it at her.

"We're offering four hundred dollars a week. Cash. We'll pay your Social Security, naturally."

Gwen's hands froze momentarily under the hot water. Four hundred dollars was one-seventy-five more than she was earning at the diner…on a good week.

"That seems like a lot of money for baby-sitting."

"You can't put a price on good child care, can you?"

Her voice lacked all conviction. In fact, the whole spiel felt scripted. Even her outfit seemed like someone else's idea of what the lady of the manor should wear when visiting one of her tenants.

"Not interested." Gwen turned off the water and dried her hands as Priscilla Lawrence observed her closely. She felt like a kindergarten teacher giving a demonstration. *This is a paper towel, you use it to dry off. Now I'm throwing it into the garbage can!*

"Regular hours," Priscilla said. "Nine to five, give or take. The important thing is that my husband not be disturbed while he's practicing."

How could she get through to this woman with porcelain skin and Ferrari nails that she'd rather mine coal than look after someone else's kid?

"I have to go," she said.

"You have the most marvelous mouth." Priscilla moved toward her. Gwen stepped back, bumping against the counter edge. "There's an alabaster fragment in the Egyptian galleries at the Met—the Metropolitan Museum, in New York?"

"I know where the Metropolitan is."

"Yes, well, there's a fragment of a woman's face with precisely your lips. They taper off to such fine points…"

Gwen fought the urge to lick her suddenly dry lips. First the woman had invited herself inside—at seven-thirty in the morning, yet. Now she was examining her like, well, like a museum exhibit.

"I really have to go," she said. She walked out of the kitchen and grabbed her car keys off the small table in the front hall. Priscilla Lawrence stayed put.

"I *said*, I have to leave."

"Four hundred is as high as I can go," Priscilla said when Gwen returned to the kitchen. She had opened a cabinet and was absently examining the set of five-and-dime glassware that had come with the house. "But we can agree on a salary review in six months. Or sooner—say, three months, after the summer."

"It's not a question of money." Gwen closed the cabinet.

"Fine, I'll speak to my father about getting you onto the Tack and Hardware payroll."

Gwen could only stare at her.

"For the health benefits," Priscilla said, her voice wearily patronizing. "You *do* want health benefits? I thought everyone was worried about medical costs nowadays."

"So I hear." The truth was, she lived in terror of Jimmy getting sick. One ear infection could wipe out her meager savings. A broken leg would mean selling the car.

"I'll need your answer by tomorrow. Nick's out of his head having to practice with the baby—Tess—always finding her way to him. It's the music that draws her, I suppose. Do you have a pen and paper? I'll give you our number."

Gwen grabbed an order pad from the diner and scribbled the Lawrences' telephone number.

"I might as well give you directions," Priscilla said, and Gwen wrote them down too.

"The house is called Penaquoit. It means fertile ground or something like that in some Indian dialect. Oh, and in case there's no answer when you arrive, the access code is six, two, three," she said. "June twenty-third, my birthday." Gwen could only guess what an access code was, and resented the *when you arrive* bit, but she wrote the code down anyway.

"Tomorrow, then," Priscilla said cheerfully. As she walked by she extended an index finger toward Gwen's mouth, tracing her lips in the air. Gwen took a deep breath and held it until she heard the front door close.

"Jesus," she said as she exhaled. "What fucking nerve."

"It's ridiculous," she told Sheila at lunch. "I mean, *me*, a baby-sitter?"

"Oh, yeah, that would be a real step down from a waitress at Mike's place."

Gwen frowned. "I used to own an antiques store. I had my own business."

"That was then."

"Anyway, I think of this job as temporary, until I figure things out."

"And taking care of the little princess is, what, permanent?"

"It would feel like a commitment, getting to know a child. Here I feel like I can walk out at any time."

"Commitments aren't necessarily bad, Gwen."

"That's what you think." Before Sheila could argue she left to wait on two men who'd taken the booth closest to the door.

"My advice?" Sheila said when she returned to the counter to pour coffee. "Take the money and the benefits and fuck Mike Contaldi."

Half the restaurant turned toward them.

"Sheila!" Gwen whispered.

"I meant that figuratively," Sheila said to the couple nearest her at the counter.

"I don't know how you survive in this town," Gwen said.

"The bank would fall apart without me, everybody knows that. Archie McGillicuddy may be the branch manager, but without me he'd be stuffing pennies in those little brown coin tubes."

"Ladies?" Mike Contaldi turned from the grill, greasy spatula in hand. "And I—"

"Use the term loosely," Gwen said.

Mike made a face and waved the spatula to indicate a roomful of people.

"Take the job," Sheila said when Mike had walked away. "Though I'll really miss you at lunch."

"But I don't like being around kids, especially babies."

"What about Jimmy?"

"Unless they're mine."

"Gwen? The customers?" She turned, saw Mike glaring at them, brandishing the greasy spatula.

"I'll miss you, too, Sheil." Gwen leaned over the counter and kissed Sheila firmly on the lips. Behind her, she heard the spatula hit the floor.

CHAPTER 4

Gwen drove up to Penaquoit's gated entrance Monday morning battling a plague of second thoughts.

In one sense the decision had been easy enough. Four hundred a week plus a health plan was just too good to pass up. But Jimmy seemed uncomfortable with the idea of her taking care of another child. He hadn't actually said anything, and that was what worried her. Jimmy normally had an opinion about everything.

"We need the money," she'd said.

"I guess."

"It's just a job, you know." And she wouldn't be a servant, exactly. At least, she'd be no more a servant than she had been at the diner.

But those gates—black wrought-iron, with some sort of gold crest in the middle where the two halves met. And the long, tree-lined drive leading up to the unseen house where she'd be working. No, she wouldn't be a servant. She'd be a fucking peon.

She rolled down her window and pushed a black button on an intercom panel to the side of the gates. Jimmy was overdue for an annual checkup, and the shots alone would cost her a half week's diner pay. So she'd swallow a little pride and watch Tess Lawrence for a while until something better turned up.

"Yes?" came a metallic voice.

"It's Gwen Amiel," she said into the small intercom. "I'm here to—" She heard a click, then saw the gates begin to open.

Several minutes and what felt like a mile later she finally reached the house, a three-story brick affair the size of most suburban high schools. Lush green ivy climbed obediently up the front, twisting around dozens of black-shuttered windows. It was all a bit too well tended. She'd gone to many an auction and estate sale at plenty of mansions, but none of them was as immaculate as Penaquoit. Everything looked slightly too bright, too vivid, like a colorized movie. As she walked to the front door she ran a hand along the top of a perfectly clipped juniper shrub; the gardener must have used a level to get it so even. If Disney World opened an attraction called Old Money, it would look and feel just like Penaquoit.

She stepped between two white pillars flanking a massive wood door clearly intended to withstand siege. It opened just as she reached for an immense brass knocker. A heavyset woman with her hair in a bun looked her up and down. Maybe the T-shirt and blue jeans had been a poor choice.

"Welcome to Penaquoit, Miss Amiel," she said. "I am Rosa Piacevic." A streak of lightning, a couple of vampire bats, and the scene would be complete.

"Nice to meet you," Gwen said, not quite knowing what struck her as so off about this woman.

"I will take you to the child."

She followed Rosa Piacevic across the marble floor of the foyer and through a succession of opulently furnished rooms and hallways. Gwen tried to take it all in as she walked: the sweeping staircase, the glittering chandelier, the murky landscapes and stern-faced portraits, the acres of Kirmans and Bukharas and Aubussons, the profusion of antique furniture—predominantly English and all genuine, she guessed. Most insistent of all was the sound of a piano, louder as they reached the end of a long hall and turned right into another even longer corridor.

"Should I leave a trail of rice?" Gwen said.

Rosa Piacevic stopped and turned. "Excuse me?"

"You know, in case I get lost." She offered a collegial smile.

"You will not get lost."

An open doorway revealed the source of the music. Nick Lawrence was hunched over the biggest grand piano she'd ever seen, intent on a very romantic-sounding piece of music. She paused to listen and watch.

"Follow, please," Rosa Piacevic said without stopping. Gwen saluted her backside and continued walking. She and her husband were Albanian, Priscilla Lawrence had said. Very hard workers.

They stopped at a playpen in a light-filled room at the very back of the house. Two long, plump-cushioned sofas, a large coffee table bearing neat piles of magazines, and a scattering of toys suggested a room actually used by human beings.

As they crossed the room, the playpen's occupant stood up and began rattling the bars. Who would keep a child cooped up in three square feet of padded cage in a house this size?

"Here is Tess," Rosa Piacevic said.

Gwen glanced at the baby, then quickly back at Rosa Piacevic. No wonder her face was so unsettling. She had no eyebrows. The skin over her dark, deep-set eyes was perfectly smooth.

"I give her breakfast an hour ago," Rosa said. "Lunch will be at noon. Keep her away from Mr. Lawrence when he practices." She looked down at the child, her features softening for a moment. "Good-bye, *zamer,*" she said, and headed for the door. Before leaving she clucked wearily and picked up several brown leaves that had fallen from a large potted ficus.

Tess rattled the cage even more insistently.

"Why don't I spring you from this joint?" Gwen said as she scooped up Tess, who touched one of Gwen's silver earrings and giggled. At least she had no problem with strangers—or was it rather that she knew only strangers? At Tess's age, Jimmy had consecrated her every departure with full-throated howling.

"Moosie?" Tess pointed to the doorway, brows furrowed. Indeed, the music had stopped.

"You're a clever one, Tess Lawrence," she said. Tess squealed and flailed her bootied feet. Gwen had forgotten how solid babies felt, their unexpected and thoroughly satisfying density. She gave Tess's thigh an exploratory squeeze, rubbed her back.

Enough! Any minute now she'd be cooing like a besotted grandmother. Falling for someone else's kid had been right at the top of her list of misgivings about taking the job.

Tess *was* cute, though, with those huge brown eyes and golden-brown curls and that one shallow dimple on her right cheek.

"I see you've made friends."

She turned to find Nick Lawrence watching them from the doorway, looking cool and fit in a white polo shirt and loosely fitting khakis. She tried to think of something smart to say as he crossed the room, something that would let him know from the start that she was no Mary Poppins. But her wit deserted her.

"We'd already met, remember? At the park, last weekend."

"I'm glad you accepted Priscilla's offer. My instincts in this area are always correct." He smiled and reached for Tess, who eagerly toddled over to him. Without the piano music the house seemed unnaturally still; she felt the burden of its enormous size, its encompassing presence. A leaf from a sagging palm in a big terra-cotta pot fluttered slowly to the floor, as if the air had thickened.

"I was just starting my morning practice," he said. "But I thought I'd welcome you to Penaquoit." He arched his eyebrows as he pronounced the name of the house. She detected a flirtatious edge to his voice and immediately resolved not to encourage him in any way. She wasn't about to repeat romantic history—which, in her case, meant falling for guys who weren't available: men terrified of intimacy, men wedded to a career or to the bottle, men secretly attracted to men. Married men.

"It sounded great," she said. "The music, I mean." He just looked at her a moment, as if she'd said something perplexing. "I heard you playing when we passed by…"

"Anything but great," he said in a deeper voice. "Some mornings I seem to bang up against my own limitations. Has that ever happened to you?"

She hoped the question was rhetorical, since she had no intention of answering it.

"It's a kind of claustrophobia," he said, placing his palms over both ears, as if pressing his head in a vise. "Like being trapped inside a room that's too small for you. You want to break out, you *need* to break out, but you can't. You know your talent is too big for the room you've been placed in, but you also know, on mornings like this, that you'll never get out of the room."

This decidedly odd revelation was delivered with the sunniest of smiles and no self-consciousness whatsoever. Yet it seemed more arrogant than intimate, as if he simply assumed she'd be fascinated by his inner self.

"Did Rosa give you the grand tour?" he said.

It took her a moment to shift gears. "Not exactly."

He nodded as if she'd said yes. "This was my father-in-law's house originally. He left a year ago so Priscilla and I could move in. He took the house next door—well, next door around here means about half a mile away. That house had been *his* father's. They keep leapfrogging back and forth, the Cunninghams. I expect we'll move next door when Tess brings home a husband."

He looked down at his daughter wistfully.

"You probably don't need to start packing just yet," Gwen said.

He glanced at her, as if startled.

"Yes, of course. It's just the…well, the inevitability of things, you know?"

Nothing in her life had been inevitable, least of all working as a nanny in Xanadu for the daughter of the most attractive man she'd laid eyes on in years. But she nodded anyway.

"Is Mrs. Lawrence home?" she said.

He looked around, squinting, as if Priscilla might be lurking behind a sofa or potted tree. No, as if the very question of his wife's whereabouts had struck him as irrelevant.

A shrug. "Somewhere."

"I'm sure we'll run into each other."

He reached down for Tess, then handed her over.

"Well, practice calls. Good-bye, beautiful." He leaned forward, lips puckered.

Gwen held her breath. *He meant his daughter, stupid.* Still, she waited until he'd kissed Tess on the cheek and left the room before exhaling.

• • •

She spent another hour in the sunroom with Tess, dimly aware of the faint piano music that accompanied their play. Around ten-thirty Tess stretched her arms, fists above her head, and yawned.

"Time for a nap?" Gwen picked her up and felt the child's head flop onto her shoulder. "Let's go find your room, then."

She retraced their steps as best she could. Nick Lawrence didn't look up when they passed the music room. She watched for a few moments, Tess almost asleep in her arms. He arched over the keyboard, his face just a few inches above his hands. Chopin, she guessed, though her knowledge of classical music was rudimentary. Beethoven, perhaps.

"Pay moosie?"

Tess's sleepy voice was almost swallowed by the music. Nick's fists crashed on the keyboard, and when he turned his eyes shimmered with rage.

"Pay moosie?"

He turned back to the keyboard, breathing hard, then faced them again, his eyes duller, forgiving.

"I'm sorry," Gwen said.

He shook his head. "Music it is." He angled his right hand to the keyboard and began to tap out a melody. "There was a farmer, had a dog, and Bingo was his name, oh. B.I.N.G.O., B.I.N.G.O."

"Nap time," Gwen said when he was done, and left the room. In the front hallway she hesitated at the bottom of the staircase, aware again of the uncanny stillness of the house without music, as if the mansion were holding its breath inside its thick, ivied walls. Only the piano seemed to bring Penaquoit out of its coma.

She climbed the stairs and carried Tess down a long hallway that traversed the second floor. Most of the doors she passed were closed. The open ones revealed a succession of bedrooms, each furnished with antiques, each carefully made up bed topped with a profusion of pillows. Finally she reached a room with a crib and, blessedly, not a piece of mahogany in sight.

She gently lowered Tess into the crib and looked around. Matching floral curtains and wallpaper, two antique pine corner cupboards overflowing with stuffed animals, a rich needlepoint carpet, two floor-to-ceiling shelf units filled with books. Tess slept in someone's fantasy of a little girl's room, she thought, a fantasy brought to reality—if not life—by the unstinting application of money. The stuffed animals, she saw on closer inspection, were all Steiff. Every single one looked new, untouched.

Jimmy had just one toy animal, his beloved panda, the only thing she'd brought with them from the city. She'd left the rest for Barry—which was all he'd ever have of Jimmy, toys and stuffed animals and the clothes he'd outgrown. They were untraceable, she and Jimmy. Vanished.

"I see you've found the nursery."

She spun around. Priscilla Lawrence stepped into the room and smiled. She had on a floor-length cotton bathrobe cinched around the waist. She looked startled, but it could be only that her hair was so tightly pulled back.

"I wasn't sure if you'd been given the official tour," she said.

Gwen put a finger to her lips. Priscilla covered her mouth with one hand and followed Gwen out into the hallway.

"Is everything going all right?" Priscilla asked.

"Everything's fine."

"Excellent." She offered a tight smile and headed toward the stairway at the other end of the long hallway. "Now that Tess is sleeping," she said over her shoulder, "you've got at least an hour to yourself."

Gwen followed a few steps behind. Was she supposed to be grateful for the time off? If so, was she supposed to *express* that gratitude?

At the top of the stairs Priscilla stopped abruptly and cocked her head. From the second-floor landing the piano sounded muted and vaguely melancholy, but then the music had traveled a long distance to reach them.

Priscilla was beautiful, Gwen decided, if unfashionably robust;

pampered, aristocratic, and extraordinarily self-possessed, with the sexy purr of money in her voice. Rich girls, if they had any brains at all, got that way somehow, no matter what genetic hand they were dealt. Gwen had met a lot of rich girls in the antiques business.

"That damn Beethoven sonata again," Priscilla said. "Honest to God, I hear it in my sleep."

"It's beautiful."

Priscilla sighed. "Not the five thousandth time it's not. It's the Lebewohl Sonata, means farewell or something. I think it's his anthem."

Again Gwen felt unsure of her role; should she pursue this rather intriguing line of conversation or stick to banalities?

Banalities were always safer. "I suppose you need to practice to get it right."

"For what?" Scorn drained Priscilla's face of its healthy glow. "It's not as if he's preparing for a concert. Let alone a recording."

"I think I'll take a walk outside," Gwen said.

Priscilla shrugged. "I have to get ready," she said. Gwen watched her pad to the end of the hallway, where she opened a door to a dimly lit room, entered, and closed it behind her.

Ready for what? Gwen wondered, feeling a bit shaken. First Nick's odd confession concerning his self-doubts, then Priscilla's venomous attack on his talent. If that's what the help got to hear on the first day…

Finally she headed back to the nursery to get the baby monitor she remembered seeing on the changing table. Priscilla had said Tess would sleep for an hour, but she didn't seem particularly involved in her daughter's day-to-day routine. She'd take the monitor along in case Tess woke up while she was outside.

The grounds were spectacular. Flawless green lawns extended in every direction, ending in rows of tall, elegant hemlock trees shaped like giant exclamation points and topped by views of distant hills. She found a pool and pool house, a tennis court, an elaborate swing set, various small sheds, and a cottage. Everything was painstakingly clipped, shaped, painted. She walked to the end of the back lawn and turned toward the house, which looked suitably secure in its fabricated landscape. From the front, at the end of that long drive, Penaquoit was certainly imposing. But literally imposing, as if it had been inflicted on the terrain. From the back it seemed more in sync with its surroundings, still grand but no more out of place than the massive oaks that provided intermittent shade on the vast, verdant lawns.

As she contemplated the house she became gradually aware of a shrill, high-pitched keening. The noise was too constant to be birds chirping; it sounded almost mechanical, like a continuous knife sharpener or lathe, and at first she thought she was imagining it. Or perhaps her own ears were ringing; she'd polished off half a bottle of wine the night before to celebrate her new status. She shook her head, swallowed. No, the noise was still there, all around her.

She headed back to the house. The baby monitor might not be effective so far from the nursery, and the strange, grating noise was starting to seem relentless. A man crossed the lawn about twenty yards from her—late middle aged, dressed in baggy overalls.

"Hello!" he called out, then changed course to intercept her. "Mett Piacevic, caretaker for Penaquoit."

"Gwen Amiel, baby-sitter for Tess."

"I thought so. Are you finding your way around all right?"

She nodded. "Are you the person responsible for keeping this place so immaculate?"

"Me and two men from the village. Day help." Like his wife he spoke with a thick, somewhat funereal accent. But his smile at her compliment was kindly, his eyes warm. "It is big job, making everything perfectly."

"Do you and your wife live here?"

"Above the garage." He pointed over his shoulder to a two-story building fairly close to the main house.

"Anyone else?"

"Live here? No, only us. Rosa gets help from a village girl twice a week."

Village girl. It was all so medieval.

"The last baby-sitter lived here, but she left. Too quiet for her, I think." He smiled. "Except for the insects."

"Insects? Is that what we're hearing?"

He crouched and picked up something from the ground. "They come only one time in seventeen years." He handed her the shell of an insect, about an inch long. It felt as light as an ash. "The trees are full with them. And the ground." He looked mournfully at the grass, which she now saw was littered with carcasses.

"Cicadas," she said, remembering an article she'd read.

"They wait under the ground seventeen years," he said quietly, leaning toward her as if imparting a scandalous local legend. "They eat sap from tree roots. When their time comes, they dig up through the dirt to the air and make the noise to bring the mates." He smiled shyly. "They like Penaquoit. So many oak trees, so much grass. Myself? I am looking forward to seventeen years of quiet."

They listened for a few moments. The whining penetrated the body like a chill.

"I don't know how Mr. Lawrence play his music with this...this sound of crying babies always in the air." Mett Piacevic sounded genuinely concerned. "But he play all the day and all the night, with no audience except for his daughter. Once I tell him, how come you don't play for the town, maybe give big concert at the high school? He look at me like I insult him, then walk away. He has moods, Mr. Lawrence. But he love his little girl, he love her like his music."

"I'm sure he and Mrs. Lawrence both love her very much."

"You think?" He shrugged. "Now I have to work some more. We take care of the old man's place too, you know." He pointed to another stand of hemlocks. "Behind there is the house." He left her and headed in that direction. "You will like it here," he said over his shoulder. "Everything perfectly. Completely perfectly."

• • •

Later she checked on Tess, who was still sleeping, then explored the house. There wasn't much else to do; she certainly wasn't about to hang out in the kitchen with Rosa Piacevic.

But the mansion was curiously uninteresting, for all its opulence. The furniture was top-notch, of course, but on the bland side, the kind of safe, pedigreed pieces a high-end decorator would choose for wealthy clients who weren't much interested in antiques. Where were the Lawrences when she'd owned the shop?

And the house offered few clues to the personalities of its inhabitants; she wouldn't be surprised to find Gideon Bibles in the Queen Anne bedside tables in the dozen or so guest rooms on the second floor.

Gwen had just entered the big living room downstairs when she heard voices through a doorway at the far end. She stepped farther into the room, curiosity overcoming an initial instinct to flee.

"...Hit it off. She's awfully pretty." Priscilla's voice.

"I suppose." Nick.

Priscilla snorted.

"Where were you earlier today?" Nick asked.

"Out." She sounded as if that one word had exhausted her.

"Out where?"

"Errands."

Gwen heard him sigh, and she easily understood his frustration. What possible errands could someone like Priscilla Lawrence have in Sohegan? Rotating the tires?

"Even when we were first dating you used to disappear, sometimes for an entire weekend."

"You never seemed to mind."

A pause, then Nick, sounding almost wistful. "Do you ever think about that first meeting?"

"What?"

"Do you ever think about—"

"I heard you. But *why?*"

"I was feeling sentimental."

Priscilla hissed, a kind of laugh, Gwen supposed. She heard the crackle of a magazine page being turned.

"I'll never forget your first words—"

"Oh, please."

"You walked into my studio for your piano lesson and announced, 'I'm your two-thirty.'"

"Brilliant." Another page crackled, then another.

"You always knew your place, Priscilla. 'I'm your two-thirty.' Amazing."

"Shouldn't you be practicing?"

"Am I boring you? Am I keeping you from your precious magazines? *Bon Appetit?* Since when do you care about cooking? *Vogue? Glamour?*" Gwen heard two thuds as the magazines hit the floor. "*Dog Fancy?*" Thud. "We don't have a goddamn dog. *Field and Stream?*" Thud. "Are you planning on taking up fishing any time soon?"

"I might."

"It's...bizarre. You live *through* these things. Get a dog if you're interested, just stop reading about it."

Gwen heard a page turn.

"Our basement is a fire hazard..."

"*Our* basement?"

"...Full of old magazines. At least throw them out when you're done."

"What if I need to look something up?" she said with placid sarcasm.

"You can't let anything go, even old magazines," he said. "I wish I knew what you were afraid of."

Gwen heard another page turn. She left the room and exited the house through the front door. She stood on the small terrace for a few moments, grateful for the warm, dry air and the agreeable silence, then explored the grounds. As she circled the side of the house she heard something from a screened porch, a low, anguished moan. She stepped a bit closer.

"Oh, God, Nick."

Gwen backed away from the porch.

"Don't stop, oh my God, don't stop!"

Priscilla's moans were intensifying into full-throated shrieks that reverberated through the tall oaks that shaded the expansive lawn.

"Don't stop. Oh, please, don't stop!"

This was a new Priscilla—animated, hungry. And very noisy. Gwen immediately thought of the uptight junior leaguers she'd had to socialize with as part of her business, the pearl-draped blondes who danced on the baby grand after the second gin and tonic and fucked the pool boy while their husbands toiled in the city. Only Priscilla's trigger seemed to be sex.

Gwen walked away, then broke into a run. Fifty yards from the house she still hadn't escaped the screaming. She spotted Mett Piacevic pruning a shrub. He looked at her, a bit shamefaced, Gwen thought, but quickly turned away when Priscilla let forth a high-pitched shriek that seemed to last forever.

Then silence.

Piacevic glanced up from the shrub as Gwen passed him on her way back to the house.

"Cicadas," he said with an embarrassed shrug.

She nodded—the lawn was anything but silent. The cicadas had resumed their wailing.

Barry Amiel felt the tap on his right shoulder as he waited to cross Fifth Avenue. *Brooklyn's* Fifth Avenue, the shabby, Bodega-lined stepchild of its Manhattan namesake. He turned slowly; his reflexes weren't what they once were, especially at ten in the morning.

"You Barry Amiel, mister?" *Meester.* Some days he thought he'd give up drinking just to hear a full sentence of unaccented English again.

"Yeah."

"I got a message for you."

His heart quickened—amazing how it could still kick into high gear after what he'd put it through. He didn't know anyone anymore, other than the other losers at the rooming house. The Puerto Rican was about twenty, maybe younger. Same height—five-nine—but heavier, *built*.

"Message?" Barry moved closer. "What kind of message?"

The Rican frowned and stepped back. Shit, even drug dealers couldn't take the liquor on his breath.

"You wanna see your kid? You wanna see Jimmy?" *Jeemy*.

Now his heart was really stoking, and his throat was closed up so tight he thought he might burst.

"Who...who the hell are you?"

"You wanna see your kid, you come to this place." He handed him a slip of paper with a Manhattan address penned in small, precise handwriting. There was a time, too: tomorrow at noon.

"Where's he? Where's my boy?"

The Puerto Rican turned and walked away.

"Where's my boy?" Barry shouted after him, almost keeling over from the effort. "Who the fuck're you?"

The kid kept walking. Barry started to go after him but his legs were wobbly. Mornings were hardest; some days it took until two, three in the afternoon to get his strength back. Someone knew where Jimmy was. The information would cost him—he was a drunk, not a fool. But he knew he'd do whatever it took to see him, reclaim him. Jimmy was his son, always had been and always would be.

The Rican didn't know where Jimmy was, but someone had hired him to deliver a message, set up a meeting. Maybe Gwen had arranged it, wanted to get some kind of visitation thing going. Nah, she'd kill him before she'd let him near Jimmy, and in a way he couldn't blame her. She took a lot of shit, Gwen did, but she wouldn't let nothing bad happen to the kid. Any kid, for that matter. She always said she didn't like children, but once, at a market near their old apartment, she saw some black dude backhand his own son and she would've slugged the guy right there in the checkout line if he hadn't caught her arm. Almost got herself punched out that time. She never could stand to see a kid get hurt.

So if Gwen wasn't the one wanting to meet him, who was?

41

Barry shrugged—what difference did it make? One way or another he'd get Jimmy back. He smiled and headed for the liquor store on Garfield, feeling something like hope for the first time in months, clutching that slip of paper so hard his hand began to shake.

CHAPTER 5

"I hate waffles."

Jimmy pushed the plate across the table to Gwen.

"Since when?"

She pushed the plate back. "At least take a few bites. You'll be hungry by ten o'clock."

This time he shoved the plate with just enough force to send it crashing to the floor.

"Damn it!" She covered her mouth to keep from saying worse, then spotted his little grin of victory. He'd never acted like this before they moved up to Sohegan. Almost never.

The grin was Barry's, of course, showing just a sliver of white teeth. Sometimes Barry's face came through Jimmy's in the most heart-stopping way, like the moment when the picture buried inside one of those 3-D images unexpectedly begins to emerge.

"Pick it up," she said. He just sat there, not even looking at the scattered bits of plate and waffle. *"Pick it up!"*

His expression was angry but unworried; he knew she wouldn't hit him, not after what he'd been through with his father. Was breaking the plate—or stuffing an entire roll of paper in the toilet, or wetting his bed a couple of times a week lately—Jimmy's agenda for punishing her? Or just venting?

The bus honked from the corner. Jimmy ran from the kitchen.

"Come on, Mom!" He stood in the hallway, holding open the screen door. She walked a few feet behind him to the corner.

"Jimmy?" He stopped but didn't turn. "We'll talk about this later," she said, then shoved a small bag of chocolate chip cookies into the outside pocket of his backpack. "In case you're starving to death at ten o'clock." He turned, unable to repress a smile—her smile, this time, the corners of his mouth turned up, a full row of top teeth visible—and ran to the bus.

She noticed an unfamiliar straw hat in the pantry at Penaquoit that morning, lying next to a tube of expensive suntan lotion. The daily routine at Penaquoit was so unvarying, she was intrigued by what she took to be evidence of a visitor. At this point, any change would be welcome. Priscilla's parents lived next door, Russell and Maxine Cunningham, yet they'd never once come by while she was working. In fact, there'd been no visitors to Penaquoit since she'd started working, other than the gardening and cleaning crews who helped the Piacevics. Sealed off the way Tess was, Gwen actually felt sorry for her, but Priscilla scoffed at her offer to take Tess to the playground in town. "We have better facilities here," she'd said.

On her way to the sunroom that morning, where Rosa Piacevic discharged the morning handoff of Tess, she paused just before crossing the open doorway to the music room. Nick Lawrence was practicing, of course, the same Beethoven sonata he'd been working on all month. Though she hadn't tired of the piece, she had long ceased paying much attention to it. Sometimes she found herself humming the slow opening bars at home, but at Penaquoit the music had become the house background. This morning, however, she stopped to listen, drawn by something different in the music, an added richness. Maybe he'd had the piano tuned.

When she passed the music room she glanced in. Perched on a footstool a few feet from the piano was a striking woman of about thirty-five, watching him play with unblinking eyes. An audience at last, she thought.

The visitor came in to the kitchen while Gwen was giving Tess lunch. She was tall and thin, with very full lips, very green eyes, and thick red hair cut in a severe, angular fashion that showed off a long, graceful neck. She wore a light blue oxford shirt over tight black leggings. Redheads were usually pale, but this woman's face and arms were tanned to caramel perfection.

"You must be Gwen," she said in an unexpectedly husky voice. "I'm Valerie Goodwin."

Gwen had been crouching in front of the high chair, trying without much success to coax some applesauce into Tess. She stood up, wiped her right hand on her jeans, and shook hands.

"I hear you're terrific with Tess," the woman said.

Gwen couldn't help feeling patronized, but she smiled. "She's not much of a challenge, except when I'm trying to feed her."

Valerie leaned over from the waist, as if bowing to royalty, wiped a streak of applesauce from Tess's chin with the tip of a beautifully manicured index finger, and inserted it into the tiny mouth. Tess smiled and pounded the high-chair tray with both hands. Smiled? She was practically cooing. Valerie took the small silver spoon from Gwen's hand and began feeding Tess from the jar.

"I haven't seen her in almost two months," she said. "You don't really think about time passing until you see them. Children, I mean. Then you realize what you've missed. You have a child of your own, of course."

"A son. He's six."

"Jimmy?"

She nodded. Surely they had better things to do at Penaquoit than talk about her and her son.

"I'm Tess's godmother," Valerie said. "It kills me to live so far away from her."

"Where do you—"

"In the city," she said quickly, as if the answer were self-evident. "I've known Priscilla and Nick since they met each other. They're like family."

"Are you a musician too?"

Valerie used the edge of the spoon to wipe a drizzle of applesauce from Tess's chin, then expertly slipped it into the baby's mouth.

"No, no. Nick has talent enough for the three of us, as I'm sure you've noticed."

"Is he preparing for a concert?"

Her hand froze for an instant in front of Tess's open mouth. "Nick is preparing for…" She seemed at a loss, finally just shook her head, and fed Tess a final spoonful. "All done!" She dropped the spoon inside the jar and handed it to Gwen.

"You said Nick is preparing for something."

"Right." Valerie moistened a paper towel in the sink and cleaned Tess's face. "He is preparing for perfection."

Give me a break.

Valerie picked up a philodendron cutting from a small vase on a windowsill. The rootless stem had turned limp and black.

"Do you mind if I take Tess for a swim?" she said as she dropped the cutting back into the glass.

"No, not at all. I have…" She had laundry to fold in the nursery, but she wasn't about to share her to-do list with Ms. Golden Tan.

After Valerie left with Tess, Gwen walked to the front hallway and up the main staircase—she made a point of avoiding the service stairs off the kitchen. She'd promised herself not to give in to bitterness over the job, and most days she kept the promise. Good pay, good benefits, good hours, good riddance in a year's time—her new mantra.

But every so often something or someone would remind her of just where she fit in on the Lawrence food chain, and bitterness boiled over. Today it was Valerie Goodwin and her silky fingernails, feeding her godchild as if she were tossing treats to a puppy and doing a goddamn good job of it.

She felt a stirring of possessiveness and promised herself she wouldn't fall for Tess any more than she already had. But the truth was, she missed having a baby to take care of, she hadn't realized just how much until Tess came along. She'd spent most of her adult life trying to avoid having anyone depend on her, and then when Jimmy was born she'd realized that being completely responsible for someone else was perhaps the most liberating thing of all. Old demons lost their power to threaten once your life's focus shifted to someone else, someone totally dependent on you. Holding Tess, she felt that same relief—Jimmy was carving out a life apart from her, but here was a child who *needed* her completely. She would have to work harder to keep from getting more attached.

In the nursery she folded Tess's clothes and arranged them in their designated drawers. Priscilla had gone out that morning, something she did two or three times a week. Gwen never knew where she went. Chores were taken care of by the Piacevics, there was no really upscale shopping available in the area, and Priscilla didn't seem to have any local friends. Occasionally she'd walk next door to see her father, cutting through the wall of hemlocks to the east of Penaquoit. Other than that she kept pretty much to her bedroom, emerging early in the afternoon for half a cantaloupe filled with cottage cheese, served by Rosa Piacevic on the patio off the sunroom.

Gwen looked out the nursery window. Valerie Goodwin and Nick, both in bathing suits, stood by the shallow end of the pool, Valerie holding a naked Tess. The adults looked uncannily fit—there was more fat on the baby than on the two of them combined. Valerie's tan skin glowed like bullion under the hot sun; that rare combination of red hair and dark skin was really quite stunning.

Valerie handed Tess to Nick, then executed a perfect racing dive from the shallow end, surfacing halfway down the pool. She did an elegant crawl stroke to the far end and back. Nick handed Tess to her. She slowly lowered the baby into the water, cradling her to her chest. Then Nick walked down the steps and joined them in the shallow end.

They stayed there for several minutes, both adults clearly focused on the child. Gwen had never seen a father so centered on his child. Mothers who obsessed that way were called overbearing or neurotic, but Nick's preoccupation with Tess was appealing, somehow. Valerie wore the same rapt expression she'd had earlier, listening to Nick play piano. It seemed unnatural, really, how plugged into Nick she was—into Nick and his two obsessions.

Gwen was about to turn away from the window when she saw Priscilla Lawrence walk across the terrace and freeze, back from

God knew where, dressed as always as if she were meeting a friend at Le Cirque: silk blouse, tailored slacks, a white sweater draped over her shoulders in that deliberately casual way some women manage to achieve. Nick and Valerie were too wrapped up in each other and the baby to notice their observer, but Gwen shuddered. Priscilla's face looked rigid even from this distance, eyes wide open in the glaring sun, mouth puckered in an oval of pure rage.

"This is the socks and pajamas drawer," Priscilla said when she entered the nursery a few minutes later to find Gwen still putting away Tess's clothes. "Didn't I mention that?" Her voice sounded shaky, as though she were barely holding it together. She bent down and started removing T-shirts from the drawer. "Isn't it time for the baby's nap?" she said over her shoulder.

The baby. "She usually sleeps somewhere between—"

"Fine, please go and put her down." Priscilla picked up a stack of shorts, started to place them in a lower drawer, then slammed them onto the top of the little dresser.

"Are you sure you don't want some help?" Gwen said.

Priscilla shook her head and continued rearranging.

Gwen left the nursery and walked outside to the pool, feeling overdressed in a heavy sweatshirt—the house was always air-conditioned to a Nordic chill.

"Isn't Tess a little fish?" Nick said when he noticed her.

"It's time for her nap," Gwen said.

"Are you tired, my sweet?" Nick said to Tess, who responded by thrashing her feet in the water. He handed her up to Gwen.

When she looked back, Valerie and Nick were swimming side by side to the deep end, their long easy crawl strokes in perfect sync.

Gwen brought Tess to the nursery and was heading downstairs when Priscilla charged past her, carrying a pile of magazines. Her face was swollen. She *had* been crying. She crossed the foyer and stopped before a closed door.

"Gwen! Open this, please." Gwen obliged, and Priscilla plunged down a dark staircase to the basement.

Gwen left the door open and went to the kitchen, where she made herself a sandwich and read a magazine while eating, enjoying the time to herself.

The phone rang. Priscilla usually answered by the second ring; after five rings, Gwen picked up.

"Russell Cunningham calling for Priscilla Lawrence," said a woman's voice.

"She's busy right now," Gwen said, wondering what kind of man had a secretary place calls to his daughter. "She can't come to the phone."

"Is she at home?"

"Yes."

"Then she *can* come to the phone."

Gwen sighed, put the secretary on hold, and walked to the basement door.

"Mrs. Lawrence?"

At the bottom of the uncarpeted staircase she found herself in a long, dimly lit hall. She headed toward a light from an open doorway and discovered a huge room full of row after row of neatly stacked magazines. She threaded her way through the room, noting some of the titles: *Architectural Digest, Modern Bride, Road and Track, Vogue, Travel and Leisure, Gourmet, American Bird.* All kind of weird for a woman who seemed interested in nothing. She recalled Nick's words: *You can't let anything go, not even old magazines. What are you afraid of?* The damp room was chilly as a cave, and the air had that sharp, stale basement odor, laced with the moldy scent of old paper. Unlike most basements, however, this one was organized perfectly. It was like a grid of mini-skyscrapers.

She heard muffled voices through another open doorway, and walked closer to investigate. Priscilla and Valerie, still wearing only a bathing suit, were standing very close to each other in the center of a room full of old furniture and large cartons. Priscilla was caressing Valerie's face with her fingertips, murmuring something. Her own face looked swollen with blocked desire.

You have the most marvelous mouth...

Gwen turned in retreat but hadn't gone two feet before she heard Priscilla call her name in a hoarse voice.

"Your father's on the phone," Gwen said quickly. "I told him..." *I told him you were busy.*

"Thank you," Priscilla whispered as she hurried past Gwen and up the stairs. Gwen started to follow.

"Everything stops for Daddy," Valerie said. "She's still his little girl. I mean, look at this room."

It was crammed with little-girl furniture: four-poster bed, rocking chair, dressers and bookshelves and night tables trimmed in pink. There were cartons of papers and photographs, and portable coat racks sagging with black garment bags.

"Nothing gets thrown away here," Valerie said. "Not even old magazines."

Gwen unzipped a thick garment bag. Inside were a dozen or more girl's dresses on identical wood hangers, exquisite confections in pastel colors festooned with bows and ribbons and satin flowers, each of them monogrammed with a delicately stitched *P.C.*

"Tess will love these," Gwen said.

Valerie snorted. "Don't tell me you think that's why they keep all this stuff."

"Why else?"

"For immortality." Valerie left the room on a breeze of chlorine and suntan oil. "They can't live forever, but they work like hell to hold on to the past."

CHAPTER 6

Valerie Goodwin was not at Penaquoit the next morning, and the house reverted to its stifling aura of hermetic isolation. Each time Gwen entered a room she felt as if she were setting off a disturbance of some kind, ruffling invisible feathers, breaking a host of unwritten rules.

Nick resumed his marathon practice sessions, Priscilla resumed residency in the master bedroom, leaving it only for lunch and the occasional midday drive. Gwen had established an easy but firm routine for Tess, who seemed to be thriving.

A few days after Valerie's visit, Priscilla asked Gwen to take a family photograph on the terrace. Priscilla held Tess; Nick stood with one arm around her waist, his smile forced and his posture oddly stiff for a man with the easy grace of a natural athlete. Gwen took several shots before handing the camera back to Priscilla. Later that afternoon, while Tess was in the music room with her father, Priscilla summoned Gwen to the music room with a shout.

"Why was she allowed near this?" Priscilla held out the camera, its back opened, the film dangling out.

"I'm..." Gwen stopped herself from apologizing for something that wasn't her fault.

"Sorry," Nick said, "I wasn't watching. We'll take more photographs."

Priscilla stormed out of the room; Gwen picked up Tess and followed her.

The next Monday morning, Gwen was awakened at home by a phone call at 7:00. She fumbled for the receiver, reassuring herself that Jimmy was safely asleep in the next room, and that no one from her old life knew her new phone number. This could not be bad news.

"Hello?"

"It's Priscilla Lawrence. We won't be needing you today. We've decided to watch Tess ourselves." Her voice sounded flat—not bored so much as distracted. "We thought it would be nice to be together as a family for a change."

Together as a family? What about the weekend that had just ended?

"Oh." Gwen carried the phone to the window and opened the shade. Wispy clouds drifted across an otherwise clear summer sky; they would burn off in an hour or so.

"You'll be paid, of course," Priscilla said. "Enjoy the day off."

"Right. I'll see you tomorrow morning."

Gwen heard a man's voice in the background. "Tell her not to come until we call her." Not Nick's voice: gruffer, deeper.

"We'll let you know," Priscilla said. "Wait until you hear from us."

Gwen went downstairs to make coffee. Were they going to fire her? Was that what this was about?

She thought of Tess, competing with Beethoven for her father's attention, ignored by Priscilla, with only the dour Rosa Piacevic for company. She spent a half hour fretting about Tess, then cursed the attachment she'd tried so hard to avoid. *Good pay, good benefits, good riddance in a year's time.* Tess survived the weekends without her. She'd survive another day on her own.

She woke Jimmy up at 7:30. "Want to play hooky with me today?"

He rubbed his eyes. "I don't know how to play."

"Trust me, it's easy. Get dressed and I'll explain at breakfast."

She made pancakes and bacon; they ate second helpings, both enjoying the unhurried time together. Weekends were filled with T-ball games and errands and housework. Today was a bonus, a warm, sunny, agenda-free bonus.

"The caretaker at Penaquoit told me about this swimming hole nearby," she said. "It's called the Devil's Ravine. Want to go?" He jumped up from the table. "My bathing suit is at work," she said, "but we can stop on the way and pick it up."

On the drive to Penaquoit she began to have second thoughts.

Priscilla's message on the phone had been clear enough: stay away. Well, she'd just run around to the pool house and grab her suit. No harm in that, surely. No one would know she was there.

She pulled up to the wrought-iron gates and briefly considered buzzing the main house for access. Instead, she punched in the access code. Six, two, three, Priscilla's birthday.

"Wow!" Jimmy said as the gates swung open. She put the car in gear and drove through, swinging around to the side of the main house and parking in front of the garage.

"One, two, three, four…they have four garages," Jimmy said. "How come?"

"For four cars, I guess." She turned off the engine and opened the door. "Wait here just a minute, I'll be right back."

"I want to come with you."

"Okay, but let's hurry."

Jimmy unbuckled his shoulder strap and got out of the car. This was the first time he'd been to Penaquoit and she wasn't happy about having him here even for a few minutes. Though if asked she wouldn't have been able to say why.

"How come they have four cars?" Jimmy asked as they circled the garage.

"I don't know, Jimmy," she said. "We need to hurry."

"*Why* do we have to hurry?" he said as she pulled him along.

The pool was at least thirty yards from the house. With luck they wouldn't run into anyone.

An elderly man emerged from the stand of hemlock trees that separated Penaquoit from the Cunningham house next door. He had a loping, determined gait, arms swinging at his side. His gray hair was cut very short, and his posture was vaguely military as well, chest thrust forward, shoulders squared. The clothes, though, were more country club than army issue: a bright madras shirt, pale yellow trousers, tan shoes.

"That must be Russell Cunningham," she whispered to Jimmy.

"Who's he?"

"He lives next door. Come on."

Just before they reached the pool area she stopped and turned toward the big house. Priscilla Lawrence was standing on the patio, wearing sunglasses, watching her father approach. When he was several yards away she practically threw herself at him, flinging her arms around his shoulders. He patted her back a few times, then seemed to push her away. They exchanged words and were joined on the patio a moment later by Nick, the tail of his white oxford shirt hanging out over a pair of jeans. Even from thirty yards away, his hair looked disheveled. He crossed to his wife and put an arm around her shoulder; then all three of them went into the house.

"Where's Tess?" Gwen said to herself, still staring at the empty terrace.

"I thought we were getting your bathing suit," Jimmy said. He didn't like her to mention Tess.

Tess was with Rosa Piacevic, no doubt…but then why the riff about spending time together as a family? And why had "family" suddenly stretched to include Russell Cunningham?

She got her suit from the cabana and hurried with Jimmy to the car. She backed out of the parking area in front of the garage, watching the rearview mirror, and caught an unexpected movement in the second-floor garage window. Rosa Piacevic was silhouetted in yellow light, not moving, her eyes on the car.

Thanks to Mett Piacevic's good directions, she easily found the Devil's Ravine on a winding back road just off Route 24. There were no other cars in the unpaved parking area he'd directed her to on Pleasant Ridge Road. They scrambled down a steep hillside, the sound of the stream and the whining of cicadas growing louder as they descended. At the bottom of the hill was a large pool formed by a natural dam of rocks and fallen trees across a fast-moving stream about twenty yards wide. From where they stood in the narrow valley formed by the stream, the forest on either side looked cool and dark, but warm sunlight streaked down into the clearing, illuminating the swimming hole as if by a landscaper's design.

"How come it's called the Devil's Ravine?" Jimmy asked.

"Don't know. It looks like paradise to me. Wait for me here while I change, okay?"

She undressed and put on her bathing suit behind a large tree a few yards away.

"It's freezing!" Jimmy shouted when she rejoined him. He had gone in up to his ankles. They held hands and waded in over large, smooth pebbles. The water was indeed icy, and as clear and silky as moonlight.

"I can still see our toes," she said when they were waist deep. "Ready to dive in? One, two, three—go!"

She dove into the water, shocked at first by the cold. She came up right away, anxious about Jimmy. He couldn't swim very well on his own, and the water was just up to his chin. He was standing, smiling, his hair slicked back.

"It probably gets deeper in the center," she said. "Want to swim with me?"

He put his arms around her neck and she floated on her back to the middle of the pool, relishing the warmth of the sun—and her son—on her face and chest, the cold of the water on her back. Even the cicadas' wailing sounded benign there, an impenetrable wall of sound between them and the world beyond. Every few seconds she touched the bottom with one foot and pushed off. They drifted like that, from one end of the swimming hole to the other, back and forth, the only two people in this bit of heaven, the Devil's Ravine. The only two people on earth, was how it felt.

She read Jimmy a story that night, then opened the shade in his room so they could observe the moon.

"It's a half-moon," Jimmy said. "But how can you tell if it's waxing or raining?"

"Waning," Gwen said, "and I don't really know. We'll have to look it up in the morning."

He seemed to fall asleep the moment she turned off the light. She hoped for the same luck as she went downstairs. She opened a book, read a few pages, then tried the television. Finally she picked up the phone and dialed. Priscilla Lawrence answered during the first ring.

"It's Gwen. I was wondering if—"

"We don't need you tomorrow." She sounded out of breath, as if she'd run for the phone.

"Are you sure?"

"Yes. I can't tie up the line."

Click.

Gwen hung up and started on the dinner dishes. She scrubbed the bottom of a sauté pan until a decade's worth of someone else's grime was gone, then kept on scrubbing until she could see her face in the copper. What the hell was going on at Penaquoit? And why the hell did she care so damn much?

CHAPTER 7

Gwen awoke early Tuesday morning after a restless sleep in which Priscilla Lawrence's fingertips read her face like braille while her chilly voice ordered her to stay away, stay away. At one point she thought she heard a baby crying. She sat up and checked the clock: 2:00 A.M. She heard the crying again, but it was only a cat yowling outside her window, probably in heat.

Worrying about someone else's kid was a hell of a way to earn a living.

The radio weather report predicted ninety-degree heat and humidity to match. A few weeks ago Sohegan had endured just such a day, and it had been unrelievedly awful. A local pilot who ate breakfast at the Mecca had once told her the air above the narrow Ondaiga Valley was a hazardous riot of strong currents. Down below, however, in Sohegan, not a twig or leaf ever seemed to stir, leaving the town to simmer in sultry, stagnant air. Sometimes Gwen would look up at the clouds moving quickly across the sky and marvel that not a whiff of current made it down below.

The phone rang just as she was leaving to walk Jimmy to the bus.

"It's Nick Lawrence. Tess isn't feeling well. Priscilla's bringing her to the doctor this morning. But I'd like you to stop by anyway to take care of her laundry and...and to straighten up the nursery."

"I'll be there at nine," she said. "What's the matter with Tess?"

Click.

She stood by the phone, hostage to a dozen questions.

"Mom, come on!" Jimmy was at the front door. "I'll miss the bus."

"I don't like this," she said when she joined him in the hallway.

"Like what?" They headed down the front walk. "Like *what*, Mom?"

"Like this heat! It's only the middle of June and we're already on our second heat wave."

"Yeah, it sucks."

She turned quickly to him but felt unable, just then, to deal with this latest addition to his vocabulary.

At 9:00 on the dot she punched in the access code at Penaquoit. Driving slowly toward the house, she noticed a filigree of brown covering the vast front lawn; the long branches on the massive elms that lined the driveway looked unusually listless. How many weeks had it been since the last rain?

She walked to the back door, slid her key into the lock, and nearly sprained her wrist trying to turn it. Damn, it didn't work. She tried again, checked the key, then tried a third time. It still wouldn't turn, but the door swung open anyway, almost taking her right arm with it.

"New lock." Rosa Piacevic turned and headed through the pantry toward the kitchen. Gwen wrested the ill-fitting key from the lock and followed her.

"Why?"

"You think they tell me?" Rosa wiped a sponge across a spotless counter. "They tell Mett to put new lock on yesterday night. I don't know how come."

"How's Tess? Mrs. Lawrence said—"

"I clean up the pool house now." Rosa furrowed her browless forehead and headed for the back door. "That's what she want me to do, clean out the pool house."

Gwen went up to the nursery. The crib blanket was in a jumble at one end, along with two of Tess's favorite stuffed animals. One sniff told her that the diaper pail hadn't been emptied since she'd left last Friday. A few toys were scattered on the pale blue carpet.

"Good morning."

She spun around.

"Sorry to startle you." Nick Lawrence stood in the doorway, wearing a wrinkled white T-shirt, blue running shorts, no shoes. His hair, though neatly combed, had an unwashed sheen. He looked exhausted.

"That's okay," Gwen said. "Where's Tess?"

"Priscilla took her to the doctor. They'll be back around lunchtime."

Three hours with the pediatrician? "What's wrong with her?"

"You know these summer colds…" He shrugged and offered a shallow smile. "Why don't you straighten up, take care of her laundry…you can go home when you're finished." He started to leave.

"I don't mind staying," she said. "I've nursed Jimmy through many a summer cold."

He turned back. "Thanks, but that won't be necessary. Priscilla gets pretty possessive about Tess when she isn't feeling well. Has to be with her nonstop." Though he managed to say this with a straight face, he turned away as soon as he was through.

"You're sure she's okay?" Gwen asked.

He stopped and turned back. "This place is…it's so dead without Tess." He glanced around the room, as if seeing it for the first time. "Penaquoit isn't exactly a warm place, I realize that. But just knowing that she's here…"

"She'll be—"

"Listen!" He touched his ear with an index finger. "Perfect silence. When Tess is here, even when she's sleeping, it's never this quiet."

To her the house *always* seemed eerily silent, whether Tess was around or not.

"I can't practice when she's not here," he said. "The music doesn't sound right, somehow."

"She'll be back in a few hours."

His head snapped up.

"Of course. Sorry to disturb your work. There's a pile of Tess's clothes in the laundry room. Once those are done you can leave."

As soon as he left, Gwen set about straightening up the room, starting with the crib. She turned to start picking up the toys on the floor and caught a glimpse through the window of Russell Cunningham, carrying a large duffel bag across the lawn. A cigarette dangled from one corner of his mouth.

About fifty yards from the house he stopped and put the bag down. He waited a few seconds, breathing hard, before picking it up and going on. Now she saw Mett Piacevic heading toward him, shouting something she couldn't hear through the closed window but assumed to be an offer of help. When the old man noticed Mett he shook his head and kept walking. Mett stood in the middle of the lawn, watching, as Cunningham reached the house and entered through the sunroom door.

Two visits in two days from the old man after a month of no appearances at all? Strange. And what was in the bag that was so precious he wouldn't let Mett Piacevic help him carry it?

She finished tidying up the nursery and headed for the laundry room, as usual taking the main stairs. As she crossed the foyer she heard voices from the sunroom: first Nick's, then the old man's.

"Fuck the police!" the old man shouted. Through a window she saw the red sports car pull up. Priscilla got out and headed for the front door. Where was Tess?

The laundry room was one of a series of chambers off the kitchen; there was also a huge pantry, an unused servants' dining room, two storage rooms stocked with a bomb shelter's worth of canned food and paper goods, and two large closets. The laundry room was a big, old-fashioned space, obviously designed for a time when a household like Penaquoit employed a full-time laundress. Three long fluorescent lights were suspended over a large porcelain sink, a giant pants presser she'd seen Rosa Piacevic use to iron Nick's khakis and jeans, a late-model washer and dryer, and two long trestle tables for folding clothes.

Next to the washing machine was a small pile of Tess's things. As Gwen crossed the linoleum floor she heard the phone ring from the kitchen. It was picked up before the first ring had ended. She began to sort the clothes by color, pushing aside a steam iron and the baby monitor to make room for the two piles. A lot of laundry for three days, she thought.

She loaded Tess's whites into the washer, poured in detergent, and closed the lid. She'd get Tess's lunch ready while waiting for the first load to finish. Three hours with a pediatrician could make anybody hungry.

Gwen entered the kitchen a few minutes later but stopped when she heard a crackling sound from back in the laundry room. She went back and saw the tiny green light flickering on the baby monitor. Someone must be talking in the nursery. Was Tess back already? Gwen lifted it and tried to raise the volume, but it was already turned up.

"Two o'clock, Route Twenty-four." Nick's voice, tense and nervous. "He said to bring a cell phone. I gave him the number."

"Where on Twenty-four?" Russell Cunningham was practically shouting. "It's probably fifty miles long, for God's sake."

"He just said Route Twenty-four, Daddy." Priscilla's voice was calm. "I guess he'll call us on the way."

"This is getting ridiculous," Nick said. "I'm calling the police."

"No!" Russell Cunningham's roar sent a shudder through the monitor in Gwen's hand. "I won't let the police screw things up again. Everything is working out. I have the money, he…or she or it, who can tell with that—what did you call it?"

"A voice synthesizer," Nick said.

"Right, that *voice* called exactly on time. We don't need the police. Once we have Tess back, then we'll talk about calling the authorities."

Gwen pressed the monitor to her ear.

"If something happens to her…" Nick's voice was higher than usual. "She asked for Gwen," he said, sounding almost wistful. "Tess asked for Gwen on the phone."

"Our sitter," Priscilla added in a deflated voice.

"You mean to tell me she asked for the baby-sitter?" Russell said.

Gwen felt a rush of anxiety. *She asked for the baby-sitter.*

"I hope you know what you're doing," Nick said.

"Leave it to me," the old man said. "This is a simple business transaction. If we uphold our end of the bargain, we have every reason to expect that—"

"Is that all you ever think about, *business?*"

"Someone has to. We can't all sit around every day tickling the ivories, now, can we?"

"It's called practicing."

"Practicing for what? I don't see any recording offers flooding in. You haven't performed or recorded a goddamn thing since you married my—"

"Stop it, both of you!" Priscilla's voice was deep and disdainful. "Save it for later, after Tess is back. Right now we have work to do." She sounded tense but composed, as if giving last-minute instructions to a catering staff. "Have you told Gwen to leave?"

"I told her she could go after the laundry was done," Nick said. "She should be through by noon at the latest."

"I still don't know why she had to come at all," the old man growled.

Gwen heard Nick sigh. "Letting her get suspicious wouldn't help in the least."

"As it is, she may talk," Priscilla said. "To the shopkeepers, her former colleagues at that diner."

Colleagues? Despite everything, Gwen had to smile.

"Better to keep her here as long as possible," Nick said. "I told her Tess was with you, at the doctor's."

"Good. And the lock?"

"Mett changed it last night. I told him I'd lost my key and had to break in through the window."

"He bought that?" the old man said contemptuously.

"He seemed to," Priscilla said. "Rosa suspects something, though. She's getting that *refugee* look again."

"So long as she keeps quiet until we have Tess back," Russell Cunningham said.

"We'll take my Range Rover," Priscilla said. "Nick, I think you should wait here, in case there are any last-minute changes. Daddy and I will—"

"*What?*"

"Daddy and I will make the transfer."

"If you think for one minute that I'm going to wait here while my daughter is—"

"*Our* daughter."

"I'm coming with you, Priss. Your father can wait here."

"The hell I will! That's my five million in the duffel bag. I go where *it* goes."

A long silence, punctuated by audible breathing. Gwen pictured them watching each other, assessing their relative positions.

"We'll all go, then," Priscilla said.

The two men mumbled their assent.

"Where were you just now?" Nick asked a moment later.

"Out," Priscilla answered.

"Out where?"

"I needed to get away for a bit. I went for a drive."

"A two-hour drive?"

"She doesn't need your permission," the old man snarled.

"I'm going to check on Gwen," Nick said.

"I think she can manage without you," Priscilla said.

"What's that supposed to—oh, fuck it." Footsteps, leaving the room.

Gwen flicked off the monitor and was hiding it in a drawer under the counter when Nick entered the room.

"How's the laundry coming?"

She had her back to him as she transferred the white clothes from the washer to the dryer.

"Fine."

"When you're done, you can go home." He sounded tentative.

She nodded, still not facing him. "Is everything all right?"

"Of course, why do you ask?"

"No reason."

He walked to the window and looked out. "Going to be a hot

one today."

Gwen said nothing.

"Did you always know you wanted a child?" he asked.

Her hands froze for a moment inside the dryer.

"No," she said softly. In fact, the pregnancy had been an unpleasant surprise, coming long after the marriage had deteriorated into angry silences punctuated by infrequent sexual skirmishes. She'd thought about ending the pregnancy every day until it was too late.

"But once he was born you felt differently, right?"

"I never wanted to be a mother, and that didn't change even after Jimmy was born."

"But you—"

"But I knew right away, the moment I saw him, that I wanted to be *Jimmy's* mother."

"Destiny," he said softly.

She shook her head. "I believe in biology."

The crumbling marriage, the virtually fail-safe diaphragm, the canceled appointments at the abortion clinic…Jimmy had willed his way into life. Maybe destiny *was* the right word. Jimmy was her fate, and she his.

"I always wanted a child," he said, still facing the window. "I always knew it wouldn't…couldn't end with me."

"*It?*"

Their eyes met.

"You have a way of seeing through me," he said. She shook her head. "No, you do. It's not what you say so much as how you look at me. You *see* things."

She turned and resumed folding. Though her back was to him and he was wearing sneakers, she knew the second he left the room.

CHAPTER 8

Alone in the laundry room, she felt so shaky she had to sit down. Someone had taken Tess and the Lawrences weren't calling the police.

She tried to piece together what she knew. Tess had been gone since at least yesterday morning. The kidnapper had broken into the house through the back door, smashing a window to unlock it from the inside. The Lawrences had been contacted at least once yesterday, when they learned that the ransom was five million dollars. The transfer was to take place that afternoon, somewhere along Route 24. They—

The dryer buzzed. She unloaded it, then transferred the other pile of clothes. She started folding the laundry, clumsily, her hands still shaking.

Should she call the police herself? She smoothed one of Tess's white cotton T-shirts with her palm, then held it to her face.

"Nothing smells clean like the laundry."

Gwen spun around to find Rosa Piacevic staring at her. How long had she been there?

"Is Tess back yet?" she asked, though she knew the answer.

Rosa shook her head, somewhat mournfully, and turned to leave.

"Wait." She turned back. "Did Mr. Cunningham have some kind of trouble with the Sohegan police?"

"Mr. Cunningham?"

"I don't mean *legal* trouble, it's just that he seems very hostile toward them." Rosa seemed to consider her for a beat, then frowned and turned to leave.

"Please," Gwen said. "It's important."

"Why important?" Rosa pivoted slowly around.

"I'm not sure, but—"

"If Mr. Cunningham is hostile at the police, why not? After that business with his son." Another mournful shake of her head.

"Mr. Cunningham had a son?"

"Russell the Third, called Russ, sometimes Trip. A year older than Priscilla. A sweet boy, but trouble. They sent him to boarding school, very expensive place, but he had the eye for the local girls." Rosa pursed her lips.

"What happened to him?"

"He comes home for Christmas holiday, twenty years ago, and one night he drinks too much with a girl, a *Sohegan* girl. They go for a drive; then a policeman, he sees the blue Lincoln Continental on the wrong side of the road. He put on his flashing light, but Russ won't pull over. He was not for nothing a Cunningham." Rosa smiled sadly. "They have a chase, then Russ and the girl go over the side of a hill, both dying right away."

"And Mr. Cunningham blames the police for his son's death?"

"He won't let them on the property, not even when we have a break-in."

Rosa turned slowly in the direction of the rear door, then back to Gwen.

"What about his wife?"

"Maxine Cunningham never gets over her son's death. Never leaves her house except to go to church on Sunday. She reads her Bible all the day long." Rosa stepped closer to Gwen. "And she drinks. Too much, I think."

"How sad."

"The old man, he keeps a pistol by his bed. I know this because I clean there, next door, once a week. And he got one for Priscilla, for her bedroom, too. 'We defend *ourselves* now,' I heared him tell her." Rosa shook her head again and left the room. "Too many guns in this place," she muttered as she crossed the kitchen.

Gwen folded the remaining items and carried the two piles of clothes up to the nursery, taking the back stairs for a change. Nick had been right: the house *was* unusually quiet. If only a breeze were blowing…

She glanced down the long second-floor hallway at the closed door to the master bedroom. Priscilla was behind that door; perhaps Nick had joined her there. Was the old man still with them? She entered the nursery and stopped short.

Russell Cunningham sat on the wicker rocking chair next to Tess's crib. His lips were slightly parted, as if he was about to say something. His eyes were wide open but unblinking. For a moment she thought he'd died right there in the nursery rocker.

He was the grandson of the founder of T & H, a product of boarding school and the Ivy League—everyone in town knew every detail of the family's story. Yet Russell Cunningham looked anything but pampered. His face had the deep creases and ruddy coloring of a man who worked out of doors, or sweated over heavy machinery in a hot factory.

She cleared her throat, got no response, and coughed. He looked at her, blinked, and started to get up.

"You must be the new girl."

New girl? She let it pass. The man was suffering.

"Gwen Amiel. You must be Tess's grandfather."

He glanced over at the crib, as if hoping to find it occupied. "What do you think of my granddaughter?"

"She's adorable. A very sweet little—"

"That's not what I'm after. Is she smart?"

She's a year old, for Christ's sake.

"Very bright, I'd say."

He squinted at her a few seconds. "Her mother went to Smith, you know."

Gwen didn't know, but nodded anyway. He flicked an ash into a small pewter cup on which Tess's name and birth date were engraved.

"And her father attended Julliard. Didn't graduate, but I expect the tough part's getting in."

Again a nod seemed in order.

"I'm a Harvard man, myself. Like my father."

She managed not to say that she'd gone to Cornell—gotten in

and graduated. She didn't think he'd care that the *new girl* was a nanny from the Ivy League.

"Tess is…" He glanced around the room, from the crib to the changing table to the corner cupboards bursting with brand-new stuffed animals. "Tess is special. I hope…" He cleared his throat. "I hope you know that."

She nodded. "Sometimes when we're outside, Tess points to your house…"

"You can't see my place from here."

"She points to the trees, actually, the ones that separate your house from Penaquoit."

"She does?"

She nodded again.

"Does she say anything?"

Gwen swallowed and plunged deeper into the lie. "'Gan-pa,' I think. Something like that."

"I never heard her even come close," he snapped.

"Maybe she—"

"But it wouldn't surprise me." His features softened. "'Gan-pa,' is it? You're sure?"

"Positive."

"Well, we're very close, you know. Birds of a feather. She even looks like me, don't you think? My hair was gold, like hers. And we both have hazel eyes."

Gwen nodded, but Tess's eyes were brown, not hazel. Surely he'd noticed that.

"If you'll excuse me, I'll just put these away."

She circled around him and carefully placed the clothes in their designated spots in the double dresser. As she left the room the old man slowly lowered himself into the rocking chair, saying "grandpa" softly as he sat.

• • •

Jimmy rolled down the back window of the Pearsons' Buick, which had a cardboard pine tree hanging from the mirror that made the car smell like the kitchen floor right after his mom washed it.

"Jimmy, did you roll that window down?" Mrs. Pearson said without turning around. "We have the air on."

Hey, I'm choking to death, he wanted to say. But Mrs. Pearson would probably scream or have a heart attack if he did—she was always worried about something. He rolled up the window and held his breath for as long as he could, noticing how the two of them looked like brother and sister: same white hair, cut short, same pink skin over the same blue collar. Pretty funny, actually. If only there was somebody to laugh with. Laughing alone wasn't much fun.

He looked out the window as they drove through downtown Sohegan. Up ahead was the diner. He kind of missed hanging out there, getting to eat all the cake and pie he wanted when his mom wasn't looking—Mike said it was their secret, man to man. The car stopped at the light in front of the diner. Jimmy pressed his face against the window to see if Mike was there.

And felt his insides go soft. There, at the table nearest the front door, right by the window. Not Mike. *Him.*

The car moved along but Jimmy felt like his face was stuck to the window, like when it's so cold metal turns to glue when you touch it. A right-hand turn, a left, and then they pulled into the Pearsons' driveway and Mrs. Pearson got out and opened his door and he practically fell out onto the ground.

"Why, Jimmy, you almost fell right—" She stepped back, put a hand on her cheek. "Jimmy, you've wet yourself." She took another step back. He got out of the car and ran to the house.

"He wet the car seat," he heard Mrs. Pearson tell her husband. "Now why would he do a thing like that?"

CHAPTER 9

It had taken Gwen only a few weeks to learn her way around Sohegan and the surrounding countryside. The long, narrow valley was divided by Route 24; if you strayed too far east or west of 24 you ran up against the bordering Ondaiga Mountains, which were sparsely populated and crisscrossed by dusty, unpaved roads. Ten miles to the north and south of downtown, LEAVING SOHEGAN signs let you know that you'd gone too far. Within these borders was an orderly grid of streets; only three intersections merited stoplights.

Gwen pulled her red Honda into the parking lot of Mario's, the town's sole car dealership, which was situated on Route 24 just north of town. The turnoff for Penaquoit was about a half mile south, so the Lawrences would have to pass directly in front of Mario's on their way to the transfer point.

She turned off the engine and checked the time: five minutes to two. Sticky heat trickled in through the open window, and within minutes the back of her T-shirt was clinging to the vinyl seat. She'd gone home, tried to forget what was happening, but couldn't. She was worried about Tess, burdened by a sense of responsibility that angered her by its intensity.

If only Tess hadn't asked for her. Why couldn't she have asked for her mother or father? Why her?

Or maybe it was only boredom, the need for *something* interesting in her life. She and Jimmy were safe in Sohegan; her job was low-stress; most nights she didn't bother locking the door. No wonder she couldn't mind her own business! So she'd driven up to Mario's; at least she'd reassure herself that things were going according to plan.

And then what?

Christ, it was hot. She wondered what Tess was wearing. One of her cotton stretchies, she hoped; Tess tended to get prickly heat, the back of her neck got all red and—

Tess was not her child. She was not her problem.

Not her child, but Priscilla wasn't exactly nurturing, and Nick's love for his daughter was too idealized to be of much practical use in a crisis. She closed her eyes and saw Tess in the middle of a vast field, all but swallowed by tall grass, crying, wailing. When she opened her eyes the field vanished but the wailing remained. The cicadas, she realized after a tense moment. The goddamn cicadas in the field behind the showroom.

She rolled up her window, started the engine, and switched on the air-conditioning, aiming the center vent directly at her face. Better. A minute later the green Range Rover drove by, moving slowly. Without thinking she put the car in reverse, backed out of the space, shifted into first, and made a left onto 24.

She quickly caught up to the car, then concentrated hard to maintain a safe distance. Nick was driving, Priscilla was next to him, and Russell Cunningham was in back. Suddenly the car veered left, making the turn at the last possible moment. Gwen braked her car until the Range Rover had completed the turn and traveled a good way into the road before she turned. As soon as she'd turned she realized she had been this way only yesterday—Pleasant Ridge Road led to the Devil's Ravine, just a mile or so ahead, on the right.

She drove very slowly; there were no other cars on this road, and the Lawrences would recognize her Honda if it suddenly appeared in their rearview mirror.

A few minutes later she saw the Range Rover on the right, about ten yards from the spot where she'd parked with Jimmy. She pulled into a long, unpaved driveway on the left, coasting a good fifteen yards before stopping where the car couldn't be seen from the road.

She got out and walked to the end of the driveway. The Lawrences' car was about twenty-five yards down the road. She waited behind a large tree until she was convinced that it was empty.

Now what?

Well, the choice was simple enough. Get back in the car and drive home. Or behave like a complete idiot and follow them into the woods. The decision took just a second.

Idiot it was.

CHAPTER 10

Gwen ran across the street and quickly found the path she and Jimmy had taken down to the ravine. The Lawrences must have used a different, parallel path. They'd be upstream from her, about twenty-five yards or so.

The woods were densely humid, pungent with decay. Gnats swarmed around her face as she walked, the cicadas humming their tuneless mating song. Sweat was soon trickling onto her forehead. She'd keep going until she reached the stream, find out what was going on, then get the hell back to the air-conditioned Honda.

She reached the top of the ridge. Below, the stream flickered through the foliage like shards of mirror, sending flashes of white light up into the treetops. She stopped and listened to the rushing water...and heard footsteps.

Twenty yards upstream, three figures made their way down the steep embankment: Nick, Priscilla, and, clearly working hard to keep up, Russell Cunningham, clutching the large duffel bag she'd seen him with yesterday at Penaquoit.

She crouched behind a tree and watched. Halfway down the embankment, Nick stopped, turned, and tried to take the bag from his father-in-law. Russell shook his head and barreled down the bank with renewed speed, though he was obviously having some difficulty with the steep grade. Now Priscilla trailed the two men, fastidiously navigating her way among the rocks and bushes, eyes fixed on the ground.

When they reached the stream, all three looked up at the surrounding forest, slowly turning around. Under the circumstances, Gwen might have expected them to huddle together, but they kept a sizable distance from each other, like three strangers waiting for introductions. The old man growled something she couldn't quite make out; the only response came from two crows feeding on the ground nearby, who took flight with raucous irritation.

A moment later Gwen heard a faint ringing sound. Priscilla placed a cell phone to her ear, listened for a few seconds, and then said something to her father, who immediately waded into the rushing stream. Nick bolted after him, trying to grab the duffel bag, but the old man ignored him, charging through the current. Nick began shouting at him; then Priscilla joined the argument, but none of it had any impact on Russell Cunningham, who squeezed the bulging bag to his chest as the water reached his hips. Nick, watching him, raised his arms and let them fall against his hips.

The old man waded to the far side of the stream and kept walking up the west embankment. The other two watched him, standing at least five yards apart. When Russell got halfway up the hill he dropped the bag and looked around. He glanced back at the bag, leaned over, and touched it, as if expressing a regretful farewell, then turned and scrambled back down to the stream, which he quickly crossed.

The reunited family once again stared at the other side of the stream, none of them speaking, let alone touching. Like competitors in a scavenger hunt, Gwen thought. The phone chirped again. Priscilla raised it to her ear, listened for a moment or two, and placed it back in her pants pocket. She said something to the two men, and immediately started walking back up the hill toward the Range Rover.

But the two men stood there for a minute, staring across the stream. Gwen followed their gaze. Nothing stirred, not even a breeze. She couldn't make out the exact spot where Russell had left the bag; the thick canopy of tall oaks and maples all but blotted out the sunlight.

After a while the old man clapped his hands, turned, and headed up the hill. Nick continued to stare across the stream, but a loud growl from his father-in-law seemed to break his reverie, and soon he too was climbing up the hill toward the car. Within moments all three were out of sight.

Gwen didn't move, eyes fixed on the spot where she thought the bag had been left. If she saw the person who retrieved it, perhaps she'd be able to identify him for the police. As long as she remained perfectly still she was at no risk, and if no one knew she was there, her presence couldn't endanger Tess in any way.

From up the hill she heard a car engine start—the Range Rover. A drop of icy sweat streaked down her neck and under her T-shirt. A shadow flitted across the stream. She looked up; a large hawk swooped effortlessly over the swath of sky above the stream, gliding back and forth on a breeze too high above ground to give mere humans relief.

She heard a sound. Footsteps? Nothing moved across the stream. That noise again, not footsteps. It sounded like…

Crying. Someone was crying. A baby.

Tess. Gwen slowly got to her feet and craned her neck toward the sound. The crying had escalated to wailing, echoing off the steep embankment in eerily hollow and plaintive waves of sound. Gwen took a cautious step down the hillside toward the stream, eyes glued to the spot where the bag had been left. Still no movement, no sign of Tess other than the pathetic sobbing.

"Gen? Gen?" The wailing was punctuated by pleas for… Gwen darted down the hill, jumping behind a thick tree trunk just a few yards from the stream. The crying continued, a succession of desperate gasps, choking coughs. She had to help her…What if she'd been left there, in this awful heat, with mosquitoes and who knew what else?

Suddenly a figure streaked across the clearing on the other side of the stream, pausing a moment at the spot where the bag had been left, then disappearing into the woods. Tall, dressed in black, possibly wearing a mask of some kind, since she couldn't make out a face. The sobbing continued.

She waited, sorting out what she'd seen. The kidnapper must have retrieved the duffel bag and fled, leaving Tess. The Lawrences had driven off—she'd heard the engine start a full minute ago. Who was going to get the baby?

She hesitated a few moments to make sure no one was across the stream. Tess's incessant wailing made it hard to concentrate, but she managed to convince herself that whoever had picked up the bag was gone. She moved out from behind the tree, walked slowly toward the stream, and waded in, eyes focused on the other side, on that clearing where the bag had been.

Halfway across she dropped into the deep hollow she and Jimmy had floated across. She swam slowly, eyes still peeled on the clearing halfway up the hillside. The kidnapper must have picked the spot upstream because he knew the old man would be able to walk across at that point without getting the money wet.

She left the stream, wet clothes clinging to her body, Tess's wailing louder and louder as she climbed the hill on the other side, alert for movement.

"Tess?" she whispered. "*Tess?*"

The crying was now a shrill, piercing wail that reverberated all around her. A few more yards and she'd be at the spot where she thought the old man had left the bag. Tess would be nearby. She'd pick her up and calm her and then—

Holy God. She froze, one hand covering her mouth. The duffel bag was still there…The kidnapper *hadn't* picked it up. Unless it was empty. *Please, God, let it be empty.* She walked as quickly and quietly as she could to the bag, unzipped it a few inches. Thick packets of bills were crammed right up to the opening.

Shit, the kidnapper must still be—

An explosion, then a whizzing sound just inches from her ear. She spun around in time to see the dark-clad figure duck behind a tree. Her right ear was ringing from the explosion—the gunshot—but as she ran for the shelter of a large boulder wedged into the hillside she realized that the woods were otherwise completely quiet: Tess had stopped crying.

She crouched behind the rock, gasping for air, trembling. Nothing moved, at least she heard nothing move; from behind the boulder she couldn't see the clearing. Where was Tess? Why had she quieted down so suddenly? What if the bullet—

Something moved behind her and she jumped. A fat gray squirrel scampered up a tree. Slowly, legs jittery, she started to stand. As soon as her eyes cleared the top of the boulder there was a second shot and an explosion just to the left of her. She felt something sting her face as she threw herself on the ground behind the rock. Blood dripped onto her shirt…She'd been hit.

No, not hit, just scratched on the neck by the spray of rock fragments. She closed her eyes for a moment, trying to think. Another gunshot. She flattened herself against the rock. This one sounded as though it came from across the stream. She slid over to the edge of the boulder and peeked out. Nick Lawrence was charging down the far side of the ravine, a gun thrust in front of him.

Still another gunshot from directly in front of the boulder. Nick ducked to the side, taking cover behind a tree, and fired back.

"Where's my daughter?" he shouted. "Where is Tess?"

He was answered by another shot, which he returned immediately. Where *was* Tess? Gwen crawled to the other side of the boulder and looked out, catching a glimpse of the kidnapper crouched behind a tree. Tall, face covered by a black ski mask, a bulky black parka disguising the contours of his body. But no Tess.

Why the hell had she gotten involved? If she'd minded her own goddamn business the kidnapper would have grabbed the money and taken off, leaving Tess behind. Now bullets were flying, Tess was ominously silent…

She peered around the side of the rock. Nick was running from one tree to another, his gun still pointed across the stream at the kidnapper, who was out of her line of sight. Nick was approaching the stream, but couldn't possibly cross it, not without making himself a clear target. And yet he was heading right for them.

"Nick, go back!" she shouted. He glanced at her and froze for a second. A shot was fired, hitting the ground a few feet from him and scattering dirt into the air. He jumped behind a tree, then emerged and plunged into the stream.

"Get the police!" she yelled. "Don't try to cross the—"

A bullet sizzled right by her face. She threw herself back behind the boulder. Her heart felt as if it were going to tear a hole through her chest. Then she heard Russell Cunningham's voice:

"What the hell is going on?" He charged down the other side of the stream, waving a gun. "Where's my granddaughter?"

Nick had managed to cross the stream and hide behind a boulder opposite Gwen, nearer the kidnapper.

"Russell, get away!" he shouted.

But the old man continued down the hill, oblivious to the gunfire as he stumbled toward the stream.

Gwen crawled to the other side of the boulder and looked out. The bag was still there, in plain sight, like some sort of prize in an athletic contest, waiting to be claimed.

"Daddy, come back!"

Shit, now Priscilla was in the act. Gwen shimmied over to the other side of the boulder and saw Priscilla running after her father.

"Daddy, don't! Come back! Daddy, listen to me, come—"

A gunshot stopped her cold. She threw up her hands, as if surrendering, her mouth an almost perfect circle. The entire forest seemed to freeze along with her, the sudden silence like a huge vacuum sucking in movement, sound, air. Even the old man stopped and stared. Nick leaned out from behind a tree, watching. A splotch of red emerged on Priscilla's white blouse, quickly spreading across her entire chest. A second shot rang out. Priscilla crumpled to the ground.

The old man bellowed something indecipherable as he charged back up the hill toward her. Still holding a pistol, Nick raced back down the hillside and into the stream, heading for his wife. Gwen listened for Tess. Surely all the gunfire, the shouting, would have alarmed her? Why was she so quiet?

A horrible roar from across the river resounded through the forest. The old man, hands akimbo, eyes facing the sky, howled until his voice gave out. Then, as if remembering something, he spun around, facing the clearing across the stream, and froze. Gwen crawled to the edge of the boulder and looked out at the clearing.

The duffel bag was gone.

Russell Cunningham collapsed to his knees as Nick Lawrence stood and turned toward the river.

"Tess!" He lunged down the hill. When he was waist deep in the stream he stumbled and fell into the water. He got up immediately, coughing, and charged ahead, paddling with his hands as he continued to shout his daughter's name.

Gwen slowly stood up, confident but not completely certain that the kidnapper had left. She made her way around the boulder, decided she was safe, and ran across the small clearing to the area where she'd heard Tess's voice.

"Tess? Tess, where are you?"

She pushed aside low branches, forearms stung by prickers. She screamed when she felt a hand on her shoulder.

"What the hell are you doing here?" Nick looked at her with fierce, panicky eyes, his chest heaving.

"I...I was..."

He turned away from her, frantically scouring the vicinity for his daughter, shouting her name over and over and over, his voice growing weak and hoarse. Finally, he leaned against a tree and slowly sank to the ground, hands bloody from the prickers.

"She's not here," he said, beginning to sob. "Oh, Tess, oh, Tess..."

Gwen walked over to him. "Do you have the phone with you?"

He shook his head. "Priscilla has...oh, God, Priscilla."

He glanced across the stream. Russell Cunningham was kneeling over his daughter's body, rocking slightly.

"Priscilla has the phone?"

He nodded slowly, still gazing across the river with wide, disbelieving eyes.

"I'm going to call an ambulance," she said, already running down the slope toward the stream. If she did something helpful, made some positive contribution, perhaps...

Perhaps what? She crossed the stream, pulling herself through the water with her arms. Perhaps she wouldn't feel responsible for what had just happened? Even then, charging through the freezing water, she knew that wasn't possible, and never would be.

Back on dry land, she sprinted up the hill and knelt beside the old man. He looked at her a beat, puzzled, seemed about to say something, then turned back to his daughter. The phone was clutched in Priscilla's right hand, covered with blood. Gwen gently slid it out from her grip—her death grip, she thought, for it was obvious that Priscilla wasn't breathing—and pressed the power button. She glanced across the stream and saw Nick, still sitting with his back against a tree, staring across the ravine at them, as motionless as his dead wife.

She hesitated before dialing. The ravine was suddenly, infinitely silent. No one spoke. The birds were quiet, the trees still, the air calm. Even the cicadas had stopped singing.

CHAPTER 11

Dwight Hawkins arrived at the ravine as an ambulance pulled up, about ten minutes after a very strange call from a woman he'd never heard of. The dispatcher had put her right through to him.

"There's been a woman killed," said a female voice. "At Devil's Ravine, it's off Route Twenty-four, just north of—"

"I know Devil's Ravine. Who are you?"

"Gwen Amiel...Please, just—"

"You say a woman's been killed?"

"Yes, a minute ago, she's—"

"How was she killed?"

"Shot, she was shot, and now her little girl is missing, the kidnapper—"

"Whoa, kidnapper?" It was sounding more and more like a hoax, although the woman would have to be a pretty good actress. "Look, the murdered woman, it's Priscilla Lawrence, okay? Priscilla *Cunningham?* She's been shot."

Dwight Hawkins grabbed his car keys. The Cunningham name got things moving in Sohegan.

He let the paramedics precede him down the hill to the stream. He used to swim at the ravine as a kid. How long since he'd been back? Thirty years? Forty? Hard to believe he could measure his past in decades. Even at sixty-one he had a tough time with sentences that began "Thirty years ago" and "Back before the war."

The paramedics reached the body, down by the stream. He could tell from their lack of urgent movement that the caller had been right: Priscilla Lawrence was dead. *Shit.* In thirty-three years on the force, fifteen as chief of police, he'd had only one contact with the Cunninghams—that business with the son—and it had been a disaster. Now he stood fifteen yards from Russell Cunningham, once again bent over the lifeless body of his child. This wasn't going to be easy.

He headed down the slope, already sweating through his shirt. According to the weather map in the paper that morning, hot humid air was blowing in from the Plains and the Ohio Valley. That's what the map said, but it felt as though the air had slithered in a while ago and just stopped dead. He'd bet the wind-speed indicator in the attic of his house read zero.

An attractive woman approached him a few yards from the body. Tall, nice figure, in her thirties, he guessed. Her T-shirt, darkened by sweat, clung to her. Her pants were streaked with dirt.

"I'm Gwen Amiel," she said.

"Dwight Hawkins, chief of police. What the hell happened here?"

"Priscilla Lawrence was shot...Her daughter Tess was kidnapped and the family came here to—"

"That's the second time you used the word kidnapped. Mind telling me what kidnapping has to do with Miss Cunningham's...I mean, Mrs. Lawrence's death?"

She nodded as she wiped tears from her face, leaving a dirty smudge across her cheeks.

"Tess Lawrence. That's her grandfather there with—"

"I know who he is."

"Anyway, Sunday night, the child was taken from her room at Penaquoit."

"Why wasn't I notified?"

As if he needed to ask. Russell Cunningham would sooner shut down Sohegan Tack & Hardware than ask the local police for help.

"I don't really know. I guess they wanted to handle it themselves."

They both spoke in hushed voices, though he sensed that the old man, just a few yards away, wasn't paying much attention to them. He walked over to the paramedics and told them not to move the body. "She's beyond help anyway," he said. Russell Cunningham was gripping his daughter's arms, as if trying to hold her down.

"Where is the granddaughter now?" he asked Gwen Amiel after rejoining her.

"I don't know. I...guess the kidnapper still has her." She looked away. He let her have a few moments to herself, noticing her bra strap through the damp T-shirt, the fine blond hairs just below her neck, the way her jeans loosely gripped her small waist, leaving gaps in front of her hipbones.

"The Sagawahnee Indians thought this river was poisoned," he said. She turned back to him and seemed to want him to continue. "They thought evil spirits bathed in the river at night, and that anyone who drank from it would have violent nightmares, and a cursed life. They named the stream the Cohoit, which means devil."

"It's not, though, is it?" she asked. "Not really poisoned?"

He shook his head. "But it is kind of unusual, I always thought, how nothing much grows around it."

She turned to the stream and nodded slowly. "I hadn't noticed before." There wasn't a tree or bush or flower within five yards of the bank. "You'd expect the riverbank to be full of life."

"Not much trout in there, either, and the other streams around these parts have some of the best fishing in the country."

His eyes caught movement on the far side of the Cohoit as a man emerged from the thick woods, running toward them. He fell forward as he crossed the stream, losing his balance a few times and disappearing below the surface. The son-in-law: everyone in town knew that face.

"Call the FBI," he shouted hoarsely as he emerged from the stream. "My daughter...she's not here, *she's not here!* You have to find her."

He stumbled up the hill, walking right past the body of his wife. He stopped just a few inches away, eyes frantic, chest heaving.

"My daughter, Tess, she's not here. You have to get help. *Now.* Her grandfather...Russell Cunningham, he'll...he'll offer a reward, he'll—" He glanced at Gwen. "Where's the phone? *Get the phone!*"

Gwen Amiel took a portable phone from her pocket, which Lawrence grabbed and thrust at him.

"Call someone. Please, my daughter…"

"Are you sure this isn't a family thing, Mr.…." Damn, *Sonny boy* was how he was known in town.

"Nick Lawrence. What do you mean, family thing?"

"Only that most kidnappings turn out to be domestic disputes, custody battles, that kind of thing."

Nick Lawrence stepped closer to him, jabbing a finger at his chest. "My wife is lying there dead…"

Dwight took a step back. "I'll call in the Feds. Meantime, are you sure the perpetrator is gone?" He looked around the woods, wondering suddenly if they were being observed.

"He ran off that way," Gwen Amiel said, pointing across the stream.

"How long ago?"

"About fifteen minutes. He took the bag and—"

"The bag?"

"The money," she said. "It was in a duffel bag. He must have taken Tess, too. I heard her, earlier, just after the money was left. She was crying and then she just…stopped."

She glanced at Lawrence, who seemed to notice her, really notice her, for the first time.

"Why are you here?" His voice was completely flat.

"I thought…I—" She covered her mouth with her hand and shook her head. Her eyes were swollen with sorrow.

"What exactly is your relationship with this family?" Hawkins asked.

"I'm Tess's baby-sitter."

She didn't look like anyone's baby-sitter, he thought. It wasn't the attractive face and handsome figure so much as the eyes— skeptical, wary. Eyes didn't get that way dealing with children.

"I'm going to radio from my car for backup, arrange for a roadblock along Twenty-four, notify the FBI. Why don't all of you come with me? The less we disturb the scene the better."

"But my daughter…"

"We'll search every inch of these woods, Mr. Lawrence. If she's here we'll find her. But that area across the stream is full of cabins and old fishing and hunting lodges. It's crisscrossed with dirt roads. The kidnapper had a fifteen-minute head start, so he's probably already in his car and on his way. There's not much you can do here, and we have to preserve the scene for the FBI. Why don't you try to get your father-in-law to let go of Mrs. Lawrence."

The man's eyes flashed, as if he remembered something suddenly, something appalling. He turned, took in the scene—his wife's blouse soaked in blood, the old man kneeling over her, one hand gripping her arm—then turned back.

"I...oh, God." He spun around and ran to his father-in-law's side.

"Maybe you can help them," Hawkins said quietly to Gwen Amiel.

One of the paramedics signaled for Hawkins, who walked over to the body.

"We found this in her right hand." He held a delicate purple flower by the stem.

"A thistle," Gwen said.

Hawkins took the flower and looked around. "Not from here. She must have brought it with her."

They both stared at the flower, at its inappropriate loveliness.

"Wonder what it meant to her," Hawkins said as he slipped it into his shirt pocket. "I'll be back in half a minute. You guys come with me."

The paramedics followed him up the embankment. The fewer people traipsing around a crime scene the better. By the time he reached the top of the hill he already felt the situation slipping from his control. The FBI would take over the search for the lost girl, then oversee the hunt for the killer. The county crime-scene unit would have to be called, and they wouldn't be too eager to leave once they were through picking over the ravine, not in a high-profile case like this. So he waited a few moments that belonged only to him, once he'd reached his car, precious moments, before grabbing the car phone and calling in to headquarters. It might well be the last independent gesture he'd make in a long, long time.

"Millie? It's Dwight. I'm going to need backup here at

Devil's Ravine."

Backup? He almost smiled. Millie Berry was one-fourth of the Sohegan Police Department and she was the dispatcher, a forty-year-old mother of three who dressed like a refugee from the fifties, beehive hair and all, and who refused to make coffee, do personal errands, or otherwise sully what she liked to refer to as her professional standing with the police force.

"I'll send Chris and Pat," she said. "They both hightailed it back here once they heard about the nine, one, one call."

As if they had anything better to do. The crime rate in Sohegan was among the lowest in the state, though the police department could take little credit. There just wasn't much worth stealing in town—everyone was as bad off as everyone else, except the Cunninghams, of course. Traffic control, domestic disputes, and the occasional DWI arrest were what kept Sohegan's finest occupied.

"Fine, we'll also need the county boys. Call Dave Sperling, tell him we have a murder scene here." He ignored an inquisitive gasp from the other end. "He'll need directions. Make sure he comes right away, we'll probably have a gaggle of rubberneckers on our hands before long. We'll also need to contact the FBI. There's a number for the Albany field office in the address book on my desk. Will you get it for me please?"

She read him back the number a half minute later.

"Thanks, Millie, and call my wife, tell her I may be late for dinner."

He clicked off before she could ask questions. Calling his wife to say he'd be late for dinner was one of Millie's most regular chores. After thirty years of marriage he still found the dinner hour the most stressful part of the day. Perhaps if they had children, or if one of them had ever lived anywhere but Sohegan. Perhaps if Elaine showed even a trace of interest in his work...

Using the car phone again, he dialed the Albany field office and gave the dispatcher the name he'd written in his address book years ago and never once called. A few seconds later a gruff male voice answered.

"Don Reeves."

Hawkins introduced himself, then briefly outlined the situation. "The kid's still missing?" The voice had a slightly accusatory edge.

"That's correct."

"Where can we land a chopper?"

"Behind the high school. It's about—"

"Secure the area, we'll be down in fifteen. Meet us behind the school."

Dwight clicked off as Gwen Amiel approached him from the woods.

"My son will be home from school in five minutes," she said. "I wasn't working this afternoon so I told the people who usually watch him…You see, he's only six. I need to be there."

He hadn't expected her to have a kid of her own. Those eyes, again, cool and observant; hard to imagine them softening for a child.

"I can't let you leave," he said. "The county sheriff's men are on their way, and the FBI. They'll want to question you."

"But my son…"

A squad car pulled up, distracting them. Chris Bernard and Pat Sykes got out, both in uniform.

"Priscilla Lawrence is down there," Dwight said, pointing. "Shot dead. Her husband's down there with her, her father, too— Russell Cunningham."

He studied their reaction, relishing it, somehow. A murder in Sohegan was big news. The murder of Russell Cunningham's daughter was something else, an epic in the making. He saw the excitement in their faces. The panic, too: everything they did from now on would have consequences.

"Both of you, secure the area, don't let anyone in or out. Get the old man and his son-in-law up here by the road and don't let them out of your sight until I get back. And try to remember the three rules of securing a crime scene, okay?" They looked blank. "Don't touch anything. Don't touch anything. And don't touch anything." A full thirty seconds later they both got it and smiled uncomfortably.

"Right, Chief," Chris Bernard said. "We won't touch anything." Bernard was only twenty-four, with a gaunt frame, prominent

Adam's apple, and pale blue eyes that looked mighty nervous just then at the prospect of being left in charge of a crime scene. "Where are you going, Chief?"

"I'm escorting Miss Amiel home," he said. "Then I'm heading out to the high school to meet the FBI helicopter."

Gwen Amiel looked at him, her face pale, eyes red-ridged. She'd just witnessed a murder, and the child she took care of was missing. And yet he saw something else on her face, something more than horror or fear or even grief.

"Thank you," she whispered.

He nodded and watched her walk toward her car. She turned back, briefly, perhaps to see if he was following her, and suddenly he knew exactly what he'd seen in her face a moment ago, in addition to the horror and the fear and the grief.

He'd seen guilt.

CHAPTER 12

Gwen drove home slowly, checking every few minutes to make sure Dwight Hawkins was following. Her heart was pumping furiously as her mind raced through the horrible events of the past hours, trying to find some way to exonerate herself, searching for a sequence of events leading up to Priscilla's murder that didn't include her stumbling onto the scene and screwing up what would otherwise have been nothing more than a transfer of money.

If only Tess hadn't cried out, and so loudly and pitifully. If only she hadn't called her name.

Jimmy was sitting cross-legged at the end of the front walk when she pulled up to the curb. She recognized the sour, accusatory expression he always wore when she was late, but his face brightened when he saw the police car park behind her.

She got out of the Honda and hugged him, letting go reluctantly.

"This is Jimmy," she said when Dwight Hawkins joined them on the sidewalk.

He offered his hand, which Jimmy shook. "Chief of Police Hawkins. Nice to meet you, Jimmy."

Gwen studied Hawkins a moment, curious about a man who would stop to introduce himself to a six-year-old when he had a fresh murder and kidnapping to deal with. His eyes were dark brown and hooded by heavy lids, his thick white hair was combed in a neat part. His lips were narrow and turned down at the edges, but the frown seemed directed inward, somehow.

"I just need to run in and make arrangements for my son." She took Jimmy's hand and practically dragged him up the walkway.

"How come the police are here?" he asked.

"Because there was some trouble at Penaquoit today," she said.

"What kind of trouble?"

Well, he'd hear about it sooner or later.

"Priscilla Lawrence, the mother of the little girl I look after? She was shot."

His eyes widened. "Who shot her?"

"We don't know, but the police want me to answer some questions. So I'm going to call the Pearsons and see if they can watch you for a few hours while I—"

"But I have to tell you something. I saw—"

"We'll talk later, okay?" She unlocked the front door.

"Today at the diner? I—"

She covered Jimmy's mouth with her hand as she pulled him to her.

"Sounds like a baby crying in here," he said when she let go.

The wailing was coming from the living room, just a few steps away.

"Go outside, Jimmy. Tell Chief Hawkins to come in here right away."

"But—"

"*Now!*"

He turned and ran outside. When the screen door closed behind him she walked to the living room. Tess Lawrence was sobbing in the middle of the living-room floor, strapped in a car seat, her arms and legs flailing. Gwen ran to her and fumbled with the strap before managing to unfasten it.

"Gen?" Tess gasped between sobs.

Tess felt hot and damp in her arms as she hugged the child to her, cooing softly. She smelled clean, though. Thank God, she smelled clean.

Tess was still whimpering when Dwight Hawkins entered the room a few seconds later.

"Is that—"

She could only nod as she stroked Tess's sweat-soaked back. "Mother of God," he said as Jimmy ran to Gwen's side and grabbed her free hand. "You have a hell of a lot of questions to answer, Mrs. Amiel."

PART II

PART II

CHAPTER 13

Gwen waited for the Pearsons to pick up Jimmy, trying to calm a still traumatized Tess. Dwight Hawkins called the crime scene to inform Nick Lawrence that his daughter was safe, and agreed to meet him later at Penaquoit. He asked Gwen to arrange for Jimmy's pediatrician to examine Tess at the estate.

"How come *she's* here?" Jimmy walked across the living room and pointed at Tess, who was fussing in Gwen's arms.

"I don't know. Why don't you wait outside like I asked?"

"But what's she doing here?" Jimmy couldn't take his eyes off the baby.

"Please, Jimmy?" Seeing the two of them in the same room, now of all times, made her very nervous.

"Where is her father?"

"Not here, okay?"

Jimmy frowned and left. She'd apologize for snapping at him later.

The Pearsons arrived fifteen minutes later and took Jimmy back to their house. Hawkins drove her and Tess to Penaquoit in his car, stopping at the high school just as a helicopter landed in the center of the football field. Two men got out the moment it touched ground and ran over to the car. Don Reeves, head of the FBI's Albany field office, was on the short side, and stocky, with a pale complexion that emphasized a five o'clock shadow so dark it formed a perfect template for a beard. He wore a shapeless black suit, white shirt, and a blue-and-red-striped tie. His associate, too, resembled a Russian bureaucrat, though Peter Annison, who introduced himself as the deputy field director, was less heavily built and looked as if he'd spent at least a few recent hours out of doors.

"We'll set up headquarters at the scene of the abduction," Reeves said as they drove. "I've got a crew on their way by chopper, should be here momentarily. I'll walk the transfer site later on."

During the five-minute drive to Penaquoit Gwen listened quietly as Dwight Hawkins reviewed the events of the past hours. Tess had fallen asleep in her arms.

"So what we're dealing with," Reeves said as they drove through the open gates of Penaquoit, "is one dead, five million dollars missing. Is that correct?"

"Well, yes, I guess that about sums it up," Hawkins said. "I had two of my men make sure the—"

"Where's the body?"

"Still at the scene. We'll take her to the county morgue, over in Whitesville, once we—"

"The father and husband?"

"Should be here at the house any minute."

Peter Annison whistled as they drove up to the mansion. "Lifestyles of the rich and famous," he said in a voice that had the flat twang of an airline pilot.

The two FBI men set up temporary local headquarters in the dining room. Soon the house and grounds were swarming with people. Teams of policemen—county men from Whitesville, Gwen guessed—dusted for fingerprints in the kitchen, along the banisters of both stairways, in the music room. Others combed the grounds in teams of three, heads down, walking slowly over every inch of the vast lawn. As she wandered, dazed, from room to room, carrying a sleeping Tess, waiting to be interrogated, it occurred to her that the house was fully alive at last—and all because of the death of its mistress.

She handed Tess to the pediatrician when he arrived several minutes later.

"Use the piano room," Don Reeves told him. "The kid's room is being dusted." Gwen started to follow the doctor but was stopped by Don Reeves.

"I should stay with her," she said.

"I'd rather you didn't," Reeves replied. He stood between Gwen and the hallway to the music room, arms folded, watching her.

"She needs me."

Reeves just stared, but the look in his eyes was anything but neutral. She turned and ran upstairs and pounded the wall on the second-floor hallway. Her hand was still throbbing when she entered the nursery and found a woman on her knees before Tess's crib, aiming a flashlight at a portion of the crib rail.

"Hello," Gwen said as she crossed the room.

"Wendy Frist, county crime-scene unit," the woman said without turning around. She was heavyset, with short brown hair, wearing a khaki shirt and pants and thick-soled black shoes. She flicked off the flashlight, dipped a tiny brush into a tin of blue powder, and gently swept it across a small portion of the rail. Gwen stepped closer.

"Don't touch anything," the agent said over her shoulder. Very carefully she placed a small length of clear tape over the powdered area, smoothed it with her index finger, and slowly pulled it off the rail. Standing a foot or so from the crib, Gwen could just make out a blue fingerprint. The agent reaffixed the tape to a blank index card and scribbled a few words on it. She immediately turned on the flashlight again and began inspecting the rest of the crib rail.

Gwen glanced at the card, which the agent had placed on top of a small pile, and wondered if the print above the words *Crib rail, left side, front* was hers, and, if so, what the FBI would make of it.

She left the nursery, went downstairs, and was crossing the foyer when Nick Lawrence and his father-in-law were escorted into the mansion by two county policemen.

"Tess?" Nick shouted. *"Where's Tess?"* The old man glanced around the big foyer with unblinking eyes, his mouth half open, as if he couldn't quite recall ever being there before.

"Tess is in the music room with the pediatrician," Gwen said.

Nick started for the hallway when Rosa Piacevic appeared, carrying Tess.

"The doctor says she is excellent," Rosa said.

Nick grabbed his daughter, squeezing her to his chest. Russell

Cunningham was still glancing around the foyer like a lost tourist.

"Mr. Lawrence?" Dwight Hawkins had emerged from the dining room. "The FBI would like to talk to you."

Nick looked momentarily dazed. "I'd like some time with my daughter," he said weakly.

"Not now," Hawkins replied.

Nick frowned and handed Tess back to Rosa, then followed Hawkins into the dining room.

They interviewed him for a half hour, then Russell. Gwen heard occasional shouts from him as she continued to roam the house, waiting her turn.

"...My daughter and five million bucks!"

"...Bet your ass I'll cooperate. Just get that son of a bitch."

"...Call the police? I'd have lost my daughter *and* my granddaughter."

When he stormed out his face was raw and red.

"Where's my granddaughter?" he bellowed at Gwen.

"Upstairs, with her father."

He took the stairs two at a time.

"Miss Amiel?" Peter Annison stuck his head out the door. "Come in, please."

They were seated around the long mahogany table: the dour and pale Don Reeves at the far end, Dwight Hawkins a few chairs down from him, and a third man she didn't recognize.

"This is Fred Barnes," Dwight Hawkins said as she sat at the end of the table nearest the door, and farthest from Don Reeves. "Detective Barnes, from the county sheriff's division."

She glanced at Barnes, who didn't take his eyes off his notepad. He was completely bald, his head perfectly round—a pink basketball with a human profile carved into one side. A bead of clammy sweat trickled between her shoulder blades.

"Why don't you start from the beginning?" Reeves said. Four sets of eyes turned to her.

"I was in the laundry room," she said, "when I heard voices over the baby monitor. I—"

"The beginning, Miss Amiel." Reeves's voice was deep but flat. "How did you come to work at Penaquoit?"

"Oh." When she lifted her right hand from the table to wipe her forehead she left a sweat imprint. Why were they interested in how she'd ended up working for the Lawrences?

"You don't think that *I* was involved in any—"

"From the beginning." Reeves's voice was like the EKG readout of a dead person.

"I was working at the Mecca Diner," she began. And the appropriate words somehow followed, though she felt curiously uninvolved in the account, as if she'd memorized it earlier and was now merely reciting it. She finished fifteen minutes later, with the 911 call.

"You said the baby was crying," Reeves said. "Yet neither Mr. Cunningham nor Mr. Lawrence recall hearing the child."

"They'd already left."

"But they came back."

"And the crying stopped."

She saw the two FBI men lock eyes for an ominous second.

"She was wailing," Gwen said. "Crying hysterically."

"In your experience with children, Miss Amiel, do babies stop crying suddenly, all at once, just like that?"

"That's why I was so alarmed, because it *is* unusual for a child to suddenly stop crying. I thought…"

"You thought what?"

"I thought she'd been smothered," she said quietly.

"You're not from around here, are you?" asked Fred Barnes, the county detective.

"No, I'm from Long Island originally. I lived in the city—New York City—up until this spring, when I moved here."

"Why did you move here?" Barnes asked. Another accusation.

"I couldn't take the city any longer," she said. "I wanted a small town, good schools…"

"And your husband?"

"We're separated. He lives in the city. What does he have to do with this?"

"Do you know much about gardening, Ms. Amiel?"

She shook her head.

"Yet you recognized the flower in Mrs. Lawrence's hand," Reeves said.

She glanced quickly at Dwight Hawkins. "A thistle, everyone knows what a thistle looks like."

Reeves arched his eyebrows. "I see. We'd like to search your house for prints. The kidnapper was there—at least once, when he dropped off the child."

At least once.

"I had nothing to do with this," she said.

"But you were at the scene. The baby was found at your house."

"*I* found Tess at my house."

"We could get a warrant," Reeves said. "I don't foresee any problems convincing a judge to issue one, but it would expedite matters if we could have your permission instead."

"Can I be there when you search?"

The FBI men looked at each other before the younger agent, Peter Annison, responded with a begrudging nod.

Dwight Hawkins observed the two FBI men as Gwen Amiel left the room. They followed her closely, eyes narrowed, lips pinched in distrust. Did they expect her to wheel around and open fire with a semiautomatic? Fred Barnes continued to scribble on his yellow pad; the county boys always walked into court with reams of notes. Through the closed French doors he heard the muted thump-thump of low-flying helicopters.

"I don't believe her," Reeves said when the dining-room door closed behind Gwen Amiel. His colleague, Peter Annison, quickly nodded.

"What don't you believe?" Hawkins asked, immediately regretting the defensive tone. Still, hadn't he been the first at the murder scene, the first to see Gwen Amiel after the shooting? She'd seemed terrified, *haunted.*

"She just *happened* to overhear her employers discussing the exchange?" Reeves said, each word hitting precisely the same tone. "She just *happened* to spot them driving along Twenty-four? She just *happened* to hear the baby screaming—when no one else did? And then she just *happened* to find the baby inside her own house?" He offered a pained smile. "I don't think so."

"She didn't have time to bring the baby to her place," Hawkins said.

"She didn't need to, the kid was there the entire time."

"But the crying at the ravine…"

"Maybe there was no crying."

"Or maybe—" Hawkins bit the inside of his lip. What was the point of defending her? He'd never laid eyes on Gwen Amiel before that day. For all he knew she had a record, abused drugs, cheated at Bingo.

And yet Gwen Amiel was local, damn it, even if she was a newcomer. These guys were outsiders, and arrogant bastards at that.

"If anyone has five million dollars in this town," Hawkins said, "we'll know soon enough. You could buy all of Sohegan ten times over with that kind of money." He waited for the smiles that never came. "We only have the one bank in town. I'll make sure they're alert for any large cash deposits."

"That would be helpful," Reeves said with a patronizing smirk. "Though the money's long gone from Sohegan, I'm certain of that."

"Then Gwen Amiel couldn't—"

"Gwen Amiel must have an accomplice."

"Nick Lawrence said he thought the voice on the phone was male."

"He also said it sounded metallic, almost mechanical," Reeves said. "The kidnapper was probably using a digital voice mask. Your higher-end DVMs can make a man sound like a woman." He smiled tightly at Dwight. "Though they're better at making a woman sound like a man."

Fred Barnes, the county man, dropped his pen and pushed the

pad away from him.

"I, for one, would like to take a look at the scene," Barnes said. "Anyone else coming?"

The FBI clones stood up together.

"Pete, have one of our boys do a trace metal on Miss Amiel, then take a criminalist over to her house," Reeves said. "I'll accompany Detective Barnes to the scene." He turned to Hawkins. "Care to join us?"

"I think I'll stay here and talk to the servants."

"Our people have already interrogated them," Annison said.

"Sometimes a local perspective can help."

"They're Rumanian."

"Albanian," Hawkins said. The Piacevics were familiar figures in town, though they said little to the shopkeepers they dealt with.

The FBI men considered him a moment. He met their gaze without budging. Finally, as if obeying a silent signal, they turned in unison and walked out of the room, Barnes close behind. They left the door open, and he became immediately aware of music from somewhere in the house. Piano music, slow and melancholy and expertly played.

"Jesus H. Christ," he said to the empty dining room. "He's playing the fucking piano."

The widower was playing the piano.

CHAPTER 14

Gwen closed the door to the breakfast room and leaned against the wall. The men in the dining room began talking the instant she left, and while she hadn't been able to make out actual words or sentences, she could guess the subject.

What was Gwen Amiel doing at the scene?

Why was she the only one who heard the baby crying?

Who had brought Tess to her house?

She wasn't even tempted to go back in to reargue her innocence. Because she wasn't innocent. If she'd stayed away, if she'd minded her own fucking business, Priscilla might well be alive.

She sat on one of the twelve chairs neatly arranged around the glass-topped table. The Lawrences ate most of their meals in the sunny breakfast room, with its framed botanical prints and built-in cupboard displaying a complete set of never-used china. She sat there for several minutes, unable to move.

The music finally roused her. The Beethoven sonata again, the one that started out so lyrically, then accelerated to near-frantic intensity. She left the breakfast room and walked slowly to the library. Tess sat on the floor by the piano, watching her father play, uncommonly still, as if she, too, was mesmerized by the sonata. Nick stared up at the ceiling as he played, rather than hunching over the keyboard in the usual way.

Even the music sounded different, at once more passionate and melancholy. She listened for a few minutes. No, not more melancholy, for the wistfulness was written into the music. The sonata—the Farewell, Priscilla had called it—sounded riper, more mature, fuller and richer in every way. It struck her, suddenly, the cruelty of the situation:

This was Nick Lawrence's greatest performance.

"Gen! Gen!"

She blinked, looked down, and saw Tess toddling toward her. She put a finger to her lips, but too late.

"Gen!"

The playing ceased, saturating the room in brutal silence.

"I'm sorry," she whispered as she scooped up Tess.

He sat there, his back to her, not moving.

"I'll take Tess…" She started to leave.

"Wait." He turned. His face was flushed, beads of perspiration clung to his hairline. His eyes were a deeper, fiercer blue than before, and though his cheeks looked dry, his eyes glistened with tears.

"I thought I'd take Tess for a while," she said. Although she should get home right away to oversee the FBI's search of her house.

"I'd like to be with her," he said quietly. He got up from the piano bench and walked toward her, extending his hands. Tess jumped from Gwen to her father, wrapping her arms around his neck.

"I'm…sorry." It was all she could say; what she wanted to do was flee.

He shook his head. "I'll have plenty of time to practice."

"I meant about your wife."

The watery gleam drained from his eyes. "Of course," he said, "thank you very much."

He sounded stiff, as if forcing out the words with great effort, but then he always spoke in formal cadences, avoiding contractions, slang, verbal shortcuts of any kind. He talked the way he played piano, with precise and practiced control.

"I'm sorry I got involved," she said, wishing she could quit while ahead, but wanting him to hear it. "If I hadn't been there, at the ravine, maybe things would have turned out differently."

He nodded slowly, staring intently into her eyes, the most attractive man she'd ever known. In spite of everything, in spite of Tess squirming in his arms, the child's mother lying in a morgue somewhere nearby, detectives at Gwen's house dusting for fingerprints…In spite of all that and much more, at that moment she was thinking that Nick Lawrence was the most attractive man she'd ever known.

"We'll have the rest of our lives for recriminations," he was saying. "Why didn't we bring in the police at the outset? Why did I open fire on the kidnapper the way I did? I think we'd all do well to look at this whole episode as somehow inevitable, preordained."

This whole episode? His daughter's kidnapping, his wife's murder— an *episode?*

"If I hadn't come—"

He put a finger to her lips and she felt a hot tension grip her body at his touch.

"But you did come," he said softly, still looking into her eyes. "The only people who should feel responsible for what happened are the people who took Tess from us."

She swallowed and wished like hell he'd show some grief about his wife, some anger, *something* other than the serene, almost decorous melancholy she'd heard in the Beethoven piece just then.

"I need to go home now, I…" Better to leave out the part about the FBI searching her house, though she doubted he'd much care.

"Of course."

She headed across the hallway.

"Say bye-bye, Tess," he said behind her.

"Bye-bye."

"Can you say, 'See you tomorrow'?"

Gwen stopped, slowly turned. "Tomorrow?"

"Nine o'clock, as usual," he said.

"But…"

"I'll need you more than ever, now, Gwen. We both will, won't we, Tess?"

He kissed his daughter's neck, forehead, both cheeks, the tip of her nose. Tess squealed happily as he carried her back into the library.

She was interrupted in the foyer by a mousy young man wearing a white shirt and khaki pants.

"Miss Amiel? Charlie Nevins, FBI?" He pushed thick tortoiseshell glasses up his nose. "We need to do a trace metal test. Would you follow me into the kitchen, please?"

"What's a trace metal test?"

"What's a—" He adjusted his glasses again, but they were already in place. "A trace metal tells us whether you've held a firearm in the past twenty-four hours."

They thought *she'd* held a gun? That she'd *fired* one?

"But I washed my hands earlier, back at my house," she said.

"Not a problem. Soap and water can't completely remove the metal molecules."

"I was wearing gloves when I fired," she said, making no effort to disguise her bitterness.

"You were—oh, I get it." He giggled nervously. "It's just an aerosol spray," he said as he followed her to the kitchen. "A couple of squirts, then we examine your hands under an ultraviolet light. We'll know the results right away."

There were two cars parked in front of her house when Gwen's taxi pulled up. Four men were shouting at the front door when she got out.

"What the hell is going on?" she yelled as she ran up the front walk.

All four turned. Dark jackets, plain ties, white-bread faces with grim expressions.

"Who are you?" one of them asked.

"Gwen Amiel. And who are you?" Though she could easily guess.

"FBI," said the same agent. "We have permission to search the premises in the matter of—"

"I know why you're here."

"Some kid won't let us in," another agent said.

"Some—oh, Christ!" She stepped up to the door. "Jimmy? Jimmy, it's me."

"Mom?"

His voice through the closed door was muted, but she heard

the panic loud and clear.

"Open up, Jimmy."

The door moved a crack and Jimmy peered out. Then he flung it open and threw himself at her.

"They...wanted to come in but you said...you said don't... don't let strangers in the house and then they said they were going to break down the door and Mrs. Pearson had already left because your car was here and she forgot you left it here and she thought you were inside and I called your name and...and..."

"It's okay, Jimmy, it's okay, you did the right thing."

She stroked the back of his head and turned to the four agents.

"You sons of bitches. He's six years old, for chrissake. Were you really going to break down the door?" She was almost shouting.

"Now calm down, miss, we were only—"

"Calm down? This is my *son*. He was home by himself..."

She'd *kill* Mrs. Pearson. The drop-off policy was written in stone: Jimmy wasn't to be left until Gwen waved from the front door, even if the Honda was in the driveway.

"May we take a look inside?" one of the agents said.

She waited before answering. If she said no, they'd get a warrant. They began to shift around, clearing their throats, glancing about. Finally, she moved aside to let them in.

"Sorry about that," she told Jimmy when they were alone on the front stoop.

"What's going on?"

"Well, someone took Tess Lawrence and left her here. The police—and the FBI—want to find out who might have done that."

"Why did somebody take her?"

"That's what they're trying to find out." She ran her fingers though his fear-dampened hair. "Come on, let's make sure these guys take good care of our house."

They watched as two agents in the living room dusted for fingerprints. Jimmy was rapt, mouth and eyes wide open, as the agents used flashlights, blue powder, and tape to collect prints. Gwen left him in the living room and went upstairs to her bedroom, where a third agent was riffling though her underwear drawer.

"Is that necessary?"

"Yep," he answered without turning around.

"I said you guys could look inside. I didn't realize that meant pawing through my underwear."

"We could get a warrant, Mrs. Amiel." He squatted and opened the bottom drawer of her dresser. "This is a kidnapping case, ma'am, and the child was…"

She found the fourth agent in Jimmy's room, searching through the few toys they'd acquired since moving to Sohegan. He held up a big plastic water gun.

"Don't worry, my son has a permit for that," she said.

He turned and started to say something. She quickly left the room and headed back downstairs. They were gone in an hour, leaving the house, though not her nerves, pretty much intact. She washed her hands in the kitchen sink to get rid of the chemical smell left over from the trace metal test. She'd passed, of course, much to the obvious disappointment of the three thousand FBI men observing the procedure in the kitchen at Penaquoit. She popped a frozen macaroni and cheese into the oven for Jimmy and poured herself a tumbler of scotch.

Sheila Stewart rapped on the kitchen door as Gwen was doing the dinner dishes. She'd finally managed to coax a still-excited Jimmy to bed just a few minutes earlier with an extra story and the ultimate bribe: chocolate chip cookies. He'd eaten them as they studied the almost-full moon from his bedroom window. His face shimmered in the moonlight, but he looked fragile and pale, with dark circles under his eyes. Times like these she was tempted to let him sleep in the bed with her, for her sake as much as his, but she was afraid it would screw him up in some way. He'd been through enough with his father.

"What in the name of God has been going on?" Sheila said

as she stepped into the kitchen. She wore a tiny black tank top and denim cut-offs. From buttoned-down banker to biker chick in just a few hours.

"You heard," Gwen said.

"The whole town's heard. Got a drink?"

"I have some orange juice, maybe soda."

"Scotch, please."

The events at the Devil's Ravine must really have been stirring things up; Sheila rarely drank anything stronger than light beer. Gwen poured them both scotch over ice and brought the glasses into the living room, where she collapsed on the sofa. Sheila sat next to her.

"So, tell."

Gwen filled her in, leaving nothing out. Just talking to someone who presumed her innocence was bracing.

"*Here?* They found the kid *here?*"

"I'll never forget how Tess looked, so helpless and *tiny*, sitting in the middle of this room like a toy someone had left behind."

"McGillicuddy at the bank is just about busting at the seams with the part he played. Old man Cunningham had him fetch the five million from a bunch of money-center banks in Manhattan. It arrived by Brinks truck this morning. McGillicuddy ran out personally to meet it. That's what passes for high finance in these parts—cash arriving by truck."

"Is it traceable?"

She shook her head. "Nobody asked us to record the serial numbers, and even if they had, there wasn't enough time to do it. We had to have the cash first thing this morning. It appears that there's a newly minted multimillionaire running around here someplace."

"Probably running as far from Sohegan as he can," Gwen said.

"Well, you wouldn't catch me here five minutes after I came into that kind of money."

Gwen smiled again. Sheila would probably stick around Sohegan with a billion dollars. She relished the role of town dyke, though she'd never admit it; she savored the stares and tsk-tsks she elicited when she and Betsy strolled through town. Not that they held hands—they weren't out to flaunt anything. But you knew they were a couple the moment you saw them—it was in their eyes and body language as much as their tight Levis and clunky hiking boots.

"How's the old man taking it?"

Gwen told her about Russell Cunningham crouching over the body, unwilling to let go.

"Later, at the house, he seemed more confused than anything else. I don't think I'll ever forget the look in his eyes."

"Losing your second child…" Sheila said. "I can't even imagine what that's like."

"Did you know his son?"

"Everyone did. The old man sent him away to boarding school, same one he'd gone to. The Cunninghams don't like their young mixing with the local riffraff. But Russ went native anyway. He was killed with a local girl, you know, the night the cops chased him over the embankment."

"Well, there's nothing 'local' about Nick Lawrence."

"Amen. Priscilla was always a daddy's girl—I went to school with her, right through junior high. She did just what her daddy wanted her to do. Went downstate and found herself an out-of-town prince, then dragged him up here on a leash."

"You talk about them as if they were royalty."

"Well? The Cunninghams may owe their fortune to this town, but they're not going to get their blood mixed up with the intermarried half-wits who live here, and I don't blame them. You know the way royalty from one European country only marries royalty from another country, since no one in their own land is highborn enough? That's the way it is with the Cunninghams."

"They find their princes elsewhere."

"Exactly. Except Nick Lawrence wasn't exactly a blue blood. He looks the part, I suppose, the genes are probably good. But he's flat broke, they say."

"Who's 'they'?"

"They? They is…us, I guess. Sohegan's a small town. If you

haven't learned that already, you're about to."

"All I wanted to do was blend in."

"Not anymore. You're about to be notorious."

Gwen sighed. "Sheila, I hope *you* don't think—"

"Don't start." Sheila drained her glass and put it on the coffee table. "You had nothing to do with this, okay?"

Gwen reached over and hugged her friend, inhaling deeply as Sheila gently patted her back. If only she could stay there in Sheila's arms, feeling trusted and safe. But the gentle pats were beginning to feel more like not-so-gentle caresses—or was she imagining it? It had been so long since anyone had held her. She pulled away and felt loneliness return like a chill.

"Thanks," she said. "I forgot how good a hug can feel."

"You need to get a life, my dear. Painting walls only goes so far."

"Do you think the trim is too bright?" She pointed to the front window.

Sheila sighed and shook her head. "I know it's slim pickings up here, but even a fling with one of our local hill apes would do you some good."

"I'm happy with things the way they are."

Sheila studied her a beat. "That husband of yours must have been a real winner." She stood up. "I can't wait until you're ready to tell me all about him. I *thrive* on that kind of story."

"Barry's the past," Gwen said. "He's out of our lives, permanently."

They embraced again at the kitchen door.

"Thanks for the inside scoop," Sheila said.

"Thanks for listening."

Sheila was halfway down the concrete steps when Gwen called her.

"He was playing piano this evening." Sheila looked puzzled. "Nick Lawrence. He was playing Beethoven, like nothing had happened."

Sheila shrugged. "The rich are different. Even the nouveau rich."

• • •

Later, trying to sleep, Gwen heard a car drive down the street, stop in front of the house, then continue toward the dead end. The headlights briefly illuminated her bedroom as the car headed back toward Union Avenue. Fifteen minutes later another car turned onto the street. She hurried to the window and pushed back the curtains. A dark minivan slowly drove past the house, with two people in the front, at least one more passenger in back. She saw the driver lean over and point to her house.

She closed the curtain and jumped back into bed, but for the next hour she was tormented by the sound of cars entering and leaving the short dead-end street, the sudden flash of light as they drove by on their way out.

Sohegan's a small town. If you haven't learned that already, you're about to.

Gwen pulled the covers over her head, tried unsuccessfully to sleep. She'd come to this jerkwater town to become anonymous, to blend in where Barry could never find them. Now her house was a local shrine.

CHAPTER 15

Nick was working on a new piece the next morning. Though she recognized the melody—another Beethoven sonata, she guessed—the music, played with uncharacteristic awkwardness, sounded inappropriate, somehow. She'd become so used to hearing the Lebewohl every morning when she entered the house. It was as if the house had been redecorated.

She found Tess in the music room, playing with a few stuffed animals as her father practiced.

"Thank God you're here," Nick said as she entered the room. "I'm working on the Pathetique for the first time and I really need to concentrate."

She tried not to look as critical as she felt.

"I need a distraction," Nick said quickly. "If I didn't have my music, I don't know what I'd be doing."

She nodded and picked up Tess. "You look like you just ran a marathon." Sweat covered his forehead and stained the collar of his polo shirt.

"The Pathetique is almost physical in its demands; it takes me out of myself like a long run."

"I'll bring Tess upstairs."

He turned back to the keyboard and pounced on a chord, following it with a string of staccato notes. As she left the room she heard someone enter through the French doors that opened onto to the patio.

"Where's Tess?" It was Russell Cunningham, and he sounded angry.

The music stopped. "With Gwen."

"Do you think it's wise, having that woman look after my... after Tess?"

Gwen stopped a few feet down the hall.

"She just lost her mother, she needs continuity."

"If she'd minded her own business, maybe Priscilla..."

The old man's voice was thin, almost whispery, his usual bluster completely gone.

Nick resumed playing, the music unexpectedly light. Gwen could imagine the old man watching, seething. She heard Nick hit a wrong note, then slam the keyboard. The chord reverberated around the house like a startled pigeon.

"Can't you leave that damn piano be?"

"How is Maxine doing?" Nick asked.

"She'll survive," he said dismissively. "She's not receiving visitors, except Reverend Leeper."

"Maybe if I brought Tess..."

"I'll call you when she's ready." The mention of Maxine had clearly annoyed Russell. Gwen sensed that only *his* loss mattered, *his* grief. What did the anguish of a boozy, Bible-thumping neurotic count next to his monumental dynastic tragedy?

"Leeper will handle the funeral tomorrow," Russell said. "Mount Hope Cemetery, ten o'clock."

So Nick would have no say in the arrangements. Eager to hear more, Gwen made a funny face at Tess to keep her happy and quiet.

"Any progress in the investigation?" Nick asked.

"Incompetents." Russell's voice came alive for the first time.

"What about the fingerprint and fiber evidence?"

"Nothing. The FBI's moving out tomorrow, going to manage the case from Albany. I told them that was nonsense. They said that in a kidnapping, once the victim's been recovered, there's no need to keep a field office open."

"But there's been a murder."

"It's a vendetta," the old man growled.

"What?"

"They can't forgive me for not calling them in the first place, so now they're only going through the motions of finding Priscilla's killer. *And* my money."

"It's more than going through the motions," Nick said. "This is already a huge case. Have you seen the papers this morning? Even the *New York Times* put the story on the front page."

"Hypocrites. Phil Robinson called this morning. My foreman," Russell added with obvious irritation that he had to identify the man for his son-in-law. "He wanted to know if he should shut the plant for the day. A sign of respect, he called it."

"Well…"

"I told him he could shut the plant for a week, just so long as no one got paid."

"Oh, Christ, Russell, he was only—"

"*Hypocrite.* You think any of them gives a rat's ass about me"—his voice broke—"or my daughter?"

No wonder he clung so ferociously to his offspring, Gwen thought. The rest of the world was the enemy.

"No one loved her the way you did," Nick said softly.

A brief silence; then the old man cleared his throat.

"About the will," he said. "I went through it this morning."

"We don't have to do this now, you know."

"She had few assets, other than some investments I made for her when she was a little girl. What she did have, she left in trust for Tess, until such time as she—"

"We talked about this, Priscilla and me."

"You won't be able to maintain this…this lifestyle without considerable assistance."

"Tess and I don't need such a big place, anyway."

"This is Tess's house," he said very slowly, as if instructing a misbehaving child. "Or it will be one day." His voice had regained its gravelly vigor. "I'm prepared to support you and Tess to any extent you please, so long as my granddaughter continues to live in this house. If you choose to live elsewhere, anywhere else, you won't get a cent."

"Sounds like bribery."

"Call it what you want. But if you take Tess away from here, I'll not only cut you off, I'll do everything in my power to get her back."

"She's *my* daughter."

Gwen could hear the old man's breathing. "I'll have you watched if you leave this place, every moment of your life. One slip and I'll sue you in court for custody."

"Slip?"

"Girlfriends, drugs, neglect of any kind." Gwen heard footsteps coming from the music room and headed quickly for the foyer, stopping when she heard Russell resume talking. "But what are we discussing here? You can't support her, at Penaquoit or anywhere. Just raise her in this house and you won't have to."

"Haven't you caught on yet?" Nick said. "After everything that's happened?"

"I don't know what you're talking about."

"You can't control the world, Russell, not even your own family."

"That's—"

"—The truth. You think you can manipulate everyone around you with your money. But you can't. If yesterday should have taught you anything, it's that."

"I may not be able to control everything," Russell said in a low, jittery voice. "But I can control you. Because I've got money, the one thing you've never had enough of. Other than talent."

"You son of a—"

"Priscilla's death ended what little freedom you had, because now I'm in charge of your life, no one else, and you'll do what I tell you to do or you'll discover just how...how insignificant you really are."

The footsteps resumed and Gwen hurried to the foyer, where she took the stairs two at a time.

"I won't lose Tess," Russell shouted. "I will not lose her."

"You already have!" Nick called after him.

A moment later the music continued, loud and clumsy and furiously fast. Gwen ran down the long second-floor hallway and into the nursery. She put Tess down and grabbed a small rubber ball, which she tossed to her. She needed a distraction from the hatred she'd just heard. The ball bounced gently off Tess's chest and fell to the carpeted floor. Tess giggled, retrieved it, and threw it back.

"Good throw!"

Tess waved her arms. "Maw," she said. More.

And so it continued. Gwen searched for some sign of distress, some indication of the trauma the child had been through. And found nothing. No screaming fits, no loss of appetite. No calls for "mama."

This last was hardest to deal with. She'd never felt at all close to Priscilla, hardly knew her, in fact. But to be so easily forgotten by one's own child…

Of course, Tess didn't understand that her mother wasn't coming back. And God knew Priscilla had been more of a specter than a living, breathing presence. Piano music continued to drift up from the first floor. Would no one mourn Priscilla Lawrence?

And then she looked up and saw the old man, watching them.

"I didn't see you."

Russell Cunningham didn't respond. The night had been cruel to him: his usually lustrous gray hair looked limp and dull, and his eyelids sagged. The yellow polo shirt and white, perfectly pressed pants seemed cruelly cheerful. But his cheeks were flushed, and his forehead glistened with sweat—from all that shouting, no doubt.

She squirmed under his relentless gaze and cleared her throat to break the spell. But he kept staring, and she soon realized that he wasn't seeing her at all.

"Tess is a very resilient girl," she said.

His head jerked, as if startled.

"Would you like to play with her?" Gwen stood up and gave him the ball. He looked as if he'd been handed a live grenade. "She can't really catch it."

"No?"

"Just throw it low enough so that it hits her tummy or legs."

He appeared doubtful as he tossed the ball. It landed a good three feet in front of Tess, who fell on top of it.

"This room is on the small side," he said, glancing quickly around.

Gwen also looked around—what else was she to do? The room

was bigger than her living room and kitchen combined.

"There's a bedroom down the hall that's half again as big," Russell said. "It's my son's room. Was. Maybe we should move the nursery there." He stepped farther into the room, almost warily, squinting at the bookshelves, dressers, and changing table. "Yes, I think the other room would be a lot more appropriate."

The ball hit him in the upper thigh.

"What the..." He stepped back.

"She wants you to throw it to her," Gwen said.

He frowned and bent over to retrieve it. "I know that," he said irritably. He tossed the ball to Tess, who tried to catch it in both hands but succeeded only in clapping.

The old man rubbed his leg. "She's got quite an arm," he said.

As if to underscore this point, Tess picked up the ball and hurled it at him, falling forward in the process. The ball skimmed the top of her changing table, toppling the baby monitor. Gwen picked it up and saw that the small plastic antenna had broken.

"I may be able to fix it," she said. "Or we could get a new one."

We. She'd probably have to pick one up herself. She couldn't imagine either Russell or Nick Lawrence getting involved in something as mundane as replacing a baby monitor. At least Priscilla had managed to keep the nursery well stocked.

"What the hell is it?"

"It's a baby monitor. So you can hear Tess crying if you're somewhere else in the house. The receiver is in the laundry room, unless it's been moved."

"The laundry room?" He shook his head slowly, sadly, as if suddenly overwhelmed by the details of raising a child.

"I'm not sure what it's doing there," she said. "In fact..."

He looked sharply at her, expectantly, as if he knew what she'd been thinking. "In fact, what?"

"In fact I'm sure I can fix it," she said, but her thoughts followed a very different track. She'd been in the laundry room when she'd overheard Priscilla, Nick, and the old man discussing the arrangements after the kidnapper's phone call. But there was no phone in the nursery, so either the three of them had hung up yesterday and immediately run to the nursery to discuss the arrangements, which was absurd, or...

She placed the monitor back on the changing table.

"Yesterday morning, when the kidnapper called, what room were you in?"

"My daughter's...the master bedroom. Why?"

"No reason." She picked up the ball and handed it to him. "Do you happen to remember seeing the baby monitor in the room when you talked about delivering the money?"

He shook his head. "I wouldn't have noticed a Mack truck in the room, under the circumstances." He sighed, picked up his granddaughter, and carried her to the window. Tess immediately tried to squirm out of his arms. Gwen held a finger to her lips and shook her head: *Don't fight him, Tess. Let him have this moment, at least.* Within seconds Tess had relaxed.

"I tried to protect her," he said softly.

"I know, I saw—"

"Not yesterday, *always*. I protected her from this place, this damn town. She never wanted to leave here, you know. I was the one who insisted she go to boarding school. For her sake—I couldn't bear to see her leave. After college she wanted to come back. She loves this place...loved it. I got her an apartment in Manhattan, a job at that auction house. She wasn't ready to take over Penaquoit, and you can't learn squat in this town. I kept her away until she was ready."

Until she'd found a husband and conceived a child, Gwen thought. Only when she was safely married off was she allowed to claim the throne.

"She loved you very much."

"She got her strength from this place." He walked over to the window, still carrying Tess.

"Why was your daughter carrying a thistle yesterday?" Russell turned to her. "Was it some sort of charm?"

His face flushed crimson as his lips opened, but he turned back to the window without speaking and pointed outside.

"See that big mountain, Tess? That's Mount Sohegan." He tried for a gentle, kid-friendly voice, but the resulting singsong sounded so insincere it verged on sinister.

The baby rapped on the window.

"That's right, you *do* see it." He glanced behind him. "She's very bright, you know." He turned back and moved his granddaughter's hand up a few inches, then tapped it against the window. "That's right, Mount Sohegan. Did you know that we own every bit of land between this very room and that big old mountain over there? You and me, Tess—every leaf, every blade of grass, every tree."

Gwen stepped out into the hall, unsure whether to cry or scream. The old man's grief was painted across his face, and yet, just then at the window, he'd been almost smug, as if he'd mentally moved on from his daughter to his granddaughter, skipping over Priscilla like a piece on a checkerboard. Now it was Tess's turn to play heir apparent, and Gwen didn't know who to feel sorry for most: Priscilla, Russell Cunningham, or Tess herself, just one year old and already saddled with the full weight of the old man's expectations.

The piano music from downstairs had turned fierce, the notes fired like bullets. Gwen glanced back in the nursery. Russell Cunningham still held Tess up to the window, surveying their property. He knew what the thistle meant, but he wasn't saying. Why?

Something else troubled her. What was the monitor doing in the master bedroom yesterday morning? Why had it been switched to the on position? Who had brought it back to the nursery? And who, for that matter, had taken the receiver to the laundry room?

Had someone *wanted* her to overhear the ransom plans?

Barry Amiel walked around the cavernous warehouse near Kennedy Airport, nervously aware of his footsteps reverberating off the corrugated steel walls. The day was bright and warm, but the empty warehouse was cold and dank, cloaked in darkness except for random shafts of grainy light from a handful of dirty windows.

He should have had a drink before leaving his room. Should have brought a bottle with him.

He'd arrived a few minutes early for the nine o'clock appointment, punctuality one of the few habits he'd brought with him when he'd left his old life in Manhattan. Left it? He hadn't left shit. He'd been thrown out, ejected, abandoned. He'd never had a chance to explain, not even a moment's chance.

He checked his watch. The big hand jerked onto the nine just as the metal door banged open and a figure in silhouette stepped into the doorway.

"You said I could see my son," he called across the warehouse. The vast space swallowed his voice. The figure stepped forward. Barry squinted through the darkness; was this the same person who'd met him back in Manhattan, offered him the first lucky break he'd gotten in ages: a hundred grand in hundred-dollar bills, his son?

"I never saw my kid; for all I know he's not even in that jerkwater town you sent me to. And you never said anything about killing anybody. I read in the newspaper about some woman getting shot at that ravine. And what the hell was Gwen doing there? You never told me she'd be there."

Holy Christ, he'd almost lost it when she'd stood up from behind that rock. Wanting Jimmy was one thing, confronting Gwen something else. But he'd played his part, nothing too demanding. He'd been involved in some rough stuff as a kid, and in his twenties, before Gwen. All he had to do was grab the bag, fire his old gun a few times into the air, then run back to the car.

The figure took another step forward, still just a black mass in some kind of long coat, the sun shimmering behind it like a vapor. A shiver ran through him, right to his gut.

"You got the money?" he asked. "Forget my son, I'll find Jimmy on my own, now I know where his mother is. You got the hundred thousand we talked about?"

He thought he saw a nod; then the right arm began to rise, real slow. Well, all those hundred-dollar bills had to be heavy.

"I'll find Jimmy on my own, now that I got some money."

A glint from next to the figure, then an explosion that he felt in his ears first, like diving underwater, then...

Then something blasted the back of his head. No, not something—he'd hit the floor, hard. He tried to sit up, couldn't. Another explosion, this one from directly above him. He saw the face then, staring down at him, the same face, and he tried to ask why.

But he knew the answer, in a flash as quick and bright and painful in its own way as the gunshots that he knew were killing him, if they hadn't already.

He tried to move his lips anyway, not to ask this time, but to explain. They were so dry, all of a sudden, glued together, they felt.

"Jimmy," he said, or thought he said. He heard nothing except a distant whooshing sound, a long, tired sigh. *It wasn't the money, Jimmy, honest. I only wanted to say, I only wanted the chance to tell you I was sorry.*

CHAPTER 16

The funeral was held on Wednesday at the Mount Hope Cemetery in Sohegan. The family huddled on one side of the mahogany casket, a few feet from the freshly dug grave: Russell and Maxine Cunningham, Nick Lawrence, and Tess. The Piacevics stood nearby, next to Gwen.

Nick had asked her to come to look after Tess. "I wouldn't bring her at all, but the old man insists." He frowned and glanced away. "And I'm in no position to refuse him anything."

Cemeteries often occupy the choicest real estate in the community, just as funeral homes are often the grandest structures in town, and the Mount Hope cemetery was no exception. It was located on a hillside overlooking the Ondaiga Valley; few private homes in Sohegan enjoyed so open and peaceful a vista. The Cunningham plot was at its highest point, with a view in all directions. There were huge granite memorials to Russell and Florence Cunningham, Priscilla's grandparents, and an even larger memorial to Russell Cunningham III, festooned with carved angels and garlands and an inscription: ETERNALLY OURS. The day was very hot, the air choked with humidity.

The small band of mourners were the focus of a thousand eyes. A large crowd had gathered at the entrance to the cemetery, which was located about three miles north of town. Two police officers kept the spectators outside the cemetery gates. Gwen saw their faces from inside the second of two rented limousines as they drove in: some familiar from her days at the Mecca, most not, all straining to see through the tinted glass, hoping for a glimpse of the town's most celebrated family, now its most notorious. Hovering above the cemetery, all but drowning out the minister's sermon, was a news helicopter.

"…Cut down while trying to save the child she loved so dearly." The Reverend Michael Leeper was tall and gangly, about fifty, Gwen guessed. Sweat poured from his face onto his prayer book, which he looked up from only to cast sympathetic glances at Maxine Cunningham. His voice held little conviction.

Gwen was just as happy to lose most of the eulogy to the clatter of the helicopter. Leeper couldn't possibly have known Priscilla any better than she had, and the empty words would only exacerbate her discomfort at being there. She studied Maxine Cunningham while Leeper carried on. Just over five feet tall, she was as thin and frail as a young girl. Priscilla had inherited her father's athletic build and strong features, his resolute jaw and sharp, almost fierce cheekbones. But she'd gotten her mother's thin, reproving lips and, most noticeably, her bird-furtive hazel eyes. Maxine's grief carried an anxious edge; every few moments she glanced up at the helicopter, as if expecting an airborne attack.

Russell Cunningham held Tess, who also gazed up at the hovering helicopter. The old man appeared more angry than heartbroken as he glowered at the flower-laden coffin. The Piacevics, standing a few feet from each other, looked sheepishly at the ground in front of them, as if expecting to be evicted with the rest of the rubberneckers.

"God in his infinite wisdom and with boundless mercy will watch over Priscilla, darling Priscilla, as she—"

"Mama?"

Leeper, mouth still open, turned to Tess.

"Mama?" Tess was staring behind her grandfather's back. Everyone turned to follow her gaze. Gwen saw the old man's face brighten momentarily, then darken when his daughter didn't emerge through the thicket of monuments and headstones.

Tess began kicking her grandfather, still crying "mama." Nick reached for her, but she turned away. Gwen stepped around the grave, and as she walked in front of Nick she saw a flash of rage cross his face, a look she'd never seen before, and would never forget. He looked almost ugly. She took Tess from the old man and hurried down the hill, away from the grave site.

Leeper's eulogy grew fainter and fainter as she walked. After a few minutes Tess was calm again. Gwen let her toddle among the headstones as she pointed out the carved angels, the crosses, the flowers.

But she saw none of it herself, not really. That expression on Nick's face as he watched his daughter call for Priscilla—what was it? Rage, yes, but at what, or whom? Could he really resent his daughter's calling for her mother rather than for him? Only when he was practicing did his features assume that darkly abstracted quality, but at the piano his preoccupation was attractive, even erotic. At the grave site just now he'd looked frightening.

"Miss Amiel?"

She turned, startled. Dwight Hawkins approached her from the main drive, wearing a tie and white shirt, a sports jacket draped over his shoulder.

"Did I frighten you?" he said.

He stopped a few feet from her. The question seemed loaded, somehow, with a hidden subtext: *Are you frightened of something?*

She shook her head.

"Kind of a small turnout for our most distinguished family."

"Mr. Cunningham requested only the immediate family."

Hawkins pointed to the crowd of spectators outside the pillared gates to the cemetery.

"Big disappointment to the peanut gallery."

"I guess they'll find some other way to express their grief."

The sarcasm seemed to stymie him momentarily. Tess yawned. Gwen picked her up.

"It's warm for June," he said, glancing around. "Eleventh day in a row above ninety, that's a record for Ondaiga County. There's a front stalled south of the Ohio Valley. Until it moves, we're going to roast." He sighed and looked at her. "The FBI ran a background check on everyone connected to Priscilla Lawrence—husband, parents, the Piacevics. And you. I was just looking over the report."

She felt her heart beat against Tess's tummy. "No prior convictions," she said, trying to sound unconcerned. "No arrests."

He actually laughed. "Yes, that *was* a disappointment. Still, you had quite a nice life downstate. Nice apartment in a nice neighborhood, nice store. Then you sold your business and moved here? Why?"

"I wanted a small town, clean air, good schools for my son."

"The schools stink," he said, and she almost laughed until she realized that he was studying her. "You'd have to go to bayou Louisiana to find worse college board scores."

"Then what are *you* doing here?" she asked.

"I have no kids," he said. "What's your excuse?"

His tone had turned aggressive, but she found herself warming to Dwight Hawkins. When he'd said "no kids" just now, he'd sounded almost apologetic.

"The truth?" she said. "I'd been driving all night, I felt tired, so I got off the highway at the first exit with a motel sign. That was here."

"You don't seem like a person who leaves things up to chance."

She felt a shiver of vulnerability. He was right, she'd always planned every step of her life. Then Jimmy was born, and her sense of control began to wane with every midnight feeding, every infant cold, every crying jag she couldn't diagnose, let alone alleviate. When things got bad with Barry, she'd tried at first to hold it together, summon that old self-reliance. It hadn't worked. So she'd exercised perhaps the last bit of control she had left to her: she got the hell out of town. From the moment she crossed the George Washington Bridge, she'd lived pretty much from day to day.

"Is there something you want?" she said.

He looked behind her. She turned and saw the funeral breaking up. Tess had fallen asleep in her arms.

"The FBI report mentioned you owned a gun."

Tess's eyes opened briefly, then closed; she must have squeezed her too hard.

"I used to own one."

"The report says there's a twenty-two caliber Browning

registered in your name, purchased in nineteen eighty-two. Did you sell it, Miss Amiel?"

"My husband, Barry, insisted I buy it, to protect me at the store. I never wanted it, and I never used it."

"Why didn't he buy it himself, then?"

"He thought I'd have an easier time registering it. He had a drunk driving charge a few years back." That, and a history of problems with the police dating back to his teenage years, when he'd been involved with a rough gang in Manhattan's Hell's Kitchen. Only when his father's cousin hired him on his construction crew did Barry find his calling. He had a genius for building things. He could grasp the scope of the most complex projects almost instantly, breaking them down to discrete components and quickly conjuring up a game plan for completing the work as quickly and inexpensively as possible. For a while there he'd been one of the most successful contractors in Manhattan. They'd met when she hired him to renovate her store. His references had been impeccable.

"The DWI charge was in the FBI report, too. Where is the gun now?"

"I don't know."

"A semiautomatic handgun isn't something you misplace."

"When I sold my store I brought it home. I left it there when Jimmy and I moved up here. My husband must have it."

"He sold everything you left in the apartment."

"He..." This was news. Not exactly surprising, but troubling all the same. An inventory flashed through her mind. The tapestry-covered sofa she'd had custom-made in a binge of extravagance, the dining-room table she'd found on a buying trip to southern France, Jimmy's dresser, which she'd stripped and painted during the last weeks of her pregnancy. "He must have sold the gun, too," she managed to say.

"Are you sure you left it in New York City?"

"Yes, I'm—what's this about?"

"The bullet that killed Priscilla Lawrence came from a Browning twenty-two." His eyes looked right into hers.

"But not necessarily *my* Browning." She would *not* mention the trace metal test. He must know she passed, and she was damned if she was going to sound defensive.

"Until we find the gun, we won't know for sure. When did you last see your husband?"

"I told the FBI, the day I left New York City."

"Not since?"

"No."

"Did the Lawrences have any visitors in the past few weeks? An unexpected delivery, strangers hanging around, anything?"

"No, life at Penaquoit is pretty dull, actually, the same thing every—wait, there was one person. Valerie Goodwin, a friend of the Lawrences from New York."

He took out a small notepad. "Valerie Goodwin? Any address?"

"No. Didn't Nick Lawrence mention her visit?"

"He might have," Hawkins said. "Did you observe anything unusual about this Valerie Goodwin?"

"She seemed…" What should she say, that Valerie seemed unusually close to Tess for a godparent? That she'd seen her and Priscilla sharing a rather intimate moment in the basement? What good could possibly come from stirring *that* pot?

"She seemed very close to all of them," Gwen said after a pause.

"Nothing else? You were about to say something more."

She shook her head and watched the funeral party heading for the limos. Nick and the Piacevics turned back frequently to watch her and Hawkins.

"Did you ever find out where Priscilla went the morning she was killed?" she asked.

"Went?"

"She was out when I got there, at nine, and didn't come back until almost eleven. Didn't anyone mention that?"

He slowly shook his head.

"Nick Lawrence was pretty upset about it, asked Priscilla where she was. She told him she went for a drive."

"With her daughter missing?" Hawkins glanced away, trying to make sense of this.

"I should join them," Gwen said.

"Of course. Just be careful, Miss Amiel."

"What do you mean?"

He looked up and shook his head at the shimmering sky, his eyes almost reproachful.

"They both think they're above the rest of us, Russell Cunningham *and* his son-in-law. They may live here, but they don't live among us. You mean nothing to them, remember that. When push comes to shove, you're not family, so you don't count."

"I'll keep that in mind," she said, then hurried around the side of the hill toward the small funeral party, moving awkwardly under Tess's sleeping weight. One by one the mourners stopped and stared at her walking away from the detective—Maxine and Russell, then Nick, then the Piacevics.

She meant nothing to them? She didn't count?

Then why were they staring at her and Hawkins, every one of them, making no attempt to disguise their interest, their faces taut with concern?

CHAPTER 17

Thursday, the day after the funeral, was disconcertingly uneventful. The FBI and county police were already scaling back their local operations, vowing to the press—and to Russell Cunningham personally—that they'd continue the search for the kidnappers from their better-equipped home bases. There just wasn't much point to sticking around Sohegan, where every possible lead had been thoroughly investigated. The kidnapper and the money were quite obviously elsewhere.

Gwen stopped in town for some groceries that morning on the way to Penaquoit and sensed a heavy air of disappointment. Sohegan was Brigadoon, settling back to sleep after a few glorious hours in the limelight. Only the half dozen or so glistening black Ford Crown Victorias attested to the FBI's continued, if diminishing, presence. Smoked-glass windows completely obscured the occupants, lending a ghostly aura to their fleeting appearances around town.

Newspaper reports of the investigation offered little new information. Priscilla Lawrence had been killed by a single .22-caliber bullet, which had pierced her heart, exited her body through her right shoulder, and lodged in a tree on the west side of the ravine—a silver birch, most articles mentioned. One other bullet was recovered, this one in the dirt about two feet from Priscilla's body. Tiny black orlon fibers had been found clinging to the bark of a tree—a Scotch pine—about five and a half feet up from the ground, also on the west side of the ravine. The gunman (or woman, the articles all noted) must have rested his (or her) head against the tree while observing Russell Cunningham deposit the duffel bag, allowing the fibers from the knit ski mask to become snagged on the bark. Shoe prints had been made, but no details of size or make had been released.

Gwen tiptoed around the mansion all day as she went about her duties, sensing some ill-defined danger in the sepulchral silence. Priscilla Cunningham's absence, it turned out, was a much more potent force in the house than her presence had ever been. Before the kidnapping, Gwen could work at Penaquoit two days straight without seeing her. Now, every time she entered a room, she half expected to see Priscilla, stern-faced, accusatory, a finger holding her place in a magazine.

"You've got a guilty conscience," Sheila informed her that evening. She'd invited Gwen and Jimmy for dinner. Betsy had cooked a runny vegetarian lasagna, which Jimmy hadn't touched. Gwen managed to eat a respectable amount by washing it down with half a bottle of Chianti. They ate at a splintery picnic table in the backyard. The lawn was more dirt than grass, and Gwen noticed several dead shrubs and leafless trees. Here and there a clump of flowers managed to thrive, flashes of color that struck her as more incongruous than pleasing. Yard work, like cooking, was clearly not a high priority for Sheila and Betsy.

"Maybe I do feel guilty," Gwen said, "but there's something else. Everything at Penaquoit is so…normal. Nick practices as much as ever, maybe more. Tess is completely adjusted; she practically never asks for her mother, and even when she does she settles right away for a warm bottle."

"What about the parents?"

"Maxine Cunningham keeps to her own house, just like she always did. Russell…well, at least *he's* acting differently. He comes over all the time now to see Tess. He and Nick basically ignore each other."

"She's all Russell has," Betsy said sadly. "The end of the Cunningham line." Everyone in Sohegan discussed the case as if it were an episode of a favorite soap opera. No last names needed: the characters were just plain Russell, Maxine, and Nick. "It's so *tragic.*"

Betsy fluffed her sable-black hair, which sprouted from a central part like twin hedges. When she had the time she liked to slather on gel and mousse and God knew what else to reshape her coif. The slower her business at the salon, the more architectural her do.

"You look like Cruella DeVil," Jimmy had said when she opened the door that evening.

"Cruella—you mean that dyke who likes dalmatian fur?" Betsy said. "Why, thank you, James."

Jimmy squinted. "Mommy, what's a—"

"Go see what's on TV in the living room," Gwen said quickly.

"They almost lost Priscilla once before, you know," Betsy said in an ominous voice over coffee. "Hodgkin's disease, wasn't it, Sheil?"

Sheila let out a sharp sigh. "Can we *please* stop talking about this?"

"Well, I'm pretty sure it was Hodgkin's," Betsy said after making a face at her partner. "She used to go down to New York City every week for radiation or chemo and whatnot."

"This isn't your hair salon, okay?" Sheila glanced from Betsy to Gwen. "Can't we find *something* else to talk about besides the local gossip?"

Betsy shot Sheila a look that was both accusatory and sad. Sheila turned away.

"Anyway, she survived," Betsy said to Gwen. "Full remission."

"I can hardly look at Russell Cunningham," Gwen said. "He tries so hard with Tess…"

"Does she respond?" Sheila asked.

"She barely knew him until this week. And the way he goes about playing with her, it's just not natural. It's like…it's like he wants her *with* him, under his watch, but doesn't really enjoy the experience, doesn't even expect to."

"He must be terrified something will happen to her," Sheila said.

"You can understand his perspective," Betsy said. "Cancer, a car accident, kidnapping. The three Cs." She started to giggle, then glanced nervously at Sheila and put a hand to her mouth. She'd had even more to drink than Gwen. "Sorry."

"I wish I knew what to do," Gwen said as she drained another glass of wine. "I mean, I make suggestions to Russell on how to play with Tess, tell him what she likes to do. But he seems completely uninterested. I don't think it occurs to him that he might actually *enjoy* his granddaughter. Or she him."

"Well, give him time," Betsy said. "He's been through a lot." She looked quite grim. "The three Cs and all." Now she completely lost it.

Sheila got up from the table and began clearing dishes.

"Look, Sheil, I don't know these people, okay?" Betsy said. "And they wouldn't have anything to do with me even if we did somehow meet."

"I don't know them either. That doesn't mean I think it's all a hoot." She took a stack of dinner plates into the house, returning a minute later with a coffeepot and three mugs on a tray. Betsy and Gwen hadn't said a word in her absence.

"How is the widower taking things?" Betsy asked as Sheila sat down.

"He looks…" Gwen shook her head and regretted the last glass of wine.

"He looks *what?*" Betsy asked.

"He looks incredibly…" She sighed. "Pass the wine, please."

"Not until you finish telling us how he looks," Betsy said.

"He looks…he looks beautiful!"

Both women snorted.

"It sounds strange, I know, but yesterday after the funeral I realized that something had changed about him. His eyes were so bright, his cheeks were darker, there was an intensity about him."

"Mourning becomes Nick Lawrence," Sheila said.

"And when I see him with Tess, the way he worships her…"

"Face it," said Sheila as she poured Gwen a glass of wine. "Some women are turned on by a man's wedding ring, some get off seeing a man acting all cuddly with a small child."

Betsy shook her head with exaggerated disgust.

Gwen frowned with more disapproval than she felt. "I didn't say I was turned on."

"You didn't have to," Sheila said.

"Hey, you two didn't have me over for dinner just to pump me for inside information, did you?"

"Gwendolyn Amiel!" Betsy put a hand to her chest. "Didn't we have you to dinner last week, *before* the shit hit the fan?"

Gwen smiled. She'd never truly doubted their sincerity.

"More coffee?" Betsy asked, getting up from the table. Gwen nodded. Betsy started to pour from the pot, then stopped. "But only if you tell us what Dwight Hawkins wanted yesterday after the funeral."

Gwen frowned. "I *knew* it."

"The whole town saw him interrogating you," Betsy said as she resumed pouring. "It's all anyone's been talking about."

By week's end, a pattern had been established. Gwen arrived at Penaquoit at eight, earlier than before the murder. She met Nick in the kitchen, where he fed Tess breakfast. He stood up and left the moment she walked in. Less than a minute later piano music, scales and arpeggios at first, filled the house.

Friday morning she spooned Tess a few remaining bits of cereal, wiped her face, and heard the music begin. The usual drill…but something was different, and it wasn't just that he'd launched right into the piece he'd been working on all week, skipping the warm-up. The music was louder, more immediate. She wrestled Tess from her high chair and carried her toward the music, walking slowly through the big pantry, down the long service hallway past the breakfast room, and, pushing open the swinging door, into the foyer.

The music was so loud, so *close*, she knew instantly that her first reaction had been correct; something had changed. She stepped into the foyer, hesitated, then walked to the other side. She glanced into the living room and felt a chill make its way down her spine.

Nick's piano had been moved to the center of the living room, displacing two sofas and a phalanx of chairs and tables. The living room was enormous, but the long Steinway still looked too big for its new location. The word "beached" came to mind, as if the piano had simply washed into the room, scattering less important furniture to the edge of the room in its wake.

But of course it hadn't washed into the room, it had been carried there, to the very heart of the house, where it could never be overlooked.

She'd wanted some tangible recognition that Priscilla was gone. She had it now.

He must have sensed their presence, for he stopped playing abruptly and turned around.

"Come in," he said. He had taken off his shirt and was wearing only loose-fitting green shorts. Sweat glistened on his back, his upper arms. His hair looked tousled and damp, as if he'd been exercising. Indeed, he had the body of an athlete, lean and efficient. Gwen stepped just inside the arched entrance.

"A lot of pianists use the Pathetique to show off," he said. "They drag out the opening, holding those half notes as if challenging the listener not to squirm. It's like a staring contest—you know, who'll blink first?"

She nodded as she put Tess down, hoping she looked as though she knew what the hell he was talking about.

"Then they really let loose in the first movement," he said. "'Look! Look how fast I can play, *look!*'"

She watched a bead of sweat run down his neck onto his shoulder. He turned completely, facing her, knees spread apart, a hand on each thigh.

"That's one advantage to performing only for yourself. Your allegiance is solely to the music. I don't have to impress anyone except myself, and my standards are very high."

Runner's legs, she thought, long and muscular. Yet she'd never seen him exercise much, other than the occasional swim.

"Do you agree?"

She blinked, felt her face flush. "I…excuse me?"

He studied her a moment, his expression more curious than anything else, though he must have known where her thoughts had been.

"I asked if you thought the piano sounded better in here."

"I'm not sure I can tell the difference."

A brief frown, which softened into a grin. "You always tell the truth, don't you, Gwendolyn? Is that your real name, Gwendolyn?"

His mouth wrapped around the three syllables like sucking candy. Always so precise in his diction: Gwen-do-lyn.

"Yes, but I never use it."

"It is very rare to find truly honest people. I hope you are the real article."

"Don't you mean the real McCoy?" He scowled and she quickly added, "Or the genuine article?"

"Are you the genuine article?" he said in an icy voice. Apparently he hated to be corrected.

"I hope so."

Though if she were truly honest she'd tell him what she really thought when she saw the tumescent Steinway in its new quarters: how she found it monstrous that he'd waited less than two days after the funeral before taking over the house, placing himself and his music at its very core. How she'd never forget her first glimpse of the Steinway beached in the center of the room, all other furniture, *Cunningham* furniture, shoved aside like so many meaningless impediments to his one true desire.

"I should really change Tess now." She turned and almost tripped over a stack of books and papers on the floor. Several volumes fell from the pile.

"Sorry," he said. "I haven't had time to organize my music."

She picked up the fallen books and placed them on a small table. A few loose papers slipped back onto the floor.

"Never mind," he said, but she picked up the papers anyway. There were notes, written in his hand, a few yellowed newspaper clippings, a receipt of some kind. She placed them on top of the books on the table.

"I've always wanted to go to Vienna," she said as she straightened the pile.

"Me too," he replied.

"Oh." She looked at the piece of paper on top of the pile.

"Doesn't 'Wein' mean Vienna?"

He stood up and examined the receipt. "Ah, the Beethoven fantasy. I haven't played that in years." He searched through the pile of music and pulled out a thin sheaf. "Here it is. Patelson's in New York must have purchased this in Vienna, for resale. See? It's a German edition."

She glanced at the music and nodded.

"I always dreamed of travel," he said quietly. "And ended up here."

"Someday I'm sure—"

"Beethoven lived in seventeen different houses in Vienna alone. I fear I shall never live anywhere but here."

She tried to look sympathetic as she knelt to pick up Tess.

"Would you like to swim?" he said suddenly.

"But I have to change Tess, clean her room…" God, she hated talking diapers to his Ludwig van Beethoven.

"Always so conscientious. And yet I don't see you as anyone's housekeeper. What were you, really, in your former life?"

"A neatness freak."

He returned her grin. When he smiled his face became handsome, but alarmingly so; such perfection always came at a price.

"Put Tess down for her morning nap, it's almost time." She was about to say something when he turned back to the keyboard. "I'll meet you by the pool in twenty minutes."

His hands crashed down on a low, angry chord, which he held for several seconds before moving on to the next.

"You see," he said over his shoulder. "I give the chord its full ration, but I will not belabor it."

She nodded at his back and left the living room, determined not to swim with him. But then, after a short gasp of silence, the somber prologue gave way to an impassioned, vigorous, almost frenzied melody. She watched him attack the sonata with his entire body, the muscles straining in his shoulders and arms and back. He would never relate as intimately to another person as he did to his music, except perhaps to Tess.

• • •

Nick was already standing by the pool when she emerged from the cabana in her bathing suit. He watched her cross the patio and she was glad she'd brought her one-piece to Penaquoit, not her bikini. Nick was wearing striped swim trunks.

"Hello again," he said, and his complete lack of surprise at her presence made her want to turn around and go back inside. Instead she looked beyond him. Milky waves of heat shimmered in the middle distance; beyond, the rounded peaks of the Ondaigas formed a dark, almost stern barrier.

"It's so beautiful here," she said.

He glanced around, eyes dispassionate. "Priscilla felt safe at Penaquoit, and never more so than when contemplating that view." He pointed to the hills in the distance. "I think she believed those mountains would keep out danger, repel the barbarians."

"Penaquoit was her Switzerland," Gwen said. But the plain, squat Ondaigas were not the Alps. The feeling of safety had been an illusion.

"The view leaves me unmoved," Nick said. "If I owned Penaquoit I'd cut down those damn hemlocks over there and have a large pond dug out in their place. In the morning it would reflect the house; in the afternoon, the mountains beyond would shimmer on its surface." His eyes turned dreamy for a moment, then refocused on her. "I like a water view—there's something incomplete about a landscape without at least a pond or lake."

He stretched his arms overhead, filling his lungs. He exhaled and caught her watching. She dove into the pool and continued underwater to the opposite end. Four laps later she stopped at the edge of the shallow end. Nick was leaning against the side.

"You must have been on the swim team," he said.

"Huntington High School," she replied, still panting. "...On Long Island."

"You should feel free to use the pool any time. Bring your son on weekends if you like."

"Thank you." She gathered her hair in one hand and squeezed out the water, then smoothed it along her neck. "Priscilla...I don't think I ever saw her use the pool."

He shrugged, looking annoyed. The reference to his wife sounded forced, but she felt the need to interpose Priscilla between them.

"I still have difficulty believing that she's dead." He glanced up at the house. "I keep expecting her to walk onto the patio for her cantaloupe and cottage cheese at lunchtime." He sounded more spooked than wistful.

"Do you think you'll stay here?" she asked quietly, though she knew what he'd be forfeiting if he left.

He let out a long, slow breath. "It's too soon to make plans. What about you? Are you going to stick around?"

"I don't know, really. This isn't exactly what I had in mind for myself."

"I hope you'll at least stay until the end of the summer. We need you, Tess and I."

She nodded. "Did you hear Tess crying at the ravine that day? After your father-in-law left the duffel bag?"

"I...no, I didn't."

She frowned. "I did, I know I did."

"It was quite windy that afternoon, perhaps you thought you heard her crying. Or the cicadas might have fooled you."

"No, it was Tess." She looked away. "I know it was." She felt her face flush.

"It's too late for second thoughts," he said softly, placing a hand on her shoulder.

"The police...Dwight Hawkins...he's talking to everyone I ever had any contact with here, questioning them about me."

"Why is he doing that?"

"He must think I was involved. I can't imagine why else he'd be asking about me."

He squeezed her shoulder; then his palm slid a few inches down her back.

"What they think and what they can prove are two very

different things."

"Prove? You don't—"

"Of course not." His hand slid down her arm. "It's so peaceful here now that the cicadas are gone—have you noticed? Well, perhaps not gone, but they've stopped that hideous noise. Their mating call, Piacevic tells me. I suppose they're through mating. Think about it, seventeen years in the cold, dark earth, waiting for just three or four weeks of copulation. The grass is littered with their shells. I asked Piacevic to get rid of them." He squeezed her arm gently, testing. She pulled away and headed toward the stairs.

"I need to check on Tess," she said. She left the pool, grabbed a towel, and hurried across the lawn. When she entered the house the cool air instantly raised goose bumps. In her eagerness to be away from him she'd left her dress in the pool house, but she didn't want to go back and retrieve it just yet. Even with a towel wrapped around her she felt vulnerable in front of him. Perhaps with Tess in her arms she wouldn't feel quite so exposed. She checked her watch: eleven-fifteen—Tess should be up soon.

She used the back staircase for a change, praying the Piacevics wouldn't encounter her wearing a bathing suit, and cursing herself for giving in to the swim.

How could he touch her like that, so soon after Priscilla's death? How could she *let* him touch her? He was getting to her, peeling away the protective shell she'd cloaked herself in when she'd driven upstate three months ago.

And it wasn't just his obvious attractiveness that was chipping away at her, though God knew that was hard to ignore. It was something else, the way he looked at her, as if he could read her like a piece of music, and find the hidden rhythms and melodies. She thought of the cicada shells on the lawn, and wondered if hers would be among them soon.

Well, she'd promised to stay at Penaquoit for the summer. Come September she'd get the hell out of there.

She entered the nursery and stopped short. "Mr. Cunningham!"

He was looking out the window, holding Tess.

"She's awake," he said, turning to her. Behind him, through the window, she glimpsed a corner of the pool.

"I was just coming to check on her."

He put Tess on the floor. She walked over and grabbed Gwen's bare legs.

"You were swimming," he said. "With my son-in-law."

"He asked me...insisted, really. I'm sorry if I—"

"I'm paying your salary now. Nick couldn't afford you otherwise." Afford her?

"I don't want you swimming while on duty, unless you're with my granddaughter."

She nodded.

"I think her diaper needs changing," he said as he headed for the door. Then he turned and added: "Be careful with my son-in-law, Miss Amiel."

"I don't know what—"

"He spent the first twenty years of his life expecting great things of himself, only to find out he hadn't the talent to achieve them."

She picked up Tess and carried her to the changing table. Russell followed her across the room.

"Disillusioned men are the most dangerous, Miss Amiel. They've already lost their dream. Remember that."

He turned and left the room.

CHAPTER 18

The weekend finally arrived, two full days away from Penaquoit. Gwen kept close to home for most of Saturday, playing catch with Jimmy in their small, fenced-in backyard, spraying him with the garden hose, drawing pictures together at the picnic table. Late Saturday afternoon they drove into town to rent a video.

While Jimmy selected a tape with his customary solemn deliberation, she began to notice that people were staring at her, occasionally pointing. Her initial reaction, that something was wrong with her hair, that she had a rip in her shorts, quickly gave way to the realization that it was her connection to the kidnapping that was attracting attention.

"Come on, Jimmy, choose something," she said. "Anything."

He frowned and grabbed a tape. At the counter she fished through her wallet for her rental card.

"Never mind, I know who you are," said the heavyset, middle-aged woman behind the counter through pale, disapproving lips. "That'll be two-fifty." Gwen handed her the exact change. The woman shoved the rental agreement across the counter. "Sign."

Gwen hesitated before picking up the pen. *She thinks I was involved. They all do.*

"The pen's right there," the woman said flatly without looking up from the cash drawer. Gwen scribbled her name on the receipt and got the hell out of there.

• • •

"Well, you're an outsider," Sheila told her on the phone after Gwen reported the video store incident. "I mean, people were suspicious of you the moment you set foot in town. Nobody moves *to* Sohegan. Especially someone with a hundred-dollar haircut and fancy clothes and—"

"Fancy clothes? They're from the Gap, for Chrissake."

"We don't have a Gap in Sohegan. Just the Army-Navy. Face it, you don't belong here, not in most people's eyes. And then you just happen to show up at the scene of a notorious murder? And then the little girl just happens to show up at your house?"

"I'm so glad I called."

"Just telling it like it is, Gwen. You want to come over for dinner?"

"I'll pass," she said. "But thanks."

She and Jimmy ate hamburgers that evening, watched the video, played go fish, then slapjack, then go fish again. By eight o'clock cabin fever had set in. She suggested ice cream cones. There was a place on Mill Hollow Road, about five miles north of town. No one would recognize her there, and the ice cream wasn't half bad.

Visibility was poor that evening, the humidity having congealed into dense clouds of fog. The scenery turned rural just a mile from town, houses giving way to farms—dairy farms, most of them, the terrain too hilly for crops.

It wasn't a charming landscape, lacking the picturesque clapboard farmhouses and rolling pastures of New England. The area had never been especially prosperous; every structure was built for utility and efficiency. The typical Sohegan house was two stories high, topped with a flat roof, had a long, sagging front porch, and needed a good scrape and paint job. There was usually a ramshackle garage out back, maybe a few rusted auto carcasses.

The small, fluorescent-lit ice cream parlor was attached to a Mobil station that shared a narrow lot with a large, run-down house set close to the road. Jimmy ran over to the ice cream freezer the moment they entered the store.

"Can I have sprinkles, Mom?" he asked as he surveyed the ice cream flavors on tiptoes.

"As many as you—" She froze in the doorway.

"As many as I want?"

Valerie Goodwin stood in front of the counter, watching a young girl scoop ice cream from large, round cartons inside the freezer. In her free hand the girl held two cones.

Figuring it was too late to retreat, Gwen walked over to Valerie and said hello.

Valerie looked up and smiled mechanically, as if she didn't recognize her. She glanced away, then whipped back around.

"You're…"

"Gwen Amiel. I look after Tess Lawrence."

"Of course." Valerie extended her hand. "I arrived yesterday. I had hoped to attend the funeral on Wednesday, but the bus schedule is so erratic. I don't drive, you know." She made this sound like a matter of principle, like not wearing fur.

"It was a small funeral," Gwen said. "Just family, really."

"I still can't believe it, that she's gone." Valerie looked paler than Gwen remembered, and thinner, if possible. Still chic—absurdly so, given the setting. But even a stranger might have surmised from her sallow complexion and tired eyes that she'd had a difficult week.

"She was my closest friend, in some ways. Every time I look at that poor child…"

She seemed about to cry as the girl behind the counter handed her the two cones. "Two-fifty," she said.

Valerie handed one cone to Gwen while she dug into her pocketbook for money. The other cone—for Nick?

"Did you know Priscilla for a long time?"

"Since she moved to New York, about ten years ago. We lived in the same building, off Third Avenue. I introduced her to Nick, in fact. We were inseparable."

She handed three dollars to the girl. "Keep the change."

The girl smiled rather inhospitably and turned to Gwen.

"Jimmy, why don't you order," she said.

"Chocolate chip with sprinkles," he said without taking his eyes off the tubs of ice cream.

"Nothing for me," Gwen said, though her mouth felt terribly dry. "I wasn't planning to come up just yet, but Nick seemed so desperate when I called."

Desperate? Nick Lawrence?

"I thought he was coping pretty well."

"Oh, Nick always seems to be coping. He can be so cool sometimes, on the outside. But he suffers terribly, do not doubt it for one minute."

Gwen nodded, trying to look as if she agreed.

"Priscilla hated him when they first met; she thought he was a cold fish. I told her to give him a second chance, then a third. I knew he'd get through to her eventually."

"How did you know Nick?"

"We'd been fixed up, on a blind date of all things." She giggled and flicked her tongue to catch a drop of ice cream. "I knew right away he was not for me—a brooding genius was the last thing I needed. He was also flat broke, which didn't help, let me tell you. But I simply knew he and Priss would be perfect. It wasn't just her money, though that was a factor, I won't deny it. She could handle him, weather his moods, give him the space he needed. You've met the father?"

"Russell? Yes."

"Well, if you can handle that bastard, you can handle anyone." She sighed and jerked back her lustrous red hair. Even now, looking vaguely neurasthenic, she was striking, almost theatrically beautiful. The girl behind the counter gaped at her as she scooped Jimmy's ice cream. Her whole look screamed "out of town."

One of the cones dripped onto Valerie's hand. She squealed girlishly as she licked it off.

"I better get this to Nick," she said. "Would you like to say hello?"

"No, I'll see him on Monday."

"I'm leaving early in the morning, so I won't see you." She pushed open the door with a bony shoulder. "Oh, there is one thing…" She leaned against the door, facing Gwen. "I understand the police found a flower in Priscilla's hand, at the ravine."

"A purple thistle."

"You wouldn't happen to know why she was holding it, would you? I mean, there of all places."

Gwen shook her head. "You were so close to her…"

"True." Valerie offered a nervous smile and let the door close behind her.

"Who was that, Mommy?" Jimmy's hand and sleeve were covered with melted ice cream. The girl leaned across the counter to hear Gwen's answer.

"A friend of Tess's father," Gwen said in a low voice. Priscilla's friend, too, she thought, remembering the scene in the basement. She walked to the window in time to see the Range Rover backing out of its parking space. Nick was at the wheel, Valerie next to him. Behind them, strapped into her car seat, was Tess, asleep.

"One and a quarter," the girl said.

Something Valerie just mentioned bothered her…

"One-twenty-five, *please.*"

"Oh, right." She handed the girl two dollar-bills.

"Keep the change?" the girl said with a fair imitation of Valerie Goodwin's throaty, moneyed voice. She handed three quarters to Gwen, who put one of them back on the counter.

"Come on, Jimmy, it's late." She placed a hand on his shoulder and they walked outside just as the Range Rover made a left onto Mill Hollow.

"Damn," Gwen said as they drove home, suddenly realizing what had bothered her.

"Damn what?" Jimmy said.

"Oh, nothing, just the heat, I guess."

The heat—and the fact that something Valerie said didn't jive with what Nick had already told her. He said that he met Priscilla when she was a student of his. Valerie said she'd fixed them up. Neither Valerie nor Nick struck her as likely to forget that kind of detail. Both were so precise in their choice of words, so fastidious in their dress—a faulty memory just didn't suit them, somehow. Which left only one conclusion.

One of them was lying.

CHAPTER 19

The Sohegan *Gazette* advertised an antiques auction on Sunday, about twenty miles south of town. Back when she'd had the store, Gwen had spent weekends crisscrossing the countryside to attend such auctions, where she'd buy furniture and bric-a-brac to replenish inventory, purchasing an occasional piece for her own apartment. Since moving to Sohegan she'd lost the desire to acquire anything for herself. Living in a rented house with someone else's furniture was unexpectedly satisfying; she could pick up and leave at a moment's notice—at least that's how it felt.

But Sunday promised to be a scorcher, and the prospect of a long drive in an air-conditioned car was suddenly quite appealing. She also figured Jimmy could use some time with a friend. He'd been pretty much a loner since coming to Sohegan, but he'd mentioned a kid named Andrew Hillman a few times, which was definitely progress. She suggested a play date with Andrew, and Jimmy hadn't objected. More progress.

The Hillmans lived in a new subdivision a mile north of town. Every tree in the densely wooded area had been chopped down to make way for the houses. The result was a gloomy, barren landscape of split-levels in mixed media—bricks, barn siding, stucco—that looked as if they'd been dropped from the sky onto a lunar landscape of small, treeless brown lawns.

Martha Hillman met her at the door, a thirtyish woman with short, no-nonsense brown hair and small, dubious eyes. Andrew joined her a moment later: tall, painfully thin, with pale skin and a blond buzz cut. He peered at them from behind his mother's legs. Jimmy, too, was hiding behind his mother, only he was clutching a handful of Gwen's skirt.

"Andrew, why don't you show Jimmy your room," Martha Hillman said. He nodded solemnly and shambled down a hallway.

"Go on, Jimmy," Gwen said. "I bet he has some cool toys." He shook his head. "I'll be back soon." She gently nudged him into the house. As he shuffled after Andrew her heart broke a little. He'd been such an independent boy, more outgoing than most, a bit of a leader, in fact. It had taken a lot to kill that, and it would take a lot to get it back. Shy, geeky Andrew Hillman was the first step.

"We'll take good care of Jimmy," Martha Hillman said with a sour smile. Gwen chose not to read anything into the woman's vaguely accusatory tone. "Take your time coming back for him."

The forty-five-minute drive to the auction was unexpectedly relaxing; no prying questions, no condemning stares. Occasionally she'd think of Valerie Goodwin and wonder why her story about how Nick had met Priscilla differed so dramatically from Nick's. But by the time she reached the auction such thoughts had all but vanished. The car was cool, Jimmy finally had a friend, and she had two hundred dollars in her pocket, squirreled away from her all-cash salary.

The auction was in the auditorium of a high school in Denby, New York. She didn't recognize anyone, but the crowd was familiar enough. The sellers were generally locals, dressed unpretentiously in jeans and T-shirts. The buyers were city folk, more fashionably attired, pulling out drawers to inspect the craftsmanship, upending china, searching for signatures on dusky oil paintings, pausing only to check off items in the xeroxed catalog. But the two groups shared a hungry, distrustful look, each eager to make a killing off the other.

She arrived in time to peruse the auction items in the school gymnasium. She saw quite a few things that she might have wanted for the store, but not much that interested her personally. She browsed through aisles of cupboards and tables and assorted bric-a-brac that only a year ago might have set her heart racing; strange to feel nothing but detached appreciation now, and perhaps a hint of sadness for a life already so remote. Acquiring things was a habit she'd lost, apparently.

Still, it was oddly fascinating to confront her former life in this way, to realize just how much she'd changed. Glancing around the crowded gymnasium, she felt neither nostalgic nor relieved, only mildly astonished that her life had once revolved around situations like this.

She sat halfway back in the auditorium, which quickly filled up. The sale items were hauled onto the small stage by a team of burly movers, and the bidding was professionally conducted by an elderly woman with the requisite knack for fast talk and gentle cajoling. The auction went fast, since most of the buyers were dealers from New York or Boston or Albany who knew the value of each lot, quickly bid up to that level, then stopped. The prices were fair—which meant they could safely be doubled at retail in Manhattan.

The one bit of excitement came about an hour into the auction, when a complete, mint-condition, nineteenth-century pine bedroom set, each piece beautifully decorated with hand-painted flowers and fruit, was bid up to forty-three thousand dollars. As soon as the gavel came down on the sale a family of overalled dairy farmers—a husband and wife and three young children—got up and headed for the door, huge grins on their faces. Gwen couldn't help smiling herself: how could they have known that grandma's old bedroom suite would fetch that kind of money?

Even she wasn't immune to the buying fever, for she found herself bidding on the next lot, a nineteenth-century pitcher and basin, white with a delicate ring of violets painted around the lip of both pieces. Bidding began at fifty dollars, she jumped in at seventy, and within moments she'd bought the lot for one hundred and eighty dollars.

Pure insanity, of course. The set was beautiful, and easily worth twice what she'd paid for it. But it would make an irresistible target for the tennis balls Jimmy liked to throw around inside the house. And what the hell was she doing, spending almost two hundred dollars on *pottery?* She should be building a nest egg, not blowing her few leftover dollars on accessories.

Ah, but the high of competing for something and winning! She'd missed that, after all. She went to claim her lot at the cashier's table and felt the tiniest twinge of regret as she handed over two hundred-dollar bills. But when the pitcher and bowl were brought to her the regret sputtered out. Her eye never failed her; the set was simply beautiful, worth every penny and then some.

She carried her purchase to her car, cradling both pieces like treasure, and decided she'd place the set in the front hallway, where she'd see it most often.

Dwight Hawkins waited until Gwen Amiel left the auditorium before approaching the cashier. He'd never been to one of these things, had never known they existed. He spent much of the auction cataloging in his mind the old furniture he and Elaine had back at the house, wondering if there was anything worth the small fortune these city folk seemed willing to pay.

He found himself fantasizing about selling the whole damn house, contents and all, and taking off for parts unknown. Hell, he was due to retire in five years. Neither of them had seen any of the world outside this small corner of New York State. They'd sell the house, drive down to JFK airport, get on the first plane out of there. The Southwest might be nice, where the *USA Today* weather map always showed bright orange—warm and dry.

He waited on the cashier's line, picturing him and Elaine on a jet crossing the country, sailing west like gods over isobars and occluded fronts and high-pressure systems, chasing the weather to its source. He'd never been on a plane—that in itself would be something.

"Lot number?" the cashier asked him.

"Excuse me?"

"What is your lot number?"

"Oh, I didn't buy anything. I..." He took out his wallet and showed his badge. "Dwight Hawkins, Sohegan Police Department. That woman you helped a few minutes ago, the one who bought the commode set?"

"Yes…" The cashier narrowed her eyes. "Is there something the matter?"

"I was wondering how much she paid for it, that's all. Or we could check the credit card receipt."

"Oh, no, detective, she paid cash. Which is pretty unusual around here." She pointed to a stack of processed credit card slips. "Pretty soon we'll just auction the cash drawer with the rest of the stuff."

"She paid cash? I don't suppose they happened to be hundreds she gave you."

"Two of 'em," the cashier said.

"Hundred-dollar bills," he said softly. If only Russell Cunningham had worked with the FBI from the start, the missing five million would be traceable by serial number. Those two bills in that strongbox could well wrap up the case.

"Anything else?" the cashier said. "I have other customers waiting."

He thanked her and headed out to his car, wondering whether to alert the FBI about Gwen Amiel's new purchase. A hundred and eighty dollars seemed like a lot of money for a baby-sitter to be spending on antiques. He felt a momentary shot of self-confidence: following her had been a smart move; he'd have to keep it up, see if she made a habit of splurging with hundred-dollar bills.

Hawkins got in his Buick and headed back to Sohegan. Yes, he'd call the FBI; they seemed to appreciate new information, no matter how trivial. Every other lead had gotten them nowhere. No sign of the money, let alone the kidnapper. Browning .22s were as common as Timex watches—millions were registered to private owners. Now, if they found the actual gun used to kill Priscilla, they could compare the barrel markings to the two shells found at the ravine.

The FBI had looked into every nook and cranny of every life even casually associated with Penaquoit. Don Reeves had personally visited Nick Lawrence's father in a nursing home near Scranton, his only living relative. What he thought he'd get out of that he didn't say, but he'd gotten zip. Nick and his father hadn't talked in years.

Gwen Amiel's story checked out—the furniture store, the sudden flight from Manhattan earlier that spring. But her husband was nowhere to be found. Reeves thought that was significant, and so did Hawkins. People didn't just disappear, and when they did they left a trail. Not Barry Amiel, though. He'd just vanished.

What else did they have? Size-ten prints of a Nike walking shoe leading from the west side of the ravine to a set of tire tracks almost three hundred yards away—Michelin radials, only moderately worn, a midsize car carrying an average load. If they found a suspect car they could compare the tread to the tire prints—good as fingerprints, almost. *If.*

Fingerprints? Every single print taken from Penaquoit had checked out against the mansion's occupants. No unexplained hair or fiber evidence, either.

Russell Cunningham was pulling every political string he had to put pressure on the Feds. He'd offered a million-dollar reward for information leading to an arrest, and had hired a detective of his own. But nothing was working. Even the county boys had left Sohegan, figuring anyone with five million dollars in cash would be crazy to stick around town, let alone try to spend it locally.

Unless, of course, the kidnapper was lying low until the case blew over. Unless the money was hidden somewhere nearby, just waiting to be claimed, untouched for the time being—except for the occasional surrender to temptation, a quick trip to the money tree. A hundred dollars here, a hundred there…Who could resist? Who would notice?

Hell, even baby-sitters need to splurge now and then.

Gwen picked up Jimmy from Andrew's house and drove home. He watched television in the living room while she unwrapped the pitcher and washbasin and placed them on the small table in the front hall. Smug pleasure, that old acquisitive high, quickly gave way to a sinking feeling; the house looked suddenly shabby and cheerless. Not to mention messy.

"Jimmy, come and put away your toys," she called to him. When he didn't respond she added, "Now!"

He dragged himself into the hallway and sluggishly gathered together several toy cars and trucks, which he carried upstairs. A minute later, in the kitchen, Gwen heard a frightened scream.

She took the stairs three at a time. Jimmy was standing just outside his room.

"Look!"

The floor was littered with every toy and book and article of clothing he owned.

"Jimmy, did you—"

"No, Mommy. And look." He pointed to his panda, Mr. Meeko. "Oh, no."

She stepped into the room. Mr. Meeko's head lay a foot or so from its body. It had been neatly severed, bits of white stuffing littering the carpeted floor.

"Who did that, Mommy?"

She shook her head and reached for him, but he wouldn't enter the room. So she turned and picked him up and carried him downstairs. He was already damp and shivering.

CHAPTER 20

Dwight Hawkins arrived ten minutes after Gwen called, but he wasn't too impressed by the injuries inflicted on Mr. Meeko. There was no sign of a break-in, though he did point out that anyone with a kitchen knife or credit card could open the locked back door. She showed him around the rest of the house, and while there was no evident damage, Gwen couldn't help feeling that the place had been searched; rarely used drawers were open just a crack, a closet that was normally open an inch or so was shut tight. Nothing concrete, though.

"It's just that the panda is Jimmy's favorite thing, the only toy we brought with us from the city. Someone *chose* that doll, someone *knew.*"

"Jimmy knew." Hawkins headed for the front door.

"Jimmy?"

"Sometimes kids do things they don't want to admit to," Hawkins said as he opened the door.

"Jimmy would never harm that doll."

"You notice anything unusual about his behavior lately?"

"Uh, no." She saw by his expression that he'd caught her hesitation.

"I'm sure you know your own son. Anyway, I'll have a patrol car watch the street for the next few days. You're a bit of a celebrity now. Local kids, they don't get much excitement."

He started to leave.

"Back in New York…"

Hawkins turned back to her.

"Back in New York my husband owed some money to…I don't know who they were, but now that my name's been in the paper I'm wondering if maybe they're sending some kind of signal."

"This isn't the kind of thing a loan shark would do, Mrs. Amiel." He hesitated a moment. "You never mentioned to the FBI that your husband owed money."

"It didn't seem relevant."

"How much money?"

"I have no idea."

He studied her for a few moments. "No one drove two hundred miles from New York City to attack a stuffed animal. I wouldn't worry about that." He smiled awkwardly and left.

She didn't sleep well that night, and Jimmy woke up twice asking for water. She spent the early morning hours sewing Mr. Meeko together with a thick needle and heavy black thread. The result looked rather ghoulish, but Jimmy didn't seem to mind the black scar around the panda's neck. He did, however, insist on taking Mr. Meeko to camp with him.

Neither Gwen nor Nick mentioned Valerie Goodwin's visit Monday morning when he handed over Tess in the kitchen, although he did seem unusually sullen. The piano music commenced a few moments after he left her—scales played furiously fast and loud.

Rosa Piacevic walked into the kitchen carrying a withered philodendron in a glazed terra-cotta pot. She dumped the plant into a garbage pail, grunting angrily as she reamed out the last bits of dirt with her fingers.

"We had a visitor this weekend." She plunked the empty pot on the counter and began to scrub the inside with a damp paper towel. "Miss Goodwin." She pounced on the first syllable: *Good*win.

"She was Priscilla…Mrs. Lawrence's best friend."

Rosa's hand froze inside the pot. Her skin was pale and wrinkled, yet soft-looking, almost pure, like an underground creature that never saw the sun.

"Is there something wrong?" Gwen asked.

Rosa dropped the paper towel inside the pot and turned. She

looked toward the door between the kitchen and the hallway, then walked closer to Gwen.

"I think she makes the play for Mr. Lawrence." Her voice was a low whisper, and she cupped one hand around the side of her mouth nearest Tess, as if to prevent the child from hearing.

"Did you…see something?" Gwen asked.

"Just the way she look at him." Her eyes moved in Tess's direction, then back. "And at the baby."

At the baby?

"Did they…" How to put this delicately? "Did they…"

"Share the bedroom?" Rosa peered at her, arching her hairless brows.

"Well, that's not *exactly* what I meant," Gwen said quickly.

"No, they did not. She use the big room next to the nursery. I see the sheets in a mess on the bed. Of course, I don't have no idea what goes on when I am in my own apartment. But she got ideas, that one."

"And Mr. Lawrence, does he…have ideas?"

"He like two things, Mr. Lawrence. Piano and daughter. Daughter and piano. He use machine to tape-record his own piano, he use it to tape-record Tessie's voice. Both precious to him. Miss *Good*win?" She made a face, as if sensing a foul odor. "Who knows? I care only for the child, my *zamer.*" She leaned over and placed a finger on Tess's forehead. "Baby-sitters, nannies…" She blew a puff of air through pursed lips. "They come, they go. I, Rosa Piacevic, they will have to drag away from this one."

"She's Mr. Lawrence's responsibility," Gwen said. "Though she is hard to resist."

They both looked at Tess, who smiled obligingly. Rosa had never said much to her in the past, but now she seemed unable to stop.

"The last girl, she said she wouldn't never leave. Mr. Lawrence, he have different ideas."

"I thought she quit."

Rosa Piacevic frowned. "One day Mr. Lawrence ask my husband to carry her suitcases to the car, then drive her to the bus station.

She was fired, leave that same day. Mrs. Lawrence, nobody asked her opinion, she was down in the city with her doctors."

"Doctors?"

"Having checkup, in case the cancer come back."

Gwen nodded, lifting Tess out of the high chair. She began pacing the room, winding Tess down for her morning nap. The little inconsistencies—the lies—were starting to pile up: How had Priscilla and Nick met? Why had the last sitter left?

"Mrs. Lawrence go crazy when she heared the girl is gone," Rosa said. "I listen that evening, I hear Mr. Lawrence tell her she quit. But I know the truth. She was fired."

"What was she like, my predecessor?"

"Mary Alice?" Rosa Piacevic shrugged. "Quiet, plain, a little much fat on the hips and the behind." Rosa turned back to the clay pot, but not before casting an accusatory glance. "She keep out of trouble."

Tess grew suddenly heavier in her arms; she was asleep, and not a moment too soon.

"Nap time," Gwen said as she headed for the front hallway.

That afternoon she swam with Tess in the pool, then pushed her on the swing set on the oak-shaded east lawn of the house. The hot weather showed no sign of letting up; the air was perfectly still, not a branch or leaf moved, as if the earth itself had stopped spinning. As she pushed Tess, Gwen began to sweat, her long cotton cover-up clinging to her damp bathing suit.

"Hello there." Nick approached them from the house, wearing only a bathing suit. Tess waved both hands at her father as Gwen contemplated the fact that the swing set and the pool were on opposite sides of the house.

"I see you two have already been swimming." He leaned against one of the swing's supporting poles. Posing, she thought. With the sun directly on him, he looked lean and supple and flawlessly tanned, as if the swing had been placed in that very spot for no other reason than to make him look irresistible leaning against it. As if the sun, too, had been positioned to flatter him.

"It's so warm…" She could think of nothing more profound to say.

"I don't mind the heat, I think I enjoy it, in some ways." He absently stroked his chest and abdomen. "It was Priscilla who insisted on keeping the air-conditioning cranked up. The house felt like a meat locker sometimes." He must have sensed her disapproval. "Not that I could blame her," he said quickly. "She always said the heat made her queasy."

Gwen nodded and gave Tess an extra-hard push.

"Do I make you nervous in some way?" he asked after a short silence. "You always seem so tentative when we're alone together, and yet when we first met, that day at the diner, there was nothing at all hesitant about you."

"It's…it's a strange situation, that's all. Your wife was…" She looked at Tess, then back at him. "It's only been a week, and you…" She shook her head.

"And I *what*…I don't appear sufficiently grief stricken?"

"I didn't say that."

"You didn't have to. The truth is, I feel dreadful about what happened. I wake up at night playing that awful scene at the ravine in my head, thinking I've been dreaming. Then I look over at the pillow next to me, and it hits me, as if for the first time. She's gone."

"I wasn't suggesting—"

"But a part of me feels liberated, I can't deny that. I can't *disguise* it. Priscilla…she lived in a bubble, her own air-conditioned bubble. I never managed to penetrate it, but I never gave up trying. Now I feel as if a burden has been lifted—I don't have to try anymore."

Tess swung back and forth in enviable oblivion.

"You knew Priscilla for a while," he said. "What was your impression?"

"I barely knew her."

"Oh, but you knew her as well as most people. Better, perhaps."

"That's ridiculous, what about"—she tickled Tess's chin

between pushes—"Valerie Goodwin?"

"I don't think Valerie ever got through to Priscilla. She's a very superficial woman. Priscilla was the perfect friend for her: their relationship never went below the surface."

"I thought you liked her. Valerie, I mean."

He seemed to think this over. Gwen stole a glance at him. His eyes were closed against the relentless sun. A vertical trail of fine dark hair bisected his abdomen.

"Valerie...Valerie had big dreams at one time. She was going to be this great actress, this fabulous movie star. The closest she got was a few modeling assignments, and now she's too old even for that. Washed up at thirty-five. She's a bitter woman. Not without her charms, but so full of regrets...I never could stand her, really."

"I'm surprised."

"She was my wife's best friend, our child's godmother. Did you expect me to treat her like an enemy?"

"No, I just thought—"

"Priscilla used to send her money every month to cover her expenses. I think that's the real reason she came up this weekend, to find out if she's still on the payroll."

Gwen grabbed Tess's ankles and held her for a moment before letting go.

"Well, the gravy boat is over, I'm afraid."

"Gravy *train*," she said.

His eyes flashed at her. "Thank you," he said icily. "Priscilla left Valerie five thousand dollars in her will, but unfortunately I am not able to continue her generosity. Five thousand dollars will last Valerie Goodwin about a week and a half, *if* she cuts back. I wonder what she'll do?" He sounded thoroughly unconcerned.

"Her affection for Tess seemed genuine," she said.

"Perhaps. She can't have children of her own. Something about her eggs."

"Oh, I..." He looked at her. "I'm sorry," she said, remembering how much Valerie had enjoyed feeding Tess, swimming with her.

"Anyway," Nick said, "I hope I don't make you nervous. I

suppose I could burst into uncontrollable sobs every few hours; perhaps that would reassure you. But I cannot pretend to feel something I don't. Priscilla did not deserve to die. And Tess deserves a mother."

"And you?"

He smiled and looked at her. "Me? I have been released from one prison only to find myself stuck in another." He smoothed back his hair with the palms of his hands, his expression darkening. "Now I think I need to cool off."

He pressed himself off the swing support and jogged effortlessly across the lawn. She watched him, tempted to follow. For the first time since last evening she'd forgotten about Mr. Meeko, about someone breaking into her house and mutilating the one thing Jimmy cared about.

Disillusioned men are the most dangerous, Miss Amiel. They've already lost their dream.

Gwen turned back to Tess and resumed pushing as Nick Lawrence disappeared around the corner of the house.

CHAPTER 21

The month passed in an easy, steady rhythm: weekdays with Tess, evenings and weekends with Jimmy. The events at the Devil's Ravine remained vivid in Gwen's mind—when wouldn't they be? But it was beginning to seem possible to move beyond that awful day, to arrive at a place where she could view Priscilla Lawrence's murder as a tragedy that had befallen a woman whom she had barely known. Just that, nothing more.

She had better locks installed at home, and occasionally she'd spot a police car driving slowly to the end of Glen Drive, then back again. Maybe it had been just a prank, the assault on Mr. Meeko. A vicious joke on Sohegan's scarlet woman—for she often thought everyone in town assumed she and Nick were lovers, had been lovers, in fact, even before the murder. Desecrating the house of an adulterer was good sport. Fitting punishment.

And yet, awakening at night from fitful sleep, she couldn't help thinking that slicing off the animal's head so neatly had taken real effort and concentration—hardly the work of a bunch of thrill-seeking teenagers. She tiptoed into Jimmy's room every night now, sometimes two or three times, just to watch him.

The murder investigation continued, of course, though she had to believe it was running out of steam. Russell Cunningham spent at least a few minutes a day at the mansion, usually before leaving for the factory, not so much playing with Tess as observing her, as if she were some kind of rare butterfly who might fly off if inadequately tended. Occasionally she'd hear him using his cell phone, often in the nursery, barking orders at a private investigator, screaming at some secretary at Tack & Hardware to *get the goddamn FBI on the phone.* But these calls were growing less and less frequent.

Nick spent his days at the piano, working through the Pathetique Sonata at least a dozen times a day. Sometimes she woke up at night hearing it, each note as sharp and precise as a migraine. She'd turn on the radio to clear it from her mind. Country and western, jazz, Christian call-in shows, she didn't care.

The Piacevics kept the house running as efficiently as ever; the refrigerator and pantry were always well stocked, the house impeccably clean, the grounds immaculate.

And Tess? She never called for her mama anymore.

July turned out to be considerably less warm than June. On the Monday following the Fourth, Gwen dropped Jimmy off at his day camp and arrived at the mansion at eight o'clock, as usual. The kitchen was empty, however, piano music already floating in from the living room. She stood in the hallway, waiting for a break in the playing. After a few minutes Nick stopped abruptly and turned; though she hadn't moved, had barely breathed, she felt certain that he'd sensed her presence in some instinctive, almost feline, way.

"Good morning," he said. He always seemed slightly dazed when he stopped playing, as if he'd just opened his eyes from a long sleep, or received troubling news. He flicked a switch on a large radio and cassette player that he kept on the piano—boom boxes, they were called in New York.

"I'm taping myself. It helps to chart my progress."

She nodded, wondering what he imagined he was progressing toward. (*He is preparing for perfection*, Valerie had said.)

"Where's Tess?" she asked.

"I brought her next door. I thought Maxine might like to see her. She's barely left the house since Priscilla died."

The mention of Priscilla felt as inappropriate, somehow, as the sight of the long piano in the middle of the living room. Neither her death nor her life were much referred to at Penaquoit any longer. He must have sensed her unease.

"Hard to believe it's been a month," he said. "Some days it feels as if she's been gone for years. Other days I can't shake the feeling that she died just yesterday."

"Do you want me to pick up Tess?"

"What? Oh, right, yes, about ten o'clock."

The gauzy white curtains that hung on either side of the French doors fluttered in a sudden breeze. The air-conditioning had been turned off since Priscilla's death, even during the hot final weeks of June. Mett Piacevic had to force open several windows with a hammer and wedge. Shades and blinds now rattled in rooms as she walked by, open windows let in the sound of birds and creaking branches. Occasionally a newspaper would blow off a table, a leaf from a potted plant would flutter to the floor. With Priscilla gone, Penaquoit felt more alive than ever.

Gwen went to the nursery and began straightening up. She waited for the music to resume, but it didn't. After a few minutes Nick entered the room.

"Aren't you bored here?" he said casually, as if continuing a conversation.

"It's not the most demanding job," she replied, resenting the rather condescending question.

"I don't mean just the job. I mean everything—this house, this town, the people here."

What the hell did he know about the *people?*

"I can't complain. I have my—"

"Tell me about Barry."

She gripped the railing of Tess's crib as blood rushed to her head. "How do you know his—"

"The FBI checked up on you. I was briefed."

She folded the pink crib blanket and draped it over the railing. "I'd prefer not to talk about him. We're divorced. I don't see him anymore."

"Separated." He stepped toward her. He wore a white T-shirt tucked into gray sweatpants, and white running shoes. He was always dressed for exercise, and indeed looked as though he worked out, though he never did. She busied herself picking up a few toys from the rug.

"I'm saving money for a divorce lawyer," she said. Which was half true. The whole truth? She hated the thought of dealing with Barry, even if it would mean being rid of him once and for all.

"You left him suddenly," he said. "Why?"

"Didn't the FBI tell you?"

That silenced him temporarily. She continued to clean up, aware of his scrutiny.

"I know this seems intrusive," he said. "But I've put my daughter's well-being in your hands. I'd like to know something more about you, especially now."

"Barry was..." No, not an alcoholic, that sounded too absolvingly clinical. "He was a drunk."

"And that's why you came up here?"

"Indirectly."

"What's the direct reason?" His voice was deep and smooth, curious but not prurient.

"He hit me," she said softly.

"Damn." He shook his head. "I'm so sorry."

"He started drinking after Jimmy was born, about five years ago. My store was doing well, his business wasn't."

"He was a contractor, wasn't he?"

She wondered if Barry knew he was being investigated. What if he used that as an excuse to try to find them? Hawkins never mentioned talking to him, and she had not the slightest interest in learning his whereabouts.

"A contractor, yes. But he screwed up on a few projects, once he began to drink. And then he couldn't get decent references. Anyway, when Jimmy was born I guess he felt pressured to support us. I was taking home enough from the store to get by, but that didn't sit well with him."

A colossal understatement. Once he'd taken a hammer and smashed every breakable object in the store. For days afterward she'd tweezered tiny slivers of glass and porcelain from her hands and legs.

"He hit you when he was drunk?"

She shook her head. "Barry was a happy drunk. Sober, he was a nightmare."

"How badly did he hurt you?" His voice was detached but kind, as if he *needed* to hear what she was saying.

"No broken bones, no stitches. Actually, I got pretty good at defending myself. Barry wasn't much taller than me, and once he started drinking he stopped working out. But he did some damage. I was bruised a lot of the time."

"You sound so matter-of-fact about it."

"Barry can't harm me anymore," she said. *Me or Jimmy.*

"You don't seem like the kind of woman who would allow any man to hurt you."

"He wasn't *any* man," she said. "Even when he was hitting me, pummeling me, I could never hate him the way he must have hated me. I'd wave a knife at him, but he knew I'd never really hurt him." She hesitated, then spoke in a fragile whisper. "I never could hurt him."

"And today?"

She straightened a picture on the wall over the changing table.

"And today?"

"Today I could kill him."

His eyes widened but he waited a moment before speaking. "Why? What changed you?"

She shrugged and looked around the room, wishing there was something left to pick up, fold, put away.

"Why did you leave so suddenly?"

"I...couldn't take it anymore," she said. "You reach a boiling point..."

He watched her for a few moments, and though she was careful to meet his gaze without flinching, she could tell he didn't believe her. He knew she was holding back. After a few tense moments he smiled gently.

"Thank you," he said. "Perhaps someday you'll trust me with the entire truth."

She turned toward the window as he left the room.

• • •

Jimmy had just kicked the soccer ball downfield when he saw the policeman standing on the side, watching the game. No, not the game. Him. He tried to follow the ball—goalies had to keep their eyes open even when the ball was all the way on the other end of the field. But every time he checked, the policeman was looking right at him.

"Nooo!"

He heard his teammates' shouts even before he saw the ball bounce right by him into the net. He just stood there, the backs of his eyes getting full with tears, like his stomach in the morning when he had to pee. *It wasn't my fault*, he wanted to shout back at them. *Don't blame me, okay? Blame that policeman over there.*

Coach blew the whistle for halftime and both sides ran to the drinking fountain near the baseball diamond. The policeman joined them after a while. Jimmy didn't want to stand there by himself, so he joined them, too.

"Mister, is that a gun inside your jacket?" Bobby Preston asked.

The policeman looked down. All the boys were staring at his shoulder holster.

"Last I checked it was." He opened the jacket to show them the gun. "It's a Smith and Wesson, same as I carried my whole career."

"It looks old-fashioned," Jason Arnold said. A couple of guys giggled at that. Coach always said Jason was a wise guy.

"It is old-fashioned. The county boys think I ought to upgrade to a Glock automatic, but I feel rather attached to this old revolver." He patted the gun like a baby's head.

Bobby stepped closer. "You ever use it, Detective Hawkins?"

The policeman shook his head. "Never fired it at anybody, if that's what you mean. But I've waved it around a few times, just to make an impression."

Everyone seemed kind of let down by this.

"You fellows must be hot from all that running," the policeman said. "Too bad there's no pool here."

"You can say that again." Jason lifted his arms and let them flop against his hips.

"Any of your counselors ever thought of taking you over to the Devil's Ravine for a swim?"

A couple of the boys shook their heads.

"Any of you actually been to Devil's Ravine?" he asked.

Two boys raised their hands. But the policeman wasn't looking at *them*. So Jimmy raised his hand, too.

"I hope it was a hot day," the policeman said. "That water's *cold.*"

"We didn't swim," said a boy named Roger. "We just threw stones."

"Did *you* swim?" the policeman said, looking directly at Jimmy, who nodded.

"Was it a hot day?"

Jimmy nodded again.

"Must have been during the heat wave last month, right?"

"I guess."

"Sorry, I didn't catch that."

"The week before school ended."

"Near the end of June," Hawkins said. "Did you go with a friend?"

"Just my mom." A few of the boys started walking away. Jimmy watched them leave. He didn't want to talk about that day. The police were asking his mom about what happened at the ravine when Mrs. Lawrence got killed. He hadn't even told her about seeing *him* at the diner that day. She seemed as though she couldn't take any more bad news. And now he wasn't even sure he had actually seen his dad. Sometimes he dreamed about him, and when he woke up his heart was going like a jackhammer and he had a hard time knowing if he'd been dreaming or not.

"Did your mom swim that day?" the policeman asked. "Grown-ups hate the cold water."

Jimmy nodded.

"Did you walk around there much? You know, explore?"

"No."

"I bet it was your idea to go there, am I right?"

"No."

"I didn't catch that," the policeman said.

"It was my mom's idea."

"Well, she's a smart lady, then, choosing a place like the Devil's Ravine on a hot day."

The policeman looked up at the sky. The other kids were back on the soccer field.

"Not today, though," the policeman said. "The front finally came through on the second, sucking down this nice, cool Canadian air."

"Can I go now?" Jimmy said.

The policeman looked at him for a while and Jimmy felt something squiggling around in his stomach. *No more questions, please?*

"Sure, run along," the policeman said.

Jimmy walked quickly back to the game, feeling the man's eyes on him like a ray gun the whole entire way.

CHAPTER 22

The Cunninghams' house was only about fifty yards from Penaquoit, but stylistically it was light-years away. A long, one-story ranch, about thirty or forty years old, it belonged in a middle-class suburb of New York City; only in a place like Sohegan would it be considered luxurious. Gwen knew from earlier explorations of the area that it was accessible from the road by a long driveway that began a few yards from the Penaquoit gates, slicing straight through a dense, dark wood.

She took the shortcut through the row of hemlocks to the east of the mansion and headed for the Cunninghams' back door, wondering about a couple who would give up a huge mansion equipped with a solarium and library and swimming pool for this modest ranch, all to accommodate their daughter and her husband and young child. An undeniably generous gesture, and yet there was something unsettling about it, like reigning monarchs abdicating in favor of the young heir, living out their lives in frugal irrelevance.

She rapped on a screen door, got no response, and opened it.

"Mrs. Cunningham?" She stepped into an immaculate kitchen, *House Beautiful*, circa 1955: linoleum floor in a brick pattern, white cabinets with sleek metal hardware, speckled Formica countertops. A clock over the small breakfast table clicked softly.

"Mrs. Cunningham?" She walked across the kitchen and entered a small foyer. Pale blue carpet covered the floor and staircase; the brass chandelier was turned off, casting the area in gray shadow. The smell of cigarettes permeated the air. She checked the living and dining rooms. Long, heavy drapes were drawn in both rooms, cloaking them in cool darkness. She followed the only trace of light into a paneled room with bookshelves on two walls.

Tess sat on the shag-carpeted floor, playing with a toy truck. On a tweed couch across from a large television set, Maxine Cunningham slept in an upright position, her head dangling forward, snoring in short, grunting bursts. Over the sofa were two large black-and-white photographs, one of a young Maxine in an elaborate wedding dress, the other of Russell in a morning suit. They were facing each other, smiling stiffly from their separate portraits.

"Hello, Tess," Gwen said.

Tess turned toward her as Maxine snorted loudly and sat forward.

"Oh!" Maxine cleared her throat and patted her hair with both hands. "Hello."

Tess ran over to Gwen, who scooped her up.

"Nick asked me to get Tess at ten."

Maxine nodded but looked disoriented. "Did you have fun, Tess?" she asked in a groggy voice. She looked tiny and frail on the sofa, skinny legs dangling above the carpet. Her gray hair was a bit disheveled.

Tess smiled. "Truck," she said, pointing to the floor.

"That belonged to our son, Russ," Maxine said. "My husband throws nothing away." She stared at the truck. "You should see our basement, full of Russ's toys and books, every award he ever brought home, every test he ever took."

Gwen almost mentioned the basement at Penaquoit. What would happen to all that stuff, now that Priscilla was gone? Would the stacks of magazines be left to molder down there, each pile topped for eternity by the July issue? She noticed a Bible on the coffee table in front of Maxine, the black leather cover worn through in places.

"What made you come here?" Maxine said, finally looking at her.

"I told you, Nick asked me to pick up Tess."

"No, I mean to Sohegan. You're from Manhattan, I believe."

Why couldn't people just accept her presence in town?

"I wanted a small town, I suppose." She put Tess down and watched her toddle over to the toy truck. "I have a young son."

Maxine frowned. "I've always hated it here. I'm from the city too, you know, raised on the Upper East Side. I met Russell at a Vassar-Yale mixer. He brought me back here after we were married. To the big house, I mean, not here."

She looked shrunken and defeated. Gwen glanced up at her wedding portrait and saw what Russell Cunningham had been attracted to. Her face had been pretty in a delicate way, her eyes slightly too large for her face, lending her an appealingly innocent, almost plaintive fragility. Now they looked haunted.

"I thought I'd get involved in the community," Maxine said. "You know, good works, ladies organizations, that kind of thing. But I quickly learned that the Cunninghams don't mix with the natives. They're the local royalty, you see. And the worst part was, there were no other royals around to mix with. Everything was family. Perhaps if my husband had brothers, sisters, *someone.*"

Gwen sat on the bench of an upright piano, plotting a quick exit.

"Family and business," Maxine continued. "If the Cunninghams had a coat of arms, that would be on their crest." As she chuckled her chest quivered beneath a blue cotton sweater; she was more bird than woman.

"You must have felt very isolated," Gwen said.

"Utterly. Of course, it got easier once the children were born. Those were the best years, when Russ and Priscilla were young. They actually went to the local elementary school—there wasn't any alternative, you see. But then we sent them to boarding school and I was alone again. My husband and I were alone together, I should say."

Gwen steeled herself for what was coming.

"After Russ was killed I...well, I didn't think I could endure. He was all I had."

"Priscilla..."

"Daddy's girl," Maxine said sharply. She paused before continuing in a softer voice. "You're raising your one child on your own, isn't that right?"

"Yes."

"Then perhaps it's hard for you to understand how...allegiances can form in families, even small families like ours. Russell and Russ, well, they were at each other constantly. I often wondered what might have happened if he'd lived. I couldn't imagine them in business together. But Russ and I…" She smiled as her eyes lost focus. "We understood each other because neither of us fit in here." The smile faded. "Priscilla and I, well, once she reached adolescence she had no time for me. I never understood why she felt so…dismissive toward me. She worshipped her father, of course. Perhaps she picked up on his disdain."

"Why was she carrying that flower at the ravine?" Gwen asked.

"Flower?" Her voice crumpled on the word.

"A purple thistle."

Maxine looked away. "I wasn't aware…"

She was lying, just as Russell had lied, but Gwen wasn't about to confront her. Tess had walked over to the coffee table and was systematically throwing magazines onto the floor. Gwen got up and grabbed her hand, grateful for the distraction.

"No, Tess, don't do that." Gwen began to collect the strewn magazines as Tess started to cry.

"I should get her home," she said. "She's long overdo for her morning nap." She picked up Tess and moved toward the door, turning back in time to see Maxine reach for her Bible. Pity flashed through Gwen, then something closer to anger.

"It's not too late," she said.

Maxine glanced up at her and smiled dimly.

"You're not a prisoner here," Gwen said. "It's not too late to change."

Maxine shook her head slowly. "You can't leave the Cunninghams, much as you might want to. My mother-in-law knew that, and I certainly caught on quickly. I believe Nick is learning that lesson now."

"But…"

Maxine shook her head slowly. "You'll find out soon enough, too," she said as she opened her Bible and held it close to her face. Gwen turned and left.

• • •

Nick met them on the flagstone terrace as they returned from next door.

"We've been summoned to the plant," he said with mock seriousness. "The old man wants to introduce the troops to the heir apparent."

"It's never too early to start a management education," Gwen said, turning to Tess, who was already sleeping in her arms. "Right, Madame Chairman?"

"We'll take the Range Rover."

She followed Nick across the yard toward the garage. After strapping Tess into her car seat, she walked back toward the house.

"Where are you going?" Nick called after her.

She turned. "I have a few things to do." Not true, of course: cleaning Tess's room and doing her laundry took about fifteen minutes a day; looking after someone else's toddler wasn't exactly hard labor.

"I would like you to come," he said.

She waited a moment for an explanation, then shrugged and walked back to the car.

"He called about fifteen minutes ago," Nick said as he drove. He lowered his voice to a harsh growl. "'Bring Tess to the plant. Right now.'"

She smiled at the uncanny imitation. "What if you'd said no?"

"Interesting question. I'm basically his employee at this point, on the payroll, you might say. So I follow orders."

"But he can't very well fire you for insubordination."

"No, but he can rein me in even further." The jocularity had gone out of his voice.

"Rein you in?"

"Cut my allowance." Nick made a left onto Route 24, heading away from the Devil's Ravine.

"How would he do that without hurting Tess?"

"Ah, my one and only trump card! I have something he needs

more than anything. An heir."

He sounded glib, almost calculating, yet his face looked uncertain, even worried.

"I doubt he'd cut your food allowance," she said.

He smiled and his face, in profile, became nearly perfect again.

"No, food isn't the problem. But he could make things difficult for me in other ways."

"How?"

He looked at her for a moment. "He could seek custody."

"But you're her father. He's seventy, for God's sake. And Maxine's not exactly…maternal."

"Maxine," he said, shaking his head. "Priscilla used to speak of her like she was a talking monkey, like it was a miracle she could even form words. She learned that from the old man—never marry somebody you respect, you'll only compromise your own position." He raised his chin.

"Why did you marry Priscilla, then, if you knew how she felt?"

He waited before answering, driving at a moderate speed on the two-lane road.

"Maybe I didn't think I merited respect," he said quietly. He glanced at her, saw her watching him, and conferred a dazzling smile. "Or maybe, just maybe, I liked her money."

She shivered and looked away. Suddenly he braked the car, glancing in the rearview mirror. She turned and saw a police car behind them.

"You weren't speeding," she said. In fact, he was a rather cautious driver.

"No? I think I might have been a bit over the limit."

The police car passed them on the left and sped on ahead. He let out a long sigh.

"The Sohegan police would like nothing more than to embarrass anyone connected to the Cunninghams," he said. "They hate us, you know. The old man thinks they're dragging their heels on the investigation, the locals and the FBI. He may have a point."

"Why would they do that?"

"Because we didn't call them in when Tess was kidnapped. I begged Russell to notify the authorities, you know. He refused. Now, as far as the police and FBI are concerned, it's not really their case. They're going through the motions, they have no choice, but without any real enthusiasm."

He turned left into a large parking lot. A sign near the road read SOHEGAN TACK & HARDWARE.

T & H occupied an enormous one-story building that had obviously been constructed in stages over the years, creating a massive, ugly patchwork of corrugated steel, cinder block, and brick. Nick drove to the visitors' lot, past acres of cars parked in neat rows.

The whole place had a grimly utilitarian feel, from the unassuming sign out front—thick black letters on a white background, no logo or decoration of any kind—to the meager strip of brown lawn surrounding the plant. Several groups of employees were picnicking under a mild July sun.

No wonder the first Russell Cunningham had built a high wall around Penaquoit. If the workers ever got a load of the luxury their toil supported there'd be class warfare. Nothing they imagined as they ate lunch on the treeless lawn by the bunkerlike plant could rival the actual splendor of the Cunningham estate.

Tess woke up as Gwen lifted her from the car seat. She was warm and sweaty from her nap, so Gwen let her walk the twenty yards to the visitors' entrance, Nick holding one hand as they crossed the lot, she the other. A few of the picnicking workers looked up and watched the happy family make their slow progress. Just inside the visitors' entrance, a middle-aged woman behind a metal desk greeted them with a chilly smile.

"Mr. Cunningham is expecting you," she said. She pointedly avoided eye contact with Gwen or Nick, fixing her eyes mournfully on Tess as they walked across the unadorned reception area. Gwen picked her up and followed Nick down a long hallway lined with small offices. Each square room contained an identical desk and chair, a puny window, and a male employee in white shirt and tie. The men glanced up as they passed. At the end of the corridor Nick stopped and knocked on the one closed door, opening it before receiving a response. Gwen put Tess down and let her enter her future office under her own steam.

Russell Cunningham's office was large and unremarkable, though compared to his employees' digs it was positively opulent. The walls were covered with dark paneling, the floors with a flat, textureless brown carpet. The old man's desk was a major piece of work: polished mahogany, probably his grandfather's originally, as big and solid as a pool table. On the walls were black-and-white photographs of various men shaking hands with various other men—she spotted Russell in a few of them, smiling next to a former New York governor in one, shaking hands with a congressman in another.

And behind the desk was Russell himself, a cigarette in one hand. He glanced up when they entered, his expression poised for admonishment. It relaxed a bit when he saw Tess toddling over.

"Took you long enough," he growled to Nick as he stubbed out the cigarette. He hefted his granddaughter onto his lap, glanced at Gwen with a puzzled expression, then turned back to his son-in-law. "Did you get lost?"

"I've been here before," Nick said.

"*Once* before." The old man turned to Gwen. "Grubby commerce—what would Ludwig van Beethoven think?"

"If we are going to trade insults," Nick said, "I'm leaving."

Gwen had noticed Nick's clothes earlier that day; she always did: white T-shirt, loose gray sweatpants, white sneakers. The casual, athletic look usually suited him. But here, at the plant, the outfit all but shouted *son-in-law*.

"I made it clear to him from the beginning that there was a place for him here," Russell said, facing Nick but talking, obviously, to her. "Priscilla had a head for business, but no interest. My son did…" He sighed as he absently stroked Tess's hair.

"I have no head for business, as you put it," Nick said. "You're better off without me."

"Oh, he has a head for business, all right," the old man said, still looking straight at Nick. "He knows the value of a buck all right. I never doubted that for a moment."

"I'll wait out front," Gwen said, turning to leave.

"No, stop," Russell said. "I want to show Tess around. You'll come with us. You too," he said sharply to Nick. "Let's go."

He picked up Tess and led them out into the corridor, at the end of which were two swinging metal doors. He pushed one open and they entered a vast factory floor, acres of machinery and conveyor belts and employees, men and women, most of them wearing plastic goggles.

"I tripled output within two years of taking over," Russell shouted as he led them down a central aisle. The noise level was astounding, a low but insistent hum that vibrated right through the body. As they walked briskly, turning corners every ten yards or so, workers would look up from their lathes and stamping machines, goggled eyes curious, suspicious, above all eager for distraction. Russell showed them a series of machines that stamped out switch plates, another group of equipment that produced metal bathroom fixtures—towel racks, toothbrush holders, soap dishes. They stopped and watched a young man stamp out four-inch-long tubes with gently tapered ends. Russell dropped the cigarette to the cement floor and ground it out with his foot.

"What's he making?" she shouted.

"Doorstops," Russell said, surmounting the din without shouting. She saw Nick smirk behind his father-in-law's back. "We sell five million a year at fifty cents apiece," Russell growled over his shoulder. "Nothing to sneer at."

Gwen was dizzy and disoriented from the noise and the activity and the curious stares. The place struck her as absurdly, grotesquely large, given the triviality of what it manufactured. It seemed more suited to producing airplanes or missiles or farm machinery. Anything but doorstops.

Tess began to fuss soon after they entered the factory floor, and within five minutes she was in the throes of a full-fledged tantrum, kicking at her horrified grandfather's midsection as he attempted to explain to her the intricacies of manufacturing decorative hardware.

Her screams were muffled by the ambient cacophony, but she was clearly unnerving the old man, who finally thrust her into Gwen's arms and stormed off ahead of them. Nick threw up his hands and followed.

Gwen waited a moment, trying to calm Tess. A lathe operator working nearby, a thin young man in overalls with dark hollows in his cheeks, said something to her.

"I'm sorry, I didn't hear you!" she shouted over the din.

"One big happy family!" he said.

She wasn't sure how to interpret his words. Then she noticed a dozen other workers staring, grinning.

"You gonna adopt the little girl?" someone yelled. "You and Nick Lawrence?"

Gwen ran after Russell and Nick, barging through the swinging doors to the office area. She leaned against the wall to catch her breath, dizzy from the sudden silence and trembling with anger. The old man charged into his office, emerging a moment later, eyes blazing, his right index finger pointing shakily at Nick.

"I'm having you investigated," he said. "My man is looking under every rock you ever hid beneath."

"Don't blame me because Tess is not fascinated by your...your empire here. She's not even a year old."

"*This* is where she belongs." Russell Cunningham stomped a foot on the floor. "Right here. You try to take her away, I'll destroy you."

"You mean you'll cut me off," Nick said.

"I mean I'll destroy you." He barreled into his office and slammed the door behind him.

Even Tess was nonplussed by the old man's rage, staring openmouthed at the closed door.

"Let's go," Nick said after a few moments. As he squeezed past her in the narrow corridor she saw that his hands were trembling. Her own hands weren't much steadier.

You gonna adopt the little girl? You and Nick Lawrence?

CHAPTER 23

Dwight Hawkins drove into the Tack & Hardware visitors' lot just as Nick Lawrence, Gwen Amiel, and the little girl were leaving the building. They made an attractive...unit, he thought as he watched them get into the green Range Rover, Gwen buckling the girl into the infant's seat in the back, then sitting up front next to Nick. Priscilla Cunningham had probably sat in that very seat on her way to the ravine.

Something was going on between those two, he'd bet his life on it. He sensed it just watching them walk, the way she kept just a little too far away from him, and slightly back. Gwen Amiel was no geisha; she stayed back because to walk side by side would be to acknowledge something, something real between them.

He waited until they drove away, then got out of his car and headed for the visitors' entrance. A warm front was moving in from the Ohio Valley, promising thunderstorms tomorrow night or early the following morning. People liked to complain about the inaccuracy of weather forecasts, but in Dwight's experience the weather was one of the more predictable things in life, certainly more predictable than human behavior.

He asked the receptionist for Russell Cunningham and wasn't surprised when, after making a call, she gave him the go-ahead. The old man was desperate for information.

He entered the big office and walked over to the desk.

"I appreciate your seeing me, Mr. Cunningham. I didn't—"

"You got my five million?" Russell didn't look up from a pile of papers on his desk, probably hated the sight of the man he blamed for chasing his son off an embankment twenty years earlier. A cigarette burned in the huge glass ashtray on his desk. "Is that why you're here, to bring me my money and tell me the killer's in custody?"

"The FBI has alerted all the banks in the country to be on the lookout for unusually large deposits of hundred-dollar bills. But the Feds figure the money is already out of the country. Could have been smuggled in ordinary luggage to some place like Switzerland, Panama, maybe the Caymans."

Cunningham growled, still not looking at him.

"Actually, I was hoping you could answer a few questions."

Now he looked up. Dwight cringed at the toll the man's daughter's death had taken. Over the past twenty years he'd caught fleeting glimpses of the old man around town, always surprised at his vigor, the strength he radiated. Now that vigor and strength were mostly gone, leaving a still handsome but diminished man, the face drawn and pale, the eyes watery and tired.

"The FBI is handling this," Cunningham said. "And my own people."

Dwight sat in one of the two chairs facing the desk. "Every lead's turned up cold. The case is still open, of course, and always will be until your daughter's killer is found. But I don't think the FBI is working overtime anymore."

Cunningham considered him for a few beats, his chest heaving with every breath.

"If the FBI can't do anything, what makes you think you can?"

A memory: twenty years ago, on the crest of Pattatee Mountain, the old man standing at the edge of the road, his face swaddled in smoke from the wreck sixty feet below that had claimed his son and namesake. Suddenly, he'd let out a roar that reverberated off the neighboring hills in that freezing January dawn.

"My gut tells me the answer is here, in Sohegan," Dwight said.

"Your gut?" His eyes finished the sentence: *Your "gut" chased my son off a cliff two decades ago.*

"The Van Slykes, for instance, they ever give you any trouble since the accident?"

"Not since I paid them off," he grumbled. "Any other theories?" Russell lit a new cigarette from the stub of the old one, which he flattened in the ashtray with his index finger.

The Van Slykes had never told a soul how much Cunningham paid them after their daughter died in the accident with his son. But the boy's alcohol level was 8.2, plenty high enough to warrant a major contribution.

"So you never had anything to do with Henry or Meg Van Slyke since…"

The old man shook his head, and Dwight decided to change tack. He'd never put much stock in the Van Slyke angle, anyway: they'd continued to live quietly after the accident, though Meg had resigned her position as payroll clerk at T & H. Neither she nor Henry seemed interested in revenge. And both had alibis for the kidnapping and Devil's Ravine incident.

"Whose decision was it not to involve the police, once you realized your granddaughter was missing?"

"I've been over this with the FBI, the county police."

Dwight waited him out.

"It was my decision," Cunningham said. "And I don't regret it, no, I do not." He stared right into Dwight's eyes.

"Did anyone protest that decision?"

A pause, then a firm "No."

"Not one word of protest? Your daughter, your son-in-law?" *Your wife*—but everyone in town knew Maxine Cunningham wouldn't stand up to a scarecrow.

"What's your point?"

"Just trying to reconstruct the—"

"I've had my son-in-law thoroughly investigated," Cunningham said. "I still have a man on him. But he didn't do this."

"How about the baby-sitter, Gwen Amiel? She claims she learned about the kidnapping from listening to a baby monitor. She heard you discussing the arrangements, right after the final phone call from the kidnapper."

"So?"

"Did you in fact discuss the plans, the three of you?"

"Of course we—wait a minute, you say she heard us through the monitor?"

"The baby monitor."

"We were in Priscilla's—what the hell was the monitor doing in the master bedroom?"

"Someone must have brought it there."

"But Tess wasn't in the house; what would be the point? Do you think she was listening out in the hallway? Or on the phone?"

"It's possible. But the Feds have looked her over pretty closely, and she's come up clean. Thinking back to the crime scene, do you recall seeing Gwen and the kidnapper together?"

"They were nearby," Cunningham said. His face had flushed, dramatically improving his appearance. "About twenty feet apart, I'd say."

"Think—did you see them at the *same time?*"

The old man squinted as the color drained from his face.

"I don't know," he said in a faint voice. "I was running down that hill to the ravine...my daughter...I think I saw two people on the other side, but I'm not really sure."

"Where did your daughter go that morning, the morning she was killed?"

Russell's eyes narrowed. "What the hell difference does that make?"

"She disappeared for two hours on the morning she was murdered. I'd like to know where she went."

"For a drive," the old man said without much conviction. "She liked to drive."

"And the flower she had with her. What was that about?"

"My daughter was murdered and you're asking me about *flowers?*"

"I take it then you don't know why she had that flower with her."

The old man looked away and nodded.

He knows something, Dwight thought as he stood up. "Well, thanks for your time, Mr. Cunningham. I'll be in touch as soon as I know anything further." He turned to leave.

"Should I fire her?" the old man asked. "The baby-sitter."

Dwight stopped and looked back. "I wouldn't do anything to alert her that she's still a suspect. *Potential* suspect. Anyway, the crime is done. Your granddaughter's in no danger from Gwen Amiel or anyone else."

Cunningham nodded but looked unconvinced. Both his children had been killed—now all he had left was his granddaughter. Why should he believe for one instant that *she* was safe?

Dwight was at the doorway when the old man called out. "Hawkins!"

He turned. Cunningham was hunched over his desk, resting his head on his elbows.

"You said you think the key to solving the murder is here in town. Why?"

"The choice of the ravine for the exchange," he said. "It's not exactly featured on tourist maps." Gwen Amiel had been to the ravine only the day before—passing along that bit of information to Don Reeves had been pure pleasure. He didn't often get the chance to show up the Feds, though in some unaccountable way he felt as if he was betraying Gwen Amiel.

Cunningham appeared to think this over, then returned to the papers on his desk. Dwight watched him a few seconds before heading for the reception area. Cunningham seemed satisfied with the lie. Or half lie—the choice of location did, in fact, suggest a local angle. But his conviction that the answer lay in Sohegan went deeper.

He nodded to the receptionist on the way out, wishing he could recall her name. He'd seen her in town a hundred times, knew her brother, Raymond something-or-other, quite well.

Whoever kidnapped Tess Lawrence and killed her mother was privy to something that only a local would know. No, not just a local but someone very close to the Cunninghams. Whoever committed those crimes had to know, or feel very strongly, that Russell Cunningham wouldn't call the police the moment his granddaughter went missing. Few people outside of Sohegan could fathom the old man's deep distrust of the police, few could guess the lengths to which he would go in order to keep them out of his life, even in a crisis.

But someone knew all about the Cunninghams, and Sohegan, and the uneasy, unavoidable relationship between them, Dwight was sure. And that someone had murdered Priscilla Lawrence.

CHAPTER 24

"I can't even pity the old bastard," Nick said as they drove back from the factory. "And I've tried, you know, I've really tried to empathize with his loss."

Gwen turned and checked on Tess, who was sleeping.

"He doesn't make it easy," she said.

He'd driven directly to the factory along ugly, commercial Route 24. But he took the scenic route back to Penaquoit, a series of roads she'd never seen before. The Ondaigas were an acquired taste. The mountains themselves were appealing in a shyly unassuming way, more like large hills, really, and frequently invisible from the tree-lined roads. But the small towns nestled in the Ondaiga Valley, including Sohegan, lacked obvious charm. Zoning was nonexistent; gas stations were shoved between houses, and convenience stores sprouted like weeds along the main roads and smack in the middle of residential areas. The entire region seemed congenitally depressed, as if prosperity hadn't deserted the valley so much as bypassed it from the get go.

And yet she was beginning to appreciate the area. The unpretentious frame houses, invariably with a rusted car or two moldering out back; the shabby but honest downtowns where parking, God knew, was never a problem; and especially the forests that climbed the sides of the humble mountains, darker and cooler than the woods she'd walked through as a child on Long Island, the odor of decay that much sweeter. The sun was bright overhead as they drove, but on either side of them the woods formed a wall of inviting darkness; she felt as if they were hurtling through a radiant tunnel amid a dense world of shadow.

"There's something almost magical about these woods," she said. "It's easy to understand why the Indians thought they were full of spirits." He didn't respond. "How did you find this road?"

"I drive around a lot by myself, listening to music. There's not much else to do."

"No, I guess not."

"I don't think he's ever stopped to consider what *I've* lost."

Back to that. "Tess lost, too," she said quietly.

He glanced at her, then nodded. "He loved the idea of Priscilla, not the reality. I don't think he's capable of making a genuine human connection. Now he loves the *idea* of Tess, his heir. That's what today was all about. But when confronted with the reality of her—a one-year-old overdue for a nap and not terribly interested in decorative hardware—he broke a fuse."

"*Blew* a fuse," she said. He shot her a look and she changed the subject.

"What was your father like?" she asked.

He didn't say anything for a while; he seemed to be answering the question silently. She concentrated on the dusky forest on either side of them, catching sporadic glimpses of distant hills.

"He was a genius." Nick spoke softly, facing the road. "In every way—music, art, even athletics."

"What did he do?"

He glanced at her and smiled. "He was a purchasing manager for a company that manufactured candy."

An interesting profession for an artistic genius, she thought as she waited for him to continue.

"His father was a plumber. There was never any money for him to develop his talents professionally, nor any encouragement. He taught himself piano, drawing. Had no formal training at all. After high school he went to work as a handyman at the plant, in Landsburg, Pennsylvania, where he was born. He worked his way up to head of purchasing, but I don't think he ever had much talent for supervising people. He trusted too easily."

He seemed to think about this for a while.

"He was determined that I would get the training and encouragement he never enjoyed. I had private piano instructors, went to Julliard. He scraped together every dime he had to buy a Steinway—it took up our entire living room."

He smiled at the memory as she envisioned the Cunninghams' big Steinway parked in the middle of the living room at Penaquoit.

"Landsburg, Pennsylvania," she said. "Is that near Philadelphia?"

"It's near nothing," he replied. "Though it's not far from here, about two hours by car."

"I have a hard time imagining you as a small-town boy."

"That makes two of us. 'You taut mebbe I was from da Bronx?'"

He was uncanny at accents. "Actually, you have no accent at all." Or was the absence of inflection an accent in its own right?

"There's a kind of twang you hear in eastern Pennsylvania, but my parents were determined that I never talk like a hick."

"They did a good job," she said as he turned into the driveway of the estate. He punched in the code to open the gates—6, 2, 3, Priscilla's birthday—and drove in silence up to the mansion.

"Practice time," he said with a sigh, but she wasn't fooled. He glanced at Tess in the backseat. "Why don't you let her sleep in the car?" Gwen rolled down two windows as he headed into the house.

The day was too glorious to waste indoors, and Tess would nap for at least another half hour. Gwen began walking around the property. Within minutes she heard the piano, the Pathetique again, third movement—she could hum the entire sonata by now. But that afternoon, Beethoven had to compete with mewling catbirds and squawking blue jays and the dolorous sighs of mourning doves. By the time she reached a neatly clipped hedge at the southern border of the lawn the birds had won.

It had never occurred to her to venture beyond the hedge; it looked impenetrable. But she noticed a spot where the foliage thinned out near the ground, creating a four-foot-high opening. An escape hatch, she thought. She ducked into the gap, stepping from manicured perfection to musky forest. The air felt ten degrees cooler, the daylight filtered by the dense foliage overhead. The contrast was disorienting; she'd never quite appreciated what an oasis Penaquoit was, never understood the effort that went into keeping the wilderness at bay.

She spotted a narrow footpath through the thick, thorny underbrush, and decided to follow it. Weeds and saplings were beginning to blur the outline of what had probably been a frequently used trail. Within a few minutes she reached a small clearing, perhaps ten yards square. Dazzling sunlight electrified a dense profusion of flowers.

The clearing was a riot of color, clusters of similar blooms straining toward the sun, as if competing for prominence with neighboring varieties. She stepped carefully among them, almost overcome by the confusion of color and shape. In one patch of velvety red flowers she noticed a green plastic stick, about six inches high, with a square of plastic attached to the top. The plastic contained a white index card on which, in Priscilla's precise hand, was written *Rose Campion*. Below, in smaller letters, were two additional words, *Lychnis coronaria*, and a date from last summer, shortly after Tess's birth.

Every other cluster of flowers was identified in exactly the same way, with the common name in large letters, the Latin name in smaller print, and a date in the lower right-hand corner. Most of the dates were from last summer, about the time Priscilla and Nick had moved back to Penaquoit with their new baby.

Gwen tried to imagine Priscilla creating the garden, tried to understand why she'd spent so much effort on this small, private place so soon after giving birth. And although she knew next to nothing about horticulture, she couldn't help but wonder at how richly mature the garden was, given that this was only its second summer. Gardens take years to fully develop; this one was absolute, fully realized perfection.

"You've found the secret garden."

She spun around. Nick stood at the entrance, watching her. How long had he been there?

"Priscilla created it not long after we moved back. Mett Piacevic had a small vegetable patch here, which she ripped out. She didn't want anyone to come here, not even Tess." He walked into the garden and yanked several purple thistles by their necks. "She died with one of these in her hand," he said, holding them out. Gwen took the flowers and bent down to read the descriptive card.

"'Thistle, *Onopordum acanthium.*' Russell and Maxine know why she carried one of these to the ravine."

"Why?" he said quickly.

"They won't say. They claim they don't know, but I could tell they knew something."

He frowned and slowly shook his head. "She wouldn't let Piacevic or anyone else near this place. She had the flats of flowers delivered to that opening in the hedge, no farther. They were always fully grown specimens. Cunninghams don't wait for nature."

"It's wonderful," Gwen said.

"I suppose..." He glanced around. "Sometimes she'd be driving along a back road and spot a group of healthy-looking flowers in someone's garden. She'd knock on the door of the house and ask the name of the flower, how much sunlight it needed, when it bloomed. Usually the owner would offer her a cutting. Gratis, of course. But Cunninghams don't wait for cuttings to take root and spread. Priscilla would offer them extravagant sums of money for the entire garden, then send Piacevic over to dig it all up." He waved his right hand over the garden. "That's what you see here, the healthiest specimens from Ondaiga County, paid for by Cunningham money and replanted by Priscilla Lawrence with her own hands."

Gwen surveyed the garden again. The colors looked suddenly garish, almost cloying. Bought, uprooted, replanted—the lush growth seemed an abomination now.

"I don't know what will happen to it now." Nick absently snapped a dead bloom from a clump of yellow and white daisies. "Piacevic asked me whether he should keep it up, and I told him not to bother. I think Priscilla would have wanted it to revert back after she was gone."

He looked around, as if seeking confirmation, then sat cross-legged on the grassy border, which was now seriously overgrown. He patted the ground next to him. She hesitated before sitting a few feet away.

"Then it all fell apart," he said. It took her a moment to grasp that he was continuing the conversation from the car. "I was two years out of college—Julliard, I think I mentioned that—when my father was implicated in a financial scandal. He lost his job, and I lost my…chance."

"What kind of scandal?"

"He was accused of taking kickbacks from some of the suppliers he used. Nothing was ever proven, and I know for a fact that he was innocent, but he never worked again." His lips curled to an angry smile. "That's when I began to work."

"What did you do?"

"Whatever I could. I wasn't trained for anything, had no skills other than music. I gave piano lessons, but that only goes so far. I was a messenger at one point, if you can believe it. And then I met Priscilla, and was able to get back to my music."

He said this so casually, so innocently. Didn't he realize that marrying Priscilla might be viewed as mercenary?

"You're thinking—how convenient," he said.

"How *fortunate*," she replied. "For both of you."

He looked at her a beat. "We were solidly middle class," he said at length. "But my father gave me the best musical education money could by. He sacrificed everything…" His voice broke. "He's in a nursing home now. He lost his will to live after the scandal. His mind's been slipping ever since. I'd always hoped he'd watch me perform one day before he lost it completely—other than at Julliard recitals. But he never did."

"You haven't mentioned your mother."

He glanced at her quizzically. "What about her?"

Gwen couldn't conceal her amazement at his dismissal of her.

"Her name was Catherine," he said after a brief silence. "She had no musical talent whatsoever. She died a few years after the scandal." He looked at Gwen. "Anything else you'd like to know about her?"

A chill ran down her spine. "I guess not."

Silence settled awkwardly between them. She focused on the flowers, imagining Priscilla seeking refuge in her secret garden, wondering what she was seeking refuge from. Father? Husband? The strangling knot of compliance and compromise that had defined her short life?

"We're a pair, the two of us," Nick said after a while.

"We're not a pair," she said quickly.

"We're both trapped, though, you and me, in Sohegan."

"I'm not trapped."

"There's no other reason for us to be here. I can't leave because the old man will cut me off and take Tess away from me."

"He can't take your own daughter from you."

He shook his head and scowled. "He'd find a way."

"She's your daughter."

"Trust me, he'd find a way."

How, though? What did Russell Cunningham have on Nick that would enable him to pry Tess away?

"Do you really see yourself spending the rest of your life here?" she asked.

"I try not to think about it."

"But Russell Cunningham is at least seventy…"

"You think he'd let a little thing like his death stand in the way of running my life? His lawyers drew up a will that ensures Tess never leaves this place." His voice dropped. "And I'll never leave Tess."

"I wish you could hear yourself," she said, her voice suddenly rising. "You're talented, you're…attractive, you've got a beautiful, healthy daughter. You have no financial worries, you live…you live in this *paradise*, and all you do is complain about how tough you have it. Most people would sell their soul for the life you have, and they wouldn't whine about their predicament afterward."

He stared at her with cold eyes. She hadn't meant to sound so harsh, but how dare he equate their situations? She was nobody's victim, not anymore.

"What's keeping you here?" he said after a long silence.

"Nothing's *keeping* me here. I want to be here."

"That's bullshit," he said. "You're hiding out from something, or someone."

She stood up and headed back to the path.

"I should check on Tess," she said as she walked. She was several yards along the path when he grabbed her shoulders and twisted her around, kissing her lips as he held her to him.

For a moment she didn't resist, though she didn't actually respond. Contact with a man's face and body felt at once so familiar and so alien, she almost swooned with confusion. When he pulled away he ran his hands along her shoulders and back.

"You've become…important in my life." He was breathing heavily.

She shook her head and backed away. "I'm the baby-sitter," she said, trying to disguise her own breathlessness. "Of course I'm important."

"More than that," he said.

"I can't."

"You can do whatever you want."

"I don't *want* to."

He studied her, his eyes reflecting the sunlight like faceted emeralds. She looked away, knowing that he'd heard the lie in her voice.

"I have to check on Tess." She turned and hurried down the path.

"Come back," he called after her, sounding more petulant than hurt. She ducked under the hedge as he called her name, then ran the entire distance to the house.

CHAPTER 25

Dwight Hawkins glanced up at the limestone facade of 222 West 83rd Street, the Manhattan building where Gwen Amiel lived before arriving in Sohegan three months ago.

The fifteen-story building looked about seventy, seventy-five years old, with a green canopy in front supported by gleaming brass poles. In the five minutes he'd been standing there, three strollers had been wheeled out, two by black women pushing white babies, the third by a frazzled-looking white woman with gray-streaked hair pushing a sleeping white child. Nice family building, he thought. Nice family neighborhood—after parking in a garage a few blocks away, he'd noticed that the West Side of Manhattan was teeming with small children and shops that catered to them and their parents.

So why had Gwen Amiel left?

That question had brought him to the city, only his fourth visit in a lifetime spent just two hundred miles away. Sohegan was about an hour north of even the most outlying suburbs, well beyond the city's magnetic field. Few residents saw anything strange in turning their backs on one of the world's great metropolises, despite its proximity. More Sohegan citizens had been to Orlando, via the Albany airport, than had ever ventured to Manhattan.

But Dwight was glad to be there all the same. The hot July sun slowed the city's pace to a tolerable rate, encouraging the neighborhood women to flaunt their fit, big-city bodies in shorts and tight T-shirts. He'd left behind a cloudy sky and the threat of thundershowers, and figured he'd crossed the front that was causing all the trouble about a half hour north of the George Washington Bridge.

The marble lobby of Gwen Amiel's old building was

unexpectedly cool. He showed his badge to the doorman, whose gray uniform had *Julio Menendez* stitched in red on the jacket pocket. He looked about sixty, with white hair, a dark complexion, and the stern countenance of a man who took his job seriously.

"Were you working here when Gwen Amiel still lived in this building?"

Julio Menendez squared his shoulders. "Fifteen years I work here. But the FBI, they already ask the same question."

"I know that." Dwight waited as Menendez opened the door for an elderly man, who slowly crossed the lobby. He knew he was retracing the FBI's steps, and that his chances of learning anything new were slim. But Gwen Amiel was at the center of the crime, he felt more confident of that every day. And if the crime had been months in the planning, as he suspected, then that planning might well have taken place at 222 West 83rd Street.

"Do you happen to recall a thirtyish man visiting Ms. Amiel— tall, well built, with light brown hair...a piano player?" The only photograph of Nick Lawrence he had was an overhead shot of Priscilla's funeral in which he was little more than a blur in a black suit and dark sunglasses. If Lawrence ever showed his face in town he might be able to get a better shot of him—or at least the press would.

"Maybe, maybe not," the doorman said. "But she have very few visitors, this I remember. You could talk to the night man, Jose DeLeon, but he don't remember so well." Menendez took a step closer to him. "He drinks."

Dwight stepped back. "Miss Amiel left this building suddenly, I understand."

"Nobody could believe it. Everyone liked her, and her boy, Jimmy." His expression softened for a moment. "She used to leave him with me sometime when she need milk across the street. Very polite boy, no problem. I let him buzz the tenants when they get deliveries."

"You haven't mentioned her husband, Barry Amiel."

He glanced at the marble floor and shrugged. "He was not so nice."

"Not so nice, how?"

"Always fighting with everybody, you know? The mail is late, he fight with the mailman. Once upon a while I forget to announce a visitor, he fight with me also."

"Did he become violent?"

"No, no, he never hit me, but I sometimes think he could, you know? He is a very tense man and..." He stepped closer. "He drink."

Dwight stepped back. "He ever get violent when he drank?"

"I never see that, but my shift ends at four in the afternoon. You ask the night man, Julio DeLeon, see if he remembers, but you have to keep in your mind, Julio, he..." Menendez stepped closer.

"I know, he drinks." Dwight turned and looked around the lobby. "Is there anyone in the building who knew the Amiels well?"

"Everyone know them like neighbors, but I don't think they had good friends in the building. Private people, you know? Gwen, Miss Amiel, she was more friendly, but..." He shrugged and looked away.

"But what?"

"I think he was not very nice to her," he said. "Barry. I think...I think he hit her. Sometime she wears dark glasses, in the rain? Sometime she have a scarf around her face even when it is warm outside. And you hear things, working the door, you know?"

"Were the police ever called in?"

"Not on my shift, but you can ask—"

"—The night man, I'll do that. What happened to their apartment after she left? I understand Barry Amiel disappeared soon after that."

"He leave a few week later, but first he sell everything in the apartment, all the furniture and paintings and kitchen pots and pans. A moving truck came one day, takes it all away. Then he leave."

"And the apartment?"

"They sell it, I think. New people coming soon."

"Gwen Amiel is selling the apartment?"

He shook his head. "I think the co-op try and sell it. The Amiels, they owe money on the apartment. When they left, the building took over. But you should talk to Mrs. Robinson, she knows what happened."

"Mrs. Robinson?"

"In seven D, the president of the building. You want me to buzz her?"

Cora Robinson opened the door to her seventh-floor apartment wearing a black leotard and panting heavily. In the background, Dwight heard a female drill sergeant: *lift your arms, punch the ceiling. Punch it! Punch it!*

"I'm...just...finishing my...step workout," she said. "Come in."

He angled past her and entered the foyer of the sunny, traditionally furnished apartment.

"I'll just...turn this off." She crossed the living room, grabbed a remote, and extinguished the television. She was about forty, very fit, with frosted blond hair and a taut, angular face.

"Julio tells me you're interested in the Amiels," she said when she rejoined him in the foyer. She was rocking gently on the balls of her feet, like a jogger waiting for a streetlight to change. "I can't say I'm eager to discuss them any further."

"Any further?" He glanced into the living room but received no invitation to sit down.

"We had a lot of trouble with them. First Gwen left in the middle of the night like some...I almost said criminal, but I suppose you can't use words like that lightly around a policeman."

She smiled and he raised his age estimate by about ten years: the body looked forty, but the lines along her mouth and eyes exposed additional wear.

"Why did Gwen's leaving cause you trouble?"

"Her leaving didn't cause us trouble per se; it was her husband's leaving a few weeks later that was the problem. He abandoned the apartment. They were already two months behind on the monthly maintenance. They bought at the peak of the market, so they had a huge mortgage and virtually no equity in the apartment."

"The bank took over the unit?"

She nodded. "But we had to cover the maintenance until we could sell the place."

"By 'we' you mean..."

"The cooperative. The apartment was a wreck. We had to have it professionally cleaned and completely repainted before we could even think about showing it." She wiped sweat from her forehead. "It's amazing how much damage a man can do in a few weeks on his own."

"So you were inside the apartment before Gwen Amiel left?"

She hesitated a beat before answering. "Once."

"Was that a social visit?"

"An official visit. There were complaints from neighbors down on three. About excessive noise. As co-op president I'm occasionally called upon to handle these situations. We'd sent the Amiels a few letters; our managing agent had called at least once. Finally, I decided to speak to Gwen myself."

"What kind of noise did the neighbors complain of?"

"Shouting."

"What kind of—"

"He used to yell at her. Like an animal, the most vile language."

"You heard it personally?"

She started to answer, then held up a finger and left him alone for a few moments. He glanced into the living room, took in the plump sofa covered in a bright floral pattern, the pale yellow walls, the piles of oversize art books stacked on every horizontal surface. In the exact center of the room, on a lush oriental rug, sat a squat plastic platform like some sort of Asian shrine. For the step workout, he guessed. Cora returned with a glass of water and took a long sip before speaking.

"I went downstairs one evening to investigate. The couple across the hall, the ones who had been complaining, called me and asked me to. So I stood out on the elevator landing and listened for a few minutes. He sounded quite out of his mind, Barry Amiel."

"Do you remember what he was yelling about?"

"Just name calling, basically. I'm not a prude, but I couldn't possibly repeat those words to you."

"This was at night?"

"Late evening, about eight or eight-thirty."

When the boy was at home. "And did you hear Gwen Amiel that night?"

"Of course. She was trying to calm him down, but having no luck. Frankly, when I later heard that she'd left, I wasn't surprised. In fact, I was relieved. She seemed like a nice person, a good mother. And her store over on Amsterdam was quite lovely; she had a very good eye, if you know what I mean. She deserved better than Barry Amiel."

"But why did she leave so suddenly?" he said. "And why would she leave everything she owned behind?"

"That I can't tell you." She glanced at a wafer-thin gold watch. "Now, I have a lunch date...Is there anything else?"

He described Nick Lawrence for her and asked if she recalled seeing him.

"That sounds like the man whose wife was killed," she said. "The man Gwen worked for."

"Ever seen him here in the building?"

"I don't think so," she said with a shudder.

"You wouldn't by any chance have a photo of Barry Amiel?"

"Why in the world would I have a—wait, I just might."

She left for a moment and returned carrying a carton filled with papers.

"One of our shareholders always takes photos at the annual building Christmas party. We run a few in the co-op newsletter." She began looking through the box. "Not that we ran one of Barry Amiel; he wasn't exactly popular here. But I do recall they attended with their little—here we go." She handed him a color photograph. "Barry's the one on the right."

Barry Amiel was taller than the other two men in the photo, with a swag of dark hair over his forehead. His eyes were also dark, and sleepy, his smile thin and cynical.

"May I keep this?" Hawkins said.

"Of course. Now, if there's nothing else…"

He walked to the front door, still glancing at the photo.

"I almost forgot," she said. He turned back to her. "I mentioned before that the Amiels owed two months' maintenance when they left. About three thousand dollars total. We had hired a collections agency, but never got very far. Then a few weeks ago we received a check for the full amount."

He walked back into the foyer. "Who signed the check?"

"It was a cashier's check."

"Was there a note?"

"Just a line to the effect that the enclosed check was to cover back maintenance. I…threw it out, actually."

He couldn't conceal his disappointment.

"Well, I didn't realize back then that she was involved in that kidnapping. Someone brought it up at our last shareholders meeting." She stepped toward him. "She *was* involved, I take it."

He shrugged, which was about as honest an answer as he could muster just then.

"I'd appreciate the name of your co-op's bank, and your account number. I might be able to trace the check, at least find out if it was drawn on a New York bank."

She frowned, left him for a minute, and returned with a slip of paper. "Our bank and account number," she said.

"Thanks." He took the paper and left the apartment, wondering how Gwen Amiel—or her husband, for that matter—suddenly acquired three thousand dollars. And why pay off the co-op now? Guilty conscience—or a keen desire not to be pursued by a collections agency?

Waiting for the elevator, he heard the step class resume.

One, two, three…don't give up, girls, lift those knees high, one, two, three. Higher, two, three. Higher, two, three.

CHAPTER 26

It's happening, Gwen decided Thursday night as she painted the trim around the door between the dining room and kitchen. Jimmy was upstairs in bed, finding Waldo with a flashlight. If she didn't get the hell out of Penaquoit, she was going to end up sleeping with Nick Lawrence.

All evening a debate had been raging inside her head.

So what if you sleep with him? Where's the harm?

"It would be wrong."

Why?

"Why? Let me count the ways. His wife died barely a month ago. I'm his kid's baby-sitter, for God's sake. I mean, this is insane."

That's two reasons, not counting insanity.

"Okay, so I'd more or less promised myself that I'd steer clear of men for a while."

Because of what that sick fuck did in New York.

"Because of Barry, yes."

Is there anything about Nick Lawrence that reminds you of him?

"They're opposites, in a way. Barry was out of control. Even before he started drinking he couldn't control his temper, couldn't say no to any kind of temptation. Nick is completely self-possessed. I get the impression that every step he takes is choreographed."

Like kissing you the other day?

"No, that was spontaneous. At least it *felt* spontaneous." Then how did he find you in the secret garden? Did he search the entire estate?

"Good question."

Well, if he's so completely different from Barry, what do you have to lose?

"I don't trust myself. I made such a horrendous decision the last time."

After Barry started drinking, all of her friends had tried to console her with the same basic line: *How could you have known he'd turn out like this? How could you have known he'd end up a drunk, and a cruel drunk at that?*

But she'd known. Oh, not about the alcohol. But she'd known his weakness from the moment she met him. Barry kept his insecurities and his anger tightly coiled inside; she knew they'd unravel eventually, and that it wouldn't be pretty when it happened. It was booze that ultimately set his demons free, but it could have been anything: drugs, a business failure, some deep personal rejection. She'd felt the danger in that coiled anger every time she held him, and she'd married him anyway.

"It's just that…"

Say it.

"It sounds like dime-store analysis, but I tend to fall for guys who are bad for me."

It's not dime-store analysis when it applies to you.

"Remember Ken, the married guy before Barry? He told me right off that he wasn't leaving his wife. Somehow I didn't care."

Years of analysis that set her back far more than a dime had yielded all sorts of explanations for her weakness for unavailable men: her parents' divorce when she was six; her mother's chronic depression after that; two much-older brothers who had basically ignored her. Even early puberty had been offered as a possible reason; she'd shot up to five-eight in the sixth grade, and been subjected to the cruelest ridicule until the boys caught up. She had a dozen explanations for always choosing men who ultimately couldn't reciprocate: married men, gay men, emotional zombies. And still she chose them.

Are you positive Nick Lawrence is wrong for you?

"No. And yet his very self-possession, that feline detachment, seems dangerous, somehow. Getting involved with a man who appears to need nothing from anyone has to be hazardous, doesn't it?"

The doorbell ended the conversation…and set her heart racing; she still couldn't think about Jimmy's panda without shuddering. She opened the curtains by the front door and relaxed.

"Am I interrupting something?" Sheila asked. She was still in bank uniform: navy suit, white silk blouse, sensible black shoes.

Gwen almost laughed. "Just a really intense conversation." Sheila looked around, puzzled. "With myself," Gwen said.

"It's the paint fumes. I mean, the dining room looked perfectly fine before you started."

"I hated the color," Gwen said.

"The color? It was white. It's *still* white."

"Ecru," Gwen said weakly, feeling a pang of empathy for the local dairy farmers and auto mechanics and contractors who applied to Sheila Stewart for loans.

"Ecru." Sheila rolled her eyes. "Anyway, I stopped by on the way home because—"

"Mama?" Jimmy called from upstairs. "I'm thirsty."

"Get a cup of water from the bathroom," she shouted back at him.

"I want *you* to."

"There's a cup in the bathroom."

"*Please?*"

She sighed as she headed upstairs. "He swears there are monsters living under the bed. At least he says he does. Sometimes I think he's just lazy."

"Men!" Sheila said as Gwen reached the second floor. She gave Jimmy a cup of water, which he gulped down as she left the room.

"Mom?"

"*What?*"

"Nothing."

"Sorry I snapped, honey. It's very late. What is it, Jimbo?"

"Does Daddy know where we live?"

"No," she said quickly. He put the cup down and snuggled under his blanket. "Why?" she asked quietly, her throat suddenly dry.

"I saw him."

"That's not possible."

"He was at the diner. I saw him sitting there, eating."

"You thought you saw him, Jimmy. Daddy doesn't know where we are."

"I guess." She saw him shrug in the dim yellow glow of the nightlight.

"Are you…I mean, do you miss him?"

"No."

She waited until his breathing slowed to sleeping tempo, wondering if he'd ever feel completely safe, if he'd ever understand that while monsters really do exist, they're not under his bed.

She went back downstairs. Sheila was still standing by the front door.

"I just thought you should know. Dwight Hawkins came by the bank the other day—our fearless police chief? He asked a few questions about the money transfer, for the ransom. I told him I'd been through this a hundred times with the FBI. Then it hit me, later in the conversation. What he really wanted to talk about was you."

"*What?*"

"The guy's got a bug up his ass for you, Gwen. He thinks you were involved in the kidnapping."

"In the murder, you mean. I *was* involved, I was there. If I hadn't—"

"In the *kidnapping*. He asked about your relationship with Nick Lawrence, whether you were in touch with your husband, if you had any hidden source of income."

"Hidden source of—Christ, look around. Does it look like I've got five million in the bank?"

Sheila glanced at the pitcher and washbasin she'd bought at the auction.

"I splurged, okay? That's not a criminal offense up here, is it?"

Sheila looked at her a beat. "You told me you didn't have a pot to pee in," she said, deadpan. "So what do you do? You go out and buy…a pot to pee in!"

Gwen felt so relieved she hugged her friend.

"Stay for a drink?" she said.

"I have to get home." They unhugged. "Betsy's into playing Susie Homemaker these days. Tonight it's vegetarian meat loaf. You should see the curtains she's making for the living room." Sheila shuddered. "I just wish she'd stop trying so hard."

Sheila smiled sadly. She was so much stronger than Betsy, far more capable. Gwen assumed that the differences between them explained the success of their relationship. Sheila was heading down the front walk when Gwen called after her.

"Sheila?"

She turned. "Yeah?"

Gwen was about to tell her about Nick Lawrence, but changed her mind. Sometimes she felt so close to Sheila, but in reality they'd only known each other a few months. Anyway, talking about Nick would make her attraction—her fear—more real, somehow.

"Thanks for coming by," she said. Sheila waved and got in her car. Gwen closed the door and felt a surge of loneliness. If she couldn't confide in Sheila, then whom could she turn to?

For advice, you mean?

The voice was back, that familiar, low-pitched summons to face facts.

"Yeah, advice."

Simple—don't get involved with Nick Lawrence. He's trouble.

"But—"

He's trouble and you're the baby-sitter.

"But I—"

You're not Jane Eyre, okay?

Gwen closed her eyes a moment and sighed. "I'm not Jane Eyre."

CHAPTER 27

Dwight Hawkins smiled as his wife, Elaine, set a plate of scrambled eggs and toast in front of him, then watched her bustle across the kitchen to fetch orange juice from the refrigerator. *Don't hurry so much*, he wanted to say, that morning and every morning. *What's the rush?*

"Thank you," he said a bit abruptly when she handed him a glass of juice. "Good eggs," he quickly added. "Really good."

She leaned against the counter next to the sink, arms folded, as he ate. She never joined him at the breakfast table, never had. Instead she played short-order cook and waitress, fussing over his eggs and pancakes and toast as conscientiously as when they were newlyweds thirty-five years earlier. He often wondered why she didn't just sit down and have a cup of coffee with him. Would that be admitting defeat for her, giving in to the fact that it was just the two of them, after all these years? Did she worry that they'd have nothing to talk about at dinner if they exhausted the conversational possibilities at breakfast?

And why, for that matter, had *he* stopped asking *her* to join him at the breakfast table, despite the irritability her constant hovering always provoked in him?

"What if we sold this place?" he said after he'd finished the eggs and toast.

"Sold?" she said from across the room. "And moved where?"

"Manhattan."

"Get out."

"No, really. Yesterday the city looked so…lively. After I retire in two years there won't be anything much to keep us here."

"Do you have any idea what apartments cost in New York? We'd end up living in a closet for what this place would fetch."

He drained his coffee cup, thinking of Cora Robinson and her perfect breasts and the dark patches of sweat on her leotard and that mound above her crotch.

Fantasizing about a fifty-year-old in leotards? *Geez.*

"We could chip in some savings."

"What?"

They had amassed an assortment of mutual funds totaling over three hundred thousand dollars, the fruits of a fruitless marriage. But she would sooner amputate a limb than touch the principal.

"Silly, I guess." He stood up. "Anyway, I'd be miserable in Manhattan after fifteen minutes. Too…" He tried to finish the sentence—too crowded, too noisy, too anonymous—but everything he came up with felt more like a benefit than a drawback. "Too expensive," he finally managed. He kissed her forehead and left.

He took the photograph of Barry Amiel from his jacket pocket and studied it as he drove into town, trying to find in that darkly handsome, slightly rakish face a hint of what would drive a woman and child away in the middle of the night. Or was it in Gwen's face that he should be searching? Perhaps the entire separation had been a charade, Act One of a drama still being played two hundred miles north of 222 West 83rd Street.

He parked in front of the Mecca. The day was warm and dry; the early morning light was sharp, almost brittle as it glinted off the elms lining Main Street, the big clock in front of the bank, the diner's polished aluminum exterior.

He sat at the counter. A middle-aged woman, her jaundice-colored hair plumped in black netting, served him coffee. Gwen's replacement, he suddenly realized. And Mike Contaldi's loss.

As if to confirm this, Contaldi appeared from the storage room behind the counter wearing a mean grimace that lingered despite the smile he managed for Sohegan's police chief.

"Everything okay?" Contaldi slid down the sugar, salt, and pepper containers, parking them directly in front of Dwight. "You need a refill?"

Contaldi still acted as if it were fifteen years earlier, when Dwight had busted him for possession of marijuana. One ounce, in Contaldi's car; he'd wet his pants when Dwight asked him to open the glove compartment. Lucky for him Dwight was an old high school buddy of his father's. Charges had been dropped, but Mike Contaldi always looked at Dwight as if he thought he was about to be frisked. And Dwight never did or said anything to put the jerk at ease.

"You remember Gwen Amiel, used to work here?" Dwight asked.

"Sure I do."

"She ever have any visitors?"

"That dyke from the bank came by a lot."

"You mean Sheila Stewart," he said. "Vice president of the bank."

"Yeah, her." Contaldi rearranged the salt and pepper.

"No one else?"

"Sometimes her son, with his baby-sitters. The Pearsons, an old couple, live out on the Muttontown Road. How come you're interested in Gwen Amiel?" He leaned on the counter, gave Dwight a man-to-man wink. Dwight shimmied as far back on the stool as he could without falling on his ass. "If you don't mind my asking."

"I'll take that refill," Dwight said.

Contaldi frowned as he grabbed the cup and saucer. When he returned a few moments later Dwight showed him the photograph.

"Ever see any of these guys around?"

Contaldi picked up the photo and studied it, shaking his head.

"Like I said, the only visitor she had was that...was Sheila Stewart from the bank. I never could figure what Gwen was doing here in Sohegan in the first place. She acted like she was too good to wipe tables or—"

"She never met with any of these men?"

Contaldi leaned on the counter again, smiled; his breath was stale and suety, as if he'd just slurped down the grease he was always scraping off his blackened grill.

"I don't think Gwen was into men, you know what I'm saying?"

"You're saying she turned you down."

Contaldi straightened up. "What's that supposed to—"

"So you never saw any of these men." He started to pocket the photo.

"I didn't say that." Dwight put the picture back on the counter. "I *said* none of them ever visited Gwen Amiel while she was working here. That's what you asked me."

"But…"

"But this guy…" He poked a stocky finger at Barry Amiel. "… This guy came in for lunch some time after she quit."

"You're sure?"

"We don't get many strangers. I served him the daily special, lasagna."

Dwight had tasted Contaldi's lasagna, just once, and felt a surge of sympathy for Barry Amiel. "When was that?"

"Had to be a Monday. Monday's Italian day."

"Ah…" Priscilla Lawrence had been killed on Italian day. "Which Monday, do you recall?"

"A while ago." Contaldi shrugged.

Dwight tapped his right foot to keep from strangling him. "But *after* Gwen left."

"I told you that already."

Tap, tap, tap. "Gwen left in late May…Could that man in the picture have visited this place in mid-June, say?"

"Sounds right."

"Could it have been the day Priscilla Lawrence was killed?"

His face brightened. "Shit, I don't know. I mean, yeah, it could have been. But, you know, he only stayed, what, twenty minutes? Who can remember that far back?"

Dwight signaled for the yellow-haired waitress and showed her the photo when she joined them.

"That's the guy was here the day that lady got killed," she said.

Contaldi scowled at her superior memory.

"You're sure about that?" Dwight asked.

"Hey, most of the guys come in here look like their parents were brother and sister, you know what I'm saying? You're just happy they got only one head." She gazed dreamily at the photograph. "This guy I didn't forget."

"Was he alone?"

She nodded. "Didn't say nothing, though. Seemed kind of moody." She shrugged. "You want more coffee?"

He shook his head, got up from the stool, and left a dollar bill on the counter before leaving. He hurried to his car, eager to get back to the office and call Don Reeves.

Barry Amiel had been in Sohegan the day of the murder, and hadn't been seen anywhere since.

Frankie Spivak saw the body first. His house was just a mile down Pleasant Ridge Road, so he knew every path leading to the Devil's Ravine. He was only nine, but he'd been swimming at the ravine for as long as he could remember. Richie and Jason were a few yards behind him. The day was cloudy and not particularly hot, especially under the trees. Maybe they wouldn't bother swimming—that wasn't the reason they came here, anyway, at least not lately. The Devil's Ravine was where that lady was killed. The coolest place in Sohegan. Every kid in town begged his parents to take him to the ravine. But Frankie lived closest. He didn't have to ask anyone for a ride, or even permission.

He stopped short when he saw the legs, feet flopped to the side. Richie bumped right into him.

"Look!" Frankie pointed to the spot ten yards down the hill, about halfway to the river.

"What is it?" Richie asked.

Jason stood behind them, breathing hard. "A body," he whispered.

Duh. Frankie squinted to get a better look. Then all three stared for a while, nobody moving a muscle. Finally, Jason poked Richie's back. "Go closer."

"Me? Why not you?"

"Cause you...you're the oldest."

"Am not," Richie said. "Frankie's older."

Frankie inched forward, but his footsteps rustled the leaves and twigs on the ground. What if someone heard? He stopped.

"What if someone's here?" he whispered. "Someone else."

All three looked around, then back at the body. They couldn't see the head, just the tan pants and the tail of a white shirt.

"Maybe it's just someone sleeping," Frankie said. He picked up a twig and threw it at the body. It landed a foot short. He threw another stick. This one hit the pants above the knee. The body didn't move.

Jason tossed a handful of pebbles. He bent down to get some more stones, but Frankie pulled on his collar.

"It's not moving," he said. "Okay?"

Jason nodded. "You think we should call the police?"

"Or we could go closer," Richie said. "Find out who it is."

"Go ahead," Jason said.

"Me! Why not you?"

"You brought it up, that's why."

"Quit arguing, okay?" Frankie said. "We stick together, okay? We all three take a closer look, or else we call the police. Together, all three of us at once."

A brief hesitation, then the three boys turned and scrambled back up the hill to the road.

CHAPTER 28

Gwen followed Dwight Hawkins down the path to the Devil's Ravine. He'd told her what to expect, and she figured she could handle it, though she'd sworn never to return to the place. Then she spotted the khaki trousers...the white oxford shirt...the green ski hat, red mittens, leather boots. She leaned against a tree, breathing hard.

"You okay?" Hawkins asked.

"They're all...all my things," she managed to say.

"Looks like another prank," Hawkins said without much conviction.

"Prank?" Someone had stolen her clothes, then stuffed them with twigs and old leaves to make a kind of scarecrow. She walked closer, her legs unsteady.

"Oh, God."

A stick pierced the shirt where the heart would be. Her heart.

"The county is sending down a crime-scene unit," Hawkins said.

"Crime..."

"This may be a prank, but someone broke into your house and stole these things. Probably that last time, when the doll was vandalized. You didn't mention anything missing, though."

"I never wear these things this time of year."

He nodded and picked up something from the ground next to one of the leather gloves.

"A thistle," he said, holding it by its stem.

She stared at the purple flower, so fragile she thought it might break apart by her breath, like a dandelion seed.

"Priscilla has a garden," she said, "behind the house..."

"Nick Lawrence took us there, after the murder."

"The thistle, the stick through the heart—Priscilla was shot though the heart…"

"The body's in exactly the same place."

"Except it's my body," Gwen said.

Hawkins looked at her. "I'm sorry about this." He turned back to the body. Gwen wiped tears from her face and sprinted up the hill.

It was a long, hellish week. She couldn't shake the vision of that… effigy at the Devil's Ravine, couldn't convince herself that it was all just a stupid prank. Someone was warning her, threatening her— what other explanation could there be?

Dwight Hawkins and his men were keeping a close eye on her house, and he'd told her not to deviate from her usual routine. Penaquoit was gated, after all; she was safe at work, and she'd be watched at home.

Not that she *felt* safe at Penaquoit. During those rare moments when she managed to forget the effigy, she found herself fixating on the Kiss, as she'd come to think of the incident in the secret garden. Scared and alone, she felt her resistance to Nick beginning to weaken.

All that long week at Penaquoit, she felt protected from her own instincts only when Nick was somewhere else. He spent most of the day at the piano; as long as she heard him practicing, and stayed clear of the living room, she was safe.

The only meaningful interaction between them was when she took Tess from him in the morning, and handed her back in the evening. He maintained a maddening serenity during these brief encounters, as if the Kiss had never occurred.

Then, around one o'clock Friday afternoon, with Tess's laundry done, her room cleaned, and Tess herself just embarked on her second nap, Gwen decided to get some fresh air. She practically bumped into him as she was leaving through the pantry door.

"I was coming to look for you," he said jauntily, as if she were a houseguest and not an employee. He was wearing only swim trunks: his hair and chest were wet, and he smelled of chlorine.

"Here I am," she said, then gritted her teeth to keep from cringing. Cleverness always deserted her in the face of his maddening self-composure.

"Were you headed for Priscilla's garden by any chance?"

She shook her head, irritated at the casual mention of the place. She'd never go back to the secret garden; there was something wrong about it, something unnatural, its lush beauty plundered from the surrounding countryside.

"I heard about what happened at the ravine," he said. "People can be very cruel."

"Someone seems to think...someone thinks I killed your wife."

"That's ridiculous."

"Do you think the thistle was from the garden here?"

"No one even knows about the garden," he said. "And no one other than the family and the Piacevics have access to the estate. Those plants could come from any garden."

"Why, though? Why the thistle?"

His expression darkened, and he waited a moment before answering. "I don't know."

She watched a droplet of pool water trickle down his right arm.

"How's Tess?" he asked. "Does she seem all right to you? What I mean is, do you think she's...Is she adapting to the loss of her mother?"

The loss of her mother. Priscilla had been relegated to *her* mother, her *lost* mother. Still, his concern for Tess sounded sincere, and his stammering was unexpected and touching.

"I think she's doing fine," she said. "Sometimes she'll ask for... for her mama..."

"I know..." He ran all ten fingers through his hair, then flicked the water from his hands. "Sometimes I wonder...if I had been the one to go, would Tess have taken it so well?"

"I think in some ways your relationship with Tess was..." *Be kind; the poor lost mother's been dead barely a month.* "Your relationship with Tess was more hands-on." He looked pleased by this, but she cut him off before he said something self-congratulatory. "Kids this age adapt really well. It's scary, in a way."

"Why scary?"

"Because if you lost a child, it would destroy you. But if your child lost you…well, he'd keep right on growing—learning to talk, learning to read, learning to love someone else. It doesn't seem fair, somehow."

He locked his hands behind his head as he continued to look right at her. He was either completely unself-conscious or an accomplished poser. She tried to avoid staring at him, but his shoulders and chest and arms seemed to obstruct every possible line of vision.

"Does your boy miss his father?" he asked.

"No."

"Are they in touch?"

"No."

"But he must have some feelings regarding—"

"He doesn't, okay?"

She headed back into the house. She heard him follow.

"Gwen…"

She stopped halfway across the pantry. He was a few feet away. Once again he seemed to occupy her entire scope of vision. "I hear Tess," she said.

"No, you don't." He placed a hand on her upper arm and slid it down to her wrist.

She stared at him, heard his breathing, smelled the chlorine on his skin.

He's trouble and you're the baby-sitter.

"Don't make me have to leave Penaquoit," she said. "Tess has been through enough."

"Leave?"

She nodded and stepped back. His hand fell to his side.

"Maybe it's being here, in my house," he said, speaking quickly. "As my employee." He sounded more curious than plaintive, as if he was genuinely fascinated, in a rather clinical way, by her reluctance. Was he so unaccustomed to being turned down? Yet he wanted her. She felt his desire in the warmth his hand had left on her arm.

"Maybe if we went somewhere else," he was saying, "just the two of us. Mrs. Piacevic could watch—"

"Please?" Her voice splintered on the word. She turned and left the room.

Later, as Gwen was changing Tess, Rosa Piacevic made a rare appearance in the nursery.

"How is my *zamer* this day?" She peered closely at Tess's face.

"She's fine. Why?"

"No reason." Rosa started to leave, then stopped and turned. "She waked up last night, from all the screaming. Mr. Lawrence called me to come be with her. She couldn't fall back to sleep. And why should she sleep, the father red and sweated like that, and the grandfather shouting like a crazy man?"

Rosa crossed to the changing table and straightened one of the socks Gwen had just struggled to put on Tess.

"What were they arguing about?" Gwen asked.

"I heared only the end," Rosa said as she put on Tess's shoes. "Mr. Cunningham has a detective. This detective, he find out something."

"About Mr. Lawrence?"

Rosa nodded and picked up Tess's silver hairbrush.

"Mr. Nick, before coming to this place, had trouble with the police in New York City."

"What kind of trouble?"

"This I didn't hear too good. Maybe drugs was involved. Medicines, you know? I heared Mr. Cunningham mention a doctor, but I didn't get his name."

She brushed Tess's short hair with quick, gentle strokes.

"Was he arrested?"

"I don't think so. But Mr. Cunningham, he say that if Mr. Nick ever make trouble, if he ever take Tess away from here, he will take him to court."

Rosa stepped back to appraise Tess's coif, made a few more quick dabs with the brush, then handed her to Gwen with a look of deep regret.

"She fall asleep on my shoulder in that chair," Rosa said, nodding toward the rocker in the corner. "But after what I heared, such anger, I didn't sleep all night, not for one minute. They hate each other, those two. This is no place for a child." She looked despairingly at Tess, shook her head, and left the room.

Jimmy had been begging for weeks to sleep over at his friend Andrew Hillman's house. Gwen had made excuse after excuse. What if he woke up in the middle of the night, homesick? What if he had a bed-wetting accident (an admittedly rare event)? The truth was, she didn't want to spend the night in the house by herself. Jimmy was the reason she'd moved to Sohegan, Jimmy was the reason she got up and went to work five mornings a week, Jimmy's was the sleeping face she kissed every night before retiring to her own room. And she was frightened of being alone, with everything that was going on—not that she'd ever mention this to him.

On Saturday, she ran out of excuses. And patience.

"Maybe in a few weeks," she told Jimmy.

"No, tonight."

"We'll discuss it in a few weeks. That's final."

His eyes narrowed and darkened. Barry's eyes. "I hate you!" he said as he ran from the kitchen. "*I hate you!*"

She followed him up the stairs. "No, you don't," she said.

"Yes, I do!" He slammed the door to his room.

She knocked twice and opened it. "Let's discuss this calmly, okay?"

• • •

Martha Hillman met her at the front door of her split-level. "Hello," she said without smiling as Jimmy ran past her into the house. She did not invite Gwen in.

Gwen resolved to remain cordial for Jimmy's sake.

"Thanks so much for having him." She glanced behind Martha Hillman, looking for Jimmy. "I just want to say good-bye."

"That's all right," she said, as if absolving Gwen from a chore. She made no effort to unblock the doorway.

"What time should I pick him up tomorrow?"

"We have church at eleven," Martha Hillman said, a touch reprovingly, Gwen thought.

"I'll come by before then."

Martha Hillman nodded and shut the door.

Driving home, she reflected on her status as a Sohegan pariah. Martha Hillman and her helmet-haired ilk didn't bother her, but she did worry about Jimmy sometimes. Not only was his mother's one local friend the town lesbian, but Gwen had been involved in the most sensational crime ever to hit town. She'd been jumpy ever since their house was broken into, and a virtual basket case since the Devil's Ravine incident. It seemed inevitable that Jimmy feel the heat.

At least he'd made one good friend in Sohegan. But he'd been so insistent about sleeping over at Andrew's. Was he really that desperate to get away from his own house, from her?

She got home, made a pot of coffee, and considered calling Sheila. No, she'd tough it out on her own, get a foretaste of life without Jimmy, a kind of inoculation against future separations. She drank the last of the coffee at four o'clock and switched to scotch.

Five hours and several drinks later, the doorbell rang. Gwen grabbed the portable phone, clicked on the dial tone, prepared to dial 911, and pushed aside the curtain on the narrow window next to the front door. Nick Lawrence, hands clasped in front of him, idly surveyed the front of her house. She unlocked the door and opened it.

"Are you on the phone?" he said.

She clicked it off and placed it on the hall table.

"May I come in?" His tone and expression implied that her response was not in doubt, and for a moment she was tempted to deny him entry, just to see what disappointment would look like on that face.

But she let him in and closed the door, wondering for a second if his showing up on the one night she was alone was a coincidence. He walked directly into the living room, the only part of the house with a light on. Wearing a white shirt, white pants, and tan loafers, he looked elegant in a completely uncontrived way; his clothes always seemed to work *for* him, never the reverse. Glancing in the hallway mirror, she frowned at her black tank top, briefly considered covering up with a sweater, and joined him in the living room.

"There's something I want you to hear," he said. "Where is your stereo?"

She pointed to the system that had come with the house, an old receiver, tape deck, and two large speakers at either end of the room.

"Perfect. I brought a tape and a CD."

He crouched before the stereo, turned on the receiver, and inserted the tape.

"Do you want something to drink?" she said.

"No, no," he answered quickly, and she realized that she'd never seen him have so much as a beer. It would be interesting to see the effect of alcohol on his impervious self-possession.

He turned to face her, and a tiny alarm tripped inside her, for she'd never seen him look that way, his poise still evident, but laced with anxiety, as if much depended on what happened next.

He crossed the room and switched off the lamp. The only illumination came from the moon, which glowed warmly through the front window.

"Please, sit," he said, gesturing toward the sofa. *Her* sofa.

She felt irritated at being dispossessed in her own house. And something else, a scary pleasure at ceding control. She sat at the end of the sofa and watched him flick on the tape player. Then he sat on the couch, just a couple of inches from her.

"Nick, I don't—"

He put a finger to her lips. "Just listen," he whispered. "Beethoven, Fourth Piano Concerto. A new recording, the Vienna Philharmonic."

Music filled the darkened room, an orchestra first, then the solo piano.

She turned to him, wondering why he hadn't mentioned the pianist. He was facing forward, eyes fixed.

"To start so…gently," he whispered, "like the entrance to a dream."

She might have laughed if he weren't dead serious, and if the music weren't in fact hypnotic. Suddenly the room exploded as a full orchestra weighed in on a series of thunderous chords. His lips curled into a half smile as the piano returned with a lovely ballad.

So many questions: Why had he come? Why this piece? What next? But his rapt expression invited no inquiries. He seemed immersed in the music, every sense shut down except hearing. She settled into the sofa, hands clasped safely on her lap, and focused on the music.

Which wasn't difficult—it really was a magnificent piece, light, almost delirious, yet still quite romantic. Before Jimmy was born she'd often listened to classical music, but she'd rarely strayed much beyond Mozart's symphonies and violin concertos, and anything by Bach. Beethoven and the other romantics had always seemed so much more demanding, too insistent, pulling her away from books, chores, bill paying.

"The most romantic piece of music ever written," he said. "First, this delirious ode to love, then the second movement, which is about to start—almost unbearably melancholy. And in the third, the rondo, a wedding march!" He smiled and shook his head. "Romantic love in a nutshell: joy, loss, recovery."

A brief pause in the music. He placed a hand on her lap. *You bastard*, she wanted to say, *you knew how frightened I've been. You set this whole scene up, you composed it.*

The second movement was slow and unexpectedly somber. She soon forgot the hand on her lap.

"Can you hear the sense of loss?" he whispered. "The piano"—he raised his right hand and made a spiraling gesture—"it swirls across the air, never touching earth."

The mood in the third movement brightened, and some bit of her evaporated in response, that part of her mind that stood outside looking in, weighing consequences, assessing outcomes. He put his arm around her shoulder and gently pulled her to him. "You have to really attack this movement," he said softly but with great fervor. *"Listen!"*

She tried, but felt only the weight of his arm on her shoulders, the warmth of his leg pressing against hers, the tensing of his biceps as the piano and orchestra charged to the finale.

Then silence. It seemed to suck the air from the room, precluding speech. She felt him all around her, and she was certain that if she moved one muscle he'd engulf her and she'd be…gone. So she sat there, frozen, hardly daring to breathe, and waited for her life to change, as she knew it would.

And then he took a deep, sharp breath and placed his free hand under her knees, his other hand still behind her back, and stood up, lifting her. Then he was kissing her, covering her mouth with his lips. And then he carried her upstairs, moving quickly.

CHAPTER 29

Gwen awoke early the next morning. Sunlight warmed her face, heightening her sense of panic. She'd lost her mind, been seduced, broken every promise she'd ever made to herself. She felt betrayed and traitorous. Victim and victimizer.

Nick slept peacefully on his stomach, arms flung across the double bed, the sheets bunched around his lower back. Even in sleep he looked self-possessed, invulnerable. She felt an escalating resentment and sat up, wishing her robe wasn't all the way across the room, hanging behind the door. Last night she'd been scared, lonely—and why not, given what she'd been through? He'd taken advantage of that.

As she stood he grabbed her waist and pulled her back down.

"You need to learn how to ask," she said.

"And you have a pretty good sexual harassment case." His voice was gravelly with sleep. "'Employer forces his way into employee's house…'"

"Violates her."

"Several times," he said. "An excellent case, but my cupboard's bare, I'm afraid."

She sighed theatrically. "Just my luck to be harassed by a pauper."

He pulled her on top of him, wrapped his arms tightly around her back, and began humming, his lips so close to her head that she felt his warm breath vibrating on her skin. She recognized the Lebewohl Sonata.

"More Beethoven," she said. "Does he always work for you?"

As he continued to hum the slow, sonorous melody, she became aware of his arousal, and then her own. But as his hands began ranging up and down her back, *playing* her, for God's sake, she felt rising indignation. *What about Jimmy? For all you know he's waking up in the next room. He could burst in here any minute, wanting breakfast.*

Or did you know he wasn't here?

She pushed off him and sat on the edge of the bed.

"What's the matter?" He sounded more curious than alarmed.

"I get the feeling you're…just taking me, like I was this available product on a shelf."

"That's not how I think of you at—"

"I have a son, Nick. Did you ever consider what he might think, finding you in my bed?"

"I'll leave, then, before he wakes up."

"He's not here," she said quietly.

"Then…"

"But you never even bothered to ask."

Slowly he traced his fingers along her spine. "I waited until I thought he'd be asleep. I *was* thinking of him, Gwen."

She crossed her arms, covering her breasts, still not facing him. If only the goddamn robe weren't all the way across the room.

"Tell me about Jimmy," he said. "Tell me why you ran from New York."

"That's two different issues."

"I don't think so."

She snapped her head around. "But—"

"You picked up and left your entire life behind. Jimmy's the only person you'd do that for."

His eyes glimmered in the morning light.

"Why do you want to know? Why now?"

"Because I need to feel close to you," he said. "And because I have basically laid bare my entire soul, and you've kept yours locked inside."

She looked away as his fingers played up and down her spine. If only men knew how incredibly seductive a few intimate questions could be, it would put every florist on the planet out of business. Just then she'd do anything for him, at least in theory. But she didn't want to tell him about Jimmy.

"Maybe someday," she said.

His fingers stopped halfway down her back. "You had to rescue him. He was in danger."

She could only nod at his intuition.

"He was in danger from your husband."

Yes.

"And you saved him."

Yes.

"What kind of danger, Gwen? What was your husband doing to him?"

And then she told him, the words gushing from her like a long-held breath.

It was an ordinary Wednesday. Since Barry's contracting work had dried up, a direct result of his drinking, she'd had no choice but to fire the baby-sitter and let Barry take over. So that Wednesday, like every other weekday, he'd picked up Jimmy at school, brought him home, and watched him until six, when Gwen closed up the shop two blocks from the apartment and rushed home, praying that Barry had managed to hold off drinking until she got there.

And, mostly, he had. Occasionally she'd catch him stumbling or slurring, but never severely enough to put Jimmy at risk. What choice had she had?

"Jimmy was past the age when he could be dropped or...I don't know, shaken." Nick gave her the reassuring nod she needed before continuing.

• • •

She'd known, of course, that the situation was untenable. But with Barry not working she couldn't afford even a part-time sitter, and the store didn't throw off enough cash to pay someone to run it for her. Letting Jimmy hang around with her in the afternoons was hazardous to him as well as the antiques. Next fall, she had promised herself, she'd find an after-school program for Jimmy. Or perhaps Barry wouldn't be drinking by then. Or maybe she'd win the lottery.

That Wednesday she came home to find Jimmy watching some cheesy cartoon on television. Barry fled, as usual, moments after she got in. She flicked off the TV and dragged Jimmy into the kitchen to keep her company while she made dinner. Where Barry went when he left them was a mystery she had no interest in solving. He gambled, she knew that much; by Tuesday or Wednesday he'd usually blown the meager amount of money she'd given him for household expenses.

Jimmy repelled all conversational forays that day, but that wasn't atypical of five-year-olds. He was fidgety but uncomplaining as he watched her prepare a pasta-and-salad dinner for the two of them. When he accidentally knocked over the bottle of salad dressing she'd placed next to him on the counter, she frowned but managed not to scold him. He apologized, haltingly at first, and then in an increasingly frantic, semicoherent monologue.

"I'm sorry, Mommy. I mean it, I didn't see it I wasn't looking it just fell I don't know how I'm sorry I'm sorry honest I'm very very sorry."

There just didn't seem to be a way to reassure him that breaking a bottle of salad dressing wasn't a capital offense. She cleaned up the mess, wondering what in the world she had ever done to him to make him react so violently.

"Pretty stupid, right? What had *I* ever done?" Nick smiled sympathetically as he gently caressed her arm.

• • •

Jimmy's overreaction was still very much on her mind a minute later as she took out a bottle of red wine vinegar from a cabinet to prepare a homemade dressing.

"No, Mommy, no!" He shimmied off the counter, landing on all fours. "I didn't mean it. I didn't mean to break it."

She stood in the center of the kitchen, holding the vinegar, as her son became someone she'd never met before, someone blubbering, trembling, panic-stricken.

"Jimbo, what's the matter?" When she crouched next to him he scrambled to his feet and ran from the room. A moment later his bedroom door slammed. She knocked gently before opening it. He was curled up on his bed, under the covers, his face pressed into Mr. Meeko, his tattered panda bear.

"Talk to me, Jimmy, tell me what's wrong."

His tear-swollen eyes peered at her from behind the panda. She started to speak, then saw something in those eyes. Fear is what she saw; not a generalized anxiety but a specific, immediate terror. She'd never done anything to provoke that fear—the fear in those eyes could never, ever come from her. Someone else, then, someone equally close…

"Did Daddy punish you today?" she asked quietly, sitting on the edge of his bed.

He shook his head, still staring at her.

"But he *has* punished you, in the past, right Jimmy?"

He waited a few moments, then moved the panda away from his mouth.

"Only when I'm bad," he said in a faint, reedy voice, and her heart broke.

"Bad? When…when are you ever bad?" The panda went back in front of his mouth. "What…do you mean, bad, Jimmy?"

"When I disturb him," he said, moving the panda a few inches from his mouth. "Like, if he's sleeping? And I drop something? Or if I don't hang up my coat? Or if I forget to clean up something?"

• • •

"Barry always told me, in our rare conversations, what a perfect angel Jimmy was. 'I don't know what the hell you're complaining about,' he'd say, 'the kid never acts up for me.'"

"And…and what does he do when…when these things happen?" she asked Jimmy.

He bit into the panda, shaking his head.

"Did Daddy tell you not to tell me?" A long pause, then a very tentative nod. "But you *can* tell me, Jimbo. I want you to."

He shook his head and kept on shaking it as she pleaded with him to tell her how he'd been punished.

"Jimmy, please, I have to know." She was trembling, too, now, trying to keep it together.

"Promise you won't…" His voice trailed off.

"Won't what?"

He glanced down at the bedspread and whispered something.

"Promise I won't what?" she said.

"Leave us?"

She reached across the bed and grabbed him before her tears erupted, holding him close until she could talk.

"I'll never, ever, ever leave you, Jimmy. Is that what he said, that I'd leave you if you told me what he did to you?"

He nodded into her chest.

"It was wrong for him to say that." She gently released him onto his pillow. "How did he punish you, Jimmy?"

He stared at his lap as he answered in a high, strained voice.

"He made me drink things."

• • •

Nick moaned and touched her shoulder, but she shrugged him off.

"The alcoholic who makes his son drink things…it's so sick it's almost perfect."

Gwen had her back to Nick, and she was glad of that, because she didn't want to see his reaction to the chill in her voice, the absence of emotion. As she told the story for the first time to anyone, she had the sense that she was narrating someone else's life, the sordid biography of some stupid, insensitive, self-absorbed woman who woke up one day to realize that she'd failed to fulfill the only meaningful prerequisite that life had presented thus far: taking care of her child.

"The vinegar triggered it," she said, "when I went to replace the salad dressing. Barry had started with vinegar, apparently, made Jimmy swallow it if he was 'bad.' Vinegar, pepper sauce…"

"Oh, God," Nick said, and rolled onto his back.

"He was clever, Barry was. If he'd slapped him, like he hit me, there would have been bruises, scars. With this technique, there was some vomiting—I used to worry about Jimmy having so many stomach viruses—but nothing that made me think he was being"— she waited until her lips could form the word—"tortured."

The first breeze of the morning drifted in through an open window. She shivered but didn't miss her robe now, wanting nothing touching her just yet.

She tried to reassure Jimmy that evening—she'd never leave, ever. But he seemed inconsolable.

"Daddy said…" He held the panda to his face.

"What did he say?"

"He said…he said he'd let the men hurt me if I told you anything."

"What men?"

Jimmy shrugged.

"What men, Jimmy?"

"Daddy owes them money. Once they took me, when he wasn't looking."

"They…" She forced the words out, one by one. "They took you where?"

"Some man's apartment. Then they called Daddy, and he came and got me."

"Did they hurt you, Jimmy?" Word by word, voice calm, even.

He shook his head. "I watched TV for a while. They told Daddy they would keep me next time if he didn't give them money. That was a couple of days ago. When we got home…"

"Tell me, Jimmy. Nothing can hurt you now."

"He made me drink Bosco. He said if I told you what happened he'd keep on giving me more Bosco."

"Bosco?" She almost gasped with relief. "Chocolate sauce? I didn't know we had any."

"No," he said, "the red stuff that burns your mouth."

"Oh," she said, "you must mean…"

Tabasco—even now she couldn't say it.

"And so we left," she said.

"Why didn't you throw him out, take him to court?"

"He wouldn't leave. I had no money for a lawyer. He'd drained every cent we had. Anyway, it was his word against Jimmy's, and when he's sober he can be incredibly convincing. He wouldn't have gotten custody, I knew that. But I couldn't take the chance that he'd get to see Jimmy even every other weekend. And what about those men Barry owed money to? I couldn't wait around to find out who they were. I had to protect my son."

She began liquidating the shop the next day, selling the furniture and bric-a-brac to other dealers for quick cash, taking a loss on most pieces. The apartment was worth far less than they'd paid for it, less than their mortgage, in fact. Even if she managed to sell it, the bank would demand repayment of the full value of the mortgage. She hadn't dared hire a van to move their things. For starters, she had no idea where they would end up. And what if someone on the co-op board saw her moving out, especially that bitch Cora Robinson, who always had her nose in everyone else's business? If the board realized she was dumping her unit they might try to stop her.

So she left at night, just she and Jimmy, two big suitcases and five thousand dollars in the dented and rusted Honda. She drove until she felt safely away from Barry, pulled off the New York State Thruway, and kept driving until she spotted the Fishs Corner Motel.

"You've had no contact with anyone from before?"

She shook her head. "My parents are dead. My brothers and I didn't speak much even before we moved. Anyway, I was afraid to leave a trail for those men. I didn't want anyone from our old life to know where we were." She shrugged. "Now you know."

"Thank you," he said. "For trusting me." He placed a hand on each shoulder, turned her around, and wiped the tears from her face with the tip of his index finger. "When do you have to pick up Jimmy?"

"Eleven."

"That leaves almost four hours." He pulled her down onto the bed and rolled on top of her. "You're safe here," he whispered as he traced his tongue along the interior ridge of her ear. "You're both safe here."

"Don Reeves? It's Dwight Hawkins, Sohegan Police."

"What can I do for you, Dwight?"

"I have some new information on the Lawrence murder. I thought I should let the FBI know as soon as possible."

"Go ahead."

"Gwen Amiel, the baby-sitter? You ever track down that husband of hers, Barry Amiel?"

"Tried. Didn't seem worth the effort after a while. We also checked up on Nick Lawrence. Turns out he was arrested on prescription drug charges a while back. Nothing came of it."

"Well, Nick Lawrence may be clear, but I have news about Barry Amiel."

"Yeah?"

"I showed a photo of him to a guy runs the local greasy spoon. Says he recognizes Amiel."

"But the baby-sitter says they weren't in contact."

"Right. But Barry Amiel was up here in Sohegan, eating Italian food."

"When would that have been, Dwight?"

"June the twelfth."

"The day of the murder."

"The day of the murder."

"I think we'll put some more manpower into finding Barry Amiel."

"Glad to hear it, Don."

"And you keep an eye on Gwen Amiel. Will you do that for us, Dwight?"

"Already happening. You heard about that incident at the ravine?"

"Lot of crazy people up there, Dwight. At least we're not the only people think she was involved. I want to know everything she does, from the moment she gets up to the moment she goes to bed. Is that okay with you, Dwight?"

"My pleasure, Don."

CHAPTER 30

Gwen led two lives that summer, and liked it that way. By day she was the baby-sitter, going about her duties quietly, unobtrusively, under the watchful eyes of the Piacevics and, for a few minutes most mornings, Russell Cunningham. She and Nick rarely interacted at the mansion, and when they did their meetings were if anything more formal than before he'd come to her house that Friday night in mid-July. He'd hand her Tess in the morning with an impassive smile and a polite inquiry as to her well-being. Something along the same lines occurred in the evenings, when she handed Tess back to him.

Her other life began late in the evening, around nine, when Jimmy was safely asleep. Nick would open the unlocked kitchen door and enter her house on cat's feet, sometimes grabbing her from behind, covering her mouth with his hand, then forcing his face into hers, in a game of surprise-the-innocent-housewife that they had both, tacitly, fallen into playing. It horrified her, sometimes, how easily she'd let herself get involved, so soon after Barry. But she'd been frightened and alone at night, wondering who had broken into her house, stolen her things, murdered her in effigy. She felt physically if not emotionally safer at night these days.

She refused to sleep with him at Penaquoit, even when Tess was napping and the Piacevics were in town on an errand. And he never pressed her to. She led two lives that summer, and that was precisely how she liked it.

• • •

On the second Saturday in August, however, several weeks into their affair, the two lives merged for a few awkward hours. She and Jimmy had no particular plans, and the day, sunny but unusually cool, seemed to call for a special activity. Nick's arrival at ten o'clock, holding Tess, saved them from having to find one.

"Anyone for fishing?" he said, loud enough for Jimmy to hear. Before she could protest, Jimmy came bounding into the front hallway.

"Yeah, fishing!"

Nick drove them in the green Range Rover, Gwen beside him in the front seat, Tess and Jimmy in the back.

"Mett Piacevic told me about this fishing hole," he said as he drove along a narrow road that snaked around a series of low hills. "'I find good hole, plenty good fishes.'"

She laughed at his perfect Albanian growl. He was brilliant at voices and accents—Russell Cunningham, Valerie Goodwin, Mett Piacevic. In back, Jimmy was playing peekaboo with a squealing Tess.

After twenty minutes he turned onto a dirt road and drove a very bumpy half mile to the end, where they got out of the car. They followed a well-beaten path that ended at a pond enclosed by dense, cool woods. In a small clearing he spread a blanket for Tess, who was still in her car seat. Then he helped Jimmy bait a hook with a worm.

"I never pictured you as a fisherman," Gwen said.

"I've done this once before, maybe twice. It's Piacevic's rod. Actually, the whole process makes me a bit queasy."

Then what were they doing there, the four of them? she wanted to ask.

He tried to show Jimmy how to cast, but bungled the first few attempts, the hook and sinker landing just a foot or so from the rocky edge of the pond.

"Let me," she said, and took the rod from him. "It's all in the wrist." She reeled in the line, drew back the rod, and executed a perfect cast, the hook and sinker landing with a dull plop in the center of the pond. She reeled it back in, repeated the demonstration, then let Jimmy have a try. After a few attempts he managed to get the line ten yards or so from shore.

"Now for the fun part," Nick said. "Waiting."

She sat on the blanket. Tess had fallen asleep in her car seat. Nick sat next to her and put his arm around her shoulder.

"Don't," she said.

He hesitated a moment before pulling away.

"You're treating our relationship like it's wrong," he said. "I'm not married, you're separated, we are both consenting adults."

"Jimmy's been through so much. He doesn't need to deal with this."

"But—"

"Not yet, anyway." She shot him a quick smile, then turned back to Jimmy, who was staring intently at the point where his line entered the pond.

"Dwight Hawkins, the police chief, came by a while ago," Nick said. "He showed me a picture of your husband."

"*What?*"

"It looked like some sort of Christmas party. There were three men in the photograph. Barry was on the right."

The building party, in the lobby of 222, eight months ago. Another life. Barry had gotten plastered that night, and when she'd gently suggested, later, that he try in the future to maintain some decorum in front of their neighbors, he'd shoved her against the refrigerator. The handle had left a bruise on her lower back.

"Did Hawkins say why he asked you to look at Barry's photo?"

"He wanted to know if I'd seen him around, before the kidnapping. I told him I hadn't."

"But Barry doesn't know we're anywhere near here."

She stood up and walked to the edge of the pond, a few yards from Jimmy. No cause for alarm: the police didn't say Barry had actually been to Sohegan; they'd only showed his picture around. She sighed. The pond smelled gassy and sour.

Where had Hawkins gotten the photo? And why the hell were the police interested in Barry of all people? Did they really imagine he had been mixed up in the kidnapping? True, someone had left Tess at her house that day, but Barry didn't know where they lived; he couldn't have been involved.

And yet, just knowing about his photograph being shown around town was enough to spoil the day. The pond felt cramped now, the woods ominously dark.

"I got a bite!"

She stared into the black center of the pond.

"Mom, look! *Mom!*"

She turned and saw a small, silver fish wriggling on the end of his line. He finished reeling it in, then let it flop onto the rocks, the hook still in its mouth.

"Well, take it off!" she said.

"I don't know how." Jimmy was gazing at his catch with wide-eyed astonishment.

She turned to Nick, standing just behind him, who shrugged.

"For God's sake." She grabbed the fish, yanked the hook from its mouth, and tossed it back into the pond. It lolled stupidly near the edge for a few moments. She pelted it with a handful of pebbles and it swam away.

"Why'd you do that?" Jimmy said, near tears. "Why'd you throw it back?"

"It was too small to eat," she said.

"But I caught it."

"What were you planning to do with it, put it on a plaque?"

Nick and Jimmy stared at her, both slack-jawed. "It wasn't a keeper, okay?" Still they stared—wasn't she allowed a bad mood once in a while? "Let's get the hell out of here."

She headed back to the car.

The FBI chopper angled down toward a large parking lot in the Astoria section of Queens, not far from Kennedy Airport. Don Reeves gazed out the small Plexiglas window as the vast, inhospitable landscape of Queens grew closer, and uglier. Block after block of semidetached houses were arranged on an infinite grid of narrow streets crossed by wider avenues. Albany, which he'd left just twenty-five minutes ago, seemed a world away. And thank God for that.

The bureau's local liaison ran up to the helicopter the moment it hit ground. Squat, fifties, in regulation dark suit and tie, never mind that it was Saturday afternoon.

"Stan McGee," he shouted over the noise of the rotors. "This way."

The chopper made a ludicrous Apache of McGee's comb-over as he hurried toward a large, decrepit warehouse across the pitted asphalt.

"I waited before entering, per instructions," McGee said.

The dispatcher in Albany had caught the tip barely two hours ago, then forwarded it to Reeves at home. A woman's voice; Reeves had a microcassette with the call in his pocket, along with a tiny tape player. He'd listened to the recording six times already.

"We couldn't locate the landlord, but I got a warrant. My guys already busted open the lock."

Two men in dark suits, legs akimbo, hands clasped at crotch level, blocked the entrance to the warehouse. Above the door was a faded sign: ASTORIA FURNITURE DEPOT.

"Guy next door"—McGee pointed to a slightly better kept warehouse fifty yards or so away—"he says this place used to be for storing furniture that came by plane from Europe. They brought it here after it cleared customs but before anybody claimed it."

"Antique furniture by any chance?"

"I...he didn't say."

They entered the warehouse through a large sliding aluminum door. The enormous space was dimly lit by the meager sunlight that managed to penetrate a half dozen small, filthy windows. Wide dust motes crisscrossed the air. When his eyes had adjusted to the gloom, Reeves saw that the place was empty, save for a few scattered piles of wood, a couple of opened cartons. A pigeon flew up from somewhere in the dark and circled anxiously overhead before disappearing.

"McGee, you take that area," Reeves said. "Ask your men to search over there. I'll look around here."

He walked slowly, kicking aside rusty nails, bits of cardboard. A dark mass in the corner to the right of the entrance caught his eye. Approaching it, he began to make out a pile of broken-down cartons, discarded chair and table legs, balls of crumpled packing paper.

And an odor that hit him as suddenly as a gust of wind. Dank and musky, it intensified as he neared the corner. He'd smelled rotted corpses before, and certainly what he smelled just then was reminiscent of that unforgettable aroma…but also different, somehow. Sweeter, he thought, vaguely redolent of alcohol and less intense than a recently dead body. If there was a corpse under those cartons, it had been there a long time, long enough even for the putrefaction process to reach its conclusion.

He kicked a carton aside and heard mice or rats scurry into the darkness. Fighting a deep reluctance, he leaned over and began excavating with his hands, tossing collapsed cartons and amputated furniture legs to the side. In less than a minute he'd found him.

He was almost a skeleton, but not quite, for bits of blackened flesh clung to his face. His clothes had been badly torn—by the rats, no doubt—but shreds of cloth adhered to his body in enough places to preserve some semblance of a human form.

The entire warehouse shuddered as a jet roared overhead. Even the corpse seemed to shimmy for the second or two it took the plane to pass over. Reeves reached into his jacket pocket, took out the microcassette recorder, and pressed the play button.

"I understand you're looking for Barry Amiel." A woman's voice, obviously disguised, perhaps with a cloth placed over the receiver. "Try the Astoria Furniture Depot, thirty-three twenty-two Atlantic Boulevard, Queens. He'll be waiting for you." A deep voice, syrupy slow, almost erotic, as if she were leaving instructions for a tryst.

Reeves clicked off the recorder and called the other men. He crouched next to the body—Barry Amiel, had to be—and squinted at a circular break in the blackened skull just over his right temple. An entrance wound.

"Aw, shit!" McGee covered his mouth with one hand, doubtless expecting a worse odor than actually existed.

"Looks like a bullet hole," Reeves said. "He's probably been here a month or more. One of you guys want to roll him over so I can check his wallet?"

The two agents glanced sheepishly at the floor.

"You, then," Reeves said, arbitrarily choosing the shorter one. The agent knelt down and, touching only the clothing bits with his fingertips, managed to lift one side of the corpse off the concrete floor, revealing a ghetto of frantic insect life. Reeves reached into the back pocket, extracted a wallet, and opened it.

"Hundred-dollar bills," he said. "At least a dozen hundred-dollar bills." He searched through the wallet—credit cards bearing Amiel's name, a photo of a little boy, aged about five, Amiel's driver's license, and a small, tattered piece of paper, folded in half. It bore a Brooklyn address, sloppily written in pencil, with *$250/month* scrawled underneath.

"Call the city," he said. "Ask for the crime-scene unit. Tell them to get here fast. And call DC and get the bug man up here while you're at it." The condition of the larvae could help pinpoint the time of death. The FBI's entomologist would earn his keep on this one. "Anyone know this address?"

He handed the paper over his shoulder, unable, somehow, to take his eyes off the body.

He's waiting for you.

"Sure, that's in Park Slope," one of the agents said.

Reeves finally looked away and stood up, brushing off his pants.

"What's this?" He bent over and lifted the flap of a carton.

"Looks like a gun," the shorter agent said.

Reeves flashed his most compassionate smile. "Brilliant." He examined the gun. "I'm no firearms expert, but my instincts tell me this is a Browning semi."

"You want me to get ballistics here, too?"

"Excellent idea," Reeves said as he straightened up. "Now, let's get the hell over to Park Slope."

CHAPTER 31

Fifth Avenue, Brooklyn: bodegas and gas stations and four-story apartment buildings, most run down, a few gentrified. The southern border of the Park Slope section of Brooklyn, Fifth Avenue was an uneasy DMZ between the yuppified neighborhood to the north and the working class—or out-of-working class—neighborhood to the south.

The address in Barry Amiel's wallet led Don Reeves and Stan McGee to a five-story tenement between Garfield and Harrison Streets. They entered the dilapidated grocery on the ground floor, flashed their badges, and showed the photo of Barry Amiel to the heavyset man behind the counter.

"Maybe I see him," he said, rubbing the dense black stubble on his jowls. "Coming into the building, leaving. But not lately."

"Which floor?" Reeves asked.

"You think I own this building? Like I would be working this piece-of-shit business if I owned this place?"

"In other words, you don't know where he lived."

He shook his head dolefully, but called after them as they were leaving.

"You try Dilianna on three."

Dilianna on three answered the door wearing a flowered kerchief around her head, a striped apron, and a wary frown. Two FBI badges did little to improve her disposition, but the photo of Barry Amiel got a reaction.

236

"You know where he is? Son of a bitch owe me two month rent. I spend three days clean up his mess, the filth you wouldn't believe. I had to—"

"He lived with you?" Reeves managed to interject.

"He was my *tenant*." She squared her shoulders and wiped her hands on the apron. Reeves noted her shapely legs and narrow waist, the way her lower lip jutted to a sultry pout. From inside the apartment came the aroma of sautéing garlic and onions. "I have four rooms I rent," she continued. "Barry was here since the spring."

Since Gwen Amiel and the kid left him, Reeves thought.

"You say you cleaned everything?"

"When he no come back after two weeks, I have no choice. Got to keep the rent coming."

"What did you do with his things?"

"I keep them in one box," she said. "Just in case he come back. You want to see?"

She led them through a dark, low-ceilinged room crammed with slipcovered sofas and chairs and one enormous television set. Reeves looked down a long corridor lined with closed doors.

"His room was second on the left," Dilianna Flores said. "My new tenant is sleeping. He drives a taxi at night." She stood at the head of the corridor, hands on hips.

"The box?" he said.

She opened a closet and dragged out a medium-size carton.

"Barry in some trouble?" she asked with what almost sounded like genuine concern as he and McGee crouched next to the carton and began rooting through it.

"You could say that," he said. McGee snorted at the understatement.

"You think I get my rent from him? He owe me two months. I have just one month from security and then there's the—"

"I'd forget about Barry Amiel," Reeves said.

She mumbled something in Spanish that didn't sound like genuine concern and padded off to the kitchen, a large, windowless alcove next to the living room.

They dug through the detritus of Barry Amiel's life. Nothing of much value, though anything worth something had probably been applied to the back rent. Two framed photos of the kid— Jerry, was it, or Jimmy?—some underwear, a few shirts, a couple of mismatched socks, a pair of blue jeans.

"He was *borracho*," Dilianna Flores shouted from the kitchen. "A drinker."

"How long has he been missing?" Reeves asked, joining her by the stove. She was stirring a large, steaming pot.

"Since June fourteen. I remember good because it was Monday, rent day. Only he no pay that Monday, not ever."

June 14 was the day Priscilla Lawrence was killed.

"Before the fourteenth, did you notice anything different about him, any unusual behavior?"

"He didn't hang out here," she said. "He come home to sleep. Sleep it off, you know? When he wake up in the afternoon he leave."

"Here's something," McGee called from the hallway. He entered the kitchen and handed Reeves a piece of white paper. "Woman's handwriting."

Reeves read the note. *Penaquoit. Two mi south of 24 on rite. 6-2-3.*

Directions to the Lawrence property, that much was obvious. The three numbers? He'd have to ask Nick Lawrence. The paper had been folded in several places. Holding it by the edges, he refolded it and placed it in his pocket—their first clear-cut connection between Barry Amiel and Penaquoit.

"I'll take this to our handwriting people," he said. "Get it fingerprinted, too." He glanced around the room. "What about visitors?"

"Did he have visitors?" She closed her eyes and made a face. "Women."

"Do you remember names? Can you give us a description?"

She frowned and shook her head. "I try not to look too closely."

He showed her a photo of Gwen Amiel. "Ever see her?"

"No."

"What about phone calls, did he receive many?"

"One or two," she said with a scowl, as if this were yet another of his shortcomings.

"Make any?"

"Sometimes."

"Did he have his own number?" McGee asked.

"You kidding, right? We have one line." She picked up a portable phone from the counter. "Tenants pay long-distance only."

"Do you have your phone bill from May and June of this year?"

"I pay it on time, first of the month."

"And you don't save the bills?"

She looked at them as if this were a trick question, and slowly shook her head.

"We'll requisition the phone records," Reeves told McGee, then leaned over the pot and inhaled.

"Did Amiel take his meals with you?"

"He drank," she said, "but he didn't eat much."

"His loss," Reeves said, sniffing the pot again.

"You want a taste? Arroz con pollo, I make the best in Brooklyn."

To his surprise he found himself nodding. She got a spoon from a drawer, dipped it into the pot, and handed it to him, pale beans and a thick orangy sauce.

"As delicious as it smells." He placed the spoon in the sink and turned to her. "We may send a crime-scene unit over to dust the room for fingerprints."

"Crime scene? This is no crime scene."

"Just a formality," Reeves said as he and McGee headed for the door.

Gwen heard the faint but unmistakable click of the kitchen door opening. The green neon of the bedside clock read eleven-fifteen; she'd been in bed for half an hour, trying to sleep, trying not to think of Barry's photograph being passed around Sohegan like some sort of chain letter from her past, linking everyone she knew to the one thing she wanted most to forget. Trying to forget that effigy at the ravine, a stake through its heart, a thistle in its gloved hand. Feeling alone, feeling scared, wishing she could work through this on her own.

A dull thud as the kitchen door closed—her heart kicked into high gear. He came every night now, in the Piacevics' Chevy, after Jimmy was asleep, and left before dawn. In the bright August sunshine she often wondered if these night visits were real, and if so, why she let them continue. In the moonlight she ached for him.

He was in the downstairs hallway now, heading from the kitchen to the staircase. She rolled onto her stomach, heart beating against the mattress. Lately she waited for him upstairs, in bed.

Now he was on the staircase, climbing slowly, deliberately, but still teasing creaks and groans from the dry wood steps. Did he know what his slow, deliberate approach did to her?

His footsteps reached the second-floor landing, hesitated for a cruel interval, then continued toward her room. She rolled onto her back just as his dark figure filled the doorway. Her heart felt as if it could rip out of her chest.

He stepped toward her, removing his shirt and tossing it to the floor. A few feet from the bed he kicked off his shoes, then slid off his pants. Pale moonlight silhouetted his naked body.

She threw off the covers and moon glow washed over her own body. He walked to the side of the bed and lowered himself onto her. Already hard, he slid easily inside. Gradually he began to thrust, gently biting her neck, then her ear, then her cheek.

She came almost instantly, just a moment before him. Within minutes he was sleeping, and then she too drifted off.

CHAPTER 32

Dwight Hawkins answered the phone at eight o'clock Sunday morning.

"Hawkins? Don Reeves. I have some news on the baby-sitter angle."

Though Dwight had been up for almost two hours, he would have appreciated an apology for the Sunday morning call at home. He awoke at six on the dot every day of his adult life. On warm mornings like this one he would take his coffee to the back patio and watch the sun rise over the Ondaiga Mountains.

"Her husband's dead," Reeves said. "Shot once in the head. We had an anonymous tip, found in him a furniture warehouse in Queens. An antiques warehouse."

"His wife's business."

"Right. The positive ID came in late last night from forensics here in New York. Time of death is hard to nail down, could be within a day or two of Priscilla Lawrence's murder. He was last seen by his landlady in Brooklyn the day before the kidnapping."

"Anything to implicate Gwen Amiel?"

"We found a Browning twenty-two near the husband. Looks like it was used to kill him. We're waiting for ballistics to tell us if it was the same gun used on Priscilla Lawrence."

"Gwen Amiel had a Browning…"

"Right, we're checking the registration. We'll know by tomorrow if it was hers. Meantime, a favor."

"Shoot."

"I want you to tell her about her husband, observe her reaction. What she was doing the day *after* Priscilla's murder?"

"I was keeping an eye on her then. She didn't leave Sohegan."

"Oh." Reeves paused a few moments. "You sure she didn't leave town?"

"Almost sure. Are we getting close to an arrest?"

"Real close," Reeves said. "Call me when you've talked to her, okay?" He recited a 212 number and hung up.

From where he was parked on Glendale Street, Dwight Hawkins could see the backyard of Gwen Amiel's house. The son was kicking a rubber ball into the air, catching it, kicking it again. Gwen sat just outside the back door, a paperback facedown on her lap.

Dwight had been there for fifteen minutes, fighting a nagging reluctance to get out of his car. He was an old hand at delivering bad news, and he wasn't even sure Barry Amiel's death was "bad news" to Gwen. No, his reluctance had to do with that kid, kicking that ball, as if getting it as high as possible into the air was the most critical thing in the world. And maybe it was, but not for long. Because things were going to get shitty for him real soon. Dwight watched the ball fly up into the blue sky, fall back down into the boy's arms, fly up again. Just then he'd give anything not to be the one to fuck it up for the boy.

He opened the car door, slammed it shut, and saw Gwen Amiel start in the lawn chair and turn his way. He waved as he crossed the neighbor's lawn to her yard.

"Morning," he said, touching the visor of his cap.

"Got any photos of my ex-husband to show me?" she said bitterly.

The sun was behind his back, forcing her to squint at him. He circled her, the better to read her reaction.

"No photos," he said. "Just some news." He checked to make sure the boy was across the lawn, still kicking that ball. "Barry Amiel was found dead yesterday afternoon."

Shock flashed across her eyes, but her composure returned

almost immediately.

"How?"

"He was shot. At a warehouse in Queens. They used to keep foreign antiques there before they were claimed."

"The Astoria Furniture Depot," she said.

Their eyes met and he nodded.

"When?"

"Difficult to say, probably back in June, just after Mrs. Lawrence was killed."

She looked beyond him, eyes unfocused.

"You called him your *ex*-husband just now," he said.

"Did I? I suppose that's how I think of him. We're not divorced."

"When did you last see him, Mrs. Amiel?"

"I've told you, the day before I moved up here, back in April."

"Never since?"

She considered him for a moment. "My husband had no idea where I was. No one did. I broke all contact with…with that life when I moved up here."

"We have information that your husband was in Sohegan the day Priscilla was murdered."

"Impossible."

She looked as if she needed to believe that.

"Why did you leave Manhattan so suddenly?"

She hesitated just a second. "Barry was cruel to my son," she said softly. "Physically cruel. I had to get Jimmy away from him as quickly as possible."

She gazed directly at his face, her blue eyes asking nothing of him, expecting nothing.

"Well, your son is safe now," he said, and immediately regretted how callous that must have sounded. Regretted the dishonesty, too; the boy was far from safe.

"Any new information on who broke into my house?"

She sounded anxious. He shook his head. The truth was, he hadn't spent much time on that angle. Once the murderer was found, the pranks would stop.

"Don Reeves, the FBI man, will be wanting to talk with you, probably tomorrow."

"I'm not going anywhere," she said, her eyes fixed on her son. He nodded anyway and headed back to his car.

Gwen managed to remain calm all morning. She called Andrew's mother to arrange a play date, drove Jimmy to his house, withstood Martha Hillman's frosty reception. She fully expected to fall apart once she was safely alone; indeed she was almost looking forward to doing so. But as she drove away from the Hillman house she found herself more bewildered than upset. She pulled over to the side of a residential street and turned off the car.

The father of her son, *her husband, for God's sake*, was dead, *murdered*. Shouldn't that…distress her?

But it didn't. Somehow, she could only dwell on practical matters, not the loss itself. When should she tell Jimmy the news, and how? What did Barry's death mean in terms of her financial situation—did it wipe out their joint debts? Maybe now, with Barry safely gone, they could move back to the city. But did she want to? And then there was the question that loomed above all others.

What had Barry been doing in Sohegan?

She shut her eyes and tried to picture Barry, tried to summon some emotion. She focused on the man she'd married, not the man he'd become: the ready smile, the lively blue eyes, the extravagant compliments that never felt like flattery. But all she could muster was a flashing image of him pouring his cheap Polish vodka down—

She opened her eyes, blinked at the early afternoon sunshine, and started the car. She wouldn't waste an ounce of grief on Barry Amiel. He wasn't worth it.

• • •

She found Nick in the living room at Penaquoit, playing the Pathetique Sonata, and for the first time ever she interrupted his playing. He turned at the sound of his name, anger distorting his face.

"I'm sorry," she said, "I needed to speak to you."

He turned to the piano, waited a few seconds, then looked back at her, handsome again.

"It's good to see you," he said, "and on a Sunday, no less."

"They think I'm involved in your...in Priscilla's murder." The words tumbled from her lips. Nick just shook his head with an amused smile.

"It's not funny," she said. "They have someone, someone who saw Barry up here in Sohegan."

"Of course it's not funny. Tell me everything." He slid over on the piano bench, motioning for her to join him.

"Tess..."

"Is napping," he said. "The Piacevics are at church."

She sat next to him on the bench and told him everything she knew.

"I've been to that warehouse," she said. "Back when I had the store I picked up furniture there from Europe. Why would someone kill him there, of all places? Why kill him at all?"

"He was garbage. I'm sure he had a lot of enemies."

"The FBI want to question me again," she said, glancing around the room, unable to focus on any one thing. "They found Tess at my house, don't forget. They think my husband was up here the day of the murder, and now they find him with a bullet through his head in a warehouse I used to visit. What's next? Five million dollars under my bed, or hidden away in—"

"Gwen, stop it." He covered her mouth with his hand. "Listen to me. You didn't do anything wrong, so you have nothing to fear. Do you understand that?"

She waited a beat, then nodded. He removed his hand.

"Don't you ever..." She shook her head and turned away.

"Don't I ever what?" he asked.

"Wonder. About me?"

He cupped her chin with his fingertips and gently turned her head to face him. Slowly, very slowly he leaned toward her and kissed her, his tongue circling the inside of her lips. When he pulled away she whispered, "Thank you" and gently caressed his cheek.

"I'm scared, Nick."

"But you're free," he said. "Barry is gone."

"But what if—" He covered her mouth again with his hand.

"Nothing bad will happen," he said softly, staring directly at her eyes. "Understood?"

This time she couldn't quite nod her agreement. He sighed, his hand still covering her mouth.

"I'll be there with you, every step of the way," he said. "You have my word." He met her gaze without flinching. "I won't let you down, Gwen," he said, and she nodded, finally, and put her arms around him.

CHAPTER 33

"Hawkins, Don Reeves. I've got an errand for you."

Dwight Hawkins took his feet off his desk and sat up. It was eight-thirty, Monday morning. He knew what was coming.

"Go ahead."

"The handwriting on that note we found in Barry Amiel's room? We had an expert evaluate it. Perfect match with Gwen Amiel."

A small knot clenched in his stomach. "What did you say was written on that note—directions to Penaquoit?"

"Correct. The Browning is registered to Gwen Amiel. Tracings line up with the bullet that killed Priscilla Lawrence. And we just got the phone records from the flophouse in Brooklyn. Seven calls to the Lawrence place, all made during the hours when Gwen Amiel was on duty there. Five of them longer than ten minutes."

"Sounds like they worked it out together, she and her husband. You still want to question her?"

"I want you to arrest her. Felony murder. I'm on my way up there, but I don't want to risk her running. You get her in custody, I'll be there by ten, ten-thirty at the latest."

What about the boy? he wanted to ask. But he kept quiet; local cops were held in low enough regard by the FBI. He'd call Frank and Clare Pearson, arrange for them to take Jimmy.

"You hold her until I get there; then we'll transfer her to Whitesville. Don't forget to Miranda her."

Miranda Who? he almost said, just to aggravate the arrogant bastard. But he did in fact take out the plastic-covered crib sheet from his top drawer. Miranda didn't get a lot of play in Sohegan.

He hung up and phoned Frank Pearson, then shouted for Pat

Sykes, who was in the outer room having breakfast at his desk.

"We got a job," he said as he stood up and crossed the room. "Come with me. And lose the uniform. You can borrow my extra sports jacket if you need one. It's hanging behind my door."

The Amiel boy didn't need to see a cop in uniform coming to get his mother. Things were going to be shitty enough for him.

"What's going on?" Sykes wanted to know.

"I'll tell you on the way, just hurry up." Reeves's arrogance was catching.

It had been twenty-four hours and still Gwen couldn't get used to the idea that Barry was gone for good. Perhaps she was unwilling to admit how unburdened she felt, the complete absence of grief. Maybe that's why Barry's death hit her like fresh news every ten minutes or so.

Or perhaps it was the fact that she hadn't told Jimmy yet, the one person in her current life who had known Barry. Maybe his reaction, whatever it might be, would make Barry's death a reality for her.

She sipped coffee in the kitchen and decided she'd tell Jimmy that morning. He deserved to know, might even feel safer. Death fascinated him, anyway, and he was a firm believer in heaven. "God drops down a rope and pulls you up to him when you die," he'd told her just before they'd left Manhattan, a theory he'd picked up last year from a friend's Trinidadian baby-sitter. Well, there'd be no rope dropped for Barry Amiel.

She had just resolved to go upstairs and have a talk when she heard him charging down the front stairs, shouting. The panic in his voice set her heart racing. A moment later the doorbell rang. When she saw Dwight Hawkins's face on the front stoop she felt more annoyed than alarmed. More questions, more goddamn questions. But when she noticed a second cop standing next to him, and when she saw both Pearsons out front, grim-faced, she knew it meant more than questions.

"Open the door, Jimmy," she said.

He obeyed. Hawkins took off his cap. The misery on his face told the whole story. She took Jimmy to the kitchen and shut the door.

"Gwen Amiel?" Hawkins said when she returned.

"You know who I am," she said quietly.

Hawkins coughed to clear his throat. "You're under arrest for the murder of Priscilla Lawrence."

PART III

PART III

CHAPTER 34

The room was a windowless rectangle with a large, battered wood table in the center under three long fluorescent bulbs, one of which was flickering. The interrogation room, Gwen decided, swallowing hard to hold down a rush of fear.

Dwight Hawkins had driven her the fifteen miles to Whitesville, the county seat, and led her through the 1950s vintage police headquarters. She noticed little as she walked, Hawkins's hand tight on her elbow. She couldn't stop thinking about Jimmy being restrained by the Pearsons as she was led to the police car. Until then she'd thought learning about what Barry had done to him was the hardest thing she'd ever have to bear.

Don Reeves of the FBI was already in the room when they arrived.

"You've heard your rights?" he asked after she was seated. He was as monochromatic as the room, with his dark suit, dark tie, and white shirt. His complexion was pale, almost translucent. She'd have to work hard to keep that detached, pitiless face from getting to her.

"I called for a lawyer," Dwight Hawkins said. "Public defender, a local guy, he'll be here any minute."

"You want to wait for him?" Reeves said in a vaguely challenging tone.

She did, but she also knew the arrest was a blunder, a joke, really, and that the sooner she talked, the sooner she'd be back with Jimmy.

"I didn't do anything."

Reeves pressed a button on a small tape recorder in front of him.

"When was the last time you saw your husband, Mrs. Amiel?"

he asked.

"April twelfth, a Tuesday."

"Are you positive?"

"Yes."

"You never saw him in Sohegan?"

"And I haven't been back in the city, either, since I moved up here."

Reeves stared at her, his right index finger lightly stroking the red record button.

"When did you last talk to him?"

"April 12th. And yes, I'm positive."

"And yet we have phone records, Mrs. Amiel, from your husband's residence in Brooklyn. To Penaquoit."

"What?"

"Calls made just days before the kidnapping and murder."

She turned to Hawkins, thinking he must be in on the joke. He looked grim.

"When we searched your husband's things we found directions, in your handwriting," Reeves said. "Directions to Penaquoit."

"That's crazy."

"Priscilla Lawrence was killed with your gun. That's a *fact*." He spit the word at her, his lips curling to a lopsided sneer.

"I left the gun in Manhattan." *With Barry*...How the hell had it turned up at the Devil's Ravine?

"You were at the scene of the murder," Reeves said. He had the flat voice of someone reading from a teleprompter. "The child was found at your house."

She wiped her wet palms on her blue jeans. "If I had kidnapped Tess, why would I bring her back to my own house?"

"I don't know," Reeves said. "Why don't you tell us?"

"I want my attorney."

"Why don't I outline it for you, then, Mrs. Amiel? You and your late husband planned this together. You were the advance man, so to speak, inside Penaquoit. You arranged the entire thing, including giving your husband directions to the estate. Barry did the actual legwork—grabbing the child, retrieving the money. If Nick Lawrence hadn't spotted you at the scene, you—"

"*Spotted* me? I heard Tess crying and tried to help her. I wasn't hiding at that point."

"That's not the way Nick Lawrence and Russell Cunningham recall it. According to them, you were hiding about fifty yards from the exchange spot. Only when Mr. Lawrence *spotted* you did you emerge from your hiding place."

Something turned over in her stomach. "Nick—Mr. Lawrence is mistaken," she said slowly. "That's not how it happened."

"How *did* it happen?"

"I went there because I was worried about Tess. I heard her cry and I wanted to help her."

"But Tess was never at the Devil's Ravine. And neither of the two men recall hearing her cry."

But Nick had told her he'd heard Tess.

"She was there, I heard her cry. So did Nick."

"He claims otherwise," Reeves said. "In any case, how did you know they'd be at the Ravine?"

"I heard Russell Cunningham and Priscilla and Nick talking about it on the monitor."

"The *baby* monitor."

"Yes."

"And yet they weren't in the nursery, where the transmitting end of the monitor is customarily kept. They were in the master bedroom."

"Then someone must have brought the monitor into the master bedroom."

"Why would someone do that?" Reeves said.

"I want my attorney."

"You never heard them talking over the monitor, did you, Mrs. Amiel? You didn't need to, because you'd planned the entire operation."

"No, I heard them on the monitor, I was in the—"

Three loud raps on the door interrupted her. It opened to

reveal a short, heavyset man carrying a huge black briefcase.

"Kevin Gargano," he said as he hoisted the briefcase onto the table. "You must be Gwen Amiel. I'm your new attorney, if you'll have me."

He extended a thick hand that, when she shook it, engulfed her own in soft, damp flesh. He looked about fifty, with only a few strands of black hair on top of his head, a jowly face, and very small dark eyes. His suit needed pressing, his tie was probably beyond cleaning, and the handkerchief he used to mop his glistening brow was the color of old newsprint. But his voice was unexpectedly reassuring, even relaxed, as if nothing ever fazed him. He introduced himself to Don Reeves, clapped Dwight Hawkins on the shoulder, and dropped into the chair next to her with a contented "aaah."

"Is that a tape recorder?" he said.

"We notified Miss Amiel of her rights," Hawkins said quickly.

"Of course you did. And now I'd like you to turn that thing off and give me some time with my client. Alone. Any objections?" He smiled, but his slivery eyes invited no argument. After a moment's hesitation, Reeves turned off the recorder, picked it up, and headed for the door.

"We'll be in the hall," he said through his teeth. Hawkins followed him out.

"Now, tell me everything," Gargano said, turning his chair to face her. "I love a good story."

When she finished she felt almost giddy, as if she'd told a fabulous untruth and, inexplicably, been believed. But her attorney looked anything but amused.

"Not exactly a rock-solid case, but it's enough," Gargano said.

"Enough for what?"

"To arraign you. Set bail." Kevin Gargano's matter-of-fact attitude, which had seemed so reassuring less than twenty minutes ago, was beginning to unnerve her.

"Bail?" She couldn't spend the night away from Jimmy, not a single night. "Look, someone has been threatening me. They broke into my house, for Christ's sake, they…" She took a deep breath and told him what had happened at the ravine. "Someone's out there doing these things!"

"Sounds like that person thinks you're guilty, and he's pretty pissed off about it."

She simmered quietly for a few moments. "Anyway, I don't have money for bail."

"The Feds will argue that you have five million dollars. Enough to fly the coop." He placed his hands on both arms of his chair and pressed slowly to a standing position, grunting. "I'm going to try to get the bail hearing scheduled for this afternoon, here in Whitesville. Kidnapping's a federal offense; they might want to move you downstate. I'll argue for a local hearing, and soon—I'll mention your son and all. Don't talk to anyone until I get back."

When he shut the door behind him she was alone for the first time in hours. She glanced around—at the pitted acoustical tile on the ceiling, at the puke-colored carpet on the floor—shaking her head each time the word *jail* jumped to mind, trying to convince herself that when the door opened Reeves or Hawkins would walk in and, avoiding her eyes in their humiliation, their shame, inform her that the arrest had been a mistake, a miscarriage, that they hoped she'd understand. *Sign here and you're free, Mrs. Amiel. Can we offer you a lift home?*

But when the door opened after ten long minutes and Reeves and Hawkins entered, they both met her gaze unabashedly. Kevin Gargano followed them into the room.

"Bail hearing's set for four-thirty," he said.

"That was fast," Reeves mumbled with a bitter chuckle.

"Not a lot of bail hearings in this vicinity. Judges are looking for things to keep them occupied." He winked at her, a gesture she couldn't begin to interpret.

Reeves stepped toward her and screwed his face into what he must have thought was a solicitous expression.

"Mrs. Amiel," he said, "you could speed things along, and help yourself, if you'd tell us everything you know. Your cooperation would look very positive to a sentencing judge. New York has just reinstated the death penalty, as I'm sure you're aware. We'd be willing to forgo the death penalty if you—"

"Death penalty?" She began to chortle, as if they'd gone one step too far in what she now realized was a very elaborate, if tasteless, practical joke. "*Death* penalty?" Still smiling, she looked from Gargano to Reeves to Hawkins and finally up at the ceiling as her laughter petered out.

"Cut the bullshit, okay?" Gargano said as he loosened his tie, then undid the top button of his pale blue shirt. "You can't cut a deal in this case—who's she gonna implicate, the dead husband?"

"I haven't had anything to do with Barry since I moved here," she said, wiping tears from her face with trembling fingers.

Gargano waved a fat hand at her. "We have nothing further to say, pending the bail hearing."

"We have handwriting analysis, Mrs. Amiel, tying you conclusively to that note. We found hundred-dollar bills stuffed in your husband's pocket and wallet. We have your gun. We have phone records."

"And my client has the right to remain silent," Gargano said. "You *did* mention that already, I trust?"

Reeves stood up and headed for the door. "We don't need a statement from you, Mrs. Amiel. You're toast already."

After Reeves left, Dwight Hawkins cleared his throat. "You'll be detained in a holding cell until the hearing, and afterward, until bail is met, you'll be remanded to the county jail." He stood up and uttered a sigh that seemed to drag his shoulders down. "I still think you're protecting someone, Mrs. Amiel."

"How can I protect someone when I didn't—"

Gargano cut her off with a karate chop through the air a few inches from her face.

"Look out for *yourself*, Mrs. Amiel," Hawkins said. "For yourself and your son. Whoever you're protecting, he's not worth it."

"I need to make a phone call," she said as he was leaving.

Hawkins turned. "Your attorney's already here."

"I want to check on my son."

Hawkins looked pensive, then motioned for her to follow. He led her down a long corridor to a pay phone on the wall next to the men's room. She could hear Don Reeves's voice from inside.

"Speak softly, okay?" Hawkins said. "Reeves probably wouldn't approve."

She looked at him, prepared to offer thanks, and saw something in his expression, an uneasiness coupled with sorrow and pity, especially pity. *He thinks I'm innocent. He knows I am.* They locked eyes for a moment; then Hawkins quickly turned away and walked a few steps down the hall.

She found a quarter in her jeans pocket and punched in the Penaquoit number. She wanted to speak to Jimmy, wanted to reassure him, but Nick would find a way to get her out of there, which was her first priority. After two rings Rosa Piacevic answered.

"Hello? Lawrence residence."

"Is Mr. Lawrence there?" Gwen said quietly.

A long pause. "No."

"It's me, Gwen. I guess you know what happened."

"We hear."

"I need to talk to him."

"He's not here."

Something in her voice...

"Who's watching Tess?"

A beat, then: "I am."

"Put her on."

"She just a baby, she cannot—"

"She loves the phone. Put her on."

Dwight Hawkins took a step toward her, looking puzzled.

"She is having nap," Rosa said.

"It isn't nap time. She's with Mr. Lawrence, isn't she? He's there, isn't he, in the house?"

"He...not home."

"Put him on!"

"He...he..."

The line went dead. She squeezed the phone until her wrist ached. *I'll be there with you, every step of the way. You have my word.* She slammed the phone in its cradle.

Dwight Hawkins walked over to her. "Everything okay?"

She shot him a look and he stepped back.

"I've thought it over," he said. "You can wait in the conference room for the arraignment. I'll have to post a man outside the door, but I don't see any reason for you to wait in a cell."

If he expected gratitude he'd have to look elsewhere.

CHAPTER 35

Gwen entered the small courtroom on the second floor of the Whitesville County Court building and almost buckled under a crushing sense of isolation. She'd survived three tedious hours in the windowless conference room by forcing herself to think optimistically: charges would be dropped, she'd retrieve Jimmy from the Pearsons, then perhaps Nick would take them both away somewhere.

But when she walked into the courtroom and saw not a single familiar face, other than her own attorney, she felt her knees start to give way. It was nearly five o'clock. Where was Nick? Where was Sheila? Where was—

And then it hit her, what she should have known all along, or had known but chose to ignore. She was alone, her life telescoped to this small, drab room and a handful of strangers who thought she had killed someone.

A female police officer escorted her to a table on the left side of the room, where she sat on a wooden armchair next to Kevin Gargano. Before she had a chance to orient herself the judge cleared his throat and began talking. He was gray-haired, probably about sixty, his shoulders hunched under a black robe. The sign in front of his desk read CHARLIE M. KOCH.

"Is everyone present who needs to be?" he said.

Gargano nodded. On the other side of the room, a young man with tightly curled black hair stood up and said, "Yes, Your Honor, we are prepared to proceed."

"The prosecutor," Gargano whispered to her. "Jason Rudolph. Major ass kisser."

Gwen nodded but couldn't help noticing the way the judge's expression softened when he looked at the prosecutor. What's wrong with a little ass kissing? she felt like asking Gargano.

The judge scanned the top of his desk, lifted a sheet of paper, and began reading.

"Gwen Amiel…" He peered briefly at her over his reading glasses. "You have been charged with felony murder in the death of Priscilla Lawrence, kidnapping of a minor, and extortion." He looked at her again, and for a moment she thought he was going to smile at the absurdity of what he'd just read. *Only kidding, you can go now.* Instead, he said, "How do you plead?"

"Felony murder?" she whispered to Gargano.

"When you cause the death of someone else in the course of committing another crime."

"But I—"

"Doesn't matter if you *intended* to kill the person. As long as he died in the course of committing a crime, you're guilty of felony murder."

"*Not* guilty," Gwen whispered.

"Mr. Gargano?" the judge said with an impatient sigh.

Gargano stood up and coughed once. "Not guilty, Your Honor." He flopped back into his chair as the judge wrote something down.

"Very well." Judge Koch dropped his pen and looked up. "Grand jury proceedings are hereby scheduled for two weeks hence, on the third of August. I trust that won't be a problem?"

Gargano shook his head as he flipped through a dog-eared pocket calendar. Even before he'd reached the first week of August, Jason Rudolph was on his feet.

"No problem, Your Honor!"

Gargano muttered something and made a notation on his calendar.

"Very well," the judge said again. "Now for the matter of bail. Mr. Rudolph?"

"Your Honor," the prosecutor said, back on his feet. "I trust you're familiar with the facts of the Priscilla Lawrence case."

"I am."

"Then I need hardly tell the court that this murder was committed in the act of kidnapping a one-year-old infant. I will, however, remind the court that five million dollars in ransom money—all cash—has not been recovered. Nor has Mrs. Amiel offered to help federal investigators locate the money. In light of these facts, and her complete and total refusal to cooperate with federal authorities, we are asking that bail be denied."

He sat down and glanced over at Gwen, breathing hard, his predatory eyes bright and unblinking. Yesterday she'd never heard of Jason Rudolph. Now he was her mortal enemy.

Gargano hoisted himself from his chair with a bovine grunt.

"Good afternoon, Your Honor."

The judge checked his wristwatch. "Or is it good evening, counselor?"

Gargano chuckled obsequiously. "I appreciate your arranging to see us at such short notice, Your Honor. The reason I imposed on your busy schedule was simply this. My client, Gwen Amiel, is the mother of a five-year-old child."

Six, she wanted to whisper. *He's six*. A tremor of dread passed through her.

"She's a single parent, I might add, so it is imperative that she not be incarcerated a moment longer than necessary."

Jason Rudolph sprang to his feet. "She should have thought of that before she murdered Priscilla Lawrence." He remained standing.

"Your Honor, we are not here this afternoon—this *evening*—to argue the guilt or innocence of my client, merely to set bail. My client works as a baby-sitter, earning…" He coughed and consulted his notes; they hadn't discussed her salary, other than to determine that *his* fee would be paid by the state. "…Earning a subsistence living for herself and her young child. Setting any bail at all would therefore be tantamount to denying bail. Which, given Mrs. Amiel's clean record, the scanty evidence in this case—"

"I thought we weren't arguing guilt or innocence," the judge said.

"Of course," Gargano replied. "But we can at least agree that this isn't a slam dunk." He glanced at the prosecutor, his eyes all but swallowed by plump folds of sallow skin. "Not by a long shot."

"Your Honor, I don't—"

"Enough," the judge said, turning to Gargano. "Proceed."

"My client is not a flight risk, Your Honor. She denies the charges against her, she is thoroughly committed to the care and upbringing of her child. And she's already been through hell... Don't make it worse for her."

"With all due respect, counselor, we're dealing with a capital case here," Rudolph said. "Or aren't you aware that our governor reinstated the death penalty two years ago."

"I feel safer already," Gargano mumbled loud enough for everyone to hear.

The judge rapped an open hand on his desk. "That'll do, Mr. Gargano." He turned to the other side of the room. "Mr. Rudolph, I *will* set bail in this case, so you might as well give me a figure."

"But Your Honor, I—"

"A figure, Mr. Rudolph?"

The prosecutor frowned. "In light of the fact that Mrs. Amiel has absolutely no roots in the community, having lived in the county less than six months, and therefore poses a very real flight risk, I recommend that bail be set at one million dollars." He sat down and again looked over at Gwen.

"My client can't afford even ten percent of that," Gargano said. "Remember her young...child."

Gwen dug her fingernails into the thick varnish of the tabletop. *He's a boy, goddamn it!*

Rudolph stood up but the judge waved a hand at him.

"Enough. Given the seriousness of the crime, a substantial bail must be set. However, in light of the absence of a criminal record, and the presence of the child, I think Mrs. Amiel poses only a modest flight risk. Bail is set at five hundred thousand dollars." He stood up as both attorneys shouted "Your Honor!" He shook his head, frowning, as he disappeared through a door behind his desk.

"How the hell am I going to come up with half a million

dollars?" Gwen said.

"I'll talk to some bail bondsmen, but it's not going to be easy. I mean, you don't even own your house. You got any kind of collateral at all, Mrs. Amiel?"

Before she could answer Jason Rudolph was standing next to them.

"Ready to deal, counselor?" His eyes had the fervent glow of the newly converted—or was it the euphoria of a lottery winner? Gwen got the strong sense that, careerwise, she was the biggest thing ever to happen to Jason Rudolph. Gargano ignored him as he gathered his notes into a pile.

"Your client pleads guilty, surrenders the cash—and I don't ask for the chair. How about it?"

"You're not going for capital, my friend, not with a female defendant." Gargano stuffed the papers into his briefcase and snapped it shut.

"Hey, I'm what they call an evolved man," Rudolph said. "What's good for the goose is—"

"Fuck you," Gwen said.

Rudolph looked at her, eyebrows arched. "Temper like that won't sit well with a jury."

"She isn't talking to a jury, Rudolph. Now, my client and I would like some time alone."

"First-degree manslaughter, then, in return for a guilty plea and restitution of the cash."

Gargano started to speak, but Gwen grabbed his shoulder and bore down on it as she stood, almost toppling him. From the corner of her eye she saw two police officers moving toward her.

"If you bring this case to trial," she said, trying hard to keep from shouting, "you'll regret it for the rest of your life."

"Why?" said Rudolph with a smirk. "You gonna kill me too?" His grin exposed an orderly string of tiny teeth topped by a good half inch of glistening pink gum.

"Because I'm innocent," she said. "And I have powerful friends in this county."

Rudolph turned and swept a hand across the empty courtroom. "Powerful and invisible, apparently."

"You'll hear from them," she said, praying her lack of conviction wasn't showing.

"I hope you don't mean the Cunninghams and Nick Lawrence," Rudolph said in a patronizing singsong. "Is that who you mean?" She raised her chin and didn't breathe. "Russell Cunningham has already called the governor on your behalf."

She let out a slow breath, biting back a smile.

"He's demanding the death penalty," Rudolph said. "And he's got lots of influence, as you just pointed out."

She felt the blood drain from her head and grabbed on to a chair to keep from keeling over.

"As for Nick Lawrence, the fact that he was fucking you, his child's baby-sitter—imagine that, ladies and gentlemen of the jury— will probably count for a lot less in his mind than the fact that he's completely dependent on his father-in-law for financial support."

"Bullshit," she said.

"Care to bet on it? Say…five hundred thousand dollars?"

She lunged at him and managed to graze his suit jacket with one fist before a male police officer yanked her away and handcuffed her wrists behind her back.

"You've got a violent streak, Mrs. Amiel," Rudolph said smoothly, but a pearl of sweat trickled in front of his left ear. "I like that in a defendant." He clapped Kevin Gargano on the arm and headed for the exit. "Call if you want to talk deal," he said over his shoulder.

Gargano stood up and hoisted his briefcase from the floor.

"I'll see about bail, but you'll probably have to spend at least tonight, probably tomorrow in jail."

No! She couldn't leave Jimmy with the Pearsons.

"Call Nick Lawrence," she said quickly, before the tears came. "He'll help with the bail."

"Doesn't sound like he has many assets, but maybe the house is in his name, who knows? You sure he's on your side?"

She nodded several times as tears began spilling from her eyes. "Can I call my son? Can I call him before they…"

Gargano glanced at the female officer, who frowned, waited a few moments, then nodded.

"Jimmy?" She smiled into the phone, struggling to keep her voice upbeat. "It's me."

"Hi, Mom."

"Things okay at the Pearsons?"

"I guess."

"I'm glad. I'm sorry you have to sleep there tonight. I'm going to try to come home tomorrow."

Silence.

"We'll go for ice cream cones, okay?"

He mumbled something inaudible.

"Jimbo, remember what I said this morning, before they took me away, about not doing anything wrong?"

"Yeah."

"Well, it's true. I know you believe that. It's so important to me that—"

"Mom?"

"Yes, Jimmy?"

"Do I have to go to camp tomorrow?"

"Don't you want to?"

"Some of the boys…"

"Some of the boys what?"

"…Said things. You know, about you and Mr. Lawrence and things."

"Don't listen to them," she said. "What happened to Priscilla Lawrence had nothing to do with you, okay? You didn't do anything wrong."

Silence.

"Jimmy, if you don't want to go to camp tomorrow, tell

the Pearsons I said you don't have to. We'll talk about it when I get home."

"Okay."

The police officer tapped her watch.

"I have to go now, Jimmy." Which was just as well, since her resolve was disintegrating, and it was beginning to show in her voice. "Sweet dreams, honey."

"But it's not bedtime."

"I know…I—"

"Can you call me at bedtime?"

"I don't think so."

"Oh."

"I love you so much."

"Mom?"

"Yes, Ji—" She cleared her throat. "Jimmy?"

"There's a three-quarter moon tonight."

"Really?"

"Uh-huh. So at eight-thirty, right before bedtime? I'll look out my window at the moon, and you can look at it at the same time."

She opened her mouth but couldn't speak. Her jaw ached from holding back tears.

"That'll be cool, right?" Jimmy said.

"Right."

CHAPTER 36

A crowd of reporters, photographers, and cameramen had assembled outside the courthouse. They shouted questions at her as she was led out a side door and into a white van.

"...Planned the kidnapping before coming to Sohegan?"

"...Intend to kill Priscilla, or was that an accident, Mrs..."

"...A sexual relationship, Mrs. Amiel?"

She prayed silently that Jimmy wasn't watching the news.

The Ondaiga County Corrections Facility was about a half hour from Whitesville. The ride in the backseat of a police car, handcuffed behind a metal grille, seemed endless. Her sense of isolation only intensified once she reached the place. She was passed from one stern-faced corrections officer to another. After her clothes were taken from her, she showered in a curtainless stall using a toxic-smelling soap for her body and hair, doing her best to ignore the unblinking gaze of a stocky guard whose name tag identified her only as *Martinson*. She dried off with a dingy towel that had the texture of a sisal rug, and was handed an orange jumpsuit, which she had to sign for.

"Afraid I won't return it?" she said, hearing a new toughness in her voice, and hating it.

Her cell was about ten feet square, with one small window, located near the ceiling, a narrow cot suspended from one wall, a lidless toilet, and a sink. She remembered little of the long walk from the shower to the cell; she felt queasily disoriented, as if she'd been spun around blindfolded.

The cell was clean, modern, and she had it to herself, thank God. Yet every time she thought of spending a second night there a constricting fear would seize her heart; she couldn't even imagine a longer stay, *wouldn't* imagine it.

She'd arrived too late for dinner. No one had offered her food, not that she had much of an appetite. At eight-thirty precisely she stood on her cot and peered up through the narrow, barred window. She couldn't find the three-quarter moon, though the night was crystal clear and white moon glow blanketed the sky. She tried every angle, and still couldn't find it. She stared at the window for close to an hour, hoping that the moon would orbit into view. It never did.

The Ondaiga Corrections Facility might be in the middle of nowhere, but the sounds she heard that night were strangely urban: sporadic shouts, the clanging of metal on metal, car doors slamming somewhere beyond her window. Throughout a mostly sleepless night she traced the path that had led her to this place. And she found that as much as she tried to blame her situation on others—on Barry, or Nick, or even Priscilla—it was she, Gwen Amiel, no one else, who had cleared the path to this place.

No one had forced her to take the job looking after Tess Lawrence. What had she been thinking? Better pay and a health plan, yes, but wasn't she also just a little bit attracted to the glamour of Penaquoit, not to mention Nick himself?

No one had forced her to follow the family to the Devil's Ravine that day. Her own vanity had sent her there, the baseless conviction that only she could save Tess Lawrence, the way she'd already saved Jimmy.

Nick hadn't raped her that first night in her house, he'd seduced her. And every seduction was a pas de deux, after all.

Her eyes skittered around the blackened cell, searching in vain for something discernible, some glimpse of light on which to focus. But the cell was a black, formless void. And the rage blazed and blistered until dawn.

• • •

Breakfast was delivered to her cell the next morning at seven-thirty: cereal, milk, watery coffee. She asked the female guard who brought the food when visiting hours began.

"Visiting hours?" she said as she continued down the aisle to the next cell. "You think this is a fucking hospital?" A chorus of cackles erupted.

Gwen swallowed a few sips of coffee and ignored the gray oatmeal and soft banana. She spent two hours pacing the small cell, one thought tormenting her above all others: what if she had to stay in there until the trial? How would she survive? Who would take care of Jimmy?

Just before ten o'clock a guard called her name and slipped Gwen's jeans and shirt through the bars.

"Get dressed," she said as the clothes fell to the floor. "You made bail."

She expected to find Kevin Gargano in the visitors' lobby once she'd signed out. But at ten-thirty in the morning the large, sparsely furnished room was eerily quiet. She found a pay phone and called Gargano's office. A secretary answered and put her right through.

"It's Gwen. How am I supposed to get home from here?"

"Home?"

"From jail?"

"Wait a minute, you made bail?"

"You mean you didn't—"

Nick. She felt a surge of something like happiness. "You must have a fairy godmother," Gargano said. "What name was on the release form?"

"I didn't look. I just assumed it was you. They showed me where to sign, I couldn't wait to get out."

"Attorneys do not make bail for their clients, at least not the ones I know. I'll call around, find out who posted bail. Meantime, sit tight. I'll be there in twenty, twenty-five minutes."

She hung up, dropped another quarter in the slot, and dialed Nick's number. Rosa Piacevic answered.

"Mr. Lawrence, please." She lowered her voice an octave to disguise her identity.

"Not home."

"Okay, Rosa," she said in her own voice. "Put him on."

"How do I put him on when he is not here?"

"When will he be back?"

"He didn't tell me nothing. I can't…"

She could hear Rosa breathing hard, as if from the effort of trying to finish the sentence. Then the line went dead.

She asked Gargano to drop her off at the Pearsons. He was fairly quiet during the half-hour drive, and she felt too anxious to talk much. First she needed to see Jimmy; then she'd deal with the future.

"One question," he said as he sailed through a yellow light near the Pearsons' street. "Yesterday, when Rudolph said something about your, uh, sleeping with Nick Lawrence?"

She'd been wondering when he'd get to that. "Yes."

"Is it true?"

"Does it matter?"

He glanced at her with reproachful eyes. "To me, no. To a jury, you bet."

"I don't see—"

"Not only did you kill Priscilla Lawrence, you had an affair with her husband. I don't suppose you've been desecrating her grave for good measure?"

"Go to hell."

He shifted noisily on the vinyl seat. The floor of his battered Oldsmobile was littered with gum wrappers, yellow sticky notes, and pink phone messages.

"Without this, we might have argued that you killed Priscilla accidentally, though granted, you killed her—*allegedly* killed her in the course of another crime. But if the jury finds out you're sleeping with the widower, it gives you a motive for killing her *deliberately*. Which makes the prosecution's premeditation argument even stronger."

She clenched her teeth to keep from protesting her innocence. She'd done that yesterday, in front of the judge. She'd never do it again.

"Our relationship began after the murder," she said quietly.

"Even so, once the jury finds out you slept with the widower, just one month after his wife's murder, you're fucked, Mrs. Amiel."

"It wasn't like that. The marriage…they weren't exactly close."

"And who will testify to that fact?" He almost passed the Pearsons' street, turned sharply left, and cursed as legal papers, candy wrappers, and a not-quite-empty cardboard coffee cup cascaded from the dashboard onto his lap.

"Nick Lawrence."

"Are you sure about that?"

"He paid my bail," she said.

"Think so? I haven't heard back from the bailiff's office yet." He parked in front of the Pearsons'. "You want a ride home?"

"No, I'll ask Henry Pearson to take me." She got out of the car, closed the door, and leaned in through the passenger window.

"What happens now?"

"We find out exactly what the prosecution has on you; then we start planning our defense."

She hated to leave with him looking so grim and disapproving. But Jimmy was just a few yards away…

"I'll call you later." She turned and headed up the Pearsons' front walk.

"Mrs. Amiel?"

She walked back to the car.

"No more surprises, Mrs. Amiel. You can't afford secrets from me, okay?"

She watched him pull away from the curb, black smoke swirling from the tailpipe of the Olds, then turned and saw Jimmy running toward her. The haunted look in his eyes, the shadows above his cheeks, the way he squeezed her when she knelt down and took him in her arms, as if he feared she'd drift up into the sky and leave him again if he relaxed one iota…

Something shifted inside her as she held him. All the fear and confusion of the past few days withered and died. She wouldn't wait for the trial to exonerate her, and she wouldn't count on Gargano to find the truth. She'd find it herself. Because she was all Jimmy had, and she'd already let him down once.

"I'm not leaving, Jimbo, not ever," she whispered.

He nodded into her shoulder, but his arms, still wrapped around her, didn't relax one bit.

CHAPTER 37

More goddamn reporters. She might have expected them—why should her house be sacred? But somehow the sight of all those people in the street outside her house was as shocking as anything that had happened to her in the past twenty-four hours.

"Don't talk to them," she told Jimmy as Henry Pearson parked in the driveway. "Just pretend they aren't here."

She got out of the car first, opened Jimmy's door, and picked him up. Cameras clicked furiously as she carried him to the front door. Questions were hurled at them in desperate voices that grew angrier as she approached the front door without answering.

"Is it true you turned down a plea bargain, Gwen?"

"What is your relationship with Nick Lawrence?"

"When did you first plan to kidnap the little girl?"

"Did you intend to kill Priscilla all along, Gwen?"

Only one day since her arrest and already she was just plain "Gwen" to them.

She fumbled for her key, the questions still coming at her, and finally managed to open the door. When she slammed it shut she realized that Jimmy was shivering. She held him until he was still.

"Are you hungry?" she said softly when she found her voice. "Want some lunch?"

He shook his head as his eyes drifted to the front window.

"Can I go somewhere else?"

"We just got home."

He nodded and stared at the floor and she marveled that after all she'd been through she had enough heart left to be broken. Who could blame him for wanting to be away from there? So what if she needed him then, needed the solace of comforting him?

She called Martha Hillman from the kitchen and arranged to drop him off.

Reporters and cameramen chased them halfway down Glendale Street as they drove off, banging on the closed windows and shouting muffled questions. She saw tears on Jimmy's face as she made a left onto Union Avenue. He opened his door the moment the car stopped in front of Andrew Hillman's house. She had to call him back for a good-bye hug.

She headed straight for Penaquoit. At the entrance to the estate she punched in the access code and put her foot on the accelerator, slamming on the brakes just before crashing into the closed gates. Cursing, she backed up and tried the code again. The gates didn't budge.

She pounded the steering wheel until the heel of her hand hurt, then backed out of the driveway and headed next door. She parked to the side of the Cunninghams' house and jostled her way through the row of hemlock trees to the back lawn of Penaquoit, then walked quickly toward the house.

"He is not home."

She stopped and turned to the voice. Mett Piacevic was watering the small rose garden about twenty yards from the house.

"So I've been told."

"It's not a good idea, coming here." Piacevic put down the hose and plucked a cicada shell from inside the bloom of a perfect yellow rose. He shook his head and ground it in his fist, scattering the pulverized husk on the ground.

"You can't go inside."

"Watch me."

She was about fifteen feet from the house when a man stepped from under the wide awning that shaded the south-facing terrace. Though the day was quite warm, he had on a long-sleeved white shirt and black pants. He was tall and heavyset, with some sort of hearing device in his right ear.

"You're trespassing," he said. "Kindly leave the property or I'll have to escort you."

"I work here," she said.

"My instructions are to keep you out."

"Your instructions?" She stepped toward the patio but he blocked her path, arms folded across his chest. "Get the hell out of my way," she said.

"You don't want any more trouble than you're already in, miss." He flaunted a condescending sneer.

"Who hired you?"

"That's none of your concern, miss. Kindly leave the property or I'll have to escort you off the grounds."

She stood facing him for a few seconds, alternately calculating the odds of doing an end run around him and fuming at being kept out like some sort of...pariah.

"Where is Mr. Lawrence?" she said.

He just stared at her with that superior smirk.

"Fuck you," she said, looking right at him, then turned and retraced her steps across the back lawn.

"How is Tess?" she asked Mett Piacevic when she reached the rose garden.

He glanced away from her, continued watering the roses.

"How is Tess?"

"She cry a lot." He shook his head and frowned. "Rosa, she is having hard time making her quiet."

He shut off the nozzle, dropped it, and walked toward the big house.

"Would Rosa let me see her, just for a minute?" she called after him. He continued walking. "She misses me and..." Mett Piacevic shrugged as he walked away.

Gwen looked up at the house and saw a figure in the nursery window. She stepped into the shadow of a nearby oak tree and looked up again.

Nick Lawrence held Tess, both of them staring out the window, motionless. At first she assumed they didn't see her. Then Tess waved a hand and rapped on the window. She moved toward the house, but almost at once they vanished. She waited, hoping he'd emerge onto the patio or from the kitchen door. After several minutes she turned and walked away, one thought on her mind: Nick Lawrence hadn't made her bail, she knew that now. Nick Lawrence wanted nothing to do with her.

She intended to return straight to her car but headed instead for the privet hedge at the south end of the property. She ducked through the opening and followed the overgrown path to Priscilla's secret garden.

The flowers were as lush as ever, despite the lack of rain. No surprise, really: these were the hardiest specimens in the county. They'd proven their mettle elsewhere, then survived transplantation. Perhaps Priscilla wanted the place to outlive her, perhaps she knew it would.

Her head felt suddenly heavy. Nick had seen her on the lawn and made no effort to reach her. The garden was beginning to cloy.

Where were the purple thistles? She stepped into the crowded flower bed and began combing through the various plants. The thistles were gone. After a few minutes she managed to find the small index card with *Scotch thistle* written in Priscilla's fastidious hand. Could the blooms have fallen off so quickly, and without a trace? A foot or so from the card she noticed a crushed cigarette butt. She flipped it over with her shoe and looked closer: no filter. Then she slowly followed the tall, silvery-leaved stems up from the index card and felt a shiver of fear. The tops of the thistle stems had been cut—no, ripped, severing the purple blossoms. Glistening drops of pale green sap clung to the uneven necks of the stems.

She glanced again at Russell Cunningham's cigarette butt, then got the hell out of there.

• • •

Sheila Stewart smiled uncomfortably and stood up when Gwen entered her office just off the main banking floor of the Sohegan Savings & Loan Society building.

"Relax, Sheila, I'm not armed," Gwen said from the doorway. After the briefest hesitation Sheila circled her desk and walked over to her, arms spread. She kicked the door shut as Gwen all but collapsed into her.

"How the fuck did you get into this mess?" Sheila said after a long embrace.

"Not by killing anyone, you have to—"

"Stop it!" Sheila looked utterly serious. "Don't insult me."

Gwen closed her eyes for a moment and thanked God for Sheila Stewart.

"Sheila, did you make bail for me?"

"No."

"Then who the hell did? I thought it might be Nick, but he won't even speak to me."

"Have you seen the local rag this morning?" Sheila got the *Gazette* from the floor behind her desk and handed it to her. The headline spanned the entire front page. BABY-SITTER ARRESTED IN KIDNAP/MURDER. There was no photo of her, thank God— but only because no one in Sohegan had taken her picture.

"You know what hurts the most?" Gwen said, staring at the headline.

Sheila nodded, frowning. "The 'baby-sitter' part."

"God, I love you. Can I have this for my scrapbook?"

"Are you sure you want it?" Sheila took the paper, flipped it over, and handed it back. Below the fold was a second, smaller headline. ACCUSED AND WIDOW WERE LOVERS.

"Oh, shit."

"Murder is one thing, Gwendolyn. Everyone feels homicidal now and then. But sleeping with a woman's husband not two months after she's been killed...Well, you've really crossed the line this time."

Gwen scanned the article, too agitated to pay close attention to what she was reading.

"You know that dream everyone is supposed to have?" she said. "The one where you suddenly realize you've studied for the wrong exam? That's how I feel right now, like this is some sort of test, only my whole life has prepared me for a different set of questions. I mean, what was Barry doing up here? I never gave him directions to Penaquoit, I never even called him. I never wanted to see him again. And who the hell posted bail this morning? I don't know anyone with access to half a million dollars."

"But they'd only need to post ten percent. I can run an activity analysis and see if anyone drew a check on the bank for that amount."

"Thanks," Gwen said.

"I'll call you later if anything turns up. In the meantime, what are your plans?"

"Apparently Mike Contaldi claims he saw Barry in the diner the morning of the kidnapping. I thought I'd talk to him." She shrugged. "The alternative is giving a press conference on my front lawn."

"I wish I could come with you, but I have an interview with a bank in Albany late this afternoon."

"Albany? I thought you never wanted to leave Sohegan."

"Me too. But this kidnapping, the murder, and now what's happening to you—the town is poisoned for me. I used to think we were kind of a blue-collar Brigadoon, the town that time and prosperity forgot. Now the whole world's watching. It's not the same."

"What does Betsy think?"

"About Albany?" Sheila picked up a printout from her desk and pretended to look at it. "She's not leaving Sohegan, if that's what you mean."

Gwen didn't have the time or the heart to pursue this.

"Well, good luck, for what it's worth." She hugged Sheila again and left.

• • •

Only when Gwen was several yards into the Mecca did she realize that people were staring. *Everyone* was staring, in fact, forks poised in midair, jaws locked midchew, lips frozen mid-sentence. Even Mike was uncharacteristically speechless.

"Can we talk for a minute?" she said, leaning over the counter. "In private?"

He looked puzzled and uncomfortable. "Nobody can hear us standing right here."

True enough. But she was beginning to sweat from the heat of two dozen eyes.

"I'd prefer the kitchen, actually. Just a few questions."

He glanced around the diner before nodding. "It's getting toward lunchtime, but okay."

The kitchen was smaller than she remembered and smelled of old grease and ammonia. Mike leaned against the slop sink and folded his hands across his chest.

"Why'd you have to come back here, Gwen? Sohegan's a small town."

A pariah at *Mike's?* She'd really hit rock bottom.

"You told the police that my husband was here, in the diner, the day of the kidnapping."

"They showed me a picture, I pointed out the guy. I didn't know he was your husband."

"Are you sure it was him?"

"Yeah, I'm sure."

"And he didn't meet anyone while he was in here?"

"Nope."

"Did he ask you for directions, mention my name?"

"Nope."

She sighed and shook her head. Well, coming to the Mecca was a long shot, she'd know that from the beginning.

"Thanks, Mike." She started to leave the kitchen.

"Who'da guessed it would end like this," he said.

"It hasn't ended yet, Mike."

"I mean, five months ago Nick Lawrence comes by for coffee,

asks about the new waitress we got here. Now that waitress is accused of—"

"He asked about me?" She wheeled around and walked back toward him.

"Sure, on a Saturday, your day off. I'd never seen him before, didn't even know who he was till one of the other customers tells me after he left."

"What did he ask about?"

"Oh, you know, your name, how long you been here, where you were from. He says he saw you around town, thought he might need a new baby-sitter. I figured he meant for nighttime work, else I wouldn't have been so helpful. Poaching another man's employees isn't right."

"But he told me his old sitter left just a few days before he asked me to work for him."

Mike shrugged. "Next thing I know, you quit."

Nick had asked about her a few weeks *before* his baby-sitter left?

"What exactly did you tell him?" Gwen asked.

"Like I said, your name, where you lived."

"Nothing else?"

"I think maybe he asked about your kid, your husband."

"*Husband?* What did you tell him?"

"Just what I knew." He scratched the side of his head.

"*Mike.*"

"You never told me squat, so what could I tell him?" His face was bright red.

"Tell me exactly what you told him. *Now.*"

"Shit." He stretched the word into several long syllables as he reamed his right ear with a pinkie. "He said he thought he might have known you, from down in the city, wanted your old address. So I showed him that application you filled out."

"You gave him my old address." *Barry's address.*

"Big deal, so he looked at the application. He said he didn't think it was the same person after all. What harm was there?"

Plenty harm, though she couldn't say exactly what. She headed for the kitchen door.

"Uh, Gwen? You mind using the back door? Some people, they don't keep an open mind like I do. Nothing personal, just—"

"Fuck you, Mike." She pushed open the swinging door and walked slowly through the crowded, suddenly dead-quiet restaurant.

She got home at one o'clock feeling hungry but completely uninterested in food. The crowd out front had thinned a bit, thank God. She managed to down a slice of bread and a few sips of milk from the carton. Then the phone rang.

"Are you sitting down?" It was Sheila. "We just had a fax from our correspondent bank in Whitesville. Guess who drew a check on the bank this morning for fifty thousand dollars?"

She sat down. "Who?"

"It's a joint account, in the name of Russell and Maxine Cunningham. The signature was hers."

"Maxine Cunningham bailed me out?"

"Your guardian angel."

Gwen thanked her, hung up, and grabbed her car keys.

"You shouldn't have come here." Maxine Cunningham, wearing sunglasses, gently rubbed her right cheek. She motioned Gwen inside the house and quickly closed the door. Gwen noticed a stack of cartons just inside the living room. Beyond them she saw a four-poster bed, a rocking chair...

"Priscilla's things," she said. "From the basement at Penaquoit."

"Russell asked Piacevic to move them over here, bit by bit. He says he doesn't trust Nick with the stuff, but..." Maxine shook her head slowly.

"But what?"

"I just think he wants to be closer to it. I've drawn the line at bringing the magazines here, but he won't hear about throwing them out."

They both stared at the jumble of furniture and boxes for a while.

"I don't know what we'll do with it," Maxine said wearily, as if, after all the tragedy she'd faced, this was the biggest challenge of her life. "Our basement is already so full."

"Is your husband home?"

Maxine shook her head. "But if he discovers you were here…"

"Why did you post bail for me?"

"You weren't supposed to find out."

"*Why?*"

Maxine took a deep, wheezing breath and let it out slowly. "Because I know you didn't kill my daughter."

God, it felt good to hear that. "Thank you," Gwen said softly.

"It wasn't charity," Maxine snapped. "With you in jail, my husband and the police and the FBI were content to stop their search for the true killer."

"But what can *I* do?"

"Find the truth and save yourself."

Gwen considered her a moment. Maxine looked thinner than ever, almost feathery, as if a stiff breeze could knock her over, or perhaps carry her up and away.

"How do you know I'm innocent?" Gwen asked. "No one else thinks so."

"Because"—Maxine pushed her sunglasses up her nose—"I saw you with Tess. I don't think you could hurt her, and taking a mother from a child is very cruel." She nodded, as if to confirm her own opinion.

"And what else?" Gwen asked.

"I don't know what you mean."

"There's something else."

Maxine was silent for almost a minute, adjusting her sunglasses every fifteen seconds or so. Gwen wished she could see her eyes.

"Come," Maxine finally said, gesturing for Gwen to follow her.

"In case Russell comes home."

She led Gwen into the family room. The drapes were closed, as always, the room lit only by table lamps. She stood in the center of the room.

"This whole…nightmare, it began a long time ago, before you came to Penaquoit." Maxine started to remove her sunglasses but left them on.

Gwen thought immediately of Nick asking about her at the diner, back in the late spring, before he'd spoken directly to her.

"You mean earlier this spring," she said, "before I even came here?"

"No!" Maxine swatted the air with her right hand. "Long before you were in the picture, *years* ago."

"Nick and Priscilla…"

"Yes," she hissed.

"What about them?"

"Something wasn't right between them, from the beginning." Maxine held up a hand. "Please, don't ask me to explain, because I can't. I simply knew that things weren't the way they were supposed to be between a young couple. It wasn't just Nick, either. Priscilla wasn't the same girl after she moved back up here. You'd think motherhood would have softened her, but it didn't, not one bit."

"Why do you think that was?"

"I don't know. But have you ever been in a room and suddenly realized that everyone else around you is in on some sort of private joke, or secret?"

Gwen nodded.

"Well, that's how I felt whenever Nick and my daughter were around, that they shared something, some important secret. It was the only bond between them, I think, whatever it was." She cocked her head slightly. "And it formed a wall around them, kept them apart from everyone else, including me."

"And you have no idea what that secret was?"

She shook her head slowly. "But I know this. Once you discover the secret, you'll know what really happened at the Devil's Ravine."

Gwen remembered what Rosa Piacevic had overheard that night at Penaquoit.

"Did Nick ever have any trouble with the law?"

She waited a beat, then shook her head.

"Are you sure? Nothing involving drugs?"

"He's my granddaughter's father," Maxine said slowly. "My only surviving…my…"

That wasn't exactly an answer, but Gwen didn't have the heart to press her.

"You said that I had to find the truth in order to save myself. Nick won't even speak to me; the police aren't exactly eager to help prove my innocence. What can I do?"

"I can't help you, I'm afraid. I've done all I can."

"But you must know something."

"No, I…"

"Please, I need help."

"You need help? *You* need help?" Maxine removed her sunglasses, revealing a purple-black bruise around her left eye.

"*This* is what I got for posting your bail. I freed my daughter's murderer, that's what *he* thinks." She put the glasses back on with shaky fingers. "I've done all I can."

"I'm so…sorry, Mrs. Cunningham."

"Enough," Maxine said. "Leave this place, now. If someone should see you here…" She walked into the foyer.

Before following her, Gwen took a photo from a side table and shoved it into her purse: Priscilla, standing on the terrace at Penaquoit, held a grinning Tess, looking a bit nervous, as if clutching an antique porcelain vase. Gwen glanced around the room for a photo of Nick but found none, not surprisingly—this was Russell Cunningham's house, after all.

"Your husband destroyed all the thistle plants in Priscilla's garden," Gwen said at the front door.

"He…" Maxine's head began to tremble.

"Why, Mrs. Cunningham? Why would he do that?"

"I don't…I really don't know." Tears emerged from behind the sunglasses. "That policeman, Hawkins, he keeps asking us about that damn flower. We don't know why Priscilla had it with her, we don't have a clue."

Oh, yes, you do, Gwen felt like saying. But if Maxine hadn't told the police, she wasn't going to tell her. Anyway, the old woman had suffered enough. She thanked her, left the house, and got in her car. She was about to drive off when the front door opened. Maxine walked gingerly to the car, as if she were barefoot, and handed a slip of paper through the half-open car window.

"Start there." She turned and headed back inside.

The paper contained a name, *Mitchell Ellikin, MD,* written in a faint, unstable hand, followed by three letters: *NYC.*

CHAPTER 38

That evening she told Jimmy that she had to go to New York City for a few days. He took it well—too well. His only concern seemed to be the Pearsons, who made him go to bed earlier than usual, and hogged their sole television set watching the Food Channel. She called Sheila and Betsy, who happily agreed to take Jimmy for a few nights. The Pearsons would pick him up from camp at three, as usual, and hand him over to Sheila at six. At least he'd be away from the reporters who had formed a dwindling but seemingly permanent outpost in front of the house.

Working until almost one-thirty that night, she finished painting the dining-room walls satin white. Covering the old, off-white pigment with fresh new paint was the only satisfaction she'd had in what felt like a lifetime. She left for Manhattan the next morning after dropping Jimmy at camp.

When she first caught sight of the Manhattan skyline from the upper level of the George Washington Bridge, at eleven-fifteen that morning, Gwen turned away, focusing determinedly on the road ahead. In the past, returning to the city from out of town made her feel like a hopeful immigrant, the Oz-like spectacle of midtown Manhattan promising excitement and opportunity. Now it made her queasy with apprehension. *Barry's gone*, she reminded herself as she merged onto the West Side Highway, heading downtown. *He can't harm either of us. Jimmy's safe.*

Was he, though? If she couldn't prove her innocence, what

would become of him? If Maxine Cunningham was right, the key to Priscilla's murder, and thus to her own future, lay in Manhattan, the place she'd fled nearly six months ago, vowing never to return.

By noon she had checked into the Boulevard Hotel on the West Side, close to where she and Barry had lived. Too close, actually, but she didn't have time to search Manhattan for an affordable hotel room; the Boulevard was convenient to Mitchell Ellikin's office, inexpensive, and clean. She left her suitcase in the room and caught the 79th Street crosstown bus on Broadway.

As she walked from the bus stop toward Ellikin's office on East 78th Street, she prayed no one would recognize her from the photograph that was circulating in newspapers and on television. The press had somehow gotten hold of a photo taken at last year's Christmas party in the lobby of her old building.

She'd stopped at an East Side newsstand and studied her face on the front page of the *Post*. Her hair had been longer then, and most of her features were in shadow. She almost didn't recognize herself, especially the tense expression on her face as she held a plastic wineglass to her lips; Barry had been drinking that night.

Ellikin's address, which she'd gotten from directory assistance that morning, led her to something called East Side Reproductive Services. It was located on the second floor of a modern apartment building just off Third Avenue, in a suite of medical offices accessible directly from the street. She walked down a long corridor until she found Mitchell Ellikin among several doctors' names stenciled on a glass door. She pressed the doorbell and was immediately buzzed in.

She crossed the waiting room to a long, waist-high counter. An attractive young black woman looked up from a very crowded appointment register.

"I need to see Dr. Ellikin," Gwen said.

"Your name?"

"I don't have an appointment."

"I'm sorry, you'll—"

"Tell him I'm a friend of Nick Lawrence."

"I'm afraid we—"

"*Tell him.*"

The receptionist frowned and disappeared through a doorway. The waiting room decor was blandly contemporary: pastel fabrics, framed art posters, stacks of old magazines, little signs indicating that credit cards were accepted, smoking wasn't. There was one patient, a woman.

The receptionist returned and asked Gwen to follow. She led her to a small, windowless examination room. A man joined her a moment later, wearing a white lab jacket over a dark blue shirt and rich burgundy tie.

"I'm Dr. Ellikin," he said. "And you are?"

Ellikin was tall and quite thin. He had glossy black hair rigidly parted on the side, revealing a line of flesh as white as the newly painted trim in her dining room. He looked to be in his mid- to late-forties, yet his pale face was unexpectedly youthful, virtually wrinkle-free.

"My name is Gwen Amiel. I think you know who I am."

He seemed ready to contradict her, but after a brief hesitation he nodded, shoulders sagging.

"What's this about?" he said. "I have a patient in my office and another in the room next door."

"I'd like to know about your relationship with Nick and Priscilla Lawrence."

He exhaled loudly and leaned against the wall. "Ancient history." His voice was deep, his tone patrician and vaguely bored. She'd never in a million years let him near her with a speculum.

"I love history," she said.

"Then try the library. Or the FBI. I've been through this with them already, and I have no desire to dredge it all up again."

She had a decision to make: play on his sympathy...or scare the shit out of him. His eyes were blue and analytical, but dark circles underneath hinted at troubled dreams.

Scare him it was.

"The Priscilla Lawrence murder is front page news," she said. "I can have any reporter I choose on the phone in five minutes. I think they might be interested in the Nick Lawrence/Mitchell Ellikin angle."

Not that she had the slightest idea what that angle might be. But when his eyes widened, exposing a grid of fine wrinkles on his pale forehead, she knew she'd struck a chord.

"I have nothing to say to you." His voice had thinned out.

She headed for the door. "Fine, I'll talk to the media, then."

"Wait!" She stopped and turned. "There weren't any charges, you know."

Charges?

"Of course not," she said slowly, "but I doubt your patients would appreciate the negative publicity. Not to mention your colleagues."

"You're just like Nick," he said, spitting the name at her. "How did you get involved with Nick Lawrence?" It was a question she'd been asking herself quite a lot lately.

"I fail to see how that is any of your business."

She was halfway down the hall when he called her name.

"I was getting divorced, for the second time," he said when she returned to the examination room, "and I had a fiancée. Ex-wives are very expensive, and my current wife isn't what you'd call abstemious. My partners and I had just opened this clinic, our overhead was exorbitant, and we got off to rather a slow start."

"What exactly do you do here?"

"Assisted reproductive technologies…infertility, basically. Artificial insemination, in vitro fertilization, gamete intrafallopian transfer."

"What's that?"

"We remove eggs from the ovaries, combine them with sperm in a petri dish, then—Miss Amiel, what the hell does this have to do with Nick Lawrence?"

"You tell me," she said.

He nodded with a condescending smile and closed the door.

"My medical work has nothing to do with Nick Lawrence, thank God. He approached me several years back with a little scheme he'd hatched. He had friends, acquaintances, really, many of them fellow musicians, who wanted a certain prescription drug, Ritalin."

"But that's for—"

"Children with attention deficit disorder. Correct. Kids with ADD don't get high off Ritalin; in fact it helps them focus, apparently—pediatrics is not my specialty, obviously. But college students have begun taking it as a study aid. It's a stimulant—sometimes they grind it up like cocaine and snort it."

"Nick Lawrence wanted Ritalin?"

"Not for himself. A lot of musicians, those who teach or hold various other day jobs, need stimulants in order to have the energy and alertness to practice. No responsible physician would prescribe Ritalin for this purpose, of course. That's where I came in. I wrote the prescriptions, and Nick managed to get them filled at a network of pharmacies he put together. Then he passed them along to his 'friends,' charging a nice markup."

"Which you split."

He glared at her before nodding. "The clinic is a gold mine today, but back then I was living hand to mouth. Nick Lawrence bought me valuable time. Unfortunately, one of his musician friends, a cellist, took too much Ritalin. I, of course, have no way of regulating how much they take. It's completely out of my hands."

He paused, perhaps waiting for absolution. Instead of providing it she focused on Ellikin's fingernails, which were polished to a pearly gloss.

"At any rate," he said, "the cellist swallowed or snorted more Ritalin than he should have and ended up in the hospital. Some sort of psychotic episode—he hadn't slept or eaten for several days. The police arrested Nick, and they located my name on a prescription in his apartment."

Ellikin picked up the crumpled plastic gown and shoved it into a garbage pail.

"The Manhattan district attorney's office offered to drop all charges against Nick if he testified against me. He refused. Nick was charged, but eventually the DA dropped the case. Small potatoes, really—all they had was that one envelope of pills found in the cellist's apartment."

"Why did Nick refuse to testify against you?"

He shrugged and shook his head. "I really don't know."

"He was willing to go to jail for you?" she said. "And you don't know why?"

"I think he knew he'd never go to jail over a handful of pills. The DA was trying to play hardball. Nick outsmarted them."

She couldn't picture Nick risking prison for anyone, least of all the imperious Mitchell Ellikin, whom he hardly knew. Then she remembered that he'd left out a key detail.

"How did you and Nick meet?"

"Meet?" He squinted and puckered his lips. "He was a messenger at the time, working for a medical imaging group I refer patients to. He delivered the x-rays and CAT scans."

"A *messenger* proposed a drug deal to *you*, the doctor?" She frowned.

"He was here virtually every day, flirting with the receptionist, the nurses. He's a very attractive man, as I think you of all people know." Ellikin's chilly smile meant he'd read the tabloids, perhaps even the JANE EYRE KILLER headline in the *Daily News*.

"When was your last contact with Nick?"

"Two years ago, when this incident occurred. I phoned him after he refused to cooperate with the police, to thank him. We never spoke again."

"And he never asked for anything in return?"

He shook his head.

"Money?"

"He wouldn't have gotten any even if he had asked."

Yeah, right. Ellikin struck her as the type who'd sell his firstborn to save his "gold mine." And Nick? Would Nick have let Ellikin walk away free and clear? He never talked about money or *things* much, but could she honestly say that he wasn't interested?

"I'm a busy man, Mrs. Amiel, and I've told the FBI exactly what I just told you. So if you have no other questions, perhaps you might answer one for me. What the hell does any of this have to do with you and your...predicament?"

"I've been accused of—"

"I know what you've been accused of. What does this...fiasco between Nick Lawrence and me have to do with your case?"

"Probably nothing," she said, fearing it was true. Yet Maxine Cunningham's words echoed through her mind. *This whole... nightmare, it began a long time ago, before you came to Penaquoit...long before you were in the picture, years ago.*

"That's precisely the conclusion the FBI reached."

Ellikin pulled a paper towel from a wall dispenser and wiped the spotless countertop. Gwen muttered a few words of thanks and left the examination room. She crossed the waiting area, heading straight for the exit.

"Miss?" The receptionist motioned her over. "We, uh, well, we generally prefer payment in full at the time of the visit." She seemed uncomfortable in the role of debt collector. "Cash or credit card."

"I doubt there'll be a bill," Gwen said.

"Let me just check." The receptionist picked up the receiver and pressed a button. A faint buzz emanated from down the corridor.

"How long have you been here?" Gwen asked as the receptionist waited for an answer.

"Just three months." Long after Nick Lawrence left the scene. "Who was here before you, do you know?"

"Before me?" She pushed the intercom button again. "Half the receptionists in the city. There's a lot of turnover."

"Why's that?"

"This place is incredibly busy." She nodded at the three women and two couples who had filled the waiting room in Gwen's absence.

"A gold mine," Gwen muttered.

"We really need a separate billing clerk," the receptionist said softly, leaning toward Gwen. "Between answering the phones, making appointments, handling the doctors' personal affairs...well, it's too much for one person."

"How many doctors work here?"

"Two REs, a couple of lab technicians, two nurses, and me."

"REs?"

"Reproductive endocrinologists, like Dr. Ellikin."

"I assumed he was a gynecologist."

"Same med school training, but then they do a two-year fellowship to learn the infertility stuff. At least that's what they tell me. Anyway, this one temp agency he once used won't even send him girls anymore, they're just—oh, yes, Doctor Ellikin? Miss... your patient is about to leave, I haven't...oh, okay." She looked puzzled as she hung up.

"You were right, no charge."

Gwen thanked her and left.

CHAPTER 39

Gwen caught the subway a block from Ellikin's office. As the number-four train clattered south toward Brooklyn she wondered how she'd tolerated the subway for so long. The grime, the noise, the gray defeat written on every face—she'd become immune to it all while living there. Now, after just five months away, it was vivid again, and oppressive.

She got off in Park Slope and headed for the address Kevin Gargano had given her on the phone that morning. Barry's last known residence had been included in the evidentiary papers the prosecution had turned over to her attorney.

She pressed the button next to the name Dilianna Flores, and was buzzed into the building a few seconds later. Climbing the dimly lit stairway to the third floor, she took in the strips of yellow paint peeling from the walls and ceiling, the rickety banister, the smudged linoleum, and felt a momentary pang for Barry, for how far he'd fallen.

To hell with pity, she decided as she reached the third floor. It was one thing to fall from grace. Barry had tried to take Jimmy down with him.

The woman who opened the door looked about forty, with a trim figure and shoulder-length black hair. Her eyes were dark and accusatory, her lipstick an angry red.

"Dilianna Flores? I'm Gwen Amiel." She extended her hand, which the woman scrutinized a few seconds before shaking. "My husband, Barry, used to live here."

"Mother of God, enough of this!" she said in a Spanish accent. "First the FBI, then the fingerprint people, then the FBI again, and now you?"

"May I come in?"

She shook her head but opened the door. "There is nothing here for you to see. They take everything, the FBI. Next thing you know, the housing police will come and close me down for not having the correct permit."

Gwen glanced around as she reached for the photograph of Priscilla and Tess in her pocketbook. The large living room had only one window, which overlooked an air shaft. A ceiling light did little to offset the gloom, but the room appeared tidy, and the mismatched fabrics on the sofas and chairs, the various patterns on the throw rugs, lent the room a jumbled liveliness.

"I have just one question," Gwen said as she held out the photo. "Did this woman ever visit while my husband lived here?"

Dilianna took the photo and studied it. "I don't think so, but..."

"But what?"

She shook her head. "Nothing."

"You were about to say something."

"I thought she look familiar, but I was wrong."

Gwen took back the photo. In truth, she'd have been surprised to learn that Priscilla had visited Barry...but she had little else to go on.

"How about a tall man, mid-thirties, handsome, blue eyes."

"No men were visiting him, just girls." Dilianna snorted and shook her head. "Mostly cheap girls, drunks like him."

She felt another pang for Barry, then resentment at her own weakness.

"Mostly?" Gwen said. "One of his girls was...different?"

Dilianna took the photo again, looked at it with a puzzled expression, and handed it back.

"Something in this picture remind me, there was this one girl, classy, you know what I mean? Not like the others. But she didn't stay long, probably got a look at the mess in his room, you know what I mean? Outta there in five minutes flat. You think I should tell the FBI man?"

"She didn't give her name?"

"To me?" Another snort. "She look like she afraid she get a disease just touching anything here, you know? She wouldn't look at me, all I saw was her legs, which were not too bad, and her red hair, which she had in a black bow."

"Red hair?"

"She have dark skin for a redhead. I remember thinking you don't see that much, red hair like that and dark skin. Usually the redheads, they have skin like mayonnaise."

"Valerie Goodwin," Gwen muttered.

"Who?"

"Did she bring anything with her, take anything away?"

"Not that I see, but who knows? Maybe I should call that FBI man, the one who liked my arroz con pollo. Eh?" She shrugged and wiped her hands on her apron. "Why bother? I mind my own business. You got any more questions? 'Cause I got things to do."

Gwen thanked her and left.

Dwight Hawkins rolled down his window and spoke his name into the square receiver in front of the gates of Penaquoit. A moment later they opened with imperious languor.

He drove slowly up the tree-lined approach to the mansion, wondering what the hell he was doing there. "Leave well enough alone," Elaine had said to him that morning as she stood sentry over his breakfast. Leaving well enough alone was her life philosophy— his too, who was he kidding? Their lives had been shaped by the acceptance of compromise, the very gradual lowering of their threshold of "enough."

The mansion loomed into view, its staid invulnerability echoing Elaine's warning: leave it alone. But he couldn't. For though the FBI seemed quite pleased with its case against Gwen Amiel and her late husband, his instincts were telling him that something wasn't right.

Which was ironic, really, since up to the moment he'd arrested Gwen Amiel Sunday morning, his instincts had shouted loud and clear: she's guilty as sin. But this morning he'd awakened to one question that wouldn't leave him: assuming Gwen Amiel murdered her husband (to avoid splitting the five million? to shut him up?), who had called the FBI to direct them to the body?

"*She* called," Don Reeves had said on the phone that morning. "Gwen Amiel figured once we'd found him dead, with a couple of hundred-dollar bills on him, we'd stop hunting down the perp. She didn't count on us finding her directions to the mansion in his effects."

"But he was her husband, Don. How could she think that finding her husband dead with ransom money—not to mention the handgun that killed Priscilla—would point suspicion *away* from her?"

"Her *estranged* husband, who she claimed not to have seen in months. So she waits until the body is practically liquified, which makes fixing the date of death impossible, and calls us. Makes sense to me. Anyway, let the defense worry about this, okay?"

"What about the break-in at her house, that effigy at the ravine?"

"Pranks, Dwight, stupid pranks. I'll tell you what, why don't you and your boys track down the perpetrators, okay, Dwight? Probably a bunch of kids, but it'll keep you occupied until this case comes to trial."

Rosa Piacevic answered the door, holding Tess in one arm. She stepped out onto the small flagstone terrace. He heard piano music from beyond the front hallway.

"Mr. Lawrence is practicing piano now," she whispered nervously. "You want me to tell him you are here?"

"In a minute, Rosa. Do you remember how I once asked you about that baby monitor?"

She nodded and stroked Tess's golden hair. A beautiful child, with her father's sharp features and even his serene self-possession.

"And you said it never left the nursery?"

"Never."

"Are you positive about that?"

"Of course I am." Creases emerged on her forehead. Her

features seemed crowded in the center of her face—perhaps it was the lack of eyebrows. "It never leave the nursery."

Which meant, as the prosecutor was going to argue, that Gwen Amiel had not "accidentally" overheard the plans for the money swap. She knew about the arrangements because she'd orchestrated them herself.

Or she had *heard about the swap through the monitor, in which case someone had deliberately moved it that morning to the master bedroom, someone who* wanted *her to hear,* wanted *her at the Devil's Ravine.*

"How is the little girl doing?" he asked, unable to take his eyes off the child.

"Tess is good," Rosa Piacevic said with a single, resolute nod. "Isn't that right, *zamer?*"

The little girl reached out a hand. He extended his pinkie and she grasped it, squeezing it with gratifying firmness in her tiny fist.

Leave well enough alone. Hawkins smiled as he gently pulled his finger from her hand and forced himself to look at Rosa.

"First her mother, now her baby-sitter...Tess must have *some* reaction to so much loss."

"Tess is lucky, her father is father *and* mother. I don't mean nothing against her, Mrs. Lawrence, but that's how it was."

"I suppose he has no choice."

She shook her head, almost angry. "Even...before, he was father and mother."

He looked back at Tess, who was growing restless in Rosa's arms. "You want me to get Mr. Lawrence?"

"I'll find him myself," he said, and followed the music into the living room. He stood in the entrance, listening. Something romantic, he thought, passionate. His eyes studied Nick Lawrence's back, hunched over the keyboard as if preying upon it. But his mind's eye was fixed on Tess Lawrence's face. Something about that face...

He cleared his throat. Nick Lawrence stopped playing and turned abruptly, eyes fierce, jaws clenched for rebuke.

"Oh, it's you." He turned back to the piano for a moment. When he faced Dwight a second time his features had regained their usual composure.

Dwight felt his stomach muscles cramp. He'd never seen a face go from ugly to splendid like that.

"What can I do for you?" Nick said.

"You remember I asked you about the baby monitor?"

"Christ, that again?"

His annoyance was justified, and yet the monitor went to the heart of the matter.

"You're positive it was in the nursery? Are you sure that no one was listening from the hallway when you and your father-in-law and your wife were talking about ransom plans?"

"As I've said a dozen times already, the door to the master bedroom was open. If someone had been listening in the hallway we would have seen them. And the monitor was not in the room. It never leaves the nursery." He seemed quite positive, and that precise diction of his, that prosecutorial inflection he was prone to, made arguing with him an unappealing prospect.

"Then Gwen Amiel knew about the ransom plans from some other source."

He shrugged and shook his head slowly. "We were sleeping together, I'm sure you know that. Had I known what she'd…" His voice broke and he took a deep breath. "She was my child's baby-sitter, do you understand that? I entrusted my daughter's well-being to this woman who…" He shuddered. Red splotches appeared on his cheeks and jaw.

"I'm sorry, Mr. Lawrence, I—"

"Dada!"

Tess charged into the room, Rosa Piacevic close behind.

"Come here, dumpling," she said. "Dada is talking with…"

"It's okay, Rosa." He scooped up his daughter and tossed her into the air, catching her in both hands and pulling her to his chest.

"Anything else, Mr. Hawkins?" He wiped tears from his eyes with the back of a hand.

"There is one more thing. The morning your wife was killed, do you recall where she went?"

"Jesus Christ, that again? The poor woman's dead. Who cares if she drove around for a while that morning?"

"So she was driving around?"

Lawrence glared at him, his chest heaving under his damp T-shirt. He was like some kind of wildcat, muscles always poised for combat.

"You're absolutely positive she was driving that morning?"

"I don't know. For the hundredth time I don't know." He sounded angry but also, for the first time, worried.

Dwight shook his head and glanced at the little girl. He was certainly no judge of infant beauty, but Tess Lawrence struck him as exceptionally pretty, with an almost magnetic intensity to her eyes. And yet there was something else he couldn't quite figure out, something in that face that disturbed him somehow. He glanced from father to daughter. The similarities were obvious, and yet there was another, deeper quality to her face that he couldn't quite fathom.

"I'll let myself out," he said, and by the time he reached the front door he heard the piano again, that same piece, the notes flowing as smoothly as before.

CHAPTER 40

Gwen rode the subway back to Manhattan, after calling directory assistance for Valerie Goodwin's address. She got off at 23rd Street and walked two blocks north to Valerie's building, feeling buoyed by accomplishment. She was saving herself.

Valerie lived in a six-story white brick building on East 25th Street, a few doors east of Lexington Avenue. Gwen pressed the buzzer next to GOODWIN and waited. The building wasn't nearly as elegant as she'd expected, given Valerie's stylishness. There was no doorman, the tiny vestibule was filthy, and the address itself was rather unfashionable.

"Yes?" Valerie's voice crackled through the antiquated intercom.

"It's Gwen Amiel."

A long silence; then the lock on the inside door clicked open. Gwen rode a cramped, jerky elevator to the fourth floor. When she got off, Valerie was standing in front of an open door, arms pressed against the frame, as if holding the two sides apart. Her red hair was gathered in a girlish ponytail. She wore a long gray sweatshirt over black leggings.

"What a surprise." An unpleasant one, her tone suggested.

Gwen replied with a smile; her goal, after all, was to be invited inside the apartment.

"I need to talk to you," she said.

Valerie kept her hands on the door frame. Her angular face and thin body had seemed chic and attractive under the warm sunlight of Penaquoit. Now, wearing no makeup, her face bleached by harsh fluorescence, she looked merely unhealthy.

"What were you doing at my husband's boardinghouse in

303

Brooklyn?" Gwen asked.

Valerie squinted, as if confused.

"I have proof you were there," Gwen lied.

Valerie waited a moment, then turned and walked leisurely through the door. Gwen followed.

The apartment was a single small room with one big window overlooking the back of a new high-rise. Yet the place was furnished in jarring defiance of its dimensions, like a plain face with too much makeup. An oversize sofa in front of the window was covered in a lush print fabric, flanked by two large wing chairs. An expensive-looking Kirmin rug extended almost to all four walls. An Empire mahogany dining table, the genuine article, Gwen suspected, was shoved into the corner nearest the closet-size kitchen. Six chairs, also Empire, also probably genuine, were crammed shoulder-to-shoulder around it.

Valerie sat in one of the wing chairs, Gwen on the sofa.

"Priscilla asked me to see your husband, as a favor," Valerie said, her voice as silky as the damask fabric on the chair. Lit by the more compassionate table lamp, she'd regained some of her chic.

"What?"

"Are you surprised? Priscilla entrusted her daughter to you; she naturally wanted some reassurance about your character." Valerie arched her expertly plucked eyebrows. "I must say, my visit to your husband's lodgings wasn't very encouraging."

"Nick hired me, not Priscilla. She didn't strike me as overly concerned about child care."

"Honestly, the poor woman's dead." Valerie may have intended to sound censorious, but she came off as eerily unemotional, almost ironic.

"How did you find Barry?" Gwen asked.

"I got the address from Priscilla."

"How did Priscilla know where he lived? Even I didn't know."

"I haven't the slightest idea." She draped one long, thin leg over the other.

Of course not, and Priscilla, conveniently, was unable to explain it herself.

"I found out yesterday that Nick was asking questions about me even before we'd met," Gwen said. "Any idea why he'd do that?"

"You'll have to ask him," she said smoothly.

"How long have you known Nick?"

"As long as he knew Priscilla, about three years."

"He told me they met when he gave her piano lessons."

"That's right."

"But you once told me that you'd introduced them."

"Did I?" She flexed all ten fingers on her lap; her knuckles crackled like lit kindling.

"Yes, you did," Gwen said. "You told me she lived across the hall."

"And I referred her to the music school at which Nick happened to be teaching."

"Somehow I can't picture Priscilla Lawrence living in this building," Gwen said. "I can't imagine Russell Cunningham *letting* her live here."

Valerie offered a dainty shrug. Her face was striking in a hard-edged way. Even her plump lips looked tough as rubber. And there was something vaguely familiar about her face…Gwen felt sure she'd seen it recently, *after* Valerie's visit to Penaquoit, perhaps in a magazine or newspaper.

"Have you ever done any modeling work?"

"When I was much younger. Nothing recent. I'm an actress," she added with a lift of her sharp chin.

Gwen nodded and stood up. "Are you in anything now?"

"No." The chin rose another inch.

"How do you support yourself, then?" Gwen asked, wondering if she'd mention the stipend she used to receive from Priscilla.

"I'm living off my savings at the moment. I worked in a gallery until recently."

Gwen glanced at a framed poster of an abstract painting over the words *Sensor Gallery.*

"What exactly did you and my husband talk about?"

"I don't recall," Valerie said. "He wasn't what I'd call lucid, I do remember that much."

"You must remember something."

She moved her head ever so slightly from side to side.

"Did you know he had been in Sohegan?" Gwen asked.

"I would have thought you'd be the one to know that."

Gwen felt her face warm. "My life is on the line," she said. "I'm accused of something I didn't do, and I believe that you can help clear me."

"I've been to Sohegan exactly twice," Valerie said. She picked up a small inlaid box and ran a manicured finger along the top. "I know nothing about your problems."

"Tell me about the purple thistle Priscilla had with her that day."

"Purple *what?*"

Gwen waited her out.

"I don't know anything about that," Valerie said, but her eyes went out of focus for a moment. Either she knew what the thistle meant, and was lying, or she didn't know, and was worried.

"You're hiding something." Gwen crossed to the front door, opened it, and turned. "You *and* Nick."

"Coming from an accused murderer, that's probably a compliment." Valerie followed her to the door.

"I'll find out what really happened at the Devil's Ravine," she said. "I have no choice."

"Do what you have to do," Valerie said lightly, but her shrug was more of a spasm, and her eyes drifted again as she contemplated some private strategy already cooking inside her head.

Gwen considered her a moment. "You're scared," she said. "You're afraid of what I'm going to find."

"You're the one who's afraid." Valerie's voice was unsteady, but her gaze was now firmly fixed on Gwen. "You're going to spend the rest of your life in prison. And you've already lost Nick." She was still laughing, deeply and without mirth, when she slammed the door.

Gwen took the stairs down to the lobby, trying to forget that laugh. Valerie Goodwin was lying through her clenched teeth. But why? Why had she gone to see Barry in early June? That bit about checking up on him for Priscilla rang false.

Pushing open the door to the lobby, she almost ran into a man standing before a row of mailboxes just inside the front vestibule.

"Sorry," she said, but the mailman was wearing headphones and didn't respond. She angled around him, opened the door to leave, and stopped.

"Excuse me? *Excuse me?*"

He looked at her and adjusted the volume on the tape player strapped to his waist. The nameplate on his pale blue uniform shirt read *Scott DeBuono.*

"Have you worked in this neighborhood for long?"

"Almost ten years."

"I'm trying to locate someone who used to live in this building. Priscilla Cunningham."

He turned from her to the mailboxes. One large horizontal door, opened by a single master key, gave easy access to all ten mailboxes at once. Labels with handwritten names had been affixed to the inside of each door; they were only visible when the master door was open. Many of the boxes had more than one name; several had layers of labels, one pasted on top of another. "She doesn't live here anymore," Gwen said as the mailman scanned the labels.

"Yeah, but I usually leave the name on anyway, in case something arrives after they're gone. Nope, no Cunningham. Don't remember the name, either. I usually do."

He resumed sorting the mail. Gwen glanced at the boxes, found apartment 4C, and saw Valerie Goodwin's name written in faded ink on a yellowed label. There was at least one label underneath.

"I think my friend lived in Four C. Mind if I look?"

He shrugged and continued filling the mailboxes. She placed a fingernail under Valerie's label and gently pulled it halfway off, revealing an even older label underneath.

The writing was badly faded, but she made out the name easily enough. She felt a sudden tightness in her chest. *You've already lost Nick.*

"Did...did Nick Lawrence live here?"

He continued sorting letters. "Sure, Four C. About three years ago, maybe longer."

"Before Valerie Goodwin moved in?"

"I don't know who lived there first. They were together when I started on this route."

"Together?" The tightness in her chest reduced her voice to a whisper.

"Sure." He stepped to the right and peeled off the entire label from the 4C mailbox. The label underneath read NICK LAWRENCE/VALERIE GOODWIN. "I was surprised when he moved out. They seemed happy enough. Sometimes they'd come down together to get the mail. You know, like they couldn't be apart for even five minutes." He put the top label back in position and pressed it with his index finger. "Then one day—pfft—he was outta here, no forwarding address, nothing."

She couldn't find the breath to thank him. She charged through the front doors to the sidewalk and gulped the warm air. Nick Lawrence had convinced her to trust him, he'd made love to her, and he'd lied to her...about Valerie Goodwin and much more. He'd lived with Valerie in that one-room apartment, then left to marry Priscilla.

And yet the three of them had remained friends...How was that possible?

She took a cab back to the hotel, staring at the gray blur of New York at dusk, the lights and shop signs and passing cars like flashbulbs popping in her face, leaving her dizzy and disoriented. She rolled down the taxi window and let the damp, sooty air wash over her face, her sense of empowerment rapidly giving way to the conviction that the closer she got to a solution to Priscilla Cunningham's murder, the worse she was going to feel.

CHAPTER 41

Gwen stood across from 222 West 83rd Street that evening and counted up six floors to her old apartment. Warm yellow lights glowed in several windows—their former living room, Jimmy's old bedroom, the guest bathroom. She felt a peculiar satisfaction in that; the apartment had been sold after all; a new life was taking root where the old one had died.

She walked east, turned down Amsterdam, and leaned against a parking meter in front of her old store, now a card shop. She'd really loved Better Times—the store's name had a bitter irony now, but twelve years ago, when she opened it, Better Times expressed not just nostalgia for the past but her expectations for the future. She could still smell the sharp, resiny furniture polish that had greeted her every morning after she'd hoisted the heavy metal window gate and unlocked the front door. Each sale had felt like a small triumph, no matter how slim the profit. There was a time, early in their marriage, when she'd race home to share the news with Barry: *I sold the Hoosier cupboard for six hundred, can you believe it?* Later, the shop had become her refuge, each sale less a triumph than a finger in the dike holding back financial ruin.

And yet she found herself curiously unable to leave. Standing in front of the card shop, she had the sense that she was looking at a vestige of someone else's life, a life at once familiar and remote, like a character from a book read long ago. Had so much of her happiness really depended on this narrow space, a thousand square feet wedged between a Korean nail salon and a take-out Chinese place? Had she really been so deluded? Once her life revolved around pine sideboards and marble-topped washstands and ladder-back chairs. Now her former sanctuary was a card shop and she felt wholly unmoved by the sight; in fact, that very absence of emotion, where surely some sentiment should be, was what kept her standing there, in a hazy, almost hypnotic state.

Eventually something brought her around. It was a face reflected in the front window of the card shop, just another pedestrian on busy Amsterdam Avenue. But a familiar face, and not a friendly one, even in reflection.

Gwen turned quickly and locked eyes for a brief moment with a startled Valerie Goodwin. Then Valerie ran toward the corner and disappeared down a side street. Gwen began to follow but had to stop on the far side of Amsterdam for ongoing traffic and gave up.

In her hotel bed that night, Gwen felt an overpowering isolation. Somehow the fact that Valerie Goodwin had been following her only added to the feeling of being totally alone. The room smelled of mothballs, old shoes, and despair. The sheets were starchy and too white. Her old life was gone; her new life, it turned out, was built on a lie. Nick Lawrence had *chosen* her, he'd lied about his past, he'd sent Valerie Goodwin to check up on her husband...and worse, she was beginning to imagine, much worse.

She didn't think she'd get any rest that night, but when she closed her eyes she found the blackness an unexpected comfort, and soon drifted off to sleep.

CHAPTER 42

Gwen entered the Sensor Gallery, on Broome Street in Soho, at ten o'clock the next morning. The gallery occupied one very large ground-floor room in a former industrial building. Its walls were bright white, the floor polyeurethaned to an icy shine. A dozen or so enormous canvases lined the gallery, depicting, in hyperrealism, tight groups of people wearing vacant expressions of postmodern apathy.

Behind a desk near the gallery entrance sat an elegantly thin woman with a gamin haircut who might have posed for one of the paintings. She smiled languidly as Gwen explained that she was seeking information about a former employee. She did manage to lift the phone from its cradle and buzz for the director, who appeared a moment later through a doorway at the back of the gallery.

"I'm Fiona Stevens," she said. "How can I help you?"

Fiona Stevens, who looked about thirty, wore a white oxford shirt, white denim pants, and white loafers. Even her skin was milk white; if it weren't for her shoulder-length black hair, she'd have no trouble camouflaging herself against any wall of the gallery. Gwen wondered if white had replaced black as the official Soho color in the short time she'd been gone.

"I'm trying to track down an old friend, Valerie Goodwin."

"Valerie hasn't worked here in several months. Janet took her place." She nodded at the receptionist, who didn't look up from the keyboard of a sleek laptop. "Have you tried the phone book?"

"She's not listed," Gwen lied, hoping she wouldn't be contradicted. "But I remember her mentioning that she worked here. Why did she leave the gallery?"

"I don't really know, and I was rather surprised, to tell you the truth. She'd been here almost three years, with practically no absences, other than that one time just after she started, when she took a short leave."

"A leave?"

Fiona Stevens looked puzzled. "Didn't you say you were a friend of Valerie's?"

Gwen tried not to flinch as the director looked her over. Before leaving the hotel she'd pulled her hair back into a short ponytail to maximize the contrast with the photographs in yesterday's editions. Her photo hadn't been in the New York papers that morning.

"We were very close at one time," she said smoothly. "But we've lost touch. What kind of leave did Valerie take?" Gwen felt the collective gaze of all those hollow-eyed urbanites on the walls—the vast room felt suddenly crowded, and hot.

"I really shouldn't discuss—"

"She was my sister-in-law, actually," Gwen blurted. "Ex-sister-in-law. My husband—ex-husband—is very ill, I just found out." She hoped her nervousness sounded like concern. "If Valerie has any sort of medical condition, she really must be tested. Our own child..." Gwen looked away, eyes downcast, trying not to overdo it.

"I'm so sorry," Fiona Stevens said. "You really don't have to worry about Valerie, though. It *was* a medical leave, but it was gynecological. She didn't go into specifics, though I do seem to recall that she'd temped for a gynecologist before coming here."

"Oh, God," Gwen said as several pieces of the puzzle slotted together. "Ellikin." Nick hadn't met Ellikin while delivering x-rays. He'd been introduced to him by the receptionist, Valerie Goodwin.

"That's right, it was a Dr. Ellikin. She was a gal Friday, basically—appointments, billing, that kind of thing."

"Are you sure she took a week off for a gynecological procedure?" Gwen asked.

"Minor surgery, I think she said. We weren't exactly on intimate terms. Anyway, why in the world does this matter? Surely her brother didn't suffer from a gynecological ailment."

Gwen looked around the gallery to avoid the woman's gaze.

The paintings were powerful in a bleak, pitiful way, each one like a photograph dropped on the sidewalk, insignificant to the person who found it, but obviously rich with meaning to the one who'd lost it.

"She kept her distance," Fiona Stevens said, glancing at a nearby canvas as if expecting to find Valerie depicted on it. "Not exactly warm, but efficient and reliable. She was very vague about her future plans—do you know what she ended up doing?"

Gwen had an idea, but kept it to herself.

Fifteen minutes later, Gwen rang the doorbell at East Side Reproductive Services. She rang again. Still no answer.

"I'll open it."

She turned and saw the attractive black receptionist from the clinic hurrying down the long corridor.

"Sorry, Metpath pickup," she said.

At the end of the corridor a uniformed delivery man waited for the elevator, holding what looked like an oversize lunch box with *Metpath* stenciled on the side.

The receptionist stopped a few feet from Gwen, a look of recognition, and then concern, crossing her face.

"I'm not here to cause trouble," Gwen said. "I just need to see Dr. Ellikin."

"I don't think you have an appointment."

"Just tell him I'm here, okay? Gwen Amiel."

"I know who you are." She unlocked the door, motioned for Gwen to follow her inside, and walked quickly behind the counter, tossing her key and a Metpath receipt onto the blotter as she sat down. She lifted the phone and punched in two numbers.

There were three other women in the waiting room, all in their late thirties, Gwen guessed, all wearing conservative suits and silk blouses. They had quickly averted their eyes when Gwen turned around—did they too recognize the notorious murderer? Or was it the fertility clinic itself that was making them edgy?

"Dr. Ellikin will see you in his office," the receptionist said as she hung up the phone. "Fifth door on the left."

Ellikin wasn't in his office when she walked in. She sat in a visitor's chair and looked around. The desk was blond wood, the chairs upholstered in an innocuous pastel pattern; the fichus in the corner behind his desk looked suspiciously robust—perhaps a fake? The only personal touch was a silver-framed photograph of a beaming Ellikin with his arm around a beautiful young woman. Must be the new wife for whom he'd risked his medical license.

Ellikin entered the room and waited until he was seated behind his desk before addressing her.

"What are you doing here?" he said, sounding more weary than curious.

"Why didn't you tell me that Valerie Goodwin used to work with you?"

"Who?"

"No more games. If I don't get honest answers from you I'm going right to the newspapers with what I know about you and Nick Lawrence."

"That's your choice. I doubt you'll find much interest in a two-year-old prescription drug case in which no charges were ever filed."

"They'll be plenty of interest now, though, given Nick's connection to his wife's murder."

She stood and headed for the door.

"Wait."

She stopped and turned. A veil of anxiety had fallen over his eyes.

"Valerie Goodwin was a temp, a receptionist. I don't know how long she was with me. What difference does it make?" His lips seemed to falter in the effort of forming a smile.

"She knew Nick. She..." Gwen sat in a chair in front of his desk. "She *lived with* Nick Lawrence."

"Fascinating."

"Valerie introduced you to Nick. She probably set the drug deal up for you."

"'Drug deal?' I think that's a bit of a stretch. We're talking Ritalin prescriptions."

"Why did you deny that Valerie worked here? What are you afraid of?"

"I'm afraid of nothing." A bead of sweat sparkled in the hollow above his upper lip.

"About two years ago Valerie had some sort of procedure done," Gwen said. "A gynecological procedure."

"Possibly, I don't remember every patient."

"But you would certainly remember a patient who used to work for you."

"She had a D and C," he blurted after a brief pause. He took a deep breath, then offered a macabre smile.

He's lying, Gwen thought. "But her employer at the time said she took a week or more off from work. Is that normal after a D and C?"

"Some women have cramping," he said, his voice clinically matter-of-fact. "Some women have psychological issues to resolve."

"Do you do many D and Cs here?"

"It's not our specialty, no." He ran a hand through his thick black hair, which fell obediently back in place.

"May I see her file?"

"Of course not. Patient records are confidential."

"Did you know Priscilla Lawrence?" she said. "Her maiden name was Cunningham."

"No," he said without hesitation, looking straight at her. "I did not know her." He checked his watch and sighed noisily. "I have patients to see. You are not one of them. Is there anything else?" He glanced at the photograph, suddenly pensive, perhaps wondering if the gorgeous young wife had been worth the risk.

Ellikin wasn't going to give her much more, though she felt certain he could. After all, Maxine Cunningham had given her Ellikin's name. Had Maxine been acting on a hunch, or did she know something concrete? Perhaps she knew only that her son-in-law had gotten into legal trouble with Ellikin, and figured the doctor was as good a place to start as any.

"I'm going to go on trial soon for murder. If you're withholding information that could exonerate me…"

"I assure you I am not. I've told the FBI everything I know about Nick Lawrence."

"Did they ask you about Valerie?"

He hesitated a beat before shaking his head. Then he stood and crossed the room to the door. "You know the way out," he said over his shoulder.

She waited a few moments before heading back to the reception area, convinced that there was more to learn there, and that once she left she'd never be allowed back in. Halfway down the long corridor to the clinic entrance she stopped in front of an open door. Inside, a man in a white lab coat peered into a sleek black microscope. He straightened up, made a notation on a white pad, and glanced at her.

"Hi," he said, smiling. "Can I help you?"

"I'm a patient of Dr. Ellikin's." The lie passed so quickly through her lips, she had no time to weigh the implications. "I was…" She shrugged, at a loss. He smiled again; at least he hadn't recognized her.

"You were snooping?"

"No, no, I just—"

"Don't worry, a lot of women snoop around here." He was handsome, about thirty-five, with a manner as warm and approachable as Ellikin's was cold and withdrawn. "I guess they want to see where their eggs end up. It must be kind of like leaving a child with a stranger. Want a peek?"

She walked hesitantly to the microscope.

"It won't bite," he said.

Gwen smiled as she bent over the eyepiece. A shallow petri dish had been placed under the lens. She looked into the microscope and waited a few seconds for her eyes to focus.

"Fertilized eggs," the man said.

Gwen began to make out discrete roundish forms.

"Harvested yesterday," he continued. "I just added a bit of prewashed sperm. Stir until completely dissolved, *et voila!* A match made in scientific heaven."

"Prewashed sperm?"

"We process donor sperm to eliminate the weaker swimmers, kind of like a college swim team. Right now I'm grading the pre-embryos to see which ones we'll end up using. See the honeycomb forms?"

"I think so."

"Those are zygotes, fertilized eggs, eight cells each."

She wasn't sure what she was looking at, but was riveted by the idea that life, a human being, was forming literally before her eyes. Eight little cells...yes, she saw them now...those eight cells, floating in a shallow dish beneath a black microscope in this windowless, Formica-clad laboratory in this cold, impersonal clinic, held the potential for a complete, unique person.

"Amazing." She straightened up and shook her head slowly.

His name tag read *Brian McDougle, Ph.D.* "Are those embryos going back to the same woman who..."

"Laid them?"

She rolled her eyes.

"Sorry," he said. "Those of us in the business hear the same bad jokes a thousand times. No, these babies...sorry...these embryos were donated. They're going to a woman whose ovaries aren't functioning properly."

"Does she know the donor?"

"In this case, yes, it's a friend. Most of our egg donors are anonymous, though. We supply relevant information, but no names."

"What kind of information?"

"Age, ethnic background, sometimes even religion. And a complete medical history, of course."

"Why would someone donate her eggs anonymously?"

"Most are college students. Some have altruistic motives, others want the money. Egg donors make several thousand dollars, even more, in some cases, if they fit a desirable demographic profile.

Excuse me."

He angled around her and peered into the microscope.

"We have one of the best success ratios in the city here at East Side," he said. "Almost twenty-five percent. Are you considering using a donated egg?" Still peering into the microscope, he skittled his right hand over the Formica counter until it located a pen. He made a note on a sheet of paper.

"Possibly," she said.

"And your doctor is…"

"Ellikin," she said quickly.

He made another notation. "Then I'm sure he'll explain the procedure. He's one of the best in the field, widely respected."

But not widely loved, his tone implied. Well, to a woman unable to conceive, success ratios probably counted for more than warmth.

"How much time would a donor need to dedicate to this process?" she asked. "You know, time off from work, away from home…"

He stood up and looked at her quizzically.

"I just want to know what the other woman is going through," she said. He nodded, smiling warmly; lying to him was neither easy nor pleasurable.

"Not an uncommon reaction, but I should probably let Dr. Ellikin explain it to you."

"Of course," she said. "It's just that he's very backed up…"

"No surprise there." McDougle shrugged. "Well, first we have to synchronize the menstrual cycles of the donor and recipient. The donor takes hormone stimulants to help her produce a high number of eggs. That involves an office visit, so she wouldn't need to alter her schedule much. Then she goes to a hospital, where she's given anesthesia. We remove the eggs through her vagina. She's usually feeling completely recovered by the next day. Once in a while there's a pelvic infection that might lead to fever, but that's rare."

"What if some day my child wanted to find out who its…who donated the egg?"

"Big issue," he said. "Big controversy. Donor names are coded by number, and the codes are kept in a special double-locked safe. Access requires the permission of two doctors. That way, the information is available, but it isn't so available that it could fall into the wrong hands."

"So my patient file wouldn't include the name of the egg donor?"

"Correct, it would indicate only that you underwent the procedure, and it would list the coded number of the donor. No nurses, lab technicians, even future doctors you might consult will know who that donor is."

"But how can you—" She heard Ellikin's voice outside the lab. "I better get back to the waiting room," she said quickly, already walking toward the door. "You've been so helpful. Thank you."

"No problem," he said as he leaned over the microscope.

She saw Ellikin enter an examination room and close the door behind him. She hurried to the waiting room, where the receptionist was typing on a computer behind the counter that separated the office area from the patients. Her back was to the room.

Gwen walked quickly to the counter, leaned over, and picked up the key that the receptionist had used to open the clinic door. She turned and walked calmly across the room. Two women and one couple watched her as she left.

CHAPTER 43

Gwen returned to East Side Reproductive Services at ten o'clock that night. Riding in a cab across town, battling panic, she'd composed the inevitable headline: ACCUSED MURDERER NABBED IN MEDICAL OFFICE BREAK-IN. She used the stolen key to unlock the front door, praying that an alarm wouldn't go off.

She held her breath and pushed open the door. Silence.

The waiting room was dimly lit by a nervous white glow from the halogen street lamps just outside the large windows behind the receptionist's area. She walked slowly and quietly, in case someone was working late.

Once she was sure the place was deserted, she flicked a light switch in the hallway, waited a beat for her eyes to adjust to the fluorescence, then began searching for medical records. She passed the lab she'd been in earlier that day, a few offices, a small lunchroom, and finally found a tiny, square, windowless room lined with file cabinets.

She located the G drawer and quickly found Valerie Goodwin's file. Holding it with jittery fingers, she began to read.

Valerie Goodwin had donated an egg on February 16 of the previous year. The recipient was not identified, in keeping with what the lab technician had told her that afternoon about ensuring donor anonymity. Valerie's physician *was* named: Mitchell Ellikin. A series of dates, handwritten, indicated several office visits, before the actual "harvesting," to hyperstimulate her ovaries. A lot of the notations were either illegible or too technical for her, but one item stood out: Valerie had returned to the office on February 17 complaining of fever; the diagnosis was pelvic inflammation.

That explained her one-week absence from the gallery last year. Amoxycillan was prescribed.

Gwen scanned the rest of the file: photocopies of bills, statements from outside laboratories, a general health report from another doctor Valerie had consulted a year or so earlier. Nothing of much interest.

She replaced the file, found the L drawer, and began searching. Audrey Lawrence...Martha Lawrence. No Priscilla.

Priscilla was in there, she was sure of it, never mind Ellikin's insistence that he'd never met her. She located the C drawer and rifled through it.

"Yes!" She started at her own voice as it reverberated off the wall-to-wall metal file cabinets.

Priscilla Cunningham's file—which began several years before her marriage to Nick Lawrence, long before she'd even met him—was much thicker than Valerie's. Gwen sat on the floor, her back against a file cabinet, and read it chronologically. By the time she reached the final entry, November of the previous year, she had become somewhat expert at deciphering Ellikin's cramped and hurried handwriting, though she still found most of his entries too technical to comprehend. But she was able to grasp the gist of Priscilla's medical history, and what she read alternately thrilled and appalled her.

She stood up, retrieved Valerie Goodwin's file from its drawer, found a Xerox machine down the hallway, and copied every page from both files. She returned them to the records room, tossed the key on the floor under the receptionist's desk, shoved the copies in a big envelope, and left.

A light drizzle was falling as she crossed the sidewalk to the curb and hailed a cab. Traffic was heavy, but every taxi was occupied. Maybe she'd have better luck on Lexington Avenue.

She turned right on 73rd Street, holding the envelope close, head bowed against the increasingly strong rain. Halfway down the dimly lit street she heard footsteps and turned. The sidewalk was empty. She walked a bit faster. More footsteps. She was turning around a second time when she felt something grip her neck, pulling her away from the street.

"What…"

Her voice was choked off by the arm pressing into her throat.

"Give it to me." A man's voice, Spanish accent.

"I don't…" But she couldn't speak, let alone scream, with the arm clamping her throat.

He had pulled her by the neck into an alcove between two brownstone stoops. As soon as they were off the sidewalk he began tugging at the envelope.

"Give it to me!"

She hugged the envelope to her chest and heard footsteps approaching on 73rd Street. He let go of the envelope and stepped back against the triangular wall formed by one of the stoops, dragging her with him. A second later she felt something dig into her lower back.

"You say anything, you gonna feel this."

She felt a sting just above her waist. *A knife.*

"Give it to me," he whispered. She felt warm breath on the back of her neck. A man walked by, heading to Lexington Avenue, the now heavy rain muffling his footsteps. A moment later, East 73rd Street was quiet again.

"Give it to me."

She shook her head. The knife stung her back, but probably hadn't broken skin.

Now what?

Give him the envelope; save your life.

Give him the envelope and those files will disappear for good. What kind of life will you have in prison?

Rain poured down her face, blurring her vision. No way he was getting those files.

"Now!" he whispered directly in her right ear with a quick poke of the knife. "Give it to me now or…just give it to me, bitch."

There! His voice was full of anger but it lacked conviction, and she saw her chance. He was about her height, obviously strong, but the arm around her neck, though it held her like a vise, was trembling. He wanted the envelope, God knew why, but he didn't want to hurt her.

"Give it to—"

She jammed her left elbow into his gut. The knife bit into her back, but his right arm slackened around her throat just enough for her to turn sideways and knee his groin. He roared, bending at the waist and cursing in Spanish as she grabbed his left arm and slammed it against the wall with her entire weight. But he held on to the knife...and was slowly straightening up, his moans growing less insistent.

She took a deep breath, leaned over, and bit into his wrist, shrieking from way back in her throat as her teeth sank into his flesh. The knife fell to the pavement. Gwen dove for it as he began to moan again. When she stood up, holding the knife, he had one hand over his crotch; the other hand, the one she'd bitten, quivered in front of his incredulous eyes.

"Hey, lady, I don't want trouble. Take your fucking papers."

Gwen spat hard, twice. No blood, at least.

"Who are you?"

He looked at her a few moments, dark eyes more fearful than angry. "You some lady, you know? How come your husband leave a lady like you?"

"My husband?"

"You Jimmy's mom, right?" *Jeemy.*

She could only nod.

"Good-looking lady, and strong." He shook his injured wrist and stepped toward her. Gwen thrust the knife at him.

"Don't worry, I won't do nothing. Keep the fucking envelope, okay? Lousy hundred bucks ain't enough to get *bit.*"

"Hundred bucks? Someone *paid* you to do this?"

"To follow you, okay? She say nothing about sticking you. I wasn't planning on using the knife, honest. She said to follow you and call her when I find out where you going. When I tell her you went into this doctor's office, this clinic place, she tells me to make sure you don't take nothing. And if you do…"

"Who paid you?"

"Some lady, lives near this…this place I work at. Don't even know her name."

"I don't believe you."

"I don't know her name, *yo juro por dios*. First she tells me to set up this meeting with someone named Barry, lives in Brooklyn, you know? Then I don't hear from her again until today."

"Red hair, dark skin…"

"Yeah, that's her. *Sinverguenza.*"

"Sin…"

"You know, bitch on wheels." He peered closely at his wrist. "You don't got no diseases or nothing, do you?"

"When did you contact my husband?"

He began edging along the wall toward the sidewalk, eyes fixed on the knife. "Early in the summer. I gave him a paper with an address, that's all. Some kind of meeting she wanted."

Gwen followed him to the sidewalk, still pointing the knife at him. But what was she going to do when he ran away, chase him brandishing a knife?

He began backing away from her, toward Third Avenue.

"Fifty bucks, I got that time, when I gave that paper to this Barry person." He turned and began to run.

"Wait, I need to ask you…"

But he kept running until he reached the corner and disappeared. She waited until her legs felt steady enough to walk, put the knife in her jeans pocket, and headed in the opposite direction.

It took her several minutes to find a cab on Lexington Avenue. She gave the driver the address of her hotel and did her best to remain calm during the ten-minute crosstown ride. Valerie had hired him to follow her, told him to grab anything she took from Ellikin's office. No surprise there. Valerie had also hired the guy to contact Barry back in June. That cleared up at least one question.

What now? Should she call the police? And if she did, what would she tell them—that a young man with a Spanish accent had shoved a knife in her back? That he'd been hired by Valerie Goodwin? Valerie would deny it, of course. And the Puerto Rican or Cuban or whatever he was would be hard to track down. Fingerprints on the knife might help, but only if he had a record. Anyway, she was a murder suspect out on bail…Who would believe her? And even if the police did buy her story, following it through would delay her return to Sohegan, and Jimmy.

She held the envelope to her chest, hands trembling. She needed to understand the truth about Tess's kidnapping and Priscilla's murder. Only then would she be out of danger. Accusing Valerie of having her followed wouldn't help; she needed to get back to Sohegan with the evidence she had just risked her life to hold on to.

Gwen felt her heart beating against the envelope. It contained merely clues, she had realized immediately, back at the clinic; the photocopies supported what she'd suspected earlier that day in the lab. Definitive proof was in her room at the Boulevard Hotel.

She entered the hotel room, double-locked the door, tossed the envelope on the bed, and retrieved the photograph from the nightstand drawer. For a moment she was afraid to examine it too closely. Winning her freedom would mean exposing an evil worse than Priscilla's murder—the theft of a soul. She would do it, of course, she would save herself. But the consequences would be ghastly for many people.

Finally she looked at the photograph: Priscilla smiled nervously, Tess in her right arm, also smiling. Perhaps it had been Nick behind the camera, coaxing those smiles as only he could. As he'd coaxed smiles (and much more) out of her. She studied Priscilla for a few more moments and decided the smile wasn't nervous at all. It was merely sad. Why hadn't she seen the sadness in that smile before?

Gwen held the photograph closer, blocking out Priscilla with her thumb, concentrating on Tess. She recalled Dilianna Flores's words as she looked at the photograph the day before: *I thought she look familiar.*

Not Priscilla.

Tess.

Slowly she brought the picture closer, then back, then closer again, as if focusing an old-fashioned stereoscope. Closer, closer still…there! Just inches from her face, Tess Lawrence came into true focus for the first time in all the months Gwen had known her. Tears began to run down Gwen's cheeks. The entire story of the Devil's Ravine was written in that beautiful face, that perfectly, perfectly beautiful face.

In Tess Lawrence's face was the truth.

PART IV

PART IV

CHAPTER 44

On the drive back to Sohegan Wednesday morning, Gwen relived her flight from New York nearly six months earlier. Then, she'd been terrified, angry, confused. Now she felt unexpectedly clearheaded. Then, it had been nighttime. Now it was a cloudless August morning. Then, she'd been fleeing. She wasn't running away anymore.

Nearly three hours after checking out of the Boulevard she left her car in front of the Cunninghams' house, sprinted around the side, through the hemlocks, and across the great lawn behind Penaquoit. This time no one tried to stop her, though it would have done little good.

The kitchen door was locked, as she knew it would be. She rapped on the window, waited, then knocked harder. A shadow moved inside; then Rosa Piacevic opened the door, expressionless.

"I need to speak to him," Gwen said.

Rosa shook her head slowly. Gwen pushed open the door and angled around her.

"Don't try to stop me, Rosa, I—are you all right?"

Rosa's eyes were red and puffy.

"They're gone," she said.

"Who?" Gwen asked, but she knew right away.

"This morning, I wait for Tess to wake up. At seven-thirty I still don't hear her, so I go up to the nursery. She is not there. I start to go to Mr. Lawrence room; then I see her favorite things, her brown bear, the little music box, they are missing too. I know then, they are both gone." She wiped tears from her face with a tissue balled up in her hands. "I ask Mr. Piacevic to check in Mr. Lawrence room. Mr.

Lawrence is gone from here too."

"When did you last see them?"

"When I give Tessie dinner last evening. Mr. Piacevic, he thinks he heared the car leave about seven-thirty. This morning, the big green car is not here." Rosa began to sob. "My poor little *zamer*, he leave all her bottles, the spoon she always like me to feed her with, even her blanket…"

"Mrs. Piacevic." Gwen touched her shoulder and shook it gently. "Mrs. Piacevic, who have you told about this?"

"My husband, he tell me to call Mr. Cunningham at the factory. He is coming here now."

Gwen charged up the back stairs and sprinted down the long hallway into the master bedroom. The bed was still made, the drapes closed, but several drawers were open, and empty. She quickly searched the night tables, the desk drawers, the garbage can, but found no clue as to where they'd gone. The room felt not merely deserted but dead, the air already thick and stale. She headed downstairs to the living room and sensed right away something was missing. In a second she knew: his music books, which usually lay in piles on the piano and on every other horizontal surface in the room, were gone.

Nick Lawrence wasn't coming back.

"Noooooooooooo!"

She jumped at the sound, a savage roar from somewhere in the house that reverberated for several seconds. Then approaching footsteps. She ran to the French doors that opened onto the terrace; she had neither the time nor the stomach for a confrontation with Russell Cunningham. Before leaving the room she looked back and confirmed a suspicion: the large tape recorder Nick always kept near the piano was nowhere to be found.

She ran across the lawn, heading toward her car next door. Halfway there she heard a second roar, then shouting.

"Where are they? *Where are they? Where the hell is my granddaughter?*"

Inside her car, heading away from the Cunninghams' house, something in the rearview mirror caught Gwen's eye. Maxine

DISILLUSIONS

Cunningham stood by the front door, waving her arms to get her attention. Gwen braked the car, reconsidered, and hit the gas.

Let Maxine hear the truth from someone else, if she had to hear it at all. Gwen had her own ass to save.

CHAPTER 45

"He set me up, from the beginning." Gwen glanced from Kevin Gargano to Dwight Hawkins. "He *chose* me."

She saw her attorney exchange a doubtful look with Hawkins. Fuck them both. Maybe she'd been wrong to drag Gargano out of a meeting in his Whitesville office and insist that he accompany her to the Sohegan police station. She'd wanted a witness to her accusations against Nick Lawrence, not another skeptic.

"Maybe you better start from the beginning," Gargano said with irritating gentleness. Gwen could have sworn he was wearing the same suit, tie, and shirt he had on at her arraignment.

"It started three years ago, in New York." She hesitated. This was the hardest part, the idea that her life, hers *and* Jimmy's, had been manipulated long before she'd ever heard of Penaquoit or Nick Lawrence. "Actually, it began before that, when Nick met Valerie Goodwin. I don't know when that was, but the two of them go way back."

"Who is Valerie Goodwin?" Gargano asked.

"Friend of his," Hawkins said. "Continue."

"Three years ago, Valerie Goodwin was working as a receptionist at a fertility clinic in Manhattan in which Dr. Mitchell Ellikin was a partner. She put the doctor and Nick together in a prescription drug scheme."

"They got caught," Hawkins said to Gargano. "No charges filed—it was some kind of medicine for kids. The FBI has been through this, Miss Amiel."

She nodded. "Valerie did something else while she was working at the clinic. She found Priscilla Cunningham, the only child of one

332

of the country's richest men. Beautiful, sophisticated, but with one major flaw." She paused and looked slowly from one man to the other. "Priscilla couldn't have children."

Hawkins leaned toward her. "But she had a—"

"Listen to me. About fifteen years ago, in her twenties, Priscilla had Hodgkin's disease. She was completely cured, but the radiation and chemotherapy damaged her ovaries. It's in Ellikin's report."

She slid the photocopies across the table. Hawkins glanced at them only briefly.

"She went to Ellikin for an evaluation, between two and three years ago, before she'd met Nick Lawrence. She was referred by her regular gynecologist. Ellikin confirmed that her ovaries were malfunctioning. Valerie Goodwin was working at the clinic at the time and must have seen the chart, figured out who she was, and set her up with her lover, Nick Lawrence."

"Whoa," Gargano said, holding up a hand. "Why would Valerie introduce her own boyfriend to Priscilla Cunningham?"

Gwen waited a moment before replying. Even she had trouble wrapping her mind around what she was about to say.

"Valerie and Nick were alike in many ways. He was a failed concert pianist, she was a failed actress. Both had big ambitions, expensive tastes...and no money." A vision of Valerie's apartment flashed in her head: a millionaire's accoutrements jammed into a single dark room. Nick had lived there with her, his dreams of international acclaim reduced to that dreary, sunless bunker. He'd even told her about it, obliquely, that strange first morning at Penaquoit:

It's like being trapped inside a room that's too small for you. You want to break out, you need to break out, but you can't. You know your talent is too big for the room you've been placed in, but you also know, on mornings like this, that you'll never escape.

"They were desperate," Gwen continued. "They were broke and had no practical, marketable skills...other than their charm. And their health."

"Health?" Gargano unbuttoned the top of his shirt and

loosened his tie. "I'm not following you."

"Stay with me," Gwen said. "In the midst of their desperation, along comes Priscilla Cunningham—reasonably attractive, fabulously wealthy, lacking only two things. A husband...and functioning ovaries. Nick would supply the first, Valerie the second."

"What?" Gargano almost choked on the word.

"Go on," Hawkins said softly.

"Valerie introduced Nick to Priscilla; he seduced her...I don't think he had much trouble." She waited a moment, remembering her own capitulation. "At some point Priscilla must have told him about her fertility problem. It must have been very difficult for her. Here she'd met the man of her dreams; now she had to tell him she couldn't bear his children. And think of the pressure on her to produce an heir. I think she'd have done anything to avoid having to tell her father that she was the end of the line."

"Nick already knew about her problem, though," Hawkins said, slowly shaking his head. "From her medical files."

"Though I'm positive he acted very surprised when she told him. In fact I'll bet Nick was incredibly understanding." He was good at empathy, a master.

"Go on, Miss Amiel," Hawkins said.

"I'm sure it was Nick who suggested egg donation. I can hear his arguments—with egg donation, it would be *his* sperm, *his* genetic contribution, to the child." She paused just a beat. "The egg, of course, was Valerie's."

"What makes you think Priscilla would agree to...to carry Valerie's child?" Hawkins asked.

"*Because she didn't know.* Read the medical reports. According to Ellikin's notes, the donor wished to remain *anonymous*. The only person who knew both the donor and the recipient was Ellikin; at least that's what Priscilla thought. In fact, Nick and Valerie both knew who donated that egg."

"And Ellikin went along with this because..." Hawkins was nodding.

"Because he owed Nick, big time, for not turning him in on the

Ritalin charges."

"Holy shit," Gargano said. "Then that little girl…"

"Tess is Nick and Valerie's child. It's in her face. I don't know how I missed it all these months."

Dilianna Flores had seen it when Gwen showed her that photograph of Priscilla and Tess. It wasn't Priscilla who looked familiar; Priscilla had never been to that boardinghouse. *Tess* looked familiar because Valerie had been there.

"Tess is Valerie's daughter," she said.

"Her face…" Hawkins said, his eyes losing focus for a moment. He'd noticed, too.

"Once the child was born," Gwen continued, "all Nick and Valerie had to do was get rid of Priscilla, now that she'd served her purpose. But they had one problem. Russell Cunningham never trusted Nick, for good reason, as it turned out. He drafted his will so that his son-in-law wouldn't get a cent in the event of Priscilla's death. That's why they resorted to the kidnapping scheme. They might not get the Cunningham inheritance, but they'd keep the five million in ransom money and get rid of Priscilla in the bargain, leaving the three of them to live as one happy, genetically related family. They knew Russell wouldn't call the police, not after what happened to his son. He'd insist on handling the ransom himself."

She glanced at Hawkins, who nodded slowly.

"All they needed," Gwen said, "was someone to grab the money at the ravine, and someone to witness the event, to testify that Priscilla had been shot while trying to help her child. And they needed someone to take the blame for the murder. As long as the case was unsolved, Nick couldn't truly relax. He had to find a plausible suspect, someone to take the fall. That's where I came in."

"This is all speculation, though," Dwight Hawkins said. "You do realize that." He sounded more perplexed than accusatory, as if he wanted to believe what she was saying, but couldn't quite.

"Nick asked about me at the diner, before I'd ever said a word to him. He even found my old address, the name of my husband. Ask Mike Contaldi at the Mecca. And Valerie hired this Hispanic kid to get in touch with my husband. Later she met with him at his boardinghouse—ask Dilianna Flores, his landlady. She said this really classy redhead had visited Barry…it had to be Valerie. Barry was up here the day of the payoff, but I never told him where Jimmy and I were living. We never had any contact with him after I left him."

"But you—"

"I'll take a lie detector test, okay?"

Hawkins sighed. "You wrote that note, giving directions," he said.

"Do you have it with you?"

"It's at the county."

"Was it torn off, as if it was ripped from a larger piece of paper?"

"Yes."

"I wrote those directions for myself, on the back of a Mecca sales check. Priscilla Lawrence dictated them to me, so I'd find Penaquoit my first day of work. The paper is light green, right?"

Hawkins nodded very slowly.

"Nick must have taken it from my house, or maybe I left it at Penaquoit the first day, I don't remember. He set this whole thing up, he masterminded it from the beginning, over two years ago. He moved the baby monitor into the master bedroom to make sure I'd hear about the payoff, he even chose a spot for the ransom that he knew I'd just been to, a place he told me about, the Devil's Ravine."

"He couldn't have known for certain that you'd go there."

"No, that's why Tess was left at my house, to make sure the connection between me and the crime was solid even if I didn't come."

"But—"

"And something else…how did he know I'd run up to the kidnapper, botch up the money transfer, and give the kidnapper an excuse to kill Priscilla? *Because of Tess's crying*…he knew I'd have to do something if I heard Tess."

"And so the kidnapper what, pinched her until she cried?"

She shook her head. "Nick…" She waited a beat until the bile subsided. "Nick Lawrence is a monster, but he wouldn't allow a strange man near his daughter, let alone a drunk like Barry. Tess is the one thing he's human about. No, Tess wasn't anywhere near the Devil's Ravine that morning. My guess is she was with her mother..." Hawkins started to say something. "...With *Valerie*, who had her the entire time, and probably left her in my house that day."

"Then who was crying at the ravine?"

"Tess! A *recording* of Tess. Rosa Piacevic told me she saw Nick taping Tess one day, *before* the kidnapping. He must have taped her crying. And at the ravine, I remember thinking that something sounded odd about Tess's voice. Last night it hit me: the thinness of it, the way it never varied in loudness. Not to mention the fact that the crying stopped the moment I crossed the stream, and I never did find Tess there. It was a recording."

"I don't suppose you've found that tape," Hawkins asked.

"The tape recorder isn't in its usual place. I checked today. But you never found the voice-altering machine, did you? And that didn't prevent you from charging me with murder."

"We never found the five million, either," Hawkins almost whispered.

"Nick *planned* to have Priscilla killed at the Devil's Ravine, he *intended* for it to go just the way it did. But he couldn't count on his wife running across the stream; he couldn't count on me doing that, either. He had to ensure that things went wrong, so he gave my husband that tape recording and told him to activate it before taking the money."

"Quite a story," Hawkins said. "But not much proof."

"How about this for proof? Nick Lawrence has run away. He's taken Tess."

"*What?*"

"I was at Penaquoit this morning. He left last night, with most of his clothes and a lot of Tess's things, too. Valerie must have called him after I told her that I knew she'd been in touch with my husband."

Hawkins's head sagged as he emitted a long, defeated sigh.

"Why would an innocent man run away? Tell me that?" Gwen

SETH MARGOLIS

leaned across the table, forcing Hawkins to meet her gaze. "Why would Nick Lawrence leave, unless he was afraid of something?"

A knock at the door saved him from replying. Gwen found she was out of breath, and only when she stopped talking did a sense of rage bubble up. A uniformed police officer stuck his head in.

"Boss, Russell Cunningham's on the horn. Wants to speak to you right away. Guy's having a fit. I think you better see what he wants."

"What *I* want is that charges against my client are dropped," Gargano said as Hawkins stood up. "Immediately. No jury on this planet will convict Ms. Amiel with the chief witness flown the coop."

Hawkins looked from Gargano to Gwen and then shook his head.

"I gotta take his call. Don't go anywhere, either of you."

Later that afternoon, after peppering Gwen Amiel with additional questions, Dwight Hawkins told her to go home and wait for his call. He sat in his office for a while, absorbing the scenario she'd outlined. His gut told him she was right. Yet every time his hand reached for the phone to dial Don Reeves in Albany, one raw thought would immobilize him: How had he missed it, what lead had he overlooked that would have taken him to where he was now?

The answer never came. He'd screwed up, and badly. There was no getting around it. When he finally called Don Reeves he spent a half hour repeating what Gwen Amiel had told him earlier that morning. Reeves asked a few questions in a flat, defeated voice.

"I'll try to find Valerie Goodwin, notify customs to watch for Nick Lawrence and his child," Reeves said when Hawkins was through. "Meantime, I'll check with our lab. We ran DNA analyses on the hair and trace from the kid's nursery. Some of the hairs matched Nick Lawrence, some Priscilla. Maybe we can use the results to prove whose daughter Tess Lawrence really is." He sounded thoroughly unenthusiastic.

338

"What about Gwen Amiel?" Dwight asked. "Do we drop the charges?"

Reeves answered after a long silence. "Let's wait for the DNA results."

Gwen felt the glass crunch under her shoes moments before she noticed the empty windowpane in the kitchen door. She froze and considered getting back in her car, then took a tentative step toward the door and turned the knob. Someone had smashed the glass, broken in.

She pulled open the door and entered the kitchen. The refrigerator hummed; otherwise the house was silent.

"Hello?" she shouted. Better to make her presence known than surprise someone who might be armed. "Hello?"

She walked slowly to the front hall, reassured by the fact that the driveway was empty.

"Hel—"

The antique pitcher and bowl were smashed to pieces on the floor. And in the middle of the disarray was a single purple thistle, garishly perfect, its long, silver-leaved stem gently arching across jagged shards of pottery.

She glanced into the living room, found it undisturbed, looked into the dining room, also untouched, then returned to the shattered wash set. Whoever had done that knew how to get to her. Nothing else in the house mattered.

Upstairs, she checked Jimmy's room, then her own. Nothing disturbed. She dialed 911 and told the dispatcher what had happened. A car would be sent over right away, the woman said. She hung up and began pacing the room. After a minute or so she ran downstairs and found the plant book on the living-room shelves.

Most species of thistle made unsuitable garden plants, she read, trying hard to concentrate. Exceptions included the Scotch or Cotton thistle, a biennial growing up to five feet with striking, sculptured leaves, covered with white cobwebby hairs and...

Where the hell are the police?

She read on. The rich purple flowers were the badge of the Stuarts and were still the national emblem of Scotland. They were cultivated in—

The phone rang. She tossed the book onto the couch and hurried to the kitchen.

"Hello?"

"It's Clare Pearson. I know this hasn't been the easiest time for you, but I think I deserve to know in advance when Jimmy has other plans. Henry and I got to the camp right on time, same as always, only to be told that Jimmy had already been picked up."

"Jimmy didn't have a play date today."

"I don't know that you'd call going over to his aunt's house a play date exactly."

"But..." Jimmy had no aunts, of course. And he would never leave the camp with a stranger, not without putting up a fight that would alert the counselors.

"Did...did anyone tell you the name of the person who took him?"

"No, they did not. But in the future I would appreciate—"

Gwen hung up and tried like hell to think clearly. She paced the kitchen, the hallway. Jimmy's...his situation was related to the broken pitcher and bowl. It had to be. But how? He wouldn't leave camp with a stranger...yet they knew so few people in Sohegan. She reviewed a mental list of their acquaintances as she gazed at the shattered wash set. The Pearsons, of course, Mike Contaldi, Sheila and Betsy, the Piacevics...

Her eyes came to rest on the purple thistle, bizarrely lovely, somehow, atop the wreckage, so deliberately placed, as if to make a statement.

And she knew.

CHAPTER 46

Gwen pounded on the front door of Sheila's house, then ran around back and tried the kitchen door. It wasn't locked.

"Sheila?" She stepped inside. "Are you home?"

She checked the entire downstairs, then the rooms above. Sheila and Betsy's king-size bed was unmade, rumpled clothes were piled all over the floor. The shades were lowered against the hot August sun, casting the room in sickly amber shadow.

She left through the back door. Halfway to her car, something caught her eye. Sheila and Betsy never paid much attention to their yard, and it showed. But at the far end of the small property, nearly obscured by a badly overgrown shrub, was a clump of unexpected color, the brightness a jarring contrast to the prevailing browns and greens.

Purple thistles. A cluster of rangy, robust purple thistles.

Gwen parked at the all-too-familiar spot and charged down the embankment to the ravine, calling Jimmy's name into the dusky woods. Her third shout was answered.

"Mom?"

She tripped over a small rock and only half noticed the hole in her jeans as she stood up.

"Jimmy!"

She charged into the clearing by the river, squinting at the sudden brightness.

"Mom!"

SETH MARGOLIS

She turned. Jimmy was waist deep in the water.

"Mom, come in! It's freezing but it's great!"

She ran toward him.

"Stop!" Sheila stepped from behind a tree. Gwen saw the pistol and stopped about ten yards from the stream.

"Back up," Sheila said. "Jimmy doesn't have to see this."

Gwen started backing up the embankment.

"Mom, come on!" Jimmy called from the water.

"There, right there," Sheila said with unsettling composure. "You're in position."

Gwen looked down, then around, and it hit her. She was standing in the precise spot where Priscilla had died.

"Sheila, I had nothing—"

"I knew you'd come. I knew you'd figure it out even without my calling." With her free hand she pulled a cell phone from her pocket and let it drop to the ground.

"The thistle," Gwen said. "Badge of the Stuarts."

Sheila—Sheila *Stewart*—nodded as a single tear glinted on her cheek. "We discovered that in junior high. We did a book report on the Stuarts."

"You and Priscilla," Gwen said quietly. Sheila closed her eyes as more tears squeezed out.

"Mom?" Jimmy was out of the water, walking toward them, shivering.

"Get back in the water, Jimmy," Gwen said.

"But I'm cold."

"There's a towel over there." Sheila pointed behind her with her free hand. Jimmy looked puzzled, but from where he stood he couldn't see the gun. He walked over to the towel and wrapped it around his shoulders.

"It was *our* badge. Priscilla..." Sheila breathed hard for a few moments. "They sent Cilly to boarding school, then to New York. They married her off...and I found Betsy. But they could never separate us. Never."

All those unexplained disappearances, Priscilla dressed so

342

fastidiously, including—

"The morning of her murder…"

"Cilly came to my house, frantic. She knew about you and Nick. She was sure you planned it, alone or with him. She was sick with worry, but Nick wouldn't let her interfere with the arrangements, and her father wouldn't call the police." She reached into her pocket and took out a thistle. "We picked this together that last morning, from my yard, so I could be with her, here, at the ravine. I never saw her again."

"Sheila, I didn't kill Priscilla, and as for Nick, he and I…"

"He and you *what?*" Her voice had dropped to a snarl.

"Nick set the whole thing up, he and Valerie Goodwin. They did it for the money. They've disappeared, Sheila, and they've taken Tess."

Her eyes flashed surprise and Gwen felt a tremor of hope. "Well, Tess is his girl," Sheila said. "All his, now."

"His and Valerie's."

The gun began to waver. "What do you mean, his and—"

"They arranged everything, back when they first met Priscilla. They did it for the money."

"But you—"

"They set me up, Sheila. They lured me to the ravine." Jimmy was headed toward her. "Go up to the car, Jimmy."

"But, Mom, I don't want—"

He saw the gun and ran to her side, wrapping his arms around her legs.

"It's okay, Jimmy. Sheila won't hurt you. Will you, Sheila?"

Sheila slowly shook her head. "Not you, Jimmy."

Gwen took a deep breath. "I didn't kill Priscilla. Even the police know that now. I found evidence, down in New York. The egg Priscilla received? It was Valerie's."

"Oh, oh, no." Sheila's voice cracked and she wiped tears from her face with the back of her free hand. "Poor Cilly. My poor Priscilla."

"Put the gun down, Sheila."

"I was sure it was you," Sheila said, "the way you mooned after

Nick. And you would never tell me why you moved up here from New York. I figured you came up here as part of the plan, the plan to take Tess. I wanted to…I wanted to kill you after what you'd done to Priscilla, after what I thought you'd done. I didn't have the nerve. I wanted to so badly but I couldn't."

"Jimmy's panda, and that…that effigy here."

"But it wasn't enough," Sheila said. "Cilly couldn't have a child, and then you took her life. I thought…"

"You thought you could take *my* child, *my* life. As if that would even the score, somehow."

Sheila stepped toward Gwen and sank to her knees. "Here, where it ended." She cleared a layer of leaves and twigs from a patch of ground near where Priscilla had died. Sacred ground, consecrated in blood. "Nobody loved her except me. Not even her father."

"Put the gun down, Sheila." Gwen stepped back, angling Jimmy behind her, as Sheila placed the thistle on the cleared dirt. An offering.

"Run up the hill!" Gwen whispered to Jimmy.

"But I—"

"Run, Jimmy, now!"

She gave him a shove and he tore up the embankment.

Sheila heard his footsteps and turned toward him, raising the gun.

"No, Sheila!" Gwen charged her. Sheila swiveled the pistol at Gwen, who stopped short. Jimmy disappeared in the dark woods above them.

"You know I wouldn't hurt him," Sheila said softly.

It was true. "Give me the gun. It's not too late. I won't press charges for breaking into my house, I swear to you. Just drop the—"

"Get away from here!"

"But, Sheil—"

"Go!" Her voice was hoarse, almost unrecognizable. "Go away. You never belonged here, never! Leave…leave us alone!"

Gwen began to back away. "I don't want to leave you here, Sheila. Please, put down the gun and come with me."

Sheila slowly shook her head as tears fell onto the bare earth where the thistle lay.

"Her parents knew about us, what we had together. They even knew about the thistle. And they did everything they could to separate us. Priscilla and I used to meet sometimes, when she lived in New York. We found this old hotel in the Catskills, practically deserted. I'd bring her a thistle from my garden. Later, when she moved back here, she took cuttings from me for her own garden. We always thought we'd be together some day, once her...once Tess was grown, her father gone. Our lives were on hold, Cilly's and mine."

On hold. Like Nick and Valerie, waiting, waiting. Cicadas, all of them, Sheila and Priscilla, Nick and Valerie, biding their time underground, year after year, all for that brief, hoped-for moment in the sunlight.

She didn't have the heart to tell Sheila that Russell Cunningham had destroyed those precious flowers, his last stab at regulating his daughter's life.

"Sheila, put down the gun."

"Just leave us alone," she said softly. Gwen didn't move. Sheila looked up, eyes unblinking, and pointed the gun at her. "Leave now," she said, the snarly voice again. "Or I'll shoot."

"Okay, Sheila." Gwen backed away, hands raised over her shoulders. "I hate to leave you here, Sheila. I wish you'd come with me." After several yards she turned and headed up the hill. Halfway to the top she stopped and called out. "Sheila! Sheila, come with—"

A single gunshot ripped through the woods.

CHAPTER 47

Gwen called the police from a pay phone on Route 24 and told them to send an ambulance to the Devil's Ravine. After the gunshot she considered running back down the embankment to help Sheila, but Jimmy was shivering with terror in the car; she didn't want to leave him alone for one more moment. Sheila had chosen her fate, as much as anyone ever does. Gwen headed home.

Jimmy had trouble sleeping that night, peppering her with questions until he was too tired to hold his head up. *Why did Sheila take me to the ravine? Was she really going to kill us? Are you ever going back to jail?* The phone rang about nine.

"Hello, Gwen."

She gasped, then almost sobbed with relief.

"Sheila…"

"I'm sorry, Gwen. I'm so sorry."

"Where…where are you?"

"Home."

"You're okay?"

"I couldn't do it, Gwen. I wanted to but…I fired once and it went over my head, and after that…"

"Does Betsy…"

"I told her everything. I told her about…"

Gwen gave her a moment to compose herself.

"I don't deserve her," Sheila said after a while. "I don't—"

The line went dead.

• • •

Gwen spent the next day trying to absorb it all: Nick's deception and disappearance, Sheila's deception and betrayal. She tried to talk things over with Jimmy, but he seemed reluctant to revisit the incident, and perhaps that showed precocious wisdom. Eventually he'd have to deal with what happened—his father's abuse, his father's death, the Devil's Ravine. But that could wait. Just then he was most concerned with his baseball swing. So she spent the early afternoon pitching whiffle balls.

"Keep your eye on the ball," she told him whenever he missed—advice she tried to follow herself. Whenever her mind strayed to Nick Lawrence she felt a sharp queasiness in her gut, a sickly light-headedness. For months now she'd assumed that what Barry had done to Jimmy had been as evil as human behavior could ever be. But Barry had been sick, unable to control himself. What Nick had done was the work of a deliberate, calculating mind in full control of itself.

"Swing level, Jimbo!" she shouted. "Keep your eye on the ball!"

One question hounded her above all others: Why had Nick seduced her? How had sleeping with her furthered his plans? Once she agreed to work in his house she was fated to take the fall for the murder...fucking her had been optional. The heat in his eyes when he looked at her, the desperate hunger of his mouth when he lapped at her breasts with his tongue, the passion he showed when he shared the music, *his* music, with her...could all that be faked?

Jimmy popped the whiffle ball over her head.

"Home run!" she yelled as she ran to retrieve it. Her own voice sounded thin and nervous.

Of course he'd faked it; she'd never be able to move on if she didn't face the truth. Nick had never really wanted her. Fucking her had been a way to stay *physically* close, keep an eye on her. Perhaps he'd even enjoyed humiliating her, relishing the power his knowledge gave him, the humiliation he knew she'd feel.

She tossed a perfect pitch. Jimmy, distracted, let it go past him. He pointed behind her.

"Sorry to interrupt the game." Dwight Hawkins crossed the

small lawn, squinting in the late-afternoon sunlight. Jimmy walked over to her, his shoulder touching her waist. She put a hand on him; he was trembling.

"Is there some place we can talk in private?" Hawkins said.

Jimmy's face was rigid with anxiety.

"My son needs to hear, too."

"We're dropping the charges," Hawkins said quietly.

Jimmy's face relaxed into a tentative smile. "For real?"

"For real," Hawkins said, also smiling.

Jimmy thrust a fist in the air, then started racing around the yard, whooping as he punched out the sky.

"The FBI had already run DNA tests on some hair evidence collected at Penaquoit. They don't have any samples from Valerie Goodwin, but they were able to rule out Priscilla Lawrence as the child's biological mother."

Gwen waited before speaking, hoping to feel at least a twinge of pleasure at being proven correct. Nothing came.

"Have you located Nick Lawrence?"

He shook his head. "What did Lawrence tell you about his background?"

She shrugged. "He was pretty vague. I got the impression he didn't like talking about his past."

"Any specifics?"

"He was from Lansburg, Pennsylvania. His father was a purchasing executive. He went to Julliard for a few years, then dropped out when his father lost his job."

"Anything else?"

"*No.*" A spark of anger, then a deflating sadness as she realized the target of that anger: herself. How could she have made herself vulnerable yet again to a man who gave so little? "Where is he?" she asked.

"London. The FBI traced his passport through Immigration. He left JFK this morning on a TWA flight to Heathrow. Interpol's been alerted."

"London…" Knowing he was an ocean away only deepened

her rage. And still she felt no safer from him.

"The FBI's sending a sketch artist up here to draw a composite." He shook his head slowly. "I was over at Penaquoit this afternoon. There's not a single goddamn photograph of him anywhere in that house. Not one."

An image flashed before her: Priscilla's camera, the roll of film dangling from it, exposed...the fiasco blamed on Tess.

"Who was he?" she said. *Even monsters have faces.*

"Even if we manage to find him we don't have a shred of evidence that he did anything."

"And the money..."

"I'm sure he's parked it somewhere where it can't be traced to him. You can't hide five million dollars in cash in this country, but there are banks in Switzerland, the Caribbean, that'll take cash deposits from foreigners without asking questions."

"And Tess?"

"She's his daughter. If we do manage to find him outside the country we're going to have trouble extraditing him from wherever the hell he is, unless we come up with new evidence connecting him to Priscilla Cunningham's murder. And that's assuming we find him in the first place. I doubt London's his final destination."

"Mom, come on!" Jimmy was swinging the bat in the air.

"I'll spend the rest of my life regretting what almost happened to you and your boy."

"Forget it." Gwen felt tears on her face, the first tears in a long time. *She'd* never forget.

"I thought they were pranks, the break-in, what happened with your clothes at the ravine."

"So many lives on hold," she said. "Sheila, Priscilla. Nick and Valerie. All those years squandered with the wrong people, holding out for future happiness. I wonder if Sheila will ever find it now."

"Well, Nick and Valerie got their reward." Hawkins glanced up at the cloudless sky. "What a day. There's a low-pressure system a hundred miles west of here, but it's not going anywhere anytime soon. Kind of like me." He looked at Gwen and smiled. "Nothing but blue sky," he said, and sang the final three words: "From now on."

"Mom, please?" Jimmy shouted.

"Mind if I throw him one?" Hawkins asked. She handed him the whiffle ball. He threw a perfect pitch. Jimmy swung and missed.

"Level swing," Hawkins said as Jimmy threw the ball back to him. "And bend your knees, yeah, that's it. Now, step into the ball."

He glanced at Gwen, smiled almost sheepishly, and threw another pitch.

She tried drinking herself to sleep that night. She lost count of the scotches, but she couldn't lose consciousness. She'd close her eyes and manage to relax for a few moments, but then faces would drift into focus, projected onto the swirling black and purple backs of her eyelids. Nick's face appeared most often, those velvet-blue eyes mocking her. Sometimes she'd see Priscilla, haunted, melancholy— but her eyes were always curiously dry. Once she saw Valerie's face, angular and smug.

But the face that appeared most often that night, the one that thwarted sleep, was Tess's, her mouth open, crying, her sobs tinny and distant, as if from a tape recorder placed at a distance.

So Gwen spent most of the night with her eyes open, trying to banish the faces by focusing on *her* life, and Jimmy's. Still they tormented her, Nick and Valerie or whatever their real names were. She thought of them latching onto Priscilla Cunningham like barnacles, sucking the life from her as they used her body to spawn their child.

At some point very early in the morning she collected the paint cans and brushes and rollers and drop cloths from the dining room and brought them down to the cellar. The kitchen and hallway looked fine as they were, just as the dining room and living room and bedrooms had. As she piled the cans in a dark corner of the cellar a thought flashed, and soon a course of action took shape.

DISILLUSIONS

At eight-thirty she dropped Jimmy off at the Pearsons' and used their phone to call Dwight Hawkins. She got the information she needed from him and began the two-hour drive to Lansburg, Pennsylvania.

CHAPTER 48

Lansburg was southwest of Ondaiga County, on the Pennsylvania side of the Delaware River, a two-hour drive along back roads that wound over gentle mountains and through sparsely populated valleys. It might have been a pleasant ride, but Gwen was blind to the scenery, unable and unwilling to enjoy the early autumn flecks of red and yellow, the occasional glimpses of glacial lakes and sun-dappled streams.

Hawkins had given her the name and address of the nursing home in Lansburg, along with a warning to move on, "let it be." But he'd sounded halfhearted, as if he knew she had to do this, and wanted her to.

The Methodist Home was just outside Lansburg, a low brick building of recent vintage surrounded by acres of brown lawn and wilting trees.

"Fred Lawrence, please," she told the young receptionist in a spacious lobby that reeked of disinfectant.

"It's only eleven," the receptionist said. "Visiting hours begin at—"

"It's an emergency, a family emergency."

"Mr. Lawrence doesn't have family," came a woman's voice from behind her.

Gwen turned to face a middle-aged woman with pouffy blond hair, wearing a pastel blue cotton suit and a synthetic smile. "I'm Agnes Marks, director of patient services. Mr. Lawrence hasn't had a visitor since he's been here." She smiled sweetly, as if this were an amusing quirk of his.

"He has a son."

Agnes Marks peered owlishly at her. "Well, yes, the FBI was here a while back asking about him. But Mr. Lawrence won't have anything to do with him, hasn't seen him in years."

"Why is that, do you know?"

"Who exactly are you?" Another sugary smile.

"My sister was married to Nick Lawrence, Fred's son."

Gwen hoped the woman hadn't followed the news stories about the Devil's Ravine incident closely enough to know that Priscilla Lawrence had no sisters. And that Gwen had been a prime suspect.

"Then you probably know that Fred Lawrence is…well, he isn't exactly communicative," she said. "His pension check is just about his only contact with the outside world."

"Pension check? I thought he was fired from his employer, some sort of scandal?"

"Not at all, he retired from Hillman Candy with full benefits. As for a scandal, Mr. Lawrence was highly respected in the community, very active in First Methodist. I have no idea where you could have—"

"May I see him?" Gwen asked. "I've come a long way."

"You won't find him very talkative." That smile again, then: "Follow me."

She crossed the reception area, pushed open a glass door, and led Gwen across a wide cement patio. Six patients sat in wheelchairs, backs to the building, facing the distant hills to the west. Agnes Marks circled the wheelchairs and walked along the row of patients, pausing in front of each one, squinting, as if trying to distinguish among sextuplets.

"Ah," she said at the fifth patient. "Mr. Lawrence, you have a visitor."

Before the old man could respond she had circled his chair and was propelling him across the patio.

"You'll have more privacy here," she said in a cloying singsong, then spun him around so that he once again faced away from the building. "Lunch is in fifteen minutes," she said to Gwen. "I hope you'll be done by then." She smiled professionally and headed inside.

Gwen carried a white plastic chair over to Fred Lawrence and sat in front of him. He looked very frail, slumped from the shoulders, his chin almost touching his chest. A few strands of yellow-gray hair were slicked over the top of his head, and what little flesh that remained on his face drooped listlessly. Gwen searched in vain for some resemblance to Nick.

"I'm here about Nick," she said. When he didn't respond she repeated the line.

"I heard you the first time." His voice was unexpectedly strong. He still hadn't looked up at her. "Go away."

"Mr. Lawrence, two people have died because of something your son did."

"I heard about that Priscilla woman. A man from the FBI was here asking questions about Nick. I told them I hadn't seen my son since he left for piano school twenty years ago."

"Julliard," Gwen said. He slowly nodded. "Why did you and Nick lose touch?"

He didn't respond, his chin still sunk in his chest. The reds and blues of his long-sleeved madras shirt looked garish against his sallow complexion.

"Did you and your son have a falling-out?"

Still no response. She was tempted to give up; indeed she was eager to get the hell out of there. But she had to know who Nick Lawrence was. The husk of a man sitting before her held the key.

"Did you ever meet his wife?"

His head slowly rose, milky brown eyes fixing on her with something like hatred.

"Priscilla Lawrence," she said. "Priscilla Cunningham, you *did* meet her, didn't you?"

His head drooped. When she repeated the question he shook it slowly.

"How about your granddaughter? Tess, your granddaughter, did you ever meet her?" She opened her purse and took out a photograph, glancing at it briefly. A perfect May sun beat down on Jimmy, holding a bat, ready to swing. In the background, watching the game, tending to younger siblings, exchanging local gossip, were the Little Leaguers' parents: two or three mothers, lots of fathers, a few grandparents. And there, just to the right of third base, standing behind a woman in a Sohegan High School sweatshirt, was Nick Lawrence, Tess in his arms.

"This is your granddaughter, Mr. Lawrence." She placed the photo under his face and pointed to Nick and Tess. Nick hadn't known he was being photographed. Indeed, he'd been just another background figure until she retrieved the photo from a kitchen drawer that morning, wondering if she'd inadvertently shot him that day in the park when she'd saved Tess from falling down from the bleacher. "Her name is Tess."

"No," he said softly.

"Yes, she's Nick's daughter."

"*No!*"

"You can see from the photo that they look very much alike, can't you, Mr.—"

He swatted the photo from her fingers. Gwen picked it up off the cement patio.

"That is not my granddaughter," he said in a low but firm voice.

"But she is, Mr. Lawrence. She's Nick's—"

"*That isn't Nick.*"

"I don't understand." She placed the photo directly under his face. Again he batted it away. This time she let it rest on the patio.

"Are you sure?" she asked. "People change over time, features change."

"Not him," the old man growled.

"Twenty years is a long time…"

He looked at her, head trembling as if from the effort of holding it up. "That is not my son's face. That is not my son's child. My son…"

"What about your son?"

He shook his head slowly but held her with a rheumy stare.

"What about him, Mr. Lawrence? Why are you so sure? Why haven't you spoken to him all these years?"

"He…Nicholas…he was sick." His voice had deteriorated to a gravelly wheeze. "Evil."

"Evil in what way?"

"He…he was…" His entire torso sagged, as if he'd expended every breath he had left. The madras shirt billowed from his chest. "Nicky never married anybody," he whispered into his chest. "Nicky has no child."

"But…" He sounded so angry, so…humiliated. "Do you think your son is homosexual, Mr. Lawrence? Is that why you refused to see him?"

His head slowly lifted, then fell. She was about to repeat the question when he lifted his head again and let it fall. Fred Lawrence was nodding.

"I don't *think*. I know. I saw him…I found him, him and a boy from the neighborhood…*evil!* " The last word splintered into a rasping cough.

"And you made no attempt to see him, after he went to New York? Your wife made no attempt?"

"She tried. Nicky…" He just shook his head.

Gwen picked up the photo and showed it to him again.

"Not him," the old man whispered. He clasped the wheels and tried to push away from her. "Not him!"

Agnes Marks appeared instantly and grabbed the handgrips behind him.

"That'll be all," she said as she wheeled him toward the door.

Gwen walked next to him, holding the photograph under his chin.

"Are you positive it's not him, Mr. Lawrence? Please look closely, it's very, very important."

"No, no, no!" His hands tried to slap the photo but missed, flopping onto his lap.

"Please, Miss Amiel, you're disturbing him." Agnes Marks walked faster.

"One question, that's all." Gwen angled in front of the wheelchair. "Take a good look at the picture and tell me—is this your son, Mr. Lawrence?"

He held the photo in his jittery right hand, just an inch or two from his face. "This man, in the picture, does he have a scar here?" He pointed to his upper right temple.

"No, he was…" He was immaculate, unblemished. "Are you sure about the scar?"

Fred Lawrence let the photo drop onto his lap.

"Are you sure about the scar, Mr. Lawrence?"

"I gave it to him!" The old man leaned forward, almost falling out of the chair. Gwen grabbed his shoulder, pushed lightly. He flopped back into the seat.

"I gave it to him," he said softly. "And others." His chin fell onto his chest.

No wonder Nick Lawrence, the *real* Nick Lawrence, wanted nothing to do with his parents. And if you needed a new identity, who better to steal from than a young boy with no family. The homosexual son of a pillar of the community, a leader of his church.

"Come now, Mr. Lawrence, it's lunchtime." Agnes Marks pushed the wheelchair around Gwen.

"Wait!" He rapped his hands on the armrests.

"The man from the FBI, he asked me about Nicky, he told me about his wife getting killed. I knew that wasn't my son they were talking about. They had no photograph, but I knew my son hadn't married a rich woman, this Priscilla." Tears trickled over the fine white stubble on his cheeks.

"Did you tell them that?"

He slowly shook his head. "I told them I haven't seen my son in twenty years. That's the truth."

And never would, most likely. Not the real Nick Lawrence, anyway.

She watched as he was wheeled inside, a pitiful creature for whom she felt no pity whatsoever. And as she drove home, slowly, in no hurry to arrive anywhere, she couldn't help glancing at that photograph every few miles, that absurd snapshot of Jimmy at bat, eyes dead serious, as if the fate of the universe depended on the next pitch, while the monster lurked behind him, scheming, even then, plotting her seduction and, eventually, her destruction.

Had Nick—whoever he was—had Nick had the entire scheme worked out back then, all the details? Had he followed her to the game that day? He'd already stolen the identity of Nick Lawrence, probably taken his life, too. But had he already chosen her?

CHAPTER 49

He finished the final bars of the Pathetique and allowed himself a congratulatory smile. Vienna brought out a deeper passion in his playing. She always had. Even a nagging nostalgia for Gwen Amiel energized his performance. She was more emotional than rational, more sensibility than sense—he'd spotted that right away, which was one reason he'd chosen her. He knew she'd come to the Devil's Ravine once she heard the plan on the monitor, the monitor he'd brought to the master bedroom that morning.

He found himself thinking about her quite a bit, actually. Perhaps it was more than nostalgia. She'd been part of the plan, but she'd become…well, part of his life. Sometimes he fantasized about having her here in Vienna with him, introducing her to the places he'd loved long before he'd ever heard of Sohegan, New York.

"Dada!"

He turned. His daughter toddled across the large sitting room, her mother just behind.

"*Liebchen*," he said. "*Kamm zum Papa.*" He extended his arms and she jumped into them. Her mother smiled warmly.

"We had a lovely stroll in the Rathaus Park, Tess and I," she said. "I mean Uta and I. The air is like silver, so clear and fresh."

"*Ein Deutche, Schatz.*" He'd warned her a thousand times—they were Austrian now, Austrian *again*. And how else would Uta—not Tess—learn her native tongue? True, his own mother, Uta's grandmother, had been English, and he'd grown up speaking both languages, but in the future it was German, only German.

"*Angewohnheit*," she said. Yes, the English habit was hard to break. No German for two years, not even when the two of them were alone together. How else to perfect their unaccented English, though admittedly neither had had much difficulty. For Analiese, speaking English without an American accent was simply a question of acting; she could also do a passable Cockney, and an excellent French. All acting. For him, the German accent had never been a problem; expunging a British accent, his mother's legacy, had been the only challenge. He still agonized over the slips that Gwen had noticed, and corrected. *Gravy boat. Break a fuse.*

"*Vien ist wie gemacht fur Dich.*"

She smiled at the compliment and began to massage his shoulders. Of course she looked her best in Vienna. She loved the city even more than he, having grown up there. He adored Vienna far more than his native Stuttgart—this was Beethoven's home for many years, after all—but he could easily imagine a life elsewhere with his music, his wife, their money. Their child.

"Beethoven moved seventeen times in Vienna alone," he said in German. "He lived in this place only a month or two." He glanced around the room, still thrilled beyond reason to be inhabiting the very flat where Ludwig van Beethoven lived and composed. Number 45 Teinfalstrasse had not inspired Beethoven in the few months he lived there; no major compositions had been written at this address. But that kept the place from becoming a museum, like so many other Beethoven residences. He'd been able to rent the top floor for a reasonable amount, just over a year ago, when Tess was born. It had been waiting for them ever since.

"And our lawyer says we are completely safe here," she said in her beautiful German. She'd cut her hair very short and dyed it back to its original dark brown. When the collagen in her lips began to dissipate she'd lose the poutiness that he'd come to treasure since she'd started having the injections two years ago, but every victory had its price.

Yes, he missed Gwen, but Valerie—Analiese—had done so much. She'd found Priscilla at the clinic, she'd persuaded Barry Amiel to help them out, she'd taken care of him at the warehouse in Queens. An inspiration, luring him to the very place where Gwen used to pick up her furniture. She'd had so many good ideas—like paying off the Amiels' back maintenance, just to cast further suspicion on Gwen. Trying to run Gwen down on the East Side, well, that had been rash. Gwen Amiel was no threat to them, then or now.

He'd found Nick Lawrence on his own, while hanging around Lincoln Center. No family, few friends, a diploma from Julliard that did little for him professionally other than secure a handful of piano students. What a pathetic creature; he'd practically had his tongue out the entire cab ride to the pier on the Hudson River, groping with sweaty hands. His wallet had contained only twenty dollars—a small down payment, in a way. But he had a driver's license, among other identification. A few "Have you seen this man?" flyers had been taped to streetlight poles on the West Side—perhaps one of his students was concerned. But they disappeared soon enough. Nick Lawrence was dead. Long live Nick Lawrence.

He vividly recalled Gwen's fine-boned face, but Priscilla's somehow eluded him. She'd never been his, really. Priscilla had another life, internal and external, that he'd never quite fathomed. Secrets—so many secrets, all those absences, and that damn thistle she'd been clutching at the ravine like a talisman. What was that about? But Priscilla's secrets would go to the grave with her, where they belonged.

Valerie, as he still thought of her sometimes, was so much like him: talented, but no genius. She, too, possessed the absolutely cruelest of gifts: a knowledge of one's own limitations. He'd known for some time that he'd amount to nothing. Julliard had taken the real Nick Lawrence, but after he'd been rejected by the academy in Vienna, he hadn't even bothered to apply in New York. No, fate had begrudged him even the dubious pleasure of fooling himself for a few years. And Valerie? A talented actress without the spark of genius that ignites success.

They shared the same dream…the same disappointment. The best they could hope for was a comfortable life filled with music, and a child who would grow up free from the disillusionment they'd both known. When Priscilla Cunningham walked into the fertility clinic two years ago, they discovered the means to that end.

Sometimes he replayed the Devil's Ravine in his mind like a favorite passage from a sonata. He heard his own voice calling Priscilla's name, saw her turn toward him, enabling him to hit her in the chest, the way the kidnapper would have. He felt the gun explode in his gloved hand, saw the look on her face, the *knowledge*, as the bullet sailed through her heart. He'd have preferred that Barry Amiel do the actual shooting. But Barry was drunk most of the time—which made him a pliant coconspirator, but an unreliable marksman. He'd been there, of course, in that ridiculous ski mask, but just to grab the duffel bag and fire a few shots into the air with his own gun. Valerie—Analiese—had kept Tess. *Uta*, their child.

Analiese sighed and ran her fingers through his hair.

"I miss you as a brunette," she said. "Even your eyebrows are blond again. And that moustache…"

He ran a finger across the hair on his upper lip, still not quite used to it. He wondered what Gwen would make of his new look—the old look, actually. Why couldn't he get her out of his mind? *It's because she resisted you early on*, Analiese had told him, back in America, when he'd confessed to a passing fascination with her. *You had to fight for a change, and you like that.*

"Uta, *mein Liebes?*" he said quietly.

She didn't look up from the little jigsaw puzzle they'd bought her. "*Uta.*"

She finally turned, drawn by the firmness of his voice, he supposed, not the name. Soon enough she'd forget all about "Tess Lawrence." She smiled at him, her eyes so richly brown, so much like her mother's, that his chest suddenly felt too small to contain his heart.

"*Uta, wurdest du gern Klavier spielen wie dein, Papa?*"

She answered by banging both hands on the second-rate piano that had come with the furnished apartment.

"*Nein, Liebes, nicht so. So!*" Like this: He held her right index finger and picked out the first notes of the Pathetique.

"*Sie ist Genie, Analiese,*" he said. And maybe she was a genius. The genes were good.

Analiese smiled affectionately and caressed his cheek.

"Klaus," she said, and he felt a shiver of pleasure at being addressed, finally, by his own name. "*Lieber, lieber Klaus.*"

CHAPTER 50

The ringing phone interrupted a dreamless sleep. Gwen hadn't dreamt in two weeks, not since the day she returned from Lansburg, Pennsylvania, knowing what she'd never know: the identity of the man who'd seduced her by playing on her tenderest vulnerabilities. She'd given the photograph to Dwight Hawkins, and told him what she had learned from Fred Lawrence. Hawkins said that Interpol was focusing its search on London, where "Nick Lawrence" had flown from New York. He could have gone anywhere from there—this was a man who had stolen another person's identity, after all. Forging a passport would be child's play. But the trail ended at Heathrow; Interpol had little hope of finding him.

She'd expected nightmares, but sleep had been seamless, and deep. "Nick Lawrence" had become a void, a faceless, nameless void. Perhaps he did inhabit her sleep, but in an empty place without color or texture.

It was the daylight hours she had trouble with. Nick had ruined so many lives, almost ruined hers and Jimmy's. Yet what tormented her was that she'd let it happen. She'd learned nothing, apparently, from the disintegration of her marriage. She put Jimmy's well-being in jeopardy a second time. *She* had, not Nick. Lust, love, loneliness—whatever the reason, she'd been weak when she'd needed to be strong.

And even now, when she thought of Nick, which she did with agonizing, she sensed something soft around the edges of her rage, a residue of longing that stoked her anger all the more. To be consumed by hatred is debilitating enough. But when some of that hatred is self-directed, it's almost crippling.

"Mommy?" Jimmy stood in the doorway to her bedroom, silhouetted by the nightlight in the hallway, a tiny figure in T-shirt and underpants. Nick Lawrence used to stand there before entering the room, silhouetted in just that way. No, not Nick Lawrence. The monster without a name.

"Mommy, the phone's ringing."

She hadn't planned to answer it. Now more than ever before, her entire life was encompassed by the house; news from outside could neither harm nor assist her. But Jimmy hadn't been sleeping well since her one night in jail; she should have guessed he'd hear the phone.

"Hello?" She glanced at the digital clock: 3:16 A.M.

She heard a very faint, rhythmic hum, like a respirator, then a dull rustling, as if someone was moving. Then—

Piano music, familiar as her own voice, the composition *and* the performance. She wanted to hang up but the music was insistent, somehow, beautiful and cruel. She motioned with her free hand for Jimmy, who hadn't moved from the doorway. He climbed onto the far side of the bed, but she pulled him to her and held him close as she listened. The melody flowed effortlessly, like water over smooth stones. Jimmy wiped tears from her face with his fingertips.

"Who are you?" she whispered into the phone, her voice as faltering as the performance was steady and confident. "*Who are you?*"

She hung up and held Jimmy closer. He was asleep within moments, but not she. As the faint light of dawn began to shimmer around the edges of the drawn shades of her bedroom, she wondered if the music would ever stop, if she'd ever enjoy a dreamless sleep again.

Every time she closed her eyes she heard it, so beautiful, so cruel. The Lebewohl Sonata. The farewell.

PERFECT ANGEL

Back at college in the '70s, they called themselves "The Madison Seven"—a close circle of friends inseparably linked by trust, loyalty, and love. Then one night, years later, they gathered at Julia Mallet's Manhattan apartment for a "Come-As-You-Were Party" and decided to play a game...

Tough, beautiful and independent, Julia Mallet feels her life is nearly perfect. She holds a high-profile executive position in an important advertising firm. She is raising a beautiful little daughter, Emily, without the inconvenience of a husband. And now "The Madison Seven" have come together once again to celebrate her thirty-fifth birthday... and to bring back a past that should have been left dead and forgotten.

Less than twenty-four hours later, a woman Julia barely knows is brutally and senselessly slain by a faceless psychopath. NYPD Detective Ray Burgess is a man pursued by shadows, a good cop who has stared too deeply into the face of evil, and his obsessive dedication is drawing him closer to Julia, even as a crazed killer strikes again and again.

The maniac has left a calling card behind that only Julia Mallet can read: the result of a post-hypnotic suggestion inadvertently lodged in six subconscious minds—the dark residue of a harmless party game gone terribly wrong. Now Julia knows without question that one of her six dearest friends is a murderer...and is coming after her next.

VANISHING ACT

When retail tycoon George Samson appears in detective Joe DiGregorio's office asking for help in faking his own death, the wary private eye knows enough to refuse. Joe D. has been having second thoughts about his move from the Long Island police force, where he'd been a lieutenant, to trying to make it as a private detective in Manhattan. Joe had made the move to be with Alison Rosen, whom he met while working a homicide case on Fire Island (*False Faces*). Though wonderful in many ways, their relationship is strained by Joe D.'s lack of work and income. The Big City doesn't seem to need one more private investigator.

But George Samson's proposition isn't easy to forget. So when Samson is found murdered, the struggling P.I. is convinced that his would-be client found another "killer." Thing is, there's no doubt the man is dead. What happened?

Intent on the truth, Joe D. offers his investigative talents to the new CEO of Samson Stores, who accepts, and Joe D. embarks on a case that could be the making of his new career—or the end of him.

FALSE FACES

Alison Rosen, a young, single Manhattan department-store buyer, first met Linda Levinson seven years ago when both answered the same Village Voice classified ad for a Fire Island "share." Since then, they've been returning to Seaside Harbor every summer weekend.

One night, after leaving Crane's, the singles bar that often serves as a pickup place, Linda Levinson is found murdered. Is her killer a spurned suitor whose advances Linda rejected? What about the mysterious lover back in the city about whom Linda had spoken but whom Alison has never met?

Long Island police officer Joe DiGregorio is assigned to work undercover on the case, posing as a yuppie accountant. Together, Joe and Alison, who is unaware of Joe's masquerade, set out to find the murderer before he strikes again. In the process, they find out that Linda was a woman of many secrets—and find themselves falling in love in an atmosphere in which nobody can be trusted.

LOSING ISAIAH

Three-year-old Isaiah has two mothers: and they both want him.

Margaret Lewin adopted Isaiah as a newborn—and she and her husband, Charles, give the boy all the love a child could want and everything that money can buy. But can even the most loving, caring white family be responsible for raising a black child?

Selma Richards is the boy's birth mother. When Isaiah was born she was illiterate, unemployed, and a crack addict. Giving up her son was the best thing for both of them—at the time. Now Selma has weaned herself off drugs, has a responsible job caring for another couple's child, and is learning to read. She's not rich and she doesn't live in the best neighborhood, but she's healed herself.

Losing Isaiah raises one of the most complex and emotional moral questions of our times, and keeps you rooting for both women until the inevitable and heartrending conclusion in which one mother ends up losing her son.

CLOSING COSTS

When Peggy Gimmel decides to sell the apartment she bought decades ago for a few thousand dollars, she's thrilled to discover that it's worth almost $2 million. But her sudden windfall triggers a cascade of unexpected events and plunges her into the dizzying orbit of Lucinda Wells, one of Manhattan's most successful and ruthless real-estate agents.

Peggy's not the only one at Lucinda's mercy. There's also the technology entrepreneur struggling to salvage his sinking company while gut-renovating his home, the socialite exiled from Park Avenue to the pullout sofa of her parents' West Side apartment, the illegal immigrant amassing a fortune printing money, and the clueless widow trying to unload a world-class collection of fake artwork. These are just some of the characters whose lives intersect in unlikely ways, all of them nearly overwhelmed by the rocketing real-estate market and the hard-charging broker who holds the key to their future.

As he interweaves these often suspenseful and frequently comical stories, Margolis captures the zeitgeist of a cultural moment, keeping us turning the pages with the rise and fall of his characters' fortunes.